RAGING HEAT
RICHARD CASTLE

 KINGSWELL

NEW YORK • LOS ANGELES

For information address Kingswell,
1101 Flower Street, Glendale, California 91201.

For publicity address Kingswell,
125 West End Avenue, New York, New York 10023.

Editorial Director: Wendy Lefkon
Executive Editor: Laura Hopper
Cover designed by Alfred Sole

ISBN 978-1-4013-2481-0
G475-5664-5-14213
Printed in the United States of America
First Edition
10 9 8 7 6 5 4 3 2 1

THIS LABEL APPLIES TO TEXT STOCK

To KB—

The stars above us, the world at our feet.

RAGING HEAT

RICHARD CASTLE

ONE

Nikki Heat wondered if her mother hadn't been murdered what her life would have been. Would she be hoofing it like this from her police precinct to a crime scene, or would she instead be on Broadway rehearsing a Chekov revival or some cutting-edge relationship exploration with whispers of a Tony? At Columbus Avenue she paused for the walk signal. Life might have intervened in other ways, too. Fate could have just as easily made her that gourmet mom sitting in the Starbucks window to her right, helping her pre-schooler negotiate a hot chocolate. Or made her a panhandler, like that guy shaking his Dixie cup of coins outside the wine store across the street. She didn't see a Steely Dan backup singer anywhere around her, but she would enthusiastically be open to that possibility, also.

A swirl of urban wind lifted some gutter trash in a mini twister and Nikki watched a plastic grocery bag, candy wrappers, and a newspaper ad spin south from Eighty-second until the spectacle lost its center and came apart into something more mundane: random garbage. It was only half past 10 A.M. Why would somebody beg outside a wine shop that was closed?

She turned back to regard the panhandler, but he turned away from her and shuffled uptown. Heat got the light and crossed. One corner down, the traffic detail chopped the air with gloved hands to keep the gawkers moving past the street barricade. But they would let her through. The NYPD's top homicide detective had a corpse to meet.

The radio call from the first uniforms on-scene had carried a spoiler. "Don't eat or drink anything en route. Seriously." One part defiance, one part caffeine jones, Heat brought along the remnants of the vanilla latte cooling on her desk and polished it off before she reached the cordon. She lobbed the cup into a city can and flashed tin at the patrol-man guarding the caution tape.

Inside the barrier, Nikki paused. To anyone else, it looked as if she were stopping to adjust her holster, which she did. But that was cover. The interval was her own moment, a ritual of one deep breath to honor the loss of a life and to connect her own experience with trag-edy. Even though Heat had closed her mother's case two years ago, she still meditated on her simple pledge every time she encountered a new body: victims deserved justice; loved ones deserved smart cops. Duly acknowledged, she exhaled and moved forward.

Scanning Eighty-first Street with beginner's eyes, she vacuumed details and opened herself to critical first impressions. Seasoned investigators were most vulnerable to missing clues because it all got workaday, if they let it. So Heat downshifted to rookie mode, playing her walk-up as if this were her first case ever.

Nikki's first ping registered a half block from the planetarium. The paramedics out front were busy. Usually medical first responders were idle by the time she arrived because the victim was dead at the scene. Occasionally, a shooting or a knife rampage left a collateral victim or two requiring treatment or transport. But this morning, the reflection of bright emergency lights bouncing off the wet pavement was bro-ken by middle school field trippers huddled around three ambulances. Even from a distance Nikki noted the signs of emotional trauma—sobs, giddiness, faraway stares. A teenage boy sat on a gurney inside one ambulance, vomiting. Outside it, a pair of girls stood holding each, wiping tears.

She passed a coach bus with Edmonton plates idling at the curb. About two dozen Canadian seniors clustered near its door, muttering gravely in the drizzle and craning for a view of the action through the trees of Theodore Roosevelt Park. By instinct, Heat looked the oppo-site way, behind them. Her inspection tracked east from the Excelsior Hotel along the block of grand apartment buildings to The Beresford, whose rooftop towers blurred eerily into the low clouds and resembled a ghost castle lurking in the mist twenty-three floors overhead. Many of the street's windows were filled with rubberneckers, some of who held up smartphones to live-Tweet the carnage from their three-million-dollar condos. She got out her own cell and snapped off some shots so, later, she could pinpoint where to send her squad to interview eyewits.

High above the gray blanket, the lazy rumble of a jet on approach to one of the airports made her think of him. Six more days, he'd be back. God, these months felt like forever. Nikki shook off the distraction and once again told her longing to take a seat.

At the cobblestone driveway to the museum's main entrance she saw it for herself and stopped cold. Riveted, Nikki stood among the evacuees and stared like everyone else. Then muttered a curse.

The mammoth six-story glass box that encases the Hayden Planetarium looked as if a meteor had smashed through the roof. But what had punched a hole in the top of the massive cube had left an explosion of blood at the jagged circle in the ceiling. On the inside wall, tongues of red extended earthward, translucent paths streaking thirty feet or more down the glass curtain. Detective Heat didn't need to role-play beginner's eyes. This went down as a first.

"Watch where you walk, Detective," said the medical examiner. But Heat had already paused on the bottom step leading down to the lower level of the giant atrium. Dr. Lauren Parry knelt on the floor in her moon suit marking evidence under Alpha Centauri. "Got pieces of this body everywhere. Some still falling. Or dripping's more like it."

Nikki tilted her head back. A hundred feet above her, drizzle and unfiltered gray light seeped through the puncture a human cannonball had made. The hole created a ragged bull's-eye in the glazed strip that framed the outer edges of the roof. Beneath the impact splatter, more blood—mixed with chunks of tissue—had not only trickled down the window, but also on one half of the giant orb nested inside the Hall of the Universe. Jupiter took a hit, too. The nearest model planet of the array suspended by wires in the cube now wore vertical streaks of red crossing its latitudinal stripes.

Elsewhere, bits of shredded clothing hung from structural tension rods where they had snagged on descent. As she looked, a gob of viscera dripped off one of the tatters and plummeted three stories, meeting the white marble floor with a splat as loud as a handclap. When it landed Detective Feller called out a long "Whooooaa!" which was followed by a chorus of rowdy guffaws from the three uniforms standing with him over near the gift shop. This time Heat wouldn't reprimand him for his habitual lack of decorum. If ever a crime scene allowed for gallows humor to dissipate trauma, this was it. And with no family, media, or civilian bystanders around to offend, she let it slide.

Heat stepped carefully into the great hall, avoiding nuggets of glass and following the route suggested by the numbered yellow markers left behind by the ME on her way across the floor. When she reached her friend, Nikki asked. "Doesn't figure as a jumper, does it?"

"First of all, you know better than to ask me that so soon. And second, thank you for not contaminating my crime scene."

"I think I know where to walk, Lauren."

"Then I have trained you well. Unlike your Detective Ochoa, who managed to slip on a piece of tendon his first minute on-scene and land on his ass. When you see Miguel, you can inform him that he is my soon-to-be-ex-boyfriend."

Nikki scanned the neighboring buildings, all visible outside of the glass. "I don't see anyplace close enough to make this drop."

"You're going to press this until I answer, aren't you." Dr. Parry stood and stretched her back. "Last week I worked a jumper up in the Bronx at the Castle Hill Houses. The rooftops of those projects are about the same height as these, OK? My victim had split open at the neck and abdomen and had gross organ protrusion, but she was, other-wise, an intact corpse.

"So there are not only no buildings close enough to reach this place, there's no structure around here high enough for a fall to do this to a body. Injuries this massive are more consistent with falls from hundred-story-plus skyscrapers."

"What about ID?"

"Our best bet will be DNA. If we get lucky, we may find extremi-ties or teeth. Any more questions before I get back to work?"

"Just one. Are you going to chill out before tonight? Because I don't want to sit through *Perks of Being a Wallflower* with you harrumphing all through it."

"*Perks of Being a Wallflower*? I wanted to see Jeremy Renner as Bourne."

"A: There is only one Jason Bourne, and, B: It's my turn to pick, so deal, lady." Nikki gave her the kind of serious look that neither could take seriously. During Rook's two-month absence on assignment for his magazine, Nikki and Lauren had set a movie night once a week, a pleasant distraction for Heat but a weak substitute for having him near. Dr. Parry signaled her acceptance of *Perks* by telling Detective Heat to get out her notebook.

"Victim is, as yet, unidentifiable with no recovered parts sizable enough to distinguish. We have tagged one shoe, a New Balance men's trainer that landed up on the First-Level elevator bridge, so we are open to the victim being male but cannot confirm without a DNA match."

"But a safe guess."

The medical examiner shrugged. "Otherwise, it's the floor on hands and knees, or cherry pickers to search the rigging. That's all I got."

"Then you'll be interested in this," said Detective Ochoa, painstakingly tracing Heat's path through the scattered remains and glass shards. Behind him, his partner Detective Raley followed, matching footfalls. "Found it over near Group Tickets." The duo, affectionately known as Roach, a mash-up of their last names, both turned to indicate the counter across the hall. "It's a piece of a finger."

"Or maybe a toe," added Raley.

The three detectives stood behind Parry while she crouched, examining the specimen with a magnifier. "Tip of a finger. Dark skinned."

Heat knelt and put a cheek near the floor for a closer look. "Let's assume black male, putting this with the men's shoe. Any chance for a print?"

The medical examiner cautiously rolled the specimen a half-turn with the blunt end of her tweezers. It reminded Nikki of checking the edge of a pancake for doneness. "Promising. We'll sure try."

"Nice one, Roach," said Heat as she stood.

Lauren tweaked her boyfriend. "Might even make up for your booty fall, Detective Clumsy."

While Ochoa made a face at her, his partner said, "Amazing. I mean that we got a whole piece like that."

"Not so unusual." Dr. Parry placed an evidence cone then bagged the fingertip. "When the human body experiences catastrophic blunt force trauma like this it separates at the joints first as it explodes."

"Giving the planetarium a brand-new exhibit for the Big Bang Theory," said the familiar voice behind them. By reflex, Heat rolled her eyes and thought, Rook. Always clowning aro—?! Heat spun, and there he stood, ten feet away, grinning that Rook wiseass grin. Nikki tried to collect herself, but all she could do was manage a breathless, "Rook?"

"Listen, if this is a bad time. . . ." He gestured widely to the carnage. "Last thing you need is somebody else just dropping in on you."

She rushed to him, wanting so much to forget who she was and where she was and just throw herself at him and kiss him. Instead, the homicide squad leader clung to her professionalism and said, "You weren't supposed to be back until—"

"—Next week, I know. Surprise."

"Uh, understatement." She took both his hands in hers and squeezed, then, frustrated, snapped off her nitrile gloves and held him again, this time feeling the warmth of his flesh. Soon a familiar rush filled her; the same intense magnetism that drew Heat to Rook three years before when he first came into her life. Nikki often reflected on how their relationship almost didn't happen. A damn journalist assigned to her for a research ride-along? No, thank you, she'd thought.

But soon enough Heat went from trying to get him reassigned because his pigtail-pulling wisecracks annoyed her, to yearning for his companionship so much she let him stay around. In time they not only became a couple, trading nights at each other's apartments, but Jameson Rook evolved into a valued collaborator on her toughest cases, notably solving the homicide of a celebrity gossip columnist, exposing a killer at the highest levels of the NYPD, helping her nail her mother's murderers, and even in saving the city from a bioterror plot. Oh, sure there had been some romantic ups and downs, including a few trial separations, but they didn't last. The pull—the magnetism—the rightness of their togetherness always prevailed. And, of course, there was the sex. Yes, the sex.

Nikki studied him. In two months he had grown thinner, tanner, more fit. And something else was different. "So. A beard?"

"Like it?" He struck a pose.

She stepped back and smiled broadly. "No. Hell, no."

"You'll get used to it."

"No I won't. You look like . . . you look like the Jameson Rook action figure."

He withdrew one hand and felt his chin to assess.

"Who told you I was here?" she asked.

"Sorry, an undisclosed source protected by my rights under the First Amendment. OK, it was Raley." The detective gave her a sheepish wave. When she turned back to Rook he leaned in close enough for her to inhale his scent and whispered, "I thought I'd kidnap you for an early lunch. Say, someplace with room service?"

What Heat wanted to do was exactly that. Only screw room service; just race across the street to the Excelsior and leave a trail of clothes from the Do Not Disturb sign to the bed. But she said, "A terrific idea. If I weren't kinda busy investigating a suspicious death, and all."

"If your job is your priority."

"Says the man who left me eight weeks ago to write a magazine article."

"Two magazine articles. Or, as my editor prefers to call them, in-depth investigations. And seven weeks. I came back early. See?" He spread his arms wide and turned a circle, which made her laugh. Damned Rook, he could always make her laugh. The other thing he always did was understand how dedication translated into deferred gratification. So without complaint, he hoisted his duffel onto the counter at Coat Check, which sat unattended but full of backpacks and raincoats left behind in the hasty evacuation.

Since the morning rain had let up, Heat decided to convene her squad meeting outside and yield the interior to OCME and Forensics, who seemed less than thrilled by all those extra personnel contaminating their scene. She and Detectives Raley, Ochoa, Feller, and Rhymer formed a loose circle on the entrance plaza between the revolving doors and the circular driveway. Rook sat on a stone bench off to the side, making no attempt to stifle his jet-lag yawns. Up the grass slope, evacuated tourists milled on the sidewalk behind the wrought iron fence. Predictably the news vans had arrived. Their raised snorkels formed portable forests at both ends of Eighty-first.

"I don't know why we got bounced out here," said Feller. "Didn't we find that finger for them?"

"We?" replied Roach, in near unison. And then Ochoa added, "Here, homes, I've got a finger for you, too."

Feller came back with, "I'm touched, Miguel. You even took it out of your nose," bringing a volley of chuckles that Heat clamped a lid on.

"Gentlemen, may I remind you we are in public at a death scene? Let's not find ourselves laughing it up on the cover of this afternoon's *Ledger*." She surveyed the street, and, sure enough, her eye caught a man snapping shots of them with a long lens. But as Nikki turned back toward her group, it occurred to her that, even though the guy seemed familiar, she didn't see a credential or recognize him as one of the usual press photogs. Where had she seen him before? Glancing again, she caught the back of his jacket getting swallowed by the crowd and shrugged it off. This was New York. The sidewalks were full of puzzler faces.

"Let's all remember," she began, "open minds. This could turn out to be an accidental, not a homicide. Either way, we are going to go about this case a little differently."

"As in, we're not looking for lurkers or suspicious persons fleeing the area," said Detective Feller. Like his colleagues, he had jettisoned the grab ass and gone all business.

"Exactly. Let's focus our efforts instead on establishing what happened. Starting with two priorities: victim ID and mode of death."

Rook raised a hand. "I'm going with *kersplat*." God, how Nikki hated and loved having him back. He read their reactions and, instead of backing off, joined the circle and doubled down. "Indelicate perhaps, but come on. The guy was basically a bug on a windshield. Except this bug actually went through the windshield, so he must have been going, what . . . five hundred miles an hour?"

"No way," said Ochoa.

"For a lawman you seem quick to doubt the laws of gravity, Detective." He appealed to Nikki, "What height did Dr. Parry say the injuries were consistent with?"

Heat felt wary of having her briefing hijacked but answered, "Over one hundred stories."

"So we're talking an altitude of at least one thousand feet. I'm surprised he didn't achieve Mach-One."

"Doubtful, Rook. An object falls at thirty-two feet per second per second until it reaches terminal velocity." Ochoa turned a few heads with that one. "What? Back in the service, I was Airborne. Trust me, before you go jumping out a cargo door you buddy-up with ol' Ike Newton."

Rook couldn't let it go. "I don't doubt your courage, but aren't we splitting hairs here?"

The detective smiled to himself, then recited, "Mach-One is the speed of sound, which is seven hundred sixteen miles per hour. Terminal velocity for the average human in free fall is one hundred twenty MPH and takes approximately twelve seconds to reach."

After absorbing his calculus beatdown, Rook paused and said, "'Approximately.' I see."

"The variable is the drag coefficient. Drag is created by things like clothing, body position . . ."

". . . Facial hair, such as a G.I. Joe beard," said Detective Rhymer.

Heat jumped in. "All right. I know how much you guys like to measure and what not, but can we just stipulate our victim fell from a height that suggests an aircraft and leave it there?" They all nodded. Then, when Rook opened his mouth, she said, "Moving on" and he closed it and gave her a smiling salute with his forefinger.

Nikki assigned Rhymer to scrub the Missing Persons database for an ID on the John Doe. "Obviously start with New York City and the tri-state," she said, "but since this poor guy probably came from an aircraft, tap the FBI and Homeland, too. Also, do a run of prison escapees and active NYPD, county, state, and federal manhunts."

She gave Randall Feller the neighborhood to canvass beginning with the tourists being held between the sawhorses on Eighty-first. "What am I looking for, though?" he asked. "I mean, since we're not seeking a lead on a perp."

"This is one of those times that we won't know until we find it," she replied. "It's the lottery. All it takes to learn something is one person who saw the fall."

"Or heard something," added Raley.

Heat nodded. "Sean's right. Plane in distress, a scream, a gun-shot, whatever. And take a platoon of uniforms to knock on doors in those apartments." She gestured to the block of pale stone encasing the Upper West Side's most fortunate and texted him her iPhone shots of the looky-loos in their windows. Next she turned to Detective Raley and said, "Make a guess."

"Show me: video cams."

"Ding-ding-ding." Rales wore the crown as the squad's King of All Surveillance Media. Over the years he had excelled at scrubbing hours of sleep-inducing closed circuit television footage of everything from neighborhood traffic cams to bank and jewelry store lipsticks, and scored major breaks in their cases. Today Nikki tasked him with finding CCTV mounts at the planetarium and the surrounding businesses and residences.

"There's a plus side," she said. "What you're looking for happens within a very tight time window.

"Detective Ochoa, I'm going to split you off from your partner to work the skies." He flipped open his notebook and took notes as she directed him to contact the FAA and Air Traffic Control for any Maydays, distress calls, or unusual activity in the local air space. "Get a list of all aircraft—commercial and general aviation—that came any-where near here around ten this morning; anything that might have veered off course or acted erratically or raised notice from other pilots."

"Like did they see anything up there or hear something on the radio that was freaky, got it."

"And don't forget the helicopters. Not just NYPD but the TV, radio, tourist, and commuter choppers." Heat looked up. The sky was brightening but still oystery. "Not sure how many of them got up in that, but if they did, somebody might have registered something."

Rook raised a hand but didn't wait to be called on. "Stowaways. Every once in a while you hear about dudes hitching a ride in the wheel well of an airliner. The pilot opens the landing gear and . . . well, you get the idea."

"Won't hurt to check, Miguel."

"Oh, and skydivers. Write that down." Rook annoyed Ochoa by tapping his finger on his notepad.

"No helmet or parachute turned up," said Heat.

"Maybe the plane banked and he fell out. Or jumped." Feeling their stares, he added. "Did anyone here see *Point Break*? Keanu Reeves dives out of a plane to chase Patrick Swayze, who left with the last parachute? Anybody?"

Ochoa clicked his pen and winked at Raley. "Skydiver one word or two?"

Heat knew it was time to send Rook home when she asked the group if they had any other theories about the victim and he didn't chime in. No speculation about an untoward application of the Monty Python cow catapult. No conjecture about a boozy wing walker stumbling off a biplane. No nothing. In fact, he had returned unnoticed to his spot on the stone bench and sat with a fixed vacant stare into the middle distance.

"Maybe you should get a nap," she told him when the others had dispersed. Logging thirty-six hours from Central Africa to Paris to JFK to that bench had finally taken its toll. He nodded blankly and she watched him amble away with his duffel after giving her an unsteady hug and a vow to catch up with her after some shut-eye. That bastard knew she was looking, too, because, at the top of the driveway, he lifted the vent of his sport coat and shook his ass. "Welcome home," she said to herself.

Back inside, Dr. Parry looked up at Heat over a grim container of human morsels and declared she would be at this for hours and that movie night was definitely off. "Although I had already assumed so now that handsome's back. Go ahead, you fickle bee-otch. Have fun."

"I will. Think I'll take him to see the new Bourne movie." Nikki turned and walked off to hide her grin.

As the detectives began to filter into the bull pen to report at the end of shift, Heat was surprised to see Rook arrive with them. "Not much of a nap," she said when he took a seat on her desktop.

"A nap'll kill ya. You want to know how an experienced traveler blows the gum out of the carburetor? Hit the treadmill, instead. Three miles and a hot shower, I'm good for, oh, another twenty minutes." He scanned the squad room. "What's with the empty desk?"

"We, um, lost one of our detectives this week." Before he could follow up, she cut him off. "A little sensitive, a little public right now, all right?"

"We won't discuss it here, then." He nodded, but continued, "Let me guess. Do I smell the handiwork of one Captain Wally Irons?" She gave him a sharp look and he put up both palms. "I think we best not discuss this here, if it's all right with you."

Detective Ochoa came over, turning pages to the front of his notebook. "No hits at the FAA or ATC. No commercial air traffic over this part of Manhattan at that time. One outbound from LaGuardia over the Bronx ten minutes before and two JFK approaches: one, five minutes after—that was over the Hudson; the second traversed the West Side at about ten-thirty." Nikki recalled the sound of that plane on her walk-up, then asked about general aviation. "Nada. Same for Maydays, distress calls. And yes, Rook, I did inquire about stowaways. None reported, plus they said it wouldn't be procedure to drop landing gear this far out."

According to Rhymer, Missing Persons didn't kick out any matches. "And still waiting on callbacks from various law enforcement on fugitives and escapees." Mindful of the polite Southern nature that had earned Rhymer the nickname of Opie, Heat directed him to be a pain in the ass with those agencies. She also suggested he widen the window on Missing Persons to include the past week; you never knew.

"Sure thing. And I'll check MP reports throughout the evening, just in case somebody comes home tonight and finds it empty by surprise." When he said it, it sounded buttery, like "bah supprahs." Opie in the big city.

Rook stood. "Hang glider."

Ochoa shook his head. "From where, the Empire State Building?"

"You're right. He'd have to get it up there undetected." But Rook kept going with it. "How about the big skyscraper they're erecting on West Fifty-seventh."

"And what happened to the actual hang glider?" asked Heat. "Rook, you should have taken a nap instead."

Rhymer beamed. "A wing suit could do it."

"*Madre de dios*, it's contagious." Ochoa stared at the ceiling tiles, shaking his head.

Rook clamped an arm around Opie's shoulder. "You know something? The halls of this precinct are going to ring with sweet laughter when one of our brainstorms leads to a break in this case."

Detectives Feller and Raley strode in together, urgency on their faces. "You're going to want to see this," said the King of All Surveillance Media.

The six of them could barely fit into the storage closet Raley had converted into his digital domain, which basically consisted of two tables resting on filing cabinets, a scrounged assortment of yesteryear's technology, and a cardboard Burger King crown, presented to him years before by a grateful homicide squad leader. "While I was canvassing the crowd for eyewits, some old dude from Canada is getting real freaked over near the tour bus, so I check him out," said Detective Feller. "He and his wife—by the way, I'm betting she's a recent trade-up, if you catch my meaning—Anyway, the two of them were posing for a video the bus driver was shooting of them in front of the planetarium."

"Makes sense," said Rook. "What's a trip to New York without a picture of Uranus?"

Feller couldn't resist joining in, adopting the voice of a tourist. "'My God, Harry, I can't believe the size of Uranus.'"

"Wanna talk massive?" said Rook. "Feast your eyes on this space junk."

Heat turned to them. "Boys." Then, admonishing Rook, "Definitely a nap next time."

Raley resumed. "The tourist couple volunteered the video so I could make a digital copy. This part's in slo-mo. Ready?" Rales didn't bother waiting for a reply. Everyone gathered a little closer to the monitor when he rolled the footage.

The screen displayed a barrel-chested senior citizen with silver hair sprayed into a meticulous pompadour embracing a buxom woman of about fifty who wore her jewels proudly and rested her head on the love of her life. Both smiles seemed frozen, but that was due to the video speed, apparent when their eyes blinked in slow motion. "Here comes," said Raley. A few seconds later, a dark form shaped like a bullet descended from the sky at a steep angle and crashed into the roof of the cube. Nobody on the video noticed or reacted, but the video room sure did, resounding with moans, gasps, and a long "Fuuuuck" from Ochoa.

"Can you zoom in?" asked Heat.

"Already done. Now, the more you zoom, the more this stuff pixilates, so it's not real sharp, but there's something interesting. Ready?"

His zoomed version excluded the couple, except for the top of the silver pompadour. Raley had also slowed the video down a step further so, as the body appeared, its movement played somewhat jerkily. A second before impact, he froze the frame.

Rhymer said, "Oh, man, headfirst."

"And check it out." Raley used a pencil to indicate the victim's hands. "Tucked behind his back."

"Who doesn't put his hands out?" asked Rook.

Detective Feller said, "Might be unconscious."

Ochoa shook his head. "If you're unconscious, your arms are all loose." He posed to demonstrate.

They all studied the image. After a few moments, Raley played it out to impact. This time it was met with silence. Which was broken by Rook. "I guess that's what the kids today mean by photobomb."

It turned out Nikki Heat's fantasy about a trail of clothes from the door to the bed wasn't so far off—the two main differences being it was Rook's loft, not the Excelsior Hotel, and they never made it as far as the bed. At least not the first time.

Separation had created a hunger and they eagerly flew at each other in a frenzy, the time apart making this reunion feel fresh. Even their familiar ways and places carried a sense of novelty and wild excitement.

And abandon. Definitely abandon. Afterward, with her head nestled into his shoulder, Nikki reflected how she had never been with a man who could make her forget everything so completely and lose herself in the instant they were creating. Of course, he could also break the spell.

"Reunion sex," he said. "Nothing like it."

"Hotel sex? Sex on the roof? And what about that time in the back of the squad car?"

"Oh, right. You know I'm very sorry to hear the NYPD is retiring the noble Crown Victoria from the its fleet. Fuel economy is one thing. A spacious and, might I say, firm, backseat is another."

"On the topic of firm backseats, how much weight did you lose?"

"Jungle travel is very slimming."

"And what is this here?" Nikki ran her fingertips down from the old indent made by the bullet he took to save her life and traced them over a jagged scar. She slid down his chest to examine it. Even in the dim light she could make out the bas-relief of crude stitchwork, recently healed.

"Later," he said, drawing her face up to his. "Let's enjoy this."

"Oo, man-of-mystery man."

"Yeah?"

Heat rolled on top of him. "Oh, yeah."

They found each other's mouths again. But this time, tenderly. The two held eye contact as she caressed him and took him inside, and then in wordless synchronicity, they spoke with only their most naked, unabashed gazes, each slowly moving, reaching for, and feeling, the depths of one another.

Rook called to order dinner in from Landmarc then stepped into the shower with her. As he soaped her back, he asked, "Now exactly which action figure do I remind you of? G.I. Joe?"

"It was just a wisecrack, let it go."

"Then perhaps one of the others in the ensemble. Storm Shadow? Snake Eyes?"

"Rook, how do you know all these? You're kinda scaring me."

"I ghostwrote a piece on Hasbro for a trade publication once. We all have a past." Then he resumed, "Shipwreck? Snow Job? I know. Firefly. I sort of feel a connection to him. Can't explain it."

Nikki turned and cupped his face in her hands. "This wasn't my favorite sport, you know."

"Don't sell yourself short. I found you downright gymnastic." But he read her, and grew serious. "I know the separation sucks."

"And I don't want to be a whiner, Rook, but two months. . . ." It had started as a mere six-day jaunt to Switzerland to file a quick and dirty glamour piece on the Locarno International Film Festival. But when his editor at *First Press* dangled an investigative cover story on diamond smugglers in Rwanda funding international terrorists, Rook smelled his third Pulitzer and hurried his rental Peugeot down the E35 to Milan, dashed through La Rinascente for tropical clothing, and hopped the next flight via Entebbe to Kigali.

"Which is why I said no when they asked me to go to Myanmar next week to cover the human rights situation."

"I hope you didn't do that because of me. Do what you have to do. I mean, you know I pride myself on my independence."

"All too well."

"That's what makes us work. We both cherish our independence, right?" Then something odd registered on his face, enough for her to study him and ask, ". . . What?"

But Rook didn't reply. He simply gave her a knowing smile and drew her close to him. After a moment, embracing skin-to-skin, under the steam, Nikki whispered, "Oh. I think a new action figure just joined us."

"Please," he said in mock indignation. "Must we cheapen this?"

The next morning, Heat brewed herself a scoop of Rook's stale coffee; and while the water sieved through the Melitta cone, she watched *Good Morning America* announce that a tropical depression off the coast of Nicaragua had now graduated to a tropical storm with a name: Sandy. Her cell phone rang and Nikki raced up the hall to the bedroom, hoping to hell it wouldn't wake him. But Rook slumbered in deep oblivion as she grabbed it and finger swiped the screen. Heat spoke in a hushed voice as she closed the door behind her. "Hey, Doctor."

"You sound out of breath," said Lauren Parry. "Please tell me I interrupted something wicked."

"He bound me to the bedposts with old typewriter ribbons. I'm lucky I could reach the phone. You still at the planetarium?"

"Oh, hell, no. But I did pull an all-nighter here at OCME with my recovery." It always fascinated Heat how professionals found a vocabulary to cope with the macabre. "I've sent good DNA samples off to Twenty-sixth Street, but that's not why I'm calling. I also came across a significant piece of remains. I'm certain it's a section of upper arm near the left shoulder. Nikki, it has a tattoo. Open your e-mail, I sent you a JPEG."

Nikki thanked her and hung up. Wincing at the outdated French roast, she watched her laptop screen fill with the ME's attachment. Lauren's photo reflected her friend's experience and attention to detail: sharply focused on the pores, lit for clarity, and no flash bounce. The dark brown skin, torn at the edges had been inked with a slogan in an ornate font: *"L'Union Fait La Force."*

"Unity Makes Strength," thought Heat. Then, always eager to use her French, said the words aloud. *"L'Union Fait La Force."*

"That's on the Haitian coat of arms." Startled, she turned to find Rook standing behind her. "My French is nowhere as good as yours, but I spent some time there after the quake to cover Sean Penn's mission."

"It walks," she said, and stood to kiss him good morning. In his jet lag haze the night before, he'd gamely attempted to unpack from his trip, but mainly just wandered stupidly, making a ludicrous job of it. "Do you even remember me catching you putting your dirty underwear in the bureau drawer instead of the hamper? You fought me all the way to bed."

"Then I must have been out of it."

Nikki offered him her coffee. Surprisingly, he drank it without reaction, while she explained the origin of the tattoo.

When she'd finished Rook said, "You know what this means, don't you?"

"Of course. There's a possibility I can ID him through the department's tattoo database."

"OK, that. And . . ." He set the mug down and became animated. "Come on, Nikki. This guy might be an alien. Do you know how easy it will be for me to pitch this to the magazine? An alien falling from the sky and crashing into the planetarium? Best. Death. Ever."

The NYPD's Real Time Crime Center maintained a computerized catalog of tattoos that proved incredibly useful identifying both suspects and victims. Initially, gang and prison tatts got the focus but, as body art gained mainstream popularity, all sorts of ink from all sorts of people got photographed by detectives and logged into the hard drives on a high floor in police headquarters. If this John Doe from the sky had any recent arrest, however minor, the likelihood that his tattoo would spit out a name and last-known address was very high. So while Rook headed off to get dressed, Heat e-mailed copies of the image to RTCC as well as to Detective Rhymer so he could share it with FBI, Homeland, and Immigration and Customs.

When Nikki went to dump her soggy Melitta grounds, she got a laugh at more hamper confusion. Resting on top of the kitchen garbage was a pair of socks and Rook's prized Comic-Con baseball cap, obvious casualties of his loopy foray into unpacking. As she rescued them, her eye caught something: a shopping bag lying underneath. It was small and of high-quality paper with braided cord handles from a jewelry store in Paris. Nikki hesitated, then, deciding it was none of her business, took her foot off the pedal. The lid dropped and she started for the bedroom with the cap and socks.

Seconds later, her toe hit the pedal again. She wondered—or maybe rationalized—what if something was in it and he had accidentally thrown away, say, cuff links? Or an expensive pen? She set the souvenir hat and socks on the counter and removed the bag, which had been folded flat. She ran her fingers on its glossy surface and felt nothing. After a hitch of minor hesitation, she opened it and peered inside, where she found a receipt for many thousands of euros.

"Nik, you haven't seen my Comic-Con hat anywhere, have you?" he called on his way from the bedroom. She stuffed the receipt in the bag and dropped it back in the trash. But not before she saw what the purchase was.

Bague de fiançailles. She didn't dare give voice to the words this time. But feeling the sudden flush on her face, she listened to her private translation reverbing in her mind: "Engagement ring."

On the elevator ride down, Rook surveyed Nikki and asked if she felt all right. She nodded, presenting the most unfazed smile she could muster, which seemed good enough for him. But, of course, she knew why he'd asked. The few minutes it took for them to get out of his loft had played out for her as a sluggish walk through a Coney Island hall of mirrors, only underwater. Her mind swirled with a cyclone of emotions. Guilt at having snooped. Exhilaration at the receipt's meaning. Fear, too. Yes, fear. And more guilt about feeling that feeling. And—fueling the icy center of the vortex—a breath-robbing, knee-jellying numbness. Because she couldn't figure out how to feel.

The sunlight cut sharp to her eyes when they stepped out of his building onto the sidewalk and he took a long inhale of Tribeca, declaring, "God, I've missed this city."

"Subway, not taxi," was all Nikki could think to say, choosing a crowded express train over the intimacy of a cab's rear seat and the conversation opportunity a venue like that threatened to open up.

As they approached Reade Street, Heat lurched into another emotional mode when she made the guy. The long lens puzzle man from the Hayden stood outside the little park in Bogardus Plaza. Only this time he wasn't holding a camera. He'd gone back to panhandling. "Keep walking," she told Rook. And when he gave her a curious frown, she repeated it, evenly but firmly. He did as he was told for once, and when he reached the corner and looked back, Nikki had vanished.

TWO

L ying there on her back in the gutter under the serving window of the Tribeca Taco Truck, all Heat could see across Reade Street were the man's boots as he came closer to find out where the hell she went. To her eye, those Lugz looked a little fresh from the box for a derelict. A hand prodded her shoulder. Nikki turned her head to look up at a sidewalk diner in a Rangers cap with the authenticity stickers still on the beak. Around his mouthful of *nopalas* burrito, he said, "Yo, lady, you sick?" Then he snatched the Ray-Bans off her face and ran. And they say New Yorkers don't care. Instead of giving chase, though, she logrolled under the chassis of the truck to the street side.

Heat waited until she saw her stalker disappear around the back of the vehicle, then pushed herself to her feet from a tripod stance, keeping her right hand on her holster. She moved swiftly, using the growl of a passing school bus to drown out her footfalls. The guy couldn't figure out how he could have lost her—Nikki didn't need to see his face to know that. As she snuck up behind him, he peered around the corner of the taco van, swiveled his head to the right to scan the opposite end of the sidewalk, then craned to survey the café tables in the plaza across Bogardus Garden.

"Don't worry, I'm right here," she said, close enough for him to feel her breath on his neck. And then, more sharply, "Ah-ah. Don't turn around. Drop the cup." Coins danced on the pavement. "Hands behind your head." Nikki slid her palm off the butt of her Sig Sauer and pressed his chest against the quilted stainless steel door of the food truck while she cuffed him.

"A little harsh for public solicitation, wouldn't you say, Detective?" said Rook on arrival. But then he saw the Smith & Wesson .40 caliber she pulled from the panhandler's waistband. "Hmm. Sir, unless that squirts water, you have some explaining to do."

The man ignored Rook. And Heat, for that matter. Just stared up at the sky, shaking his head like he was mad at himself. He bristled even more when she plucked his wallet and opened it. Now it was Heat's turn to shake her head. "You have got to be kidding me."

"Nikki Heat. This is a nice surprise." Zach Hamner's voice annoyed her even more this time. As usual, he oozed the casual jauntiness of a no-worries, above-the-fray networker enjoying his high rung on the political ladder at One Police Plaza. But this time an extra helping of duplicity seeped through the phone along with something new from the senior administrative aide to the NYPD's deputy commissioner for legal matters—a whiff of apprehension.

"Let's keep it real, Zach. This is neither nice nor a surprise." From his end came rustling, and then a door close. Heat waited him out, surveying her bull pen, empty so far, except for Rook, across the room filling his espresso maker with fresh water.

After some throat clearing, Hamner said, "That's a hell of a 'good morning,' Detective."

"Want to know what my wake-up call was? Busting the Internal Affairs Bureau doofus you sent to shadow me."

His denial reflex started to kick in, and she cut him off. "And don't insult me further by playing innocent. When I threatened to parade him through the Twentieth and lock him up in front of my squad, he talked like a starlet on *The View*."

Even though she called him a doofus, Heat blamed herself for not acting the day before when the IAB detective caught her attention outside the planetarium. Sure, he had changed out of his panhandler's disguise, put on a hat, and acted like he belonged with the news snappers, but when the sonar ping had sounded for Nikki, she dismissed it, breaking one of the cardinal rules of investigation that she preached to her squad: Always notice what you are noticing.

"All right," said Hamner with a sigh of resignation. "Let's stipulate I was doing some background on you—"

"You had me tailed."

"—But I had a reason."

Count on that, thought Nikki. Zach "The Hammer" Hamner always had a reason. Or, more likely, a strategy.

"I'm waiting," she said.

"You're sorta blindsiding me here. I'm still herding my ducks." He chuckled, trying to regain footing. "Can you meet at our usual deli for breakfast, say, tomorrow or early next week?"

The seasoned interrogator kept his feet to the fire. "Background on me for what? Tell me now, or I'll start asking around."

Nasal breeze crossed his phone's mouthpiece. Then came the creak of executive leather as he sat. "A job, since you insist on squeezing me. A promotion. Again."

His "again" carried some stank. Three years before, Zach identified Heat as a rising star and campaigned for her to take command of her precinct after the death of the beloved Captain Montrose. The ugly politics of the process gave her second thoughts, however, and she left him at the altar, declining both her promotion to captain and the command, to remain a street detective. A gamesman has a long memory, she decided. And yet, he still played the game. Why this time?

It had to be Wally Irons. The man who took the precinct command Heat had declined proved himself to be an inept self-promoter with no copsense nor any clue how to manage people. Captain Irons's sole talent rested in his astonishing ability to survive in the face of his gaffes, usually buffoonish or egregious. The whole squad bet that the exposure of his secret affair with one of his homicide detectives, Sharon Hinesburg, would trigger the end of his command. Especially since his lover turned out to be a mole for a terror organization. Yet, after two weeks of intensive meetings downtown and a monthlong leave of absence, the Iron Man returned to flip on the lights in his precinct commander's office without so much as a wink about his transgression—or a hint of how he kept his post.

The tongue-in-cheek speculation ran to holding blackmail photos of the mayor. Rook theorized Wally was like Kafka's Gregor Samsa, "a human cockroach, only freakishly mutated. Like that deviant species they discovered that survives chemical spills, nuclear meltdowns, and Real Housewives marathons."

These were Nikki's thoughts as she eyed the empty desk in the bull pen. The desk that had been assigned to Sharon Hinesburg's replacement, a grade-three who transferred from the Organized Crime Unit, a gifted, instinctive investigator whose single drawback turned out to be her bust size. And when years of innuendo from Captain Irons turned to harassment, and finally, an "accidental" grope, Detective Camille Washington just didn't show up one day last week. Now, Nikki assumed Irons was out and she was Zach Hamner's candidate—again.

She was mistaken.

"The commish directed the head of Counterterrorism to create a new task force, and he wants you on it. You do remember Commander McMains?"

Of course she did. Nikki especially recalled how he stepped in to help her shut down that bioterror plot. "Good cop. Good person."

"He thinks the same. Which is why your name tops his short list. This is big, Heat. We're definitely thinking outside the boroughs with this job. We need someone who can liaise with our foreign law enforcement partners to meet the challenges of all cross-border criminal activity that impacts New York City."

Nikki wondered, was he reading this? Probably not. Most likely, Zach wrote it and accessed his talking points from memory.

"Under McMains, you would be *the* NYPD point person working directly with Interpol, New Scotland Yard, the Joint Threat Research Intelligence Group, and a slew of others. And I hope you know where your passport is, because you're going to be spending a lot of time in London, Hamburg, Tel Aviv, Lyons, Mexico City, Rio . . ." The implications resonated immediately and Hamner's words fuzzed while she watched Rook fiddling with the espresso maker across the squad room. Something cold and melancholy poked her gut.

". . . You there? Hello?"

"Uh, yeah." She gathered herself and tried to reset the course of the call. "Listen, you still haven't explained why you spied on me."

"Due diligence is not spying, Detective Heat." The Hammer was not only back in his wheelhouse but strutting the deck. "This is proper vetting for a key position. We needed to see who you are associating with to make sure we don't have any surprises. Like gym rats turning up naked and dead on your parlor floor."

Heat wished Zach was there so she could throttle his face to a bloody pulp with the phone. Don—a hero and ex-Navy SEAL—had no longer been her no-strings sex partner that night he came over to shower after a combat-training workout. Instead of rising to the bait, though, she calmly replied, "My personal life is my own. But we both know that man took a shotgun blast instead of me, and I'm here now because of him."

"Un-fucking-flappable. See, this is why we need you, Heat." Maybe it would be worth the drive to headquarters to give him a beatdown there. "And so you know, I've taken the step of confidentially clearing your transfer with your precinct commander."

"What? Irons knows?"

"Transparency. We're your NYPD." And then, proving the fine-tuning of his antenna, Hamner said, "I'm vibing hesitation. You are aboard for this, right?"

He broke her pause with, "I've been down this road with you once already. You only get so many of these. This is last call, Heat."

She swiveled her chair from her view of Rook. "I get it. Tell me when you want to meet."

"Excellent," he said.

The moment she hung up, Rook came up behind her and startled her. "Who the hell ground decaf in this when I was gone? Smell." He held out his coffee grinder. "What did The Hammer say about your IAB tail?"

Nikki mulled their conversation of the night before about Rook's travel absences—then thought about the ring receipt—and punted. No sense making waves right then. "You know him. Double-talk. He says it was just some Internal Affairs zealots getting out of hand. You know how those men in black are." Before Rook could question her further, she gave the grinder a cursory sniff. "Want me to dust it for prints?"

" 'Unity Makes Strength,' " translated Rook to the squad as Heat posted a hard copy of the tattoo JPEG on the Murder Board. Hearing him say those words made it difficult for her to meet his face when she turned to continue her briefing. But she did, and the corners of his eyes crinkled from that smile that made her heart skip again. And then flutter once more from the pair of secrets she held: the job offer that threatened to make her the globe-trotter for a change and finding the engagement ring receipt in his Simple Human trash can. Neither was so simple to Nikki.

Just before the meeting, Rook had cornered her in the break room, telling her that they needed some Us Time and asking how she felt about canoodling in their favorite booth at Bouley that night at nine o'clock. Her bobblehead nodding felt stupid and inadequate, so she'd said yes loud enough to turn heads in the hallway. "I'll take that as a yes!" he'd bellowed back, then inhaled deeply. "Mm, Bouley. I can already smell the wall of apples in the vestibule."

Randall Feller got a text, jogged out of the meeting, and returned in less than a minute holding a cellophane evidence bag. "Look what CSU found." He lofted it like an auction item on his way up front to hand it to Heat. "A nylon zip tie. Those of us who've worked crowd control and riot duty will recognize this puppy as a double-cuff disposable wrist restraint. And it's got blood on it."

"Where'd they make the find?" asked Nikki.

"Food cart vendor who works Eighty-first and Central Park West reported it. Apparently, the bloody zip tie landed in his chestnuts."

"*Schproing*," said Ochoa, kicking off the inevitable gallows laughs.

Rook joined in with, "I can eat around the nylon, but is blood gluten free?"

Heat didn't have to settle them down. Detective Raley accomplished that by observing the wrist restraints would explain why the victim's hands were tucked behind him when he crashed into the planetarium. The room grew very still indeed.

"Gentlemen, I believe we are leaving the realm of accidental death as a possibility," said Heat as she block printed WRIST RESTRAINTS on the whiteboard.

While Feller stepped out to get the evidence bag to Forensics for labbing, Rhymer reported no missing persons hits yet, even though he'd been checking in hourly with all the agencies. Detective Ochoa had met with similar dead ends on the aviation front. He said he contacted all the local airfields for lists of takeoffs and landings, then followed up with the pilots, and tower personnel, none of whom reported any unusual activity, visually or over the radio. The only aircraft over the area during that time were radio station traffic, government, and police helicopters.

"What about the tourist choppers?" asked Rhymer.

"All grounded. Low ceiling, no customers."

A lull of contemplation ended with Ochoa saying, "Come on, Rook, let's hear it. *Close Encounters* castaway? Rocket pack malfunction? Bring it."

But Rook remained pensive. "Sorry to disappoint, but I know as well as you do, it's going to be tough to speculate on a means, let alone a motive, without knowing who our victim is."

"Buzz killer," said Raley. "I was kind of hoping for more, you know, Rook signature whack theories."

"Oh, they'll come," said Nikki as she dismissed the squad. "Meantime, you all know the drill. Keep thinking, keep digging, keep checking, repeat as needed."

Taking her own advice, Heat worked the phones, too. She struck pay dirt with the Real Time Crime Center. "Listen up, everybody," she announced walking to the center of the bull pen. "Turns out our John Doe's ink is in the tattoo database. It took a while to process because this is far from the only Haitian coat of arms tatt in the system, but the detectives down at RTCC gave it some extra scrutiny and, thanks to spotting a small scar creating a ridge in the slogan, we have a match. Our alien now has a name." She uncapped a dry erase and recited as she printed it on the board. "Fabian Beauvais."

"Which is the identical name the fingerprint lab just gave up," said Detective Rhymer, cradling the phone at his desk. "Hey, two hits at the same time. Are we supposed to hook our pinkies, or something?" Opie got a sense of the room and blushed. "Forget I said that."

"See how this jibes with your info, Ope." She referred to her new spiral notepad, the red Clairefontaine *Pupitre* that Rook brought her as a souvenir from France. "Beauvais was indeed Haitian. An illegal who got in the system with a prior arrest for trespassing."

Rhymer nodded. "They busted him and some of his pals for Dumpster diving on private property. Midtown North turned him over to ICE for processing and a hearing date. Beauvais bonded out then . . . surprise, surprise . . . bail skipped."

As Roach saddled up to check out the Haitian's last-known address in Flatbush, Captain Irons waddled in from his office. "Patrol just responded to a call about a home invasion on West End Avenue and discovered a fatal." He turned to go, then added, "It's a pretty exclusive block. Let me know if it's a VIP so I can do my thing."

Everyone knew Wally's thing was a press announcement. For the Iron Man, getting on TV was more than a duty; it was his passion.

Always thinking in contingencies, Heat knew this would happen eventually: dueling cases and a short staff. It was one thing to lament Detective Washington's empty desk, another to be prepared when it came time to divide and conquer. Nikki beckoned Detectives Raley and Ochoa over. "Calling an audible. You two think you're ready to take the point on this new case, the home invasion?"

She already knew the answer. And the pair, who recently had been asking to be given more responsibility, didn't need to debate. Raley said, "Better than ready."

Ochoa finished the thought. "Roach-Ready."

"Good. Bring along Detective Rhymer as support, but this is your show." Heat couldn't help but notice the two seemed a little taller when they rolled to West End Ave. "Detective Feller, you set for a ride with me to Flatbush?"

But it was Rook who answered, "You bet." And, as he saw Feller approach, he added, "Shotgun."

Rush hour crept the opposite way when they came out of the Battery Tunnel, so the unmarked Taurus Police Interceptor sailed along through Red Hook and Gowanus, turning off Flatbush Avenue onto Avenue D a mere thirty minutes after Heat, Rook, and Feller buckled up outside the precinct. "You don't care that I have a tendency to get carsick," said Rook from the rear seat.

Detective Feller didn't turn around, just said, "Only if you blow chunks on the back of my head."

Nikki caught a glimpse of Rook appealing to her in the mirror, and when she ignored him and went back to looking for the address, he added, "I don't know if I can live in a world where shotgun doesn't mean shotgun."

They drove right past the building the first time because the street numbers had been pried off the doorframe, leaving only half of a brass 4 dangling sideways from a nail. Heat killed the engine and surveyed the flophouse, a six-story walk-up of graffitied brick, sections of which had been slathered over by brown paint in a sorry attempt to hide the tags. Some teenage girls, huddled clannishly on the stoop, registered the cop car, and split for the bodega next door. A plastic bag of trash flew out an upstairs window. It broke apart on the dead lawn and Feller said, "Home, sweet home."

"You might think about waiting here."

Rook groaned in protest. "This again? Really?"

When he had first started riding along, before they were in a relationship, Heat made him wait in the car for fear of liability. And later, because he meddled. Then she gave it up because he had—more or less—proven he knew how to behave himself. Sometimes. Why did she revert today? She glimpsed him again in her rearview and knew why. That jewelry receipt. It impacted her more than she knew. Nikki was worried something could happen to him.

"Maybe I should go back where I'll be safer, like hanging off a broken footbridge in the Congo."

"Stay close, writer boy," was all she said.

They passed some chalky dog turds on the landing of the third floor, and, as they trudged up one more story toward Fabian Beauvais's room, Rook asked what they guessed the monthly rent ran in an apartment building like this. Feller said, "You don't go monthly here, dude. This is weekly, at best. No lease, no ID, no job, no prob."

"It's an SRO," said Heat.

"Right. Single-room occupancy."

Detective Feller scoffed. "More like squalid, wretched, odious."

"Uh, actually," said Rook, "that would be SWO."

Feller stopped on the top step of the fourth floor and turned to look down at him. "You're still pissed I got shotgun, aren't you."

"No, I write for a living, and, with all due respect to the erroneously dubbed three Rs, wretched isn't spelled with an R, but with a—"

"Hey!" called Heat just as two men the size of NFL tight ends rushed from the hallway at Feller's back, shoving him from behind. He flew forward, his body plowing into Heat and Rook. All three tumbled as the pair leaped over them and bolted down the stairwell, skipping half the steps. Detective Feller grabbed the banister and pulled himself off Heat, who rolled herself to her feet and sprang off in pursuit.

Flying around the turn on the second floor landing, Nikki heard the entry door slam below her and so wasn't surprised when she reached the front stoop and saw the men had already gained fifty yards on her. She ID'd herself and called a freeze as she sprinted after them, now with Feller and Rook a dozen paces behind.

At Kings Highway the men separated and, just as Heat hand signaled for Feller to take the one who split left, something unusual happened. Each hopped into a waiting car—one of two nondescript, plateless sedans that sat waiting for them—and then sped off, roaring with far more muscle under their hoods than those little cars should have packed. One of them, a Japanese import, cut a wild, bounding diagonal across the concrete median and fishtailed with the other into the distance until the sound of their souped up engines faded like dying flies.

They returned to the fourth floor more quietly. Attentively, too, with Heat and Feller resting hands on holsters. Rook hung back on the landing while the cops flanked the door to listen. They shook no to each other. Nikki examined the lock for jimmy marks, but the serially abused relic had more scratches than shine. The two detectives shared ready nods. Heat turned the key the manager had given her and in they went, announcing "NYPD" and fanning out textbook-style to clear the compact room, closet, and lav.

In contrast to the grubbiness of the building, the Haitian's SRO revealed itself to be tidy and immaculate when Feller peeled the aluminum foil off one of the windows to let in the sun. The futon on the floor was neatly made with a week's worth of T-shirts, underwear, socks, and a pair of jeans folded and stacked in the blue plastic basket beside it. A so-called kitchen, really just a thirty-six-inch Formica counter with a puny, stainless steel sink dropped into it, gleamed. There was no stove, not even a hot plate, but the old microwave oven, which Heat popped open, was empty and smelled like the Mr. Clean with Febreze on the shelf above it.

Rook said, "This place would go for five thousand a month in Manhattan," then pressed PLAY on the portable CD unit on the empty bookcase. Rap Kreyol from Barikad Crew blasted and made them jump. He switched it off and said, "Sorry, sorry."

"What's your take?" asked Feller after a quick once-over of the place.

"You mean beyond the fact that Fabian Beauvais was a neatnik and liked Haitian rap?" Heat turned a circle in the middle of the room. "No personal effects, no pictures, no books, no magazines, only take-out containers in the trash? I'd say he hardly lived here."

"How does an illegal who resorts to Dumpster diving afford a place he doesn't live in? Doesn't make sense."

They spread out to search the room. It wouldn't take long with three of them and a place that size. Heat took the kitchenette, Feller the shelves and boxes, Rook went into the tiny closet, which lacked even a door. As was the case throughout the whole SRO, the primary repair element was duct tape. It was wrapped around the spigot of the kitchen faucet, it held the empty curtain rod up above the bed, and where Rook stood in the closet, dusty, gritty, and gummy old pieces of it held down the curling linoleum on the floor. But a one-foot strip of shiny and new silver tape was plastered in one corner. "What do you think?" asked Rook. When they joined him, he said, "One of these things is not like the others."

Heat and Feller got on bent knees. She took a documentary shot with her iPhone. The other detective took out his blade and cut the length of the tape, opening up a seam in the flooring that curled up. He pulled it back, exposing a rectangular hole in the under-boards, and nested in it was an envelope. Even though she wore gloves, Heat plucked the envelope out by the edges. It was thick and unsealed. And there were several fingerprints on it in what appeared to be dried blood. She folded back the closure, knowing what she'd find, just not knowing the amount.

"Are they all hundreds?" asked Detective Feller over her shoulder.

"Looks to be," she said, leaving the money inside. "If so, there are thousands in here." Nikki riffled the stack and stopped when she came upon a lump that created a bookmark in the middle of the cash. Feller extracted the tweezers from his Swiss Army knife, and with them, Heat drew out of the money a small piece of scratch paper with an address and a phone number written in ballpoint. And underneath, a word scrawled in pencil. "Can you read this?" She held it out to the other detective who squinted and tilted his head, trying to make it out.

"Conscience," whispered Rook in her ear. Startled and blushing, Nikki turned to him. But he was only deciphering the scrawl. "It says, 'conscience.'"

The crime scene unit tagged-in and Detective Heat left them to scour Fabian Beauvais's rental for more clues. She had not turned up a cell phone and asked them to alert her if one surfaced. Meantime, she, Rook, and Feller left to work the new leads. Once more the homicide squad leader felt hamstrung by her personnel shortage. Nikki's preference would have been to leave a detective to canvass the building and neighborhood, but with Roach and Rhymer deployed on the home invasion, she brought Randall Feller back to the Two-Oh with her to get the envelope labbed for a potential fingerprint and blood match with the dead Haitian's and to run serial numbers on the ten grand that turned out to be inside it. She would track the phone number and the address herself.

Of course, the pair of goons that bowled them over in the stairwell deserved some scrutiny, also. Heat called ahead to book a police-sketch artist to meet at the precinct so they could generate some pictures to follow up the Be On The Lookout notice she had transmitted. When she hung up, Rook asked them why they thought the two men had been there.

"Could be the money," said Feller. "Whatever they were up to, we surprised them."

"Actually," said Heat, "I believe we were the ones who got surprised." She made a note that when Raley got free, she'd have the King of All Surveillance Media scrub traffic cams in Flatbush for hits on the two getaway cars, although she didn't hold much hope there. Their escape setup smelled like a pro execution. Combining that with ten grand and a mysterious note hidden in the floor of a closet told Heat something more was going on than a guy falling out of an airplane. She pressed the gas pedal, as if that would help her find out sooner what it was.

Back in the bull pen, Nikki hung up her phone and crossed over to the Murder Board. "Bingo." Rook and Feller joined her there and she pointed to the eight-by-tens of the bloody envelope and the note she had posted there. "As you know, there wasn't any area code with this phone number, but a telecom records crunch scored a match with the address written there, which turns out to be in the Hamptons. I had them run it twice, and the phone listing is definitely to the same residence."

"Show-off," said Rook.

Feller tried to peek at her spiral notepad. "You get a name?" Without answering, she uncapped a red dry-erase marker with her teeth and printed it in big block letters. When she finished, Randall said, "Whoa. . . ." Rook simply had two brows arched in surprise.

"What about Keith Gilbert?" asked Wally Irons from the doorway of the bull pen. The precinct commander's fishbowl office looked out upon the Homicide Squad Room, and the VIP name had attracted his immediate attention, even from behind the glass. As a rule—and a sound one—Heat kept the captain out of the loop on most investigations until they closed. The Iron Man had too great a knack for gumming the works, at best; monkey-wrenching the whole deal, at worst. Trapped now, she sketched out the case in its leanest bullet points and explained how she came to identify a rich and powerful Port Authority commissioner as someone she wanted to interview in a suspicious death inquiry.

"You sure that's a smart play?"

"I'm taking it you don't, sir."

Irons peered over his gut to check the shine on his shoes. "I am not going on the record telling you not to follow a lead, Detective. But." He raised his face to hers. "Keith Gilbert is golf buddies with the fucking mayor. You watch the news, you read the papers. Every night he's in a tux making rounds at cocktail parties with the biggest political donors in this city, getting greased up to run for senator. Like he needs their Goddamn money."

His face clouded and he turned to Rook, as if just realizing he was there. "All this is off the record, right?"

The journalist winked and mimed a lock and key to his lips.

Heat had to acknowledge that, for once, her captain's aversion to stirring trouble was more than his default stance of self-preservation and sycophancy. Keith Gilbert was a force of nature not to be taken lightly. Scion of a wealthy shipping magnate who had let his cargo business go to rust in his old age, young Keith had dropped out of his Harvard MBA program to grab the reins of the family business from his father. Against odds, advice, and common sense, he not only held on to the broke company, he doubled down by committing a fortune to expansion, gambling his own inheritance on a dream.

Gilbert spent and spent, first renovating the outmoded cargo fleet. Then he spent more, buying up cruise ships from weak players to create a new income stream in tourism, which paid off richly. Through a series of canny moves, luck, and legendary toughness, he boldly saved the broke company and made it flourish.

He also did it with style. Over the past decade Gilbert's winning face commonly stared out from multiple covers at newsstands: paragliding the western mountains of Norway; skippering a yacht in the America's Cup; holding hands with his society bride at their storybook wedding on the Amalfi Coast; or, more recently, laughing as the charismatic guest at dinner parties inside the Beltway with the DC power elite. As if resurrecting a decaying business wasn't enough of a challenge, the shipping millionaire had set his compass heading for Washington.

But charming as he was known to be publicly, the once and future knight of the next Camelot also had a reputation as a bullyboy. Behind his back—always with a look over the shoulder—critics knew he took no prisoners. One joke making the rounds speculated that the environmental affront floating in the middle of the Pacific known as the Great Garbage Patch was really just the remnants of anyone who ever said no to Keith Gilbert or got in his way.

Heat knew all that. But she also knew doing her job meant not being afraid of uncomfortable places and the powerful that inhabit them. "Sir, I appreciate your caution. And I hope you recognize that I would never approach anyone disrespectfully, whether they were wealthy and connected like Keith Gilbert or poor and marginalized like Fabian Beauvais."

"Who?"

Rook pointed to his name on the Murder Board and mouthed, "Victim."

"You're gonna do this aren't you, Heat."

"The address and phone number of his summer mansion was written on an envelope containing ten thousand dollars hidden in the floor of a dead man's apartment. I think it's good police work to at least ask Commissioner Gilbert a few questions."

At a loss, Irons said, "Keep me looped in," and retreated toward his fishbowl.

"As always, Captain," said Heat. Detective Feller smirked and returned to his desk.

Rook seemed lost in the ozone. "Weirdest thing. All this talk made me flash on this vivid dream I keep having. You are a senator." He shook it off. "Senator Heat. Where'd that come from?"

By late morning, the police artist finished his sketches of the two men who fled the Flatbush SRO, and Heat, Rook, and Feller unanimously agreed they were good likenesses. Heat tasked Detective Feller to get them transmitted, then to return to Avenue D in Brooklyn to canvass the building and neighborhood for anyone who might have known Fabian Beauvais.

"Flash those new sketches around, too," Heat added as Feller was on his way out, but he already had copies with him for that purpose and lofted them over his head as he disappeared through the door.

"You thinking about lunch?" asked Rook.

"I'm thinking about sitting right here until I get a call back from Keith Gilbert's office." She checked her watch. "Talk about the runaround. I can get his home number in the Hamptons in less than ten minutes, but I can't get connected to his office on Park Avenue South after two hours. Reception ships me to voice mail. I call back. They bicycle me to media relations." She picked up her phone again. He put his hand on hers and returned it to the cradle.

"I think you should stop calling."

"Are you kidding me? You, Mr. Dogged Investigative Reporter?" Then she noticed Rook was looking past her. Nikki turned and couldn't believe what she saw.

Or, more accurately, whom.

An administrative aide escorted the tall man in the chalk, pinstripe suit into the bull pen and gestured to Nikki. "Detective Heat?" The commissioner smiled and extended his hand as he came to her. "Keith Gilbert. You wanted to talk with me?"

THREE

Keith Gilbert made full eye contact when he shook her hand—
something Heat always paid attention to. In her line of work, the
eyes were not only the windows to the soul, they also afforded a
panoramic view of its darker regions. But she registered none of
the shifty tells like floor staring, sideways averting, or the dead-fixed
glare. Framed by deep creases in his lean, sun-weathered face, Gilbert
smiled openly and took her measure, too, making Nikki wonder if the
guileless reading she got from him was as carefully masked as the one
she was returning.

"This is Jameson Rook," Nikki released his hand and the two men
gripped.

"Commissioner," Rook said as they sawed air. "It was a few years
back, but we met briefly at—"

"—The Robin Hood Foundation gala, right?"

While Rook beamed at Heat, Gilbert stroked the short bristles of
his goatee. "Trying to remember which year, but I do recall you were
in a very serious huddle with Tom Brokaw and Brian Williams when I
busted things up."

"'Oh-nine. And you tried to strong-arm us to pony up twenty
grand apiece to race Sir Richard Branson to Halifax on your sailboat."

"It's a ninety-foot Trimaran, and the privilege of crewing was all
for charity." Then he winked an aside to Nikki. "Never ask a journalist
to pay for anything."

While Rook and Gilbert enthused about Aretha Franklin filling
the Javitz Convention Center with "Bridge Over Troubled Water," it
bought Heat time to gather herself from the Port Authority commissioner's unexpected drop-in. She had not yet organized her questions
but had no desire to postpone and risk losing him to his busy schedule

or wall of handlers. Then, behind his back, she spotted the Murder Board in plain view with the ink still drying on his name in big fat letters. "You know what?" she said, already steering him to the door. "We should go someplace we can speak more privately."

She ushered him into the conference room, much less onerous than one of the mirrored interrogation boxes. Rook followed them. To further keep things respectful, Nikki ignored the long table and indicated the trio of cloth chairs in the corner as an informal seating area. As he took one of them and set his slim briefcase on the floor, Heat said, "I'd offer you coffee, Commissioner Gilbert, but it's kind of stale, and you caught me by surprise."

"My chief of staff said you'd left three calls. I wanted to find out why all the urgency."

"Not that I mind the personal visit, but it's kind of heroic."

"I was on the Henry Hudson anyway. Quite literally in the neighborhood, coming back from a disaster survey of the George Washington Bridge."

Rook leaned forward. "Problem with the GWB?"

"I should have said 'readiness survey.' Reporters . . . Look, I know you work with Detective Heat from those *First Press* articles you wrote about her. Impressive."

"Thank you."

"I meant Heat," he said as another playful aside to Nikki before he turned back to Rook. "But since you asked, as chair of Security and Operations, I am charged to make sure all bridges, tunnels, airports, seaports, rails, and other Port Authority assets are ready in the event we get hit by this Sandy."

Nikki flashed on the *GMA* update she'd seen that morning. "That thing all the way down around Nicaragua?"

"The computer tracking for 'that thing' has put us on alert for a potential Category One or Two hurricane to make landfall somewhere in the Northeast within a week. It could strike the tri-state, if you follow the European models."

Rook wagged a Groucho air cigar. "I followed a European model once. Until she tazed me." He felt Commissioner Gilbert's cool stare and let the mimed stogie fall from his fingers.

"Detective, I have a teleconference with FEMA, the Office of Emergency Management, and two nervous governors this afternoon, so perhaps you could simply tell me what you need to talk to me about."

"Absolutely. Let's get right to it." She gave Rook a cautionary glance to lay back, and he acknowledged it. "You own a mansion out in the Hamptons, is that right?"

"Yes . . . well, I have a second home there. I'm not sure I'd call it a mansion." His eyes narrowed in bemusement. "Did something happen to it?"

"No, not that we are aware."

"Then, if you'll pardon me, this doesn't seem like getting right to it." His demeanor remained pleasant, but he was unsubtle enough to check his wristwatch, an expensive, chunky outdoorsman's piece with more dials than the Mercury space capsule. Respect notwithstanding, Heat was determined not to let him run her meeting. She wanted to know how the address and private phone number of a man of his stature ended up bookmarking a wad of cash hidden in the floor of a poor immigrant's flophouse.

But she also knew she couldn't come at it straight on. Taking as much time and cooperation as he'd give, Nikki set out to start with a wide circle, then angle her way to the central question, learning perhaps more that way than serving his impatience. Or stature.

"Do you go there often?"

Resigned that she would follow her own tack, he answered, "As often as I can. Why are you so interested in Cosmo?"

Succumbing to the urge, she reached for her pen and notepad. "Who is Cosmo, please?"

He laughed. "Cosmo is the name of the property."

Rook was unable to restrain himself. "It's not a mansion, but it has a name?"

"Every place out there has a name."

"Cosmo . . . is unique," she said.

"The name of the first ship I bought when I took over my father's cargo business and expanded Gilbert Maritime into cruise liners. Unfortunately, like the old ship it's named for, Cosmo is a money pit. I spent more on renovation and upkeep this year alone than I did to buy it. I lost a roof to Hanna in 2008 and a second one last year to Hurricane Irene. I've decided next time it would be cheaper just to reshingle with thousand-dollar bills."

"I assume you're able to afford it," she said and watched him grow colder.

"My assets are public record, or will be, now that I'm filing for candidacy. Moving on?"

"Is the house occupied while you're away?"

"No, unless it's my wife, who never goes there. Otherwise, I have some maids who come once a week, a gardening staff, and a caretaker."

"Are they all local?" she asked.

"No, I chauffeur them out from Park Avenue." His face pinked, probably realizing how One Percenter that came off. Dropping his flash of sarcasm, he replied, "Yes, all locals who've been with me for years."

If true, that eliminated the potential domestic-worker connection she was wondering about between him and Fabian Beauvais. But the mention of his shipping line triggered something new to explore. "Where do your cruise lines go, may I ask?"

"Sure. Caribbean, mostly. We experimented in some high-end, smaller vessels to do some of the European rivers and exclusive Mediterranean ports, but the real business is the Gulf and the Caribbean."

"Jamaica?"

"Absolutely."

"Puerto Rico? Aruba? Turks and Caicos?"

"Yes, yes, and yes. Nevis and St. Kitts, also."

"Haiti?"

He scoffed. "Not a lot of vacationers eager to put in there. Why?"

Nikki pursued another line. "Have you had any burglaries, trespassers, or anything like that at Cosmo?"

"Nope. College kids had a zombie party on the beach. Some sort of *Thriller* flash mob, it's called. They knocked down some of my dune fencing and chewed some lawn with their dance, but that's about it."

"Any problem with stalkers?"

He shook no.

"Getting any strange phone calls?" Same no. "Take your time, Commissioner. Any hang ups with nobody there, weird voice mails? Think about it."

He gave it a ponder and wagged his head.

"No unknown cars hanging around? Loiterers?"

"I have protection for that sort of thing."

"You mean a gun?"

"Oh, sure I have a gun—registered, of course. But that's not what I mean. My protection is Topper. My German shepherd."

Heat decided it was time to try out the name. "Are you acquainted with a Fabian Beauvais?"

"I assume that's a person and not a wine or perfume," he said with a chuckle and a nod to Rook.

"Fabian Beauvais," she repeated, not joking.

He blew out some air and closed his eyes. "Nope," he said when he opened them. "Detective, I came here to help you, and now I don't think it's unreasonable of me to ask you tell me why. Please." He didn't make it sound anything like a question. She would have preferred to hold off until she made some more blind inquiries, but rather than lose him, she doled out the headline version, parsed for holdbacks, which was standard.

"We are looking into the death of a Haitian illegal named Fabian Beauvais, which we deem suspicious." Nikki studied him for reaction and got that same unselfconscious eye contact from when he'd first walked in. "In his personal effects we found the address and phone number of your home in the Hamptons."

"That's just weird. I never heard of this guy." Heat mentally noted the repetition. Could be a tell. Maybe not.

"How'd he die?"

"The medical examiner hasn't given a final ruling yet." In her periphery, Rook's head turned to her, reacting to the holdback. "In the meantime, we're just doing our job, covering bases. Last thing." She unfolded hard copy sketches of the two goons from the SRO stairwell. "Do you recognize these men?" As he held them for examination, she added, "And it could be from anywhere. New York City, the Hamptons, around your cruise line, maybe passengers, maybe workers."

When he said no, she handed him a mug photo. "That is Fabian Beauvais."

He laid it on top of the sketches and gave a shrug. "I'm not being much help, am I?" he said as he handed the pictures back.

"You did just fine," she said, rising. "Would it be all right if we contacted Human Resources for your shipping line to see if they know any of these three?" He eyed the printouts and said that would be fine.

"One more question before you go. Do you own an airplane or a helicopter?"

"That's an odd thing to ask."

"In the job description, I'm afraid," she said, sloughing it off. "Well, do you?"

"I have a seaplane at my place in Vancouver."

"And a helicopter?"

"A Bell JetRanger. Sounds elitist, I know, but I couldn't perform my Port Authority responsibilities without it—which, if you don't know, are *pro bono*."

"But you do have income from your shipping business."

"I am drawing from other resources at the moment. I had to place Gilbert Maritime into a blind trust this summer when I received my appointment to Port Authority. It's all about avoiding conflict of interest. The Authority receives decades of my expertise; I receive, well, nothing."

"Still, a JetRanger makes that commute from the Hamptons a snap," said Rook, reloading Heat's topic.

"Did you use your copter yesterday morning?" she asked.

"Yes, I did. I was flown from Southampton to a speaking engagement in Fort Lee for a Port Authority readiness seminar concerning the George Washington Bridge. Same drill I just mentioned. Why?"

"What time was that?"

"Let's see . . . early. The pilot got me there at seven-thirty for the seven forty-five meeting."

"And how long were you there?"

"Until four in the afternoon." A time span that would have alibied Gilbert from being anywhere near the Upper West Side when Beauvais fell. "Why so interested in my comings and goings to Fort Lee?"

"Like I said, just in the job description. Thank you for your cooperation, Commissioner Gilbert. Most appreciated."

"Happy to make the acquaintance of the famous Nikki Heat." He gave her a double handshake and enveloped her hand warmly. She escorted Gilbert as far as the lobby then doubled back to him before he got outside to his waiting black Suburban. "Oh, one more question: Does the word 'conscience' mean anything to you?"

He laughed heartily. "Lady, I'm a politician. Are you serious?"

On her way back to the bull pen, Rook met her with a briefcase. "The commish left this in the conference room."

Heat hustled through the lobby and saw he was still out there, engaged in a sidewalk phone call. When she came through the door, he had his back to her and was speaking sharply, nothing like the affable charmer she'd just interviewed. "I don't care if he's in a goddamned meeting. You get me Fred Lohman—now." Then he spotted Nikki in his periphery, flashed a winning grin, rolled his eyes, and said of himself, "What an idiot." He took the briefcase mumbling something about getting distracted.

On her way back inside, Heat wondered why Keith Gilbert so urgently needed to speak with one of Manhattan's top criminal attorneys. As he slid into the rear passenger seat of his gleaming SUV, the Port Authority commissioner caught her eye and held it briefly. In that unguarded moment she saw something foreign on him.

Strain.

Then he pulled the door closed and left.

"Roach on your desk," said Rook as Heat returned to the bull pen. She pushed aside her mail and picked up the landline.

"You two better not be messing this up."

Her detectives chuckled on the other end. "Oh, did we have an assignment or something?" said Ochoa.

"Here's the thirty-second drill," added his partner. "Doorman got overpowered from behind by multiple assailants in the middle of the night and locked up in the mail room."

"He's OK; he's the one who called it in," added Ochoa from their speakerphone.

"They forced the tenth-floor apartment door with a crowbar. Which was also used on the victim, Shelton David, eighty-six-year-old male, Dead On Scene, blunt force bleed-out is the ME's prelim. He was in his pajamas and had a Louisville Slugger beside him on the floor. Probably heard the noise and grabbed it to defend himself."

Heat nudged aside the burnished mental image of her mother's pool of blood on her kitchen floor and asked, "Any eyewits?"

"None yet. We've got some unis canvassing the building and, of course, we're already scoping for cams that might have picked up something." Ochoa's sure-footed rundown made her feel proud of these guys for seizing the moment. "CSU is here now, dusting and tweezing."

"This old guy was a prime target. A retired broker from the Gordon Gekko days who had plenty to show for it." Detective Ochoa drifted off mic. Heat could picture him surveying the apartment as he spoke. "The place has been tossed pretty good, but we contacted his insurer so we can get an inventory, in case somebody tries to fence anything."

"Good move," she said. "He was a stockbroker, so you might also check past clients or business partners. Gekko's gone. We're in the Madoff era now, so maybe somebody was getting revenge."

Raley said, "Ahead of you," and she could hear his smile at being able to say it. "Opie's got a buddy at the First Precinct who's the Wall Street go-to. His pal's already doing some legwork for us."

"Well, you guys are making me feel sort of unnecessary."

"Just doin' our jobs, ma'am," said Ochoa before they hung up. "Just doin' our jobs."

The second she cradled her phone Rook took a seat on her pile of mail. "What's your take on Commissioner Gilbert?"

"You really want to know?" she asked. Heat mulled the numerous possibilities she had been weighing and said, "Too soon to tell."

He grinned and stood. Then he made a show of extracting a

five-dollar bill from one pants pocket and putting it in his other. "I bet myself that's what you'd say."

"You're a wiseass, know that?"

"Wise, smart, irresistible, whatever. This ass is all yours, Nikki Heat."

Even clowning like he was, that declaration sparked another chest flutter, an echo of the one she'd felt that morning when she found the receipt. Nikki diverted by clearing her e-mail. "Check this out from Forensics." He leaned in, his shoulder gently brushing against hers as they shared the screen. She didn't move away. "The lab found residue of chicken blood and chicken feathers on that New Balance trainer from the planetarium."

"You know what this means, don't you?"

"Rook, I swear if you say he was a trying to be a birdman. . . ."

He pulled a face. "Birdman? Where the hell did you come up with something as whack as that? I was going to say voodoo sacrifice."

She hung her head and shook it. "All right," he said, "you doubt me? Fire up your search engine and type in "Haiti" and "chicken blood" and see if Mr. Google doesn't slap you with a page of voodoo links."

"I don't need to, Rook, I'm sure that's so. But I had a more practical thought. An illegal immigrant needs a job, right?" She entered a search for chicken slaughterhouses in the area and came up with three. "I remember passing one of these places once in Queens and a lot of alien day laborers were hanging around outside hoping for work. Now, I won't rule out some voodoo connection, but with two of these places so near to Flatbush, don't you think we'd be smarter to put our limited manpower there first?"

"Well," he said. "I suppose I can humor you."

"You from the Health Department?" hollered the woman. The screen door of the run-down corner market slammed behind her and she rushed across the road toward the undercover car, nearly getting clipped by a lumber-supply truck. "The fuck took you so long? I been calling."

Their second slaughterhouse that afternoon, and this marked the second complainer to accost them on arrival. An amused Rook came around to join Nikki on the sidewalk, which was wet in a radius around a coiled hose and tinged pink from rinsed blood. "No ma'am, I'm with the police."

"Even better. Bust these fucking assholes." She gestured with her cigarette to the slaughterhouse behind them, an orange, one-story, boxy industrial that was probably an auto body shop at one time. It had no windows, and its rolling metal garage door, prolifically tagged, was closed. "I put together three-fifty for a nice condo, and I gotta listen to the fucking squawking all day and night. And the fucking stink. I want them out of here."

Nikki assessed the moment and said, "I'll see what I can do," sympathetic to the woman's gripe but not disposed to deal with it, either.

They were let in an aluminum door cut into the metal roller, and when Heat showed her badge, about a half dozen of the workers, observing warily through the hazy glass partition, shrunk back in the warehouse and, most likely, exited out the rear. While they waited for the general manager, she gave Rook the same advice Lauren Parry had shared on her first visit to the basement autopsy room. "Breathe through your mouth, it'll trick your brain." It worked, sort of.

Standing at the glass, Rook surveyed a line of chickens hung on hooks by their feet, headless and bleeding out, waiting to be plucked. "So much for Emily Dickinson. She called hope . . ."

". . . the thing with feathers," said Heat. "Yes, I know."

"I can't let you go out onto the floor," said the GM, a doughy guy in whites with JERRY stitched on the left breast above a pocketful of pens and a quick-read thermometer. "I've got sani-caps for you both, but he'd need a beard net." Which got Nikki to tilt her head and regard Rook with a pleased grin.

"Fetching," she said.

"We're good out here," said the Jameson Rook action figure.

Heat showed the Beauvais mug shot. "We won't take much of your time. I was wondering if you could tell us if you recognize this man."

"Sure, that's Fabian." He pronounced it like the fifties rock-and-roll star instead of the Island French, but the ID hit was all Nikki cared about. In her excitement, she drew a nasal inhale and tasted death.

According to Jerry the GM, Fabian Beauvais was a dayworker like most of his crew. The immigrant community liked the job because he paid fair and didn't ask a lot of questions. Beauvais had come there nine months ago, referred by some of his Haitian buddies, and was one of his best workers. "He pulled a no-show, Jesus, must have been end of August. Then came back, I dunno, about five days ago, all nervous and stooping like he was really hurt."

"Did he say what happened?"

"Like I said, you don't ask a lot of questions here. But he was hurting, for sure. And jumpy. Fabian was always kind a cool and easy-peasy, but this guy came back totally paranoid. Is he in some kind of trouble? Is that why he disappeared on me again?"

"When did he disappear?"

"Yesterday he pulled another no-show."

Rook asked, "Did he ever say where he was or what he was doing during those two months he was gone?"

"That much I know. Said he scored a steady job doing manual labor. Construction helper, I'm thinking. I just figured he fell off a ladder, or something."

Nikki poised her ballpoint over her notebook. "Where was that job?"

"Not sure where exactly. All he said was the Hamptons."

FOUR

"Hi, Bouley? Jameson Rook. I need to cancel my dinner reservation, party of two, for this evening?" He nodded as he listened to the reservation agent. "Thank you. Yes, I'm sorry, too. My lady decided her career is more important than Us Time."

"Rook."

"Relax, he'd already hung up. That last part was for your benefit. Bite?" He held out his Italian sub, but even though it was two growls past lunchtime, she didn't like to eat behind the wheel.

The decision to drive to the Hamptons didn't come easily. In truth, there was never a good time to leave the city when you were working a case. Heat had two of them going. Plus, she was down a detective. But Raley and Ochoa had risen to the challenge of the home invasion, which definitely relieved some pressure. And Randall Feller, the best street cop she'd ever seen, had Beauvais's Brooklyn neighborhood covered. He'd even texted his plans to branch out and spend the afternoon circulating his picture around the Haitian cafés and diners concentrated near Flatbush Avenue. Her decision to go came out of the axiom drummed into her by her late mentor, Captain Montrose: "When in doubt, follow the hottest lead."

Right now, that pointed to the East End of Long Island, even though Keith Gilbert's helicopter alibi had checked out. The JetRanger dropped him in Fort Lee, New Jersey, at seven-thirty, and he led a Port Authority conference there until four-fifteen yesterday afternoon.

"Made good time," Rook said as they crossed over the canal from Hampton Bays into Shinnecock Hills. "An hour-fifteen, even without a siren, which—I'm just sayin'—would have been kind of awesome."

Rook balled the wrapping from his Jersey Mike's Number Thirteen and stuffed it in the bag with her untouched turkey and provolone. The heart of the season had passed and only light traffic laid ahead of them. Hints of autumn color painted the trees flanking the Sunrise Highway and the sign advertising pick-your-own apples ahead at the Milk Pail took her back to the fragrant vestibule of Bouley and the dinner that might have been. The grain of truth hidden in Rook's joke wasn't that she had chosen work over Us Time; she had postponed a landmark occasion in their relationship. Nikki rested a hand on his, knowing she would just have to live a while longer with the ache of curiosity.

Detective Sergeant Inez Aguinaldo greeted Heat enthusiastically in the vestibule of the Southampton Village Police Department. "Appreciate the courtesy call. We don't always get that when outside enforcement comes to visit."

"You're welcome. But this is more than a courtesy call. You can help me with a case I'm working."

Aguinaldo's face brightened, but with no golly factor. Even though she was the lead detective of a small-town force, the plainclothes sergeant gave off the coolheaded ease of military seasoning. She nodded smartly then held the inner door open. "Is your partner coming in, too?"

"No, he's . . . He's good out there." Rook had volunteered to wait in the car. Odd, for sure. Then Nikki glimpsed him jumping right on his cell phone during her walk through the lobby and wondered what he was up to.

Detective Aguinaldo arranged the mug shot of Fabian Beauvais and the sketches of the two goons from the Flatbush SRO in a spread array on her desktop. "I don't recognize any of these men." She studied them some more and said, "If you text me digitals, I'll circulate them. With your permission, I mean." Nikki liked this woman. There were too few cops who pulled off the professional command but were still human beings. Heat respected that, and felt immediately comfortable trusting her. Something she demonstrated by texting Aguinaldo the JPEGs right then and there.

Nikki's instincts about her counterpart received validation by silence. Although clearly curious, Inez Aguinaldo let things rest there. She confirmed receipt of the photos on her iPhone, set it aside, and paused, leaving it up to Nikki whether to tell her more about why she was in Southampton. Heat ran it down in bite-size chunks. From the ghastly fall from the sky to the discovery of the money in the floor of the SRO. Then she took a pause, studying the local cop carefully as she mentioned the name of one of Southampton's wealthiest and connected residents, Keith Gilbert.

"To be clear," continued Nikki, "I'm not saying Commissioner Gilbert is even involved in this. Or, if he is, whether he is a victim of some kind of crime himself, or. . . ." She let it go unsaid.

"First off, I appreciate your candor. Keith Gilbert's about as big as they come. But know this: I don't care." For emphasis, she turned her palms upward. "You work in a wealthy town like this, pretty soon you learn two things. One, do your job. Two, do your job. We don't have two sets of laws, regardless of how much money somebody has or who they think they are."

"Or, in fact, are," said Nikki.

"Back to not caring, Detective. Not looking for trouble, not looking to hide from it, either. So how can I help?"

Ten minutes later, Heat started up the car armed with a set of directions to Keith Gilbert's estate and an ally who said she would personally review any official complaints from Gilbert, as well as all traffic stops, altercations, noise reports, or strangers in the vicinity of his neighborhood over the last six months. Further, Detective Aguinaldo pointed out that if Fabian Beauvais had been in the village to do casual labor, it's possible he never got on their official radar. Frequently, if they had a benign encounter with someone, say a minor disorderly or a nonbelligerent drunk—as long as they were not behind the wheel—the officers would deal on-scene without an arrest. The sergeant said she would discreetly talk to her uniforms to see if Beauvais sparked any recollection. It wasn't quite the Real Time Crime Center, but it would do.

Heat updated Rook as they rolled through the Village Center, a quaint ideal of what small-town main streets should feel like, where people who seemed so problem-free ambled the sidewalks past a succession of designer boutiques, stylish galleries, and tea cafés nested in landmark buildings of stone and brick. When she finished, he said,

"Aren't you going to ask what I did? You don't have to. I called and made us a rez tonight for dinner—and lodging—at the renowned 1770 House in East Hampton."

"That's what you were up to? You stinker. Sounds lovely."

"The food is Barefoot Contessa-approved. And, if you think the restaurant is romantic, wait until you see the rooms."

She regarded him. "How would you know the rooms are romantic?"

"I think we should focus on my rescue of Us Time."

"Rook, I'm not so sure I like the idea of reliving some romantic getaway you once had in the Hamptons."

"Hey, Gin Lane, this is your turn." He snatched up the map in a move to check the conversation. "We'd better concentrate." They followed the quiet drive for a while, passing sprawling estates, each, it seemed to her, more opulent than the prior. "Not sure, but I believe I came this way once when I was doing a cover story on Madonna. . . . You don't mind that I had a business reason for being here before you, I hope."

"Not as long as I don't have to sleep on the same road."

"Beckett's Neck," he said. "This looks like it." She pulled onto a wide sandy spot on the shoulder and they got out. A vast pond lay across the lane behind them. Five or six smaller estates ringed its shore. They would be considered large by any standard, if they hadn't been dwarfed by the mansion before them, whose three Gothic chimneys rose up from behind a nine-foot hedge clipped so meticulously, its top edge looked sharp enough to cut.

"Come on." Nikki began walking the length of the boundary shrub and he fell in step with her. In the Hamptons these manicured greens were more common than walls for privacy. As for security, she made out the grid of chain link fencing embedded in the bushes, painted dark to match the branches. They covered about two hundred yards before they came to the corner of the hedge where it angled a hard right turn and continued along a service path on a neck of sand, rocks, and sea grass that jutted out into the Atlantic.

"Behold Beckett's Neck," said Rook. "Stunning."

The two of them retraced their steps past her undercover Taurus and continued walking another hundred yards to the opposite corner of the property front line. He never asked Heat what she was doing because he knew all about beginner's eyes and her need to let first impressions be felt. They heard a car, notably the first they'd encountered on this exclusive stretch of road, and a BMW 760 rounded the bend, slowing as the driver gave these strangers a head-to-toe once-over, making no effort to hide it. Nikki wondered if an SVPD cruiser would be summoned. Or if the man in the Bimmer had Keith Gilbert on speed dial.

They came to the main gate, framed by artisanally crafted granite pillars accented with brick. A thick timber crosspiece formed an arch overhead. Implanted in its center sat a rectangular steel plate whose white paint showed weathering and blossoms of rust. The sign, cut from the hull of an old ship, read in black letters COSMO.

Rook appraised the gate, which was made of heavy wood that matched the crossbeam. "We could get over this."

"And get arrested."

"Then it's a good thing you made a police friend."

When she protested again, he said, "Come on, Nik, we can't come this far without a healthy peek. You think I got two Pulitzers by waiting in the Humvee because some sign said keep out? Although, I can't read Russian, so I had plausible deniability."

Heat ignored him and pressed the call buzzer on the code box. He checked his watch face. "Fine, but exactly one minute, and you're giving me a boost."

A dead bolt snapped and the gates parted in the middle wide enough for the man to step out. He had graying hair poking out from under his Carhartt cap and wore a tan, long-sleeved shirt and pants that matched. No stretch for Nikki to take him to be the groundskeeper. "Help you?"

Heat showed her ID and, without any mention of Keith Gilbert or the circumstances, explained she was looking for information on someone. His face tightened, and he said, "I'm just the caretaker." She had encountered men like him before. Middle-aged pool cleaners and house painters, mostly. Emotionally fragile types not wired for life's interactions. A lot of them had an unhappy history of desk jobs, and working outdoors alone provided a way to drop out in plain sight. In deference to his unease she kept it simple.

"I'd just like you to look at a picture."

When she held out the mug shot his eyes barely swept it; then he said in sort of a plea, "I'm only here today to shutter up in case we get that hurricane." Heat tried to read him for a reaction. Was that blinky look away stress or something more?

"Have you ever seen him?"

"I don't like to get involved in stuff that's not my business. I'm just the caretaker," he repeated.

"Have you ever heard the name, Fabian Beauvais?"

He closed his eyelids as he said, "You should talk to my boss."

Then Nikki got distracted. Behind the caretaker's back, Rook flashed her an impish grin and tiptoed through the gap in the gate. What the hell? The man started to look over his shoulder. She drew his attention back. "What about your boss? Has Mr. Gilbert ever mentioned his name?"

He never answered. Behind the gate they heard an urgent bark and Rook's more urgent "No!"

When they got inside the German shepherd had a mouthful of Rook's right leg. Sharp teeth took hold of his calf above the Achilles'— but only clamped firmly without biting. It served its purpose, freezing him in place while the guard dog awaited further instructions. "Call him off?" said Rook, trying to keep his cool. The caretaker drew a forefinger across his throat like a TV director's cut sign, and the guard dog let go. Then he tapped his thigh twice and the shepherd left Rook and trotted off to heel and sit on alert at the man's left knee.

"You got lucky. Topper here's all about strangers."

The dog's ears flicked when he heard his name but remained locked on Rook, who inched his way back beside Heat. "Sorry. Really. The gate was open and I just thought it was OK."

Nikki took the opportunity to study the mansion. Keith Gilbert downplayed it, but with all its grandeur, its multiple gables, its widow's walks, its nineteenth-century windmill looming over the topiary garden, the gazebo by the pool, and the outbuilding that housed what looked like four sea kayaks, a pair of Lasers and a Hobie Cat, it could only be called the M-word. The caretaker interrupted her survey. "Going to be dark in an hour, and I've got chores to finish. I'll close the gate after you."

As soon as the dead bolt slid behind them she said, "This is why I make you stay in the car."

"And, if I had, you'd have never seen that place. Did you get a load of that garden? Straight out of *Architectural Digest*."

"I want to try the neighbors." Nikki crossed the road, trying to find a house close enough to be considered neighboring. She chose the nearest, a sore thumb of a Moroccan modern situated on the pond.

Rook didn't miss a beat as they walked toward it. "How could Gilbert not call that a mansion? Jeez, it's the size of a hotel. No, it's Downton Abbey's little brother, only of wood. And did you see the color variation on the roof and siding? That must be the post-Irene repair work he was complaining about."

Actually, Nikki had made note of the new shingling, too, first on the old windmill, then on the house and roof; the older squares appeared slightly darker than the replacements. "Lot of work got done on that place since spring." Meaning a Rook Theory couldn't be far off.

"Here comes."

"Hey, I don't think it's tinfoil hat time to postulate that our dead Haitian's manual labor job was rehabbing Cosmo. In fact, are you ready for a hypothesis?"

Heat said no, but he voiced it anyway, one that she herself had been percolating. "You've got a guy about to run for political office. Lots of scrutiny. Everybody sniffing through every aspect of his life. And what's one very damning skeleton he could have rattling in his closet? Employing an illegal alien."

"So you think the ten grand was hush money to Beauvais?"

"Got you thinking, haven't I?" Then he stretched and grinned. "Validation. Hello, my old chum."

Alicia Delamater invited them in. As Heat put away her ID, the woman said, "You didn't strike me as religious solicitors. Not that you'd get many converts on this stretch of road. Can I offer you anything?" Nikki noticed the half glass of red on the black lacquered hutch where she must have parked it when they rang the bell.

"That's very kind. We'd just like to ask you a few questions, then we'll be off."

"Sure. But can you come with me? You caught me in the middle of something." They followed her from the foyer into the dining room, which had been converted into a home office. "I'm downloading a bunch of baby pictures to make posters for a client's surprise seventieth for her dad." She moved around to her Cinema Screen monitor and frowned. "Can you believe people still use DSL? So East Ender."

Outside of, maybe, pizza, a meal hadn't been served in that room for a long time. It bespoke ordered chaos with surfaces and shelves full of large-format planning calendars, catering menus, three-ring binders with client last names on the spines, and event photos with socialites and celebrities. Rook said, "I take it you're a party planner."

"Planner, executor, part-time shrink to the wealthy dysfunctional. I'm also not above valet parking a few Bentleys, if it makes the host happy." Alicia Delamater radiated a gameness for just about anything. Beyond energy and ambition, she gave off an up-front lustiness, like a skinny-dip or a margarita in a red cup was never out of the question. Nikki took her to be about her age, but showing some mileage that must have gone with the lifestyle. "I'm all yours," she said, surrendering to the sluggish bit rate.

"Do you mind if I ask if you've been around here long?"

"About two years. Got sick of the corporate insanity and chose my own brand. Moved here, started my own business, and, Geronimo."

"You must be doing all right," said Rook.

"Not getting the call from Sean Combs to revive his White Party all right, but all right enough." She let her gaze linger on the handsome journalist in frank assessment.

Heat broke that right up with the photo. "Sometime in the last few months would you have seen this man?"

The woman let out a throaty laugh. "Oh my God, are you kidding? Sure. That's Fabian." Then she gave Heat a worried glance. "This is a mug shot. Is he in some kind of trouble?"

Nikki remained nonchalant, but Rook moved closer in his excitement. "And do you know his last name?"

"It's one of those French-Haitian ones. Not Bouvier but close."

"Beauvais?" offered Heat. And Alicia affirmed with a nod. "How or where do you know him?"

"He worked here for me. I had a lot of high-water damage after Irene that I just lived with through the winter. I hired Fab in the summer to get the property in shape."

Rook joined in. "When was the last time you saw him?"

"Exactly two weeks ago. He cut his leg on the power clipper. I offered to take him to the ER but he refused. Probably paranoid because he was illegal." An idea struck her. "You're not here because I hired an alien . . . ?"

"No," Nikki assured her. "We're just trying to piece together his movements. "Did he have any other interaction around here, perhaps do some work for some of the neighbors?" She held her breath, waiting for the Keith Gilbert connection. But Alicia shook her head.

"No way. I kept him too busy here, believe me."

"Did Beauvais tell you where he was going when he left?" asked Rook.

"Back to New York was all he said."

Heat turned a page on her notebook. "And what about visitors, did anyone come by?" The woman wagged no again. "Did he ever mention any problems or conflicts with anyone?"

"No, I'm sorry, Detective. He was just a nice guy who worked on my property and left. Not much else to tell."

They walked down her driveway in silence. Heat churned conflicted feel-ings. Not just the surface disappointment that Fabian Beauvais's connection pointed to Alicia Delamater, not Keith Gilbert, but the wariness she felt that of all the places the Haitian could end up in an area the size of the Hamptons, it was with Gilbert's neighbor. As he so often did, Rook voiced her thoughts. "Did that pass the smell test for you?"

"She never asked why we were interested in him."

"But you never told her, either. Is that a holdback, Detective?"

"I want to knock on some more doors."

They got no answer at the first four places they canvassed. They agreed to try one more before dark and were greeted on the driveway of a best-selling author, a mystery writer who routinely held the top spots on airport bookracks.

"Sure, I can spare a minute. Got Connelly, Nesbø, and Lehane waiting for me at Nick & Toni's, but that's all right. Good for humility." He chuckled, and it softened his brawny good looks, making that iconic face appear like his early author photos, the ones before he started wearing sunglasses and black leather coats in a dark alley. He gave a polite nod of recognition to Jameson Rook when Nikki introduced him, but the crime novelist seemed more keen on Heat and her police interview.

"No, I can't say that I've seen this guy. But there's a battalion of casual laborers through here. On any given day, somebody's building something or tearing something down. Have you tried Beckett's Neck? I swear Gilbert's been single-handedly turning the economy around this summer."

"We didn't get anybody who could help us there," said Heat. "Aside from you, the only person we've talked to is Alicia Delamater, his neighbor."

The author seemed to find that funny. He repeated "neighbor" and made air quotes then leaned forward, as if he could be overheard on his four-acre estate. "Try substituting 'mistress' and you'll have it."

"Aha," said Rook. "So there's been a little hedge jumping?"

"And then some. Rumor is Keith Gilbert was doing her when she worked at his shipping company. Must be good because he installed her out here and set up her business."

Rook nodded. "That's what I call a golden petticoat."

"Stick to magazines," said the author.

When she opened her door to find Heat and Rook, Alicia Delamater's smile seemed forced. "You back to check on my download? Still cooking, can you believe it?"

"I had a few more questions, if that's all right."

Alicia shrugged fine and smiled a little more. Heat made it a point to hold her pen over her notebook. "I was wondering, how did you come to hire Fabian Beauvais?"

Alicia pursed her lips and let her eyes roam the beadboard on the porch ceiling. Nikki prodded her. "I mean, could you give me the name of the agency? Or did you drive by and pick him out of the crowd of immigrants who hang out near the train station?"

"Hmm, can't remember. But I've got your card; I'll call you when I do." Heat sensed uneven breathing and decided to push.

"Are you currently, or have you been, in a relationship with Keith Gilbert?"

"I . . . I think you should go." And Alicia Delamater closed her front door.

"I'm no detective," said Rook, "but I would definitely mark that down as a yes."

The hostess at the 1770 House gave them the most romantic spot in the restaurant, a table for two against a pony wall for privacy right near the antique fireplace for atmosphere and coziness. "I feel sort of weird checking into a special place like this without luggage," she said after they sat.

"See?" said Rook. "A first." He reached across the linen and took her hand. "You're not still perseverating on the fact that I've been here before."

Heat surveyed the subdued dining room's exposed beams, tasteful oil paintings, and period china displays that adorned the walls. As she watched the hearth's goldenness flicker on Rook's face, Nikki felt a warmth and anticipation spread inside her and slid her other hand to caress his. "I can be distracted," she said.

Aware of the small world of East Hampton, they had decided in the car not to discuss the case in an open setting, which was difficult because the afternoon had raised as many questions as it answered. But that would wait. A bottle of Lucien Crochet Sancerre sat on ice and the pressing order of business for Heat and Rook was to choose between pan roasted Atlantic cod or the organic chicken with mashed potatoes and kale.

Rook made a face. "Problem with chicken after today?" she asked.

"What's all the excitement about kale? Know what kale is? Kale is the pubic hair of greens."

"Shh." Nikki swept the other tables, but nobody else heard.

He leaned in and lowered his voice. "Seriously. Know what kale tastes like? The Jolly Green Giant's nether regions. Don't ask how I know."

They laughed and made a lovers' tink of their wineglasses. Nikki studied him, fighting her anticipation, just as she also embraced it and felt its thrill. Then her phone buzzed. She stole a discreet look and the caller ID told her it was Detective Ochoa. "I'm sorry."

"Please. Take it."

Heat excused herself and whispered, "Hang on," during her walk to the inn's reception area. Both Ochoa and Raley were on the call and eager to fill her in.

Ochoa began, "We still haven't turned any eyewits, and the security cams aren't pointed in our favor. As for the Wall Street check, so far this guy was a candidate for sainthood. But we'll still mine that shaft."

"Now for the strange. Want to talk odd socks?" asked Raley, employing the term she had coined to instruct her squad always to look for things at a crime scene that don't match or feel right. "We've spent the day here combing through everything with CSU and the inventory specialist from the victim's insurance company. Nothing valuable got taken. And there's plenty here. Jewelry, collector paintings, sculptures. Even some gold Krugerrands in a cigar humidor."

"Anyway," continued Ochoa, "drawers have been emptied, bookcases pawed, closets ransacked, you get the picture. But all this valuable stuff around, and nothing seems to have gotten boosted."

Raley added, "Oh, and even the maid's room got tossed. Which is odd. It's pretty spare. Just some clothes and makeup. And no wall safe in there."

"Somebody was looking for something," she said.

"And we can't tell if they found it."

"What about the maid?" asked Heat.

"Nowhere to be found," said Ochoa. "Missing as missing can be."

"And here's reason we called. The maid's not only Haitian, but in her room we found a picture of a guy who could be a boyfriend." Raley paused. "He's got a tatt on his shoulder." In butchered pronunciation he said, "'L'Union Fait La Force.' Pardon my French."

FIVE

They surrendered their fireside table, checked out of the room—unused—and drove west, pausing only for a pit stop in Sagapanack for takeout at Townline BBQ. "So much for our romantic dinner," she said.

"I don't think of it so much as a romantic dinner as an incursion. But that's fine. Rain check tomorrow night," said Rook as they joined the red ribbon of taillights on 495. "How do you feel about an intimate rooftop supper for two? I'm sure Alton Brown has something in his *Good Eats* repertoire. I'll look in the index under 'Fussy, and Travels Well Up a Fire Escape.' "

"Or you could just consult Alicia Delamater. I'll bet she's carried more than one covered dish across the lane to Casa Cosmo."

"I'd say a hot dish. Sure explains why Keith Gilbert said his wife never goes there."

"Come on, Rook, it's obviously the other way around. The wife never goes there, so it's the perfect place to stash his mistress."

"Not so stashed, as it happens. That's the way it is with secrets; we both know that. Sooner or later, it all comes out."

There it was, served up like a big softball: Nikki's opening to come clean about the task force and relieve the pangs that had troubled her all day. She almost seized it, but held back, telling herself it was too speculative, to wait and see. In truth she knew it wasn't the job's hypothetical nature, but its disruptive one. Her emotions were swirling enough about his potential marriage proposal, why open the touchy subject of a new gig involving lots of absences for international travel?

"Wonder if it's possible Fabian Beauvais sniffed out Gilbert's illicit relationship and that's what bought him a skydive without a parachute," he said. "Like, could that money be a blackmail payoff?"

"What is that, theory number ten?" Even though Heat teased him, she had already added that notion to her growing list of maybes. But Nikki kept that list stowed away. She had seen too many detectives fall in love with one theory too soon and shut the door to all the other possibilities.

"An observation?" she said. "Keith Gilbert has to know by now that we were nosing around out there. If his caretaker didn't tell him, Alicia certainly did. That was almost three hours ago, and yet, no reaction. No call, no text, no thunder from the department's brass mountain."

"You know, Detective, it gets curiouser and curiouser. I had no idea when I pitched this case as a story to *First Press* it would end up being so juicy. An alien crashing to earth from the heavens now could herald the fall of a rising political star. Writes itself, doesn't it?" And then he quickly added, "They don't, just so you know. They never do."

If Detectives Raley and Ochoa felt tired, it didn't show on them when Heat and Rook ducked under the caution tape and entered the apartment on West End Avenue later that night. The exhilaration of piloting their own case had made the day timeless for Roach, who were on opposite sides of the living room, each conferring with a different CSU tech near bright portable work lights that made it feel more like noon than midnight.

"Oh, sure, you guys flit off to the Hamptons on a mini-vacation and leave the heavy lifting to us," said Ochoa as the four of them gathered near the bloodstain.

Heat wanted to get right to the potential tattoo connection, but engaged in the ritual cop game of playing against emotion in response to the masked thanks he'd just offered for the opportunity. "Yeah, well, until you rudely interrupted, we were hobnobbing with J-Lo and Jerry Seinfeld and Martha Stewart. We only came back to laugh at all the evidence you two overlooked."

Protocols met, Roach began the recap with a tour. The shambles matched Roach's phone description. The luxury apartment looked as if a bear had gotten into a cabin and clawed every possible hiding place for food. Bookcases, clothing armoires, and furniture had all been scraped, dumped, or slashed. Valuables—and there were plenty left behind by the burglar or burglars—had been photographed, inventoried, and filed in banker's boxes labeled NYPD Forensics. CSU technicians were still dusting for prints and plucking fibers in the maid's quarters when they got there.

Heat asked, "Did we flip the mattress like that?"

"Found it that way," answered Detective Raley. And then, sensing the graveness that descended on his squad leader as she stooped to inspect the modest personal belongings scattered on the floor—a hairbrush, a small crucifix, store-brand makeup, and a shattered votive candle—he added more gently, "We found bimonthly stubs in the victim's checkbook made out to her. The name's Jeanne Capois."

"Yeah, I got it on your missing persons call alert." She rose up and went to the window. "Was this locked like this?"

Ochoa nodded. "And no sign of exit."

"Any blood in here?"

The tech in the hairnet and sterile suit said, "No. But still checking."

Nikki said, "What about the picture?"

"Pulled these off the floor underneath the box springs." Ochoa held out three cellophane evidence envelopes. The first two contained group photos of friends: one at a nightclub; another from Battery Park with Lady Liberty in the background. "Must have gotten knocked off the bulletin board."

Heat noted the small corkboard, askew on the wall, with a tropical sunset photo push-pinned into it above a trio of faded rectangles where these shots had been posted. Only one woman was common to both pictures. Black, mid-twenties, beautiful. The third shot was a solo of a black man, also mid-twenties. It had been taken on the Coney Island boardwalk, and he had his shirt off. On one of his shoulders the Haitian tattoo faced the camera.

"We'll get this to Forensics to verify the tattoo match," said Raley, anticipating her.

"Anybody in the building know her or see her recently?" asked Heat. Her answer came with a big Roach grin that said yes. "It's almost like you guys know what you're doing."

Wilma Stallings, an elderly housekeeper from an apartment up the hall had identified Jeanne Capois when Roach knocked on doors during their routine canvass earlier in the day. She repeated to Heat and Rook that she hadn't heard any of the commotion because, at seventy-eight, she'd become hard of hearing. QVC blasting in a back room might also have been a factor. "Such a shame. Mr. David was a wonderful man. I told the other detectives he should have just let them take what they wanted. Are you sure you won't sit? The couple I work for is away at their place in Stowe."

They followed her to the living room and Nikki doubled back over ground Roach had covered with her, to get her own take on the missing woman and her life. Wilma had last seen Jeanne Capois about ten the evening before. "She seemed upset. Usually that young lady had a bright smile and all the time in the world. But when I saw her in the hall she was poking that elevator button like it was video blackjack. And not so much as a hello in return."

"Did she have anything with her," asked Heat.

"No, just her purse."

"Did it seem particularly full or unusually heavy?"

"What a peculiar question. . . . No, not that I noticed." Of course, Heat was fishing to see if Jeanne Capois's hurry was all about getting some unknown object out of the apartment. That is, assuming that's what the invasion was all about.

"Did she have any visitors recently or talk about anyone bothering her?"

The old woman shook her head.

Rook asked, "Do you know how she came to this particular job?"

"Oh, yes. An agency." Then she stared and stared. So long, in fact, Nikki wondered if she was having some sort of episode. Then she came back from the ozone and said, "Happy Hazels. Knew I'd remember it." She grinned and held up a hand, which Rook high-fived. Then Wilma squeezed her eyes tight behind her thick glasses and slapped her knee joyfully. "I'm on a roll. Something else came to me. Those young detectives showed me a photograph."

Nikki had snapped a shot with her iPhone of the Coney Island man, Fabian Beauvais. She held it out to Wilma and traded a quick hopeful glance with Rook. "Yes, that one. I just remembered. I have seen him before, after all. This fella brought Jeanne to the apartment one night last month. Or June. I don't know. Mr. David was away in Florida, I know that."

Nikki calmed herself in the face of the old housekeeper's big connection. She handed the photo to her for closer inspection. "But you are completely sure it was he?"

"Absolutely." She tapped an arthritic finger on her temple. "Sometimes it comes late, but it always comes right."

"How did they act? Did they seem to know each other well?" asked Rook.

"They had their tongues down each other's throats."

"Well enough then," he said.

First thing the next morning, Heat addressed her squad from the Murder Board. "Thanks to a photo hit from a witness found by the Detectives Roach, we now have a solid link between Fabian Beauvais and the home-invasion homicide of Shelton 'Shelly' David." Raley and Ochoa sat hunched in their chairs, each swollen-eyed and wearing the previous day's clothes. In the gap between photos of the two dead men she posted a blowup of Jeanne Capois, vignetted from the Battery Park selfie. "Roach?"

Raley side nodded to his partner and Ochoa stood to tag in on the briefing. He ran down the findings at the crime scene, including the odd sock of a home invasion without an apparent theft.

"And you don't think the ransack was just to cover the murder of the vic?" asked Randall Feller.

Ochoa nodded. "We were liking that. Even had Opie do the drill on the old broker through his First Precinct contact. That's still in progress, but the game changed when we drew the missing maid's connection to Splat Man." Even without turning he could feel Nikki's disapproving stare boring into him and amended, "I mean, Mr. Beauvais." Then he faced Heat and added, "We've pulled Detective Rhymer off the Wall Street assignment so we can detail him to track Jeanne Capois."

Raley joined in: "Logic being, she's now the hot lead. Whether she has information, is in danger, or is a player. Just wanted you to know."

Heat said the wisest thing she could have to them. "Your case, your call."

Detective Rhymer reported that he had already started working the same agencies he'd contacted on his ID search for Beauvais. "Got her picture out to airports, transit, and subways, too. The Happy Hazels voice message says they don't open until seven-thirty. I'll pay them a visit then to see if they have any alternate addresses or emergency contacts on file for her."

"Still no video around West End Avenue of the home invaders?" Heat asked Raley. And when he shook no, she said, "Have you thought about re-scrubbing those security cams for Jeanne Capois to see where she might have gone after leaving the apartment?"

"I have now." The room chuckled, but then immediately quieted when they all saw Rook entering the bull pen for the day. He was carrying his coffee and her vanilla latte. And he was beardless.

He read the silence and said, "I miss something?"

"Yeah, like half your face, homes," said Ochoa. "Did you at least save a lock for me?"

During the burst of catcalls and rowdiness, he handed Nikki her Starbucks and she mouthed, "I like it," which made him smile—with lips she could actually see now. After West End Ave., they'd gotten to his loft after 1 A.M., too wired to sleep, so they carried glasses and a bottle of Hautes-Côtes de Nuits to the bathtub. He mentioned that, on the plane, he had seen a Bond Girl shave Daniel Craig in a preview of *Skyfall* and, after their second glass, Nikki straddled him with a razor. It wasn't the warm water and the Burgundy that excited her (well, maybe a little). It was the thrilling intimacy of the act and Rook's complete trust as he rested his head back on the edge of the tub while she ran sharp steel down his throat to his naked chest. Their kiss at the end gave her his old mouth back, and they finally found sleep after surprising each other with a newfound intensity.

"Welcome back, face," she said as Rook rolled a chair over to join the meeting. Heat briefed the group on Keith Gilbert's unannounced visit then connected the dots from the chicken slaughterhouse to the Hamptons, including the encounters with Alicia Delamater, who claimed Beauvais worked for her, not her lover.

"Nice and tidy," said Detective Feller, giving voice to all their instincts. "Not saying there isn't something there, but for me, coincidence is like air freshener. It only masks the odor. The trick is to know of what." He recapped his walking tour of Flatbush, "making friends with the islander folk, and handing out business cards to anyone who'd talk to me. No hits on the mug shot or the sketches, although my gut tells me a few people recognized the dude. I'll work it some more today."

Heat said, "Take the picture of Jeanne Capois along, too."

"Maybe I should stop at CVS and get one of those cute little photo albums." His Galaxy buzzed. He checked it and held the screen out to her. "Three-four-seven area code. Could be a callback from Flatbush. Better take it." Feller hustled off to his desk across the room for quiet. With no new clues or theories developing, Nikki released the squad to work their assignments. She refreshed her computer and found a new e-mail from Forensics at the top of her stack.

"Rook, check this out." She turned to summon him but he was already right there on her shoulder. "You're very stealthy when you're clean-shaven, you know that?"

"I am all sleekness like the fabled ninja. I am made of wind and smoke, not flesh and bone. Well, except for that little trick in the bath-tub, if you catch my reference."

Nikki covered her ears. "Ew? Please? Ew?" She rotated the monitor so he could read the report along with her. Forensics had labbed clothes from Fabian Beauvais's SRO. One pair of jeans was dappled with dried spatters and abrasion transfers of a hardened resin commonly used to shellac exterior wood as a weather seal.

"You know what this means, don't you?" said Rook. "He shellacked shingles by the seashore. Which means Alicia Delamater lied. Her faux Moroccan eyesore is all stone with no exterior wood to speak of."

"Slow down there. He could have picked up that shellac anywhere, not necessarily from singles on the shea—forget it. You know what I mean."

"I do. You're applying the transitive law of mathematical logic to tell me that C minus A does not equal B if C is not the sea. Get it? Sea?" Heat elbowed him. "Hey, read what else they found."

But in her eagerness, she quoted the next section for him. "Spectral analysis revealed nonparallel rows of indentations, including several slight punctures of the denim at the calf of one leg. See: attached photo."

She opened the attachment and both reacted to what they saw: "A dog bite."

"Not a bite, exactly. Having just received one of those message-chomps myself, I'd say that's a warning hold from Topper. What are you doing?"

Nikki talked while she typed. "Replying to Forensics. To see if they can detect or ID any dog hairs by breed."

"While you're at it, you might also ask if they can test the bite for a possible DNA match to my German shepherd pal." She shrugged why not? and keyed that in, too. "The manager at the slaughterhouse said Beauvais was injured. Is it possible it was from the dog?"

"Always possible. But no mention of blood. Not on these pants, anyway. I'll have them double-check all his other clothes."

"Yeah, I'll bet those lab types love it when street detectives tell them to be thorough."

A telltale rustle of plastic announced the arrival of Wally Irons carrying a crisp white uniform shirt and blue jacket in dry cleaner bags. The camera-ready captain always kept spare wardrobe handy in the event of a news conference or photo opportunity. But instead of unlocking his office, he entered the bull pen and came directly to Heat's desk.

Normally obsequious to the press, he didn't even acknowledge Rook. "Guess what I've been doing the last fifteen minutes, Detective. No, I'll tell you. Sitting in my car in the parking lot getting an ear-ful from the Office of Emergency Management. And why? Because some pissant tropical storm near Jamaica just bumped up to a Category One hurricane, and there seems to be a strong sentiment that a witch hunt being conducted by my precinct is distracting key planners from readying this city for a potential landfall."

"And let me guess. One of those key planners is Keith Gilbert?"

"You tell me, Heat. Have you been stomping around outside your jurisdiction, dogging the heinie of a respected Port Authority commis-sioner when this entire region is about to go on storm watch?"

So there it was. Nikki wondered how it would come down. She'd half expected another drop-in by the commish. Or a phone call. But the squeeze came through channels. Back channels, actually, utilizing a high-level proxy to apply Gilbert's pressure. "Sir, I object to the term witch hunt."

"Tell the mayor's man from OEM. He's the one who used it." Wally shifted the clothes hangers to his other hand and examined the pink indents the hooks had left on his porcine fingers.

"Storm or no storm, sir, I am conducting an investigation into a suspicious death, which has now been linked to a homicide." She paused to let that seep through the crust and mantles of Wally's skull. "I have no doubt that Commissioner Gilbert finds it unsettling to have the police looking into his potential involvement in this matter, but you know how it goes here, Captain. We always follow the evidence wherever it leads without fear or favor."

She could see that registered as a platitude on the political survivor standing before her. But the other edge of the sword facing Wally was to keep his skirts clean if some future probe into his handling of a murder case put him on the record as an obstructionist. Heat was savvy enough to see that and applied her own pressure from that angle. "Sir, are you telling me to cease my investigation because it involves a highly placed member of government?"

This time Irons did seem quite aware of Rook. He glanced from the journalist back to Nikki and said, "Absolutely not. I'm apprising you of all angles . . . as you move forward." The words fell dead from his tongue. But all Heat needed was to hear them.

"Most appreciated, Captain." Heat and Rook flashed celebratory faces behind his back. "Oh, and Captain Irons? I'd also like you to sign off on getting a warrant to search Keith Gilbert's phone records."

"OK, Heat, now you're pushing it."

"But, sir, if I'm going to—"

"No way," he snapped, cutting her off. "I said you can pursue your investigation. But I am not waking the lion by getting any warrants against the commissioner, not after the phone call I just had." The Iron Man started off but had an afterthought and U-turned back to them. "In case you haven't considered it, OEM is in overlap mode with

Homeland Security and other agencies. This all works because we're all in the same sandbox and we all talk to each other."

"Sir?"

"I'm sure Counterterrorism is in the mix some way." He gave her a meaningful stare. Butterfly wings brushed her stomach in fear that he would take this conversation to the next step and out her secret in front of Rook.

Nikki shifted, physically placing herself between Rook and Irons, trying to alter the dynamic. "Thank you again."

"I'm just saying. Careful where you poke." Panic rose in her. And then out it tumbled. "You just might kiss off that job offer for the international task force." He nodded and clucked his tongue, then headed for his office, sorting out keys.

Rook's face, so much more readable without the beard, drew into itself. "What job? What was he talking about?"

Heat led him into the break room where they sat at the lone table. Given the circumstances, she might have been more at home in one of the interrogation boxes. At least Nikki didn't have to see herself in a mirror while she confessed. He watched her passively while she told him about the true reason for the Internal Affairs tail and the conversation it led to with Zach Hamner at One PP. "I really want you to know this has been tearing me up. I don't keep secrets from you, but this just came up on the heels of our . . . thing . . . about you being gone so much that I . . . didn't feel comfortable telling you just then. It was wrong of me for a lot of reasons, including this. This is worse."

But she did hold one other secret, after all. Her accidental discovery of the ring receipt. That one, Nikki could better forgive. Or, at least, rationalize.

"Let's get past you holding this back. For now," he said, and a measure of relief filled her. It was only temporary. "What's your thinking about taking this job?"

"It hasn't been formally offered."

"Nikki. You know it's coming. It's why you lied to me."

"I didn't lie."

"By omission."

"Is this what you call getting past this?"

"Where do you stand? Are you thinking about it? I'm sure it's a big promotion. Very exciting. Lots of responsibility, lots of fulfillment . . ." He let it hang there for her to fill in the Mad Lib.

"Lots of travel." She bobbed her head gravely. "International travel. I'd be gone a lot."

"But I'm asking, will you be?" The question hung there in the space between them. Because they were built of fabric that dictated rising to calls and making personal sacrificing for duty, both knew where she was leaning without the words being spoken. Indeed, it was the whole reason she'd hidden the offer from him in the first place.

For Nikki Heat, the die was cast. She'd crossed the Rubicon the day her mom was killed and she decided to be a cop. "There's a part of me that would like to hear some congratulations."

The face that had trusted her so completely, so memorably, in the tub when she shaved him now clouded. He quietly replied, "I think the time for that would have been yesterday when you hung up from the offer and told me all about it." And then he added, "But honestly, I do hope it's good for you."

Heat's phone buzzed. She showed him FELLER on the caller ID, and he left her there to take it. Nikki's heart clinched watching his back going through the door to the bull pen without a wisecrack or a funny face for her. Or even a glance.

"I'm about to hit the tunnel to Hipsterborough." Detective Feller harbored an open contempt for the millennials who had annexed Brooklyn, as he put it, "spoiling a perfectly decent working borough that doesn't need any more artisanal pickle stores or boutiques mixing home-crafted microbrews with curated vinyl LPs." His car window was down. She could hear he was moving fast. "Got a call from a guy who knows a guy I talked to on my canvass in Flatbush. Thinks he saw those two goons we chased. They were asking around for Fabian Beauvais a few days ago."

"That's great, Randall."

"We shall see. These folks weren't such big talkers yesterday."

"Use your innate charm."

"More fun to beat it out of them, but OK. I'll keep you looped."

Heat pressed END and went into the squad room to share the news with Rook. She found him packing up his laptop and notes over at his squatter's desk.

"Going somewhere?"

"Actually, yeah. I have lots of work to do on this article, and I'm not getting any writing done here. I'll catch up with you later on."

Nikki wanted more. Wanted conversation. Wanted a smile. Wanted it all back, clean. But standing there in shame and awkwardness, all she could manage was, "Sure. Your place? Mine?"

"I don't know. Let's check in." The idea of the rooftop and candles became a hope that sank, plummeting without comment, featherless.

Heat tried calling Rook when they found the body of Jeanne Capois, but his phone went straight to voice mail. Not the sort of news you leave on a message, so she let it go with, "Big development. I'll be in the field on my cell." She resisted saying call me. Too needy.

Detective Ochoa spotted her and strode toward her unmarked Taurus when she pulled up in front of the prep school on West End Avenue. Nikki paused for a ritual breath then met him on the sidewalk. "School custodian made the find," he said, escorting her to the black iron gate between the granite school building and a mixed-use apartment with a dental practice on the ground floor. "Garbage pickup is today. He was rolling the trash barrels to the walk, and there she was, dumped behind them. Lauren says there's so much blood, no doubt she was done here."

Dr. Parry crouched over the corpse, running tests and directing the CSU tech where to take photos. "This is a bad one, Nikki."

"Sadistic shit," said Detective Raley. He knew Heat wasn't big on profanity but let it out. "Sorry for that, but this is pretty fucked up."

Nikki leaned over the ME for a peek and quickly turned away. "This goes beyond blood loss from a beating," said Lauren. "My totally prelim cause of death is asphyxia. See the choke marks on the neck? As yet, I see no signs of sexual assault, so I can only imagine it was either deviant behavior or torture."

Ochoa said, "Based on the ravaging of the apartment she lived in, my money's on torture."

"Mine, too," said the medical examiner. "Come closer. See the fingertips? That damage was caused by pliers—see the grooves made by the grippers inside the pincers? And her eyes . . . It looks like some sort of toxic or corrosive liquid was poured into them. The bright stain on her blouse could be from automotive antifreeze. I'll test it." Heat turned away again, standing up straight to look at the bright yellow leaves waving on the fall trees while she contemplated the horror of Jeanne Capois's last moments alive. "She also has abrasions around her mouth where they must have gagged her. There are also numerous burns about her breasts and the soles of her feet."

"What about these here?" asked Nikki. "The marks just above her wrists."

"These are consistent with some sort of restraint biting into her skin."

"Like disposable cuffs?" Ochoa said it, more than asked it. All three detectives went right to the bloody zip ties recovered from the vendor outside the planetarium where Fabian Beauvais crashed.

Lauren Parry, the scientist among them, said, "It's highly possible. To be certain, I'd want to examine more carefully back at OCME."

"Disposable cuffs it is," said Ochoa.

"Can you venture a time of death?" asked Detective Heat.

As the medical examiner slipped brown paper bags over the victim's hands to preserve DNA and particle evidence, she said, "The body's been here two nights, I'd say. As for the hour, that's tricky. I'm going to need my lab work to give us a window. That would make it the night of the home invasion, if it tests out."

Nikki looked down at Jeanne Capois's soft, kind face; such a contrast to the brutal agony she endured. What was her life like? The photos found in her room portrayed a joyful, young woman with lots of friends, a smile that lit up the world, and a boyfriend. A boyfriend who had also died in a most horrific fashion. Heat thought about an immigrant woman in her twenties, coming to New York, as so many did, to gain a toehold on the American Dream. And this is where it ended. In an enclosure where they kept the trash. Destined for a stainless steel table in the basement autopsy room on East Thirtieth. How did this happen? What was she into? One thing Heat knew for sure: Given the timing and her relationship with Fabian Beauvais, there was something more to all this than a first-genner seeking a better life.

The detectives huddled on the sidewalk while the OCME van backed up to the gate of the garbage area. Even though the prep school closed for the day following the discovery, technicians tented the area for privacy while the body got loaded. "TOD before or after the apartment ransack?" Heat asked.

"I could see it either way," said Raley. "Scenario-one, they nab her after she leaves the building at—what time did the elderly housekeeper say?"

"Ten P.M."

"Right. And they bring her here—or catch her hiding out here—and go to work on her, trying to get her to give up whatever it is they wanted to find."

Ochoa shook his head. "But then why go and rip the hell out of the apartment?"

"Maybe she didn't tell them what they wanted," said Heat. "Or she lied."

The metal legs of the Stryker collapsed as the gurney got loaded. And they all just stopped talking and thought about the strength of will that woman must have had in the face of a professional interrogation job like that.

"Gentlemen, still your case. What next?"

Ochoa started without hesitation. "I want to get a bunch of unis to comb the four blocks between here and that apartment to see if anybody saw or heard anything that night. If she was being chased, she had to make some noise. Had to make some here, too, even if they gagged her."

"And since I am still reigning as the King of All Surveillance Media," said Rales, "I'm hunting me some cams."

Heat remained at the crime scene. It had become the hot lead. Nonetheless she was careful not to bigfoot Roach, and stood aside to let them organize deployment of Detective Rhymer, the uniforms, and the plainclothes borrowed from Burglary. She did suggest putting a detail on the homeless people who routinely set up cardboard cartons for sleeping on the steps of the church at the corner. They were the owls of the night, and their misfortune did not make them any less important as eyewitnesses.

While examining a piece of torn cloth found by a CSU tech, her phone vibrated and she jumped.

"Detective Heat? Inez Aguinaldo from SVPD." In other words, not Rook calling back. "I wanted to follow up on those checks I said I'd make for you. Is this a good time?"

"I'm at a homicide site, but I can talk."

"Then I'll keep it brief," said the lead detective from Southampton. "First of all, I checked records of calls and complaints since last April near Beckett's Neck. One of the calls, I personally responded to after we got an alarm for an intruder at Keith Gilbert's home. When we arrived Mr. Gilbert was with a woman who was clearly spending the night."

"Alicia Delamater?"

"Yes. Gilbert was holding a gun—which we verified as legally registered—on the intruder who turned out to be a very drunk mystery writer from up the neck who said he found the wrong house."

"So many look alike around there," said Heat.

"The rest are only a few routine traffic stops—all local residents. Another complaint for a dispute at the home of the same mystery writer—this time he keyed the paint on the car door of his editor—plus some loud music complaints for a sorority beach party that got out of hand."

"The *Thriller* flash mob?"

"You are certainly tapped in."

"I heard about it from Keith Gilbert."

"So did we that night." She laughed. "Let's just say the *Thriller* was gone. And pretty quickly. I also showed the sketches and the mug photo to the local patrol officers. That's the beauty of a small town. My patrol sergeant is away on vacation, so I'll have to show him when he gets back, but I got no hits on the pair of bad guys. One patrolman said he may have seen the man in your photo walking to the late train to New York a while ago, but he can't be certain. It was nighttime and he found him staggering along the road. The officer thought he was drunk, but the man said he had a bad case of the flu. He seemed lucid, although difficult to understand because he had a foreign accent, so he was a catch and release."

"That could be Beauvais. When was that?"

"Nine days ago. Is this helpful?"

"You know how it goes, Detective Aguinaldo. You never know until you know." Heat thanked her for her cooperation and hung up to snag an incoming call.

Detective Feller began without a hello. " 'K, here's the deal. The night manager of a diner that serves Island food on Church Ave. here in Flatbush got braced about six days ago by the pair of goons from our sketches. I didn't talk to him yesterday, but I did speak to his cousin who works the day shift, and he passed my card along to this guy."

"Did he know Beauvais?"

"Says he doesn't. Told them that, too, and they thought he was bullshitting them, so they got a little rough with him. So when they left, he wrote down their plate. Just for safekeeping."

Heat said, "I wonder if it's one of the getaway cars from the SRO."

"It's not. I ran it."

"Randall Feller, you rock."

"Just wait. The plate came back belonging to a Chevy Impala. Ready? It's registered to the Port Authority of New York and New Jersey."

After telling Detective Feller to stay in Flatbush to continue working the Haitian community, Nikki sat on the galvanized metal steps beneath the school's service door for a moment to take stock of this new information. She wasn't sure where it would lead, but Heat knew something bigger than she could yet see was going on. And now this Port Authority connection made it increasingly more difficult not to leap to the conclusion that beckoned her with increasing urgency.

Nikki fogged out the work of the CSU team before her. Shut out the street noise and chatter. Quieted, undistracted, creating solitude amid the chaos, she conjured a mental picture of the Murder Board six blocks away and, in reviewing every development that surfaced in this case, she began slapping imaginary Post-its on the eight-by-ten photo of one Keith Gilbert.

Whose Hamptons' address and phone number did they find with all that money in the Haitian's closet? Slap. Whose dog most likely left those bite marks on Fabian Beauvais's jeans—the jeans splattered with shellac that probably came from the renovation at Cosmo? Slap. Whose Southampton neighbor-slash-mistress far-too-coincidentally claimed to employ Beauvais? Slap. Whose organization owned the car driven by the two thugs searching for Beauvais—who also fled his SRO in Flatbush? Slap. In Heat's imagination, enough pastel sticky notes ringed the head shot to make it look like Gilbert wore a Hawaiian lei.

But that was far from a collar.

Knowing where this all pointed wasn't enough to act upon. These were indicators, for sure. Incriminating? Not yet. Forget the fact that she had not discovered a motive. Or even a mode of Beauvais's death to establish means. Heat did not have one solid connection implicating Keith Gilbert in anything more sinister than hiring an illegal day laborer to reshingle a second home.

That was, until Detective Rhymer's urgent text.

"I found it here inside this one," said Rhymer when Heat arrived. He indicated the yellow sidewalk box dispensing freebie catalogs for the Gotham Writers' Workshop. The plastic newsstand was wedged between a red one with free copies of the *Village Voice* and the blue container for handouts of *Big Apple Parent*. "I said, 'OK, what if she wasn't captured but was on the run, in a panic,' you know? Since we didn't find her purse at the murder scene, I thought maybe, if she didn't drop it, or if the bad guys didn't take it, maybe she stashed it on the fly. I walked the beeline from the home-invasion building, checking tree limbs, trash cans, even the roofs of parked trucks. Two blocks into it, dang."

His Southern accent came out on that last word, making Heat think of little Opie Rhymer, a boy in the hills with a bloodhound. With work like this, maybe he didn't need one.

Ochoa had pull up the Roach Coach and, with gloved hands, he carefully placed the contents of Jeanne Capois's purse on the hood.

Raley powered up the inexpensive pay-as-you-go cell phone inside it as Heat and Rhymer looked on. The purse items seemed to be standard fare, including a lipstick and compact, hair scrunchies, chewing gum, a MetroCard, ring of keys, grocery list, a few random business cards, and a stick pen. Her wallet still had cash in it: just a few dollars and some U.S. and Haitian gourde coins mixed together. In the photo windows were a picture of a middle-aged couple, most likely her parents, and a smiling shot of Fabian Beauvais standing proud over a barbecue of grilled fish.

"Uh, Detective," said Raley, holding out the phone, "you're going to want to look at this." Nikki took it from him and shielded the screen from the sunlight so she could read the text he had opened. The message read: RUN. KG THING GO BAD. RUN NOW! *JE T'AIME.* FAB.

The other two detectives came around to flank her so they could get a peek. Opie let out a low whistle. Ochoa kept his usual cool. "Huh," he said. "I might call that a nexus."

Heat read the text again and turned to her team. "I think it's time to have another chat with Keith Gilbert."

SIX

Detective Heat wanted to surprise Keith Gilbert same as he had with her. To Nikki, off guard meant guard down, and she didn't want him to see her coming by phoning ahead. Even if the commissioner would consent to an appointment, he had shown his hand by applying pressure through his crony at the Office of Emergency Management. Not the move of a man in the full-cooperation mode he professed.

The Port Authority headquarters were on Park Avenue South, but before Heat took a ride down there she made a quick surf of Gilbert's Web site for his exploratory campaign. Up top she found a Save the Date posting for a policy speech he was making that morning at a businesspersons' forum sponsored by a local radio station. Leaving Detective Rhymer in charge of the ongoing search of West End Ave., Roach followed Heat's car to the Widmark Hotel in Times Square. Another light drizzle was falling, reminiscent of the morning Fabian Beauvais smashed into the planetarium. When they parked and met on the sidewalk, Ochoa put his face to the mist and said, "Sure doesn't feel like a big storm's coming."

"You sound like Noah's neighbor when he saw him building the ark," said Raley. On the escalator ride from the hotel lobby to the mezzanine, he was still on the topic of Sandy. "Plus this thing's supposed to be, what, five days away? Monday or Tuesday, I hear."

"My partner the weatherman." But Nikki only half listened. Her attention went to the dark-suited security trio at the doors to the Fraunces Meeting Room. Mainly because their attention was on her.

"Do you have tickets?" asked the woman at the reception table. There were fewer than a dozen unclaimed name badges arrayed before her. The amplified voice of the afternoon drive-time newscaster boomed out of the room when one of the doors opened briefly and someone slipped out. Heat noted the new arrival was a fourth security person.

Heat showed her ID and said, "I'm not here for the forum. This is police business," which caused the young woman to chew her lip and present a "now what?" face to the security detail.

The man who had joined them from behind the door stepped forward, smiling without particular joy. He brought the scent of Old Spice and Altoids to her. "Is there a threat we should know about, Detective?"

"No, not at all." She introduced herself and Roach. The front man showed his Port Authority PD credential, but his cohorts didn't. "We're investigating a case in NYPD jurisdiction."

"I respect that." His topic sentence set a tone of obstruction. "However, PAPD is assigned to this event, and we are only to allow ticketed guests."

"I respect that," she replied in kind, "but we're not here for the speeches. We just want to conduct an interview."

"With?"

This dance had become tiresome to Heat who nonetheless kept things pleasant. "I'm sure as a cop yourself, you can understand not disclosing details of an ongoing case."

"That is certainly your prerogative," he said. Then he folded his arms to send the message that's as far as it goes then.

"We're here to see Commissioner Gilbert."

"He is not seeing anyone. The commissioner is preparing remarks to give after the breakfast."

Behind her, Ochoa cleared his throat and said, "We can wait."

"Sorry, right after, we're hustling him to Port Newark to make sure the container cargo docks are ready for Sandy." The detective reached in his side pocket and came out with a business card for Heat. "Here's the number of his office. I'm sure his assistant will compare calendars with you."

"That chaps my hide," said Raley when they descended to the lobby. "Those guys have no jurisdiction here. PAPD covers Port Authority assets. Last I heard, that did not include the Widmark Hotel."

Heat shrugged. "The Port Authority asset they're covering is the commissioner, whatever real estate he stands on. Unless you're pre-pared for a skirmish, those guys were not going to budge."

"What?" asked Ochoa. "You're just giving up?"

Not for the first time that morning, Nikki thought about Rook. But on this occasion it was not about his departure from the squad room and his not answering her calls. Heat flashed back a few years to when they had to get past security in a hospital outside Paris and he told her that nobody challenges you if you carry something or, even better, are eating. She grinned at Ochoa and picked up a house phone. "Catering manager, please."

Five minutes later Nikki stood in the hotel kitchen amid the controlled frenzy of banquet service for seven hundred guests. The manager accepted the sealed envelope from NYPD Homicide detective Heat, placed it under the stainless steel dome covering Keith Gilbert's breakfast plate, and directed the server to take it to the commissioner immediately.

Her message, in her neat printing on a Widmark note card, was succinct: UNLESS YOU WANT A VERY PUBLIC CONFRONTATION BETWEEN POLICE FORCES WHEN I ESCORT YOU OFF THE PODIUM, YOU'D BETTER SEE ME. NOW.

The Widmark Hotel had named its events facilities after American Revolutionary-era taverns and pubs. Clockwise from the Fraunces on the mezzanine came Slaters, Buckman's, The Green Dragon, and the one banquet hall sitting vacant that morning, the Bull's Head. That is where Heat stepped into the dimly lit, cavernous space with a dining capacity for fifteen-hundred to find Keith Gilbert standing alone in silhouette in the middle of the empty room. Her footfalls were barely audible on the carpet as she crossed to him. He spoke to her the whole way there.

"Your imposition into this event is not only extraordinary and rude, Detective Heat, but there will be consequences for your intrusion."

She had only closed half the distance, and he kept talking. "I came to your precinct on my own volition to make a good faith effort to answer your questions and help you put your investigation on the right course. And now this?" They were close enough for him to drop the

Widmark envelope at her feet when she stopped. "An extortion note with my eggs Benedict? Really?"

"I tried the front door. It was blocked."

"I have an office."

"You're here. And so am I. And I want some answers." She made sure to hold his gaze without flinching while he sized her up.

"Me, too. Like why are you on a such a holy mission to go after me? Is this aggressiveness your normal style? Or are you getting pressure? Is someone in city government rummaging for something so they can fire a preemptive strike at my candidacy?"

Of course Heat resented the implication that she would act as a partisan for anyone, but she was experienced enough to see it for what it was. A clever psychological attempt to put her on the defensive and dominate the interview. Well, maybe not so clever. Instead of rising to the bait, she calmly took out her notepad and said, "If you're finished, we can proceed. Don't want to make you late for your speech."

In the semidarkness of the room, she could see his jaw muscle flexing. "There are a few inconsistencies I want to give you a chance to clear up. When I told you the other day that we'd found your Southampton address and phone number in the personal effects of Fabian Beauvais, you denied knowing him."

"That's right."

"And you didn't recognize him from his picture."

"Stipulated."

"You holding to that? Because I went to Beckett's Neck yesterday and, from what I've learned since, I want to give you an opportunity to think and decide if that's still your answer for the record."

"The fuck you talking about? Speak English."

"Your neighbor, Alicia Delamater, said Fabian Beauvais worked for her recently. Kind of a coincidence." Heat raised her hand. "By the way? Not so big on coincidences. Except as red flags."

"So maybe she gave him my phone number."

"Why would she do that?"

"Ask her. See? You're fishing and trying to hold both ends of the tackle. Are we done?"

Once again, Nikki took the pushback in stride. "Thank you, I will be asking her. But, in the meantime, you're saying that Mr. Beauvais was across the lane from Cosmo this summer, and you never once saw or spoke to him?"

"That's correct."

"Even though he was supposedly in the employ of your mistress?" Her turn to poke at the defenses. Keith Gilbert was either a cool one or he could be taken at face value. All he gave up was a demi-smile.

"Sounds like you talked to some of the village gossips while you were out there, too." And then the amusement left him. "I do not have a mistress. I have a strong, long-standing marriage and embrace the value of family. I'm also prepared for the unfounded smears that can rise in a political contest." He shrugged to dismiss them.

Heat stayed on her facts. "What if I told you I had physical evidence placing Fabian Beauvais on your property?"

"What evidence?"

"Would you still hold to your statement that you didn't know him?"

"I would. What evidence?"

For Heat, the shellac stains and dog-bite marks were a definite holdback. Instead of responding, she turned a page of her spiral. "The two men I showed you the sketches of."

"Who I also don't know."

"An eyewitness in Flatbush identified them after they came into his diner asking around for Fabian Beauvais."

"Sounds like they're your lead."

"You could be right. He wrote down their license plate. They were driving a car registered to the Port Authority, Commissioner."

Finally, a reaction. Not a big one, but busy eyes while he processed the news. And how to answer it. He composed himself and chuckled. "Do you have any idea how many cars we have at Port Authority? Thousands. What's that mean? If a Metropolitan Transportation Authority car was around, do you roust the MTA commissioner?"

"Maybe if his address and phone number turned up in a bloody envelope of cash hidden in a dead man's closet." And then she watched him keenly, adding, "Or if a text about him from the dead man warning his girlfriend to run was found on her cell phone."

"What are you talking about?"

Nikki had achieved what she'd hoped for, putting him off balance. She continued to press. "Tell me about Jeanne Capois."

"Who?"

"You don't know her, either, I suppose."

"You said my name was on some woman's cell phone?"

"It was a warning text. We found it looking through her effects—after she'd been murdered."

The commissioner found his calm again and said, "I still don't see what this has to do with me."

"You were mentioned in the text."

He appeared stunned. "Me? By name?" Gilbert had her on thin ice there. His initials in that text message were not the same as naming him. He sensed her hesitation and leaped at the opening.

"Here." He thrust out his arms, presenting his wrists to her. "If you have something solid, cuff me." Then it became a taunt. "Come on. Slap 'em on, Detective." His voice grew loud enough to echo among the stacked chairs and tables at the rim of the empty hall. "Come on, do it!" He came closer, leaning into her like a batter taunting an umpire for a called strike. "Ha ha, you won't because you can't. You smell blood but you don't know whose. You got shit's, what you got."

But then his wildly manic performance jerked to a stop. Yet his face remained close to hers, and he spoke in a quiet, chilling tone. "This is no game, Detective. Do not try to browbeat me. Do not come to me with bullshit. Do not go further with this. Because you aren't man enough, and I am not to be fucked with."

She rose to her full height, unshaken. "I am getting to the bottom of this, no matter what."

"You know, my father used to butt heads with a rival in the shipping business. A guy named George Steinbrenner. Steinbrenner had a way with words when people pushed him. Like, 'Next time you drive me to the wall, I'll throw you over it.'"

"Steinbrenner was always quotable. Are you borrowing his words to threaten me?"

He smiled. "Don't take that as a threat. It's just information."

And then he left to make his speech.

———

Nikki discovered a voice mail from Rook on her way back to the car and cursed at missing his call. "Hey, it's me. Sorry to be off the grid, but I'm in the work cave, you know how that goes. Hate to do this, but I don't think that dinner's going to happen tonight. I'll explain later." So damned . . . neutral sounding. No anger, no hurt. No warmth, either. Just the facts ma'am. She decided against calling him back and rolled with the Roach Coach back to the precinct motivated by a strong desire to fulfill Keith Gilbert's wish and slap on those cuffs.

More out of habit than hunger, Heat sat at her desk picking at a turkey sandwich from Andy's Deli while she worked the phones. One inquiry was spurred by Gilbert's comment about the number of vehicles that populated the Port Authority motor pool. The Authority, a joint agency of the states of New York and New Jersey, not only oversaw the operation of area airports, air cargo, marine terminals, major bridges and tunnels, key bus terminals, cross-Hudson railroads, and the new World Trade Center, it also had its own highly respected police force of 1,700 officers—four of which Heat had the pleasure of dealing with that morning at the Widmark. Far from begrudging that detail for picket fencing her and Roach, she saw them as police professionals doing their duty. Given reverse roles, she might have done the same. Certainly they had been effective, even somewhat polite.

PAPD also has a Criminal Investigation Bureau of a hundred detectives, and Nikki's call was to one of the CIB supervisors.

"Inspector, just doing some I dotting and T crossing," she began. "One of my detectives investigating a Haitian immigrant named Fabian Beauvais heard that another pair of men had also been working Flatbush looking for him recently. I'm not sure who these two are, but their description made me wonder if they could be plainclothes cops, so I'm making the rounds of other PDs to make sure we're not stepping on brother detectives' toes anywhere."

Inspector Hugo said he appreciated the professional courtesy and that he'd check and get back to her. Heat didn't mention the nature of her case or the commissioner. She also left out the fact that the men were linked to a Port Authority-registered car. But it struck her as due diligence to make this outreach in the event the Impala was a CIB undercover. If Beauvais was part of a PAPD investigation, that would be game-changing information. Their behavior and demeanor—especially knocking them over fleeing the rooming house—was not very coplike, but there was also something about the staging and precise execution of their dual car escape that smelled like training to her.

A half hour later, Heat convened a catch up at the Murder Board with Raley, Ochoa, and Rhymer to report that PAPD called back and said they have no investigation into a Fabian Beauvais.

"It still leaves the open question of, what was a Port Authority car doing there?" said Ochoa.

"Well, the link to Gilbert is pretty cozy." Heat flicked a thumb to the plate number on the whiteboard under the sketches of the two men. "We've sent the plate out on the alert system, so if we get a ding, we may get our answer."

Detective Rhymer had made contact with the staffer at Happy Hazels, the agency that placed Jeanne Capois as the housekeeper. "Nothing earth-shattering. Kinda sad, though. They loved her, and had all good things to say. Also Fabian was more than a boyfriend. The both of them apparently came from Haiti at the same time and were engaged. But they said the only thing Jeanne cared about was to somehow get back home for the wedding."

"I found an anomaly of sorts on Jeanne Capois's MetroCard," said Raley. "Her pattern on days off was to take the Three line from the Seventy-second Street station to Saratoga Avenue in Brooklyn, which was the nearest station, I guess, to her fiancé's place near Kings Highway in Flatbush. You could set your clock to that, twice a week, for half a year. But a few weeks ago, she started using the card to round trip it on the One train from Seventy-ninth and Broadway to the Fourteenth Street stop in Chelsea, then come back to the Upper West Side the same day."

"Were these at repeating times and days?" Heat knew the value of breaks in habit. Big things like changes in lifestyle and income were key indicators to look for in an investigation, but you sometimes got the biggest breaks from the smallest things, like switching gyms or altering subway stops. "I'm wondering if she had some kind of appointment. Like maybe she was pregnant. Or had medical issues. Is there a clinic near there? Physical therapy, maybe?"

"The trips were all at different times, both day and night."

"Tell you what I'd like to do," said his partner. "I say we Roachify this."

Heat cocked her head to Detective Ochoa. "Did you just say Roachify?"

"I did. As in getting all over this. I want us to go back through her purse, her room, everything, to see if something links up to Chelsea."

"When you put it like that," said Nikki, "I'd be foolish to say no."

She had set her iPhone on her desktop and she caught the thing side-creeping across her blotter from the vibration when she came back from the restroom. Once again, not Rook. Detective Feller was calling in from Flatbush.

"Got one for you," he began. "A detective goes into a bar."

"Yeah?"

"And comes out with a clue."

"I'm listening." By reflex, she flipped to a clean page in her Claire-fontaine notebook. Feller liked to clown around, but Heat knew he wouldn't have called unless it mattered. Did it ever.

"There's kind of a dive spot around the corner from Beauvais's flop-house. I know it's early in the day, and all, but I thought I'd go in and see what kicks. So the bartender doesn't seem to want to talk but wants to at the same time; you've seen those types, right?" She had. "So I noticed there were some guys at the bar, chins over their beers, who he may not want to share in front of, so I ask him if he could come outside and give me directions to the BQE. When I get him alone, sure enough, he knows Beauvais from the neighborhood and says one night about a week ago he comes in about last call, acting like he's drunk, but he's not. He's got blood on his shirt, and says he's been shot."

"Did you say shot, as in gunshot?"

"One and the same. Beauvais says no 911 call, refuses a trip to the ER, but remembers the barkeep has a friend who's a doctor."

"Did you get a name?"

"Already spoke to him. And guess what? He'll cooperate," said Randall Feller, keeping his record unassailable as Nikki Heat's most-esteemed street cop. "I'm heading there to interview him now."

"I want to be there when you do. I can be there in half an hour."

"He's on Cortelyou near East Sixteenth." He gave her the street number, repeating it for clarity. "Look for the Klaus's Auto Parts store."

"The doctor's next door?"

"Negative. That's where he works. Ask for Ivan."

En route to Brooklyn, Heat tried calling Alicia Delamater to give her a chance to clarify her statement that Fabian Beauvais had injured himself with hedge clippers. Or, more to the point, to present Gilbert's neighbor-mistress an opportunity to recant it and come clean about her lie. She got no ring, just an insta-dump to voice mail: "This is Alicia. Away for a while. If it's urgent, call this number . . ." Nikki called it and got her attorney.

Vance Hortense of Hortense, Kirkpatrick, and Young sounded like the male version of Siri when you asked your iPhone to do something off the menu. His tone was neutral, dispassionate, and unaccommodating—which, to Heat, might have been a better name for the law firm. "Ms. Delamater has left the country."

"Where did she go?"

"Somewhere she is out of touch."

"Did she leave a number where I can reach her?"

"I'm sorry, she didn't."

"Are you saying you wouldn't know how to reach her if you had an emergency?"

"If she checks in, I'll pass on your request."

"Do you expect her back soon?"

"I can't say."

And won't, she thought.

"Please, I am not in trouble, I hope," said Ivan Gogol. His eyes, which were set in meaty lids under a constellation of moles, darted nervously from Heat to Feller. "A man need help, is all, so I help." His palpable fear in a police interview reminded Nikki of every Cold War-era spy movie Rook addictively Netflixed where the KGB breaks a hapless citizen in two while he confesses to anything they want.

"Let me put you at ease," Heat said in as reassuring a way as she could. "Your cooperation is quite appreciated. We are not here to investigate you, but simply to hear about your experience with this man."

He took another look at the photo of Beauvais and nodded, relaxing only slightly in his chair. Under the fluorescent lighting of the cluttered office the auto parts manager had let them use, his beard seemed like a dark blue tattoo beneath his pasty white skin. He had told them he was thirty-eight, but his baldness added twenty years. Or maybe it was the toll of a life spent in paranoia.

Her first question felt obvious but, knowing it was an inherent stressor, she approached it offhandedly. "I was surprised when Detective Feller said to meet you here."

"This is my work. How I pay my way," he said. "In St. Petersburg, I left medical academy knowing to be doctor of medicine, yes? But when I come to United States, the, what is it . . . ? The criteria . . . for doctor license not so easy. In Russia, I would have own clinic. Coming here to be with my wife, surprise. I drive cab or work this. Someday I take board exams and have practice in Brighton Beach."

"So you aren't technically a doctor," said Feller, and Ivan's eyes started darting again. She jumped in.

"Which makes your service to friends who can't afford doctors so admirable." She paused while he took out a cigarette and then put it back in his pocket. "Is that how the man in this picture came to you?"

Gogol recounted the late-night call from the bartender, all the details matching up with Feller's source. "So I dress and get my satchel to drive to the bar where this man, Fabian, is in the back kitchen. He is in pain and not well."

Heat asked, "How severe was the wound?" Feller had taken a cue and taken a seat beside the desk to observe.

"The wound itself not life threat. He had stopped own bleeding with compression like this." Ivan held both palms to his rib cage and pressed. "But skin is very thin at ribs and many nerve endings radiate from spine. Very painful."

"What kind of bullet was it?" And then she added with anticipation, "Did you keep it?"

"Was no bullet. The wound slice like a cut. Slice, not puncture, you see?" Feeling more in control of things, he tore a blank off a Klaus's

Auto gummed pad and drew an anterior outline of an upper torso. To her surprise, his sketch was precise and expert, neater than some drawings she had seen in autopsy files. He added a slash where the bullet struck Beauvais.

"A graze."

"That is it, graze. But close to heart. Was lucky man."

For a while, anyway, she thought. "Did you talk at all?"

"*Da*. His accent make hard, but yes," he said in his own variant of English.

"Did he say who shot him?"

Both detectives studied him as he shifted in the seat. "No." Then Ivan fixed his stare on his little drawing and he fussed with it, smoothing down the page with the side of one hand. The silence unnerved him and he filled it.

"All he tell me was earlier that night somewhere in Hamptons."

"Did he tell you exactly where?"

"Mm, no."

"In a bar, a house, in the street?"

"I do not know this."

Feller joined in. "What town?" All he got was a shrug from the Russian before he went back to fiddling with his sketch, which he then slid to Heat as an offering.

"Help me understand," she said. "Did he not see who shot him, or did he not say?"

"I did not ask him so many questions as you ask. This is best, I think."

It struck Nikki that she was getting about as far with him as she had with Alicia Delamater's lawyer on the drive over. Same obfuscation, the difference being the fear she sensed from Ivan Gogol. Was it his own nature or was it the plight of the immigrant to be ever wary, careful beyond measure? Or was he hiding something? "I want you to know that you can share anything with us without worry."

In response, he stood. "I must go back to work. I have carburetors to deliver."

One last try. "Fabian Beauvais was murdered. Whoever did that is still out there." Nikki watched that sink in as she gave him her business card. "If you remember anything more, call me anytime, day or night. I will help you." She smiled but he broke eye contact and left the room.

When Heat and Feller stepped out onto the sidewalk, Ivan was waiting by their cars. "When I finished stitching his wound, this Fabian left but came back in. He said there was a car and he waited for it to go. He was very scared. He said he wanted to tell me who did this in case something happened to him. And now you say something did?"

Nikki knew better than to speak and fracture this man's delicate moment of truth. He took a long moment to gather his courage before his leap.

But he took it.

"He said it was a powerful man. And he is. Because I have seen him on the TV. Mr. Keith Gilbert."

To be honest with herself, Heat had no idea yet how getting shot by Keith Gilbert had anything to do with Fabian Beauvais's eventual—and more lethal—plummet from a high altitude into the planetarium. But she did have enough experience in homicide to know a few things. Two attempts on Beauvais (one of which was successful), plus the torture death of his fiancée, plus a wad of hidden cash, plus the ransacking of an upscale apartment in a home invasion smelled strongly of a cover-up and conspiracy. And something Heat also knew from experience: The thing about a conspiracy is that there's always someone behind it. Someone with power. The sum of all that math told her it was time to bring in the prime suspect.

Getting a warrant would take some doing; she knew that. The DA sign-off presented enough of a hurdle. A high-profile arrest like a commissioner on the Port Authority, especially one like Keith Gilbert, who was so prominent and well connected, would require approval at the highest level downtown. But Heat trusted the courageous impartiality of the district attorney and felt confident in asking. The problem was on a much lower rung.

Her precinct commander's face went florid when she asked his permission to call the prosecutor for the arrest order. The overworked springs of Big Wally's executive chair groaned as the skipper tilted backward, jaw slack, eyes big as cue balls as he mentally played out the risks-versus-rewards of this action. To nudge him along, Heat led him from his office to the Murder Board to recap the main points, persuasively and, most importantly—ploddingly—laying out her case against Keith Gilbert as if to a first grader. He listened without interruption, bobble-heading in a way that made Nikki feel she had at last fracked through the thick insulation of fat encasing his brain.

But she had underestimated the power of organizational survivor instinct.

"Answer me this," said the captain. "Your cause of death on the flying Haitian was smacking into the planetarium, right? And now you want an arrest warrant for Gilbert because some Russkie sawbones with a sewing kit and no license claims the commissioner blasted the guy? The gun didn't kill him, gravity did."

Once again, her precinct commander fabulously displayed his lack of street experience. Nikki knew how cases get solved. You pick up a piece of the puzzle here, an odd sock there, a coincidence that doesn't make sense. . . . You stick with it, and soon, as you get more pieces, you get a whole picture, and the truth is revealed. It never dropped cleanly into your lap the way Wally fantasized.

She made another run. "Captain, come on, he shot the man. And I believe the gunshot was a first attempt. When that failed, Gilbert found some other way. Or had somebody do it." Irons kept shaking his head. "I want a warrant for his arrest and search warrant for that gun."

"No sale," he said when she had finished. "Not with my neck on that cold marble." Behind his back, the squad pelted the skipper with a barrage of disparaging looks. Heat put her own scorn aside and focused on rescuing the warrant.

"Maybe I can go back over some of these points, if I didn't make it all clear, sir."

"Oh, I get your points, just fine. But from where I sit? This is one jumbo button to push. And no way I'm pushing it without the one thing you're missing." He made a sweeping gesture to the Murder Board, which had a dismissive feel. "I see no hard link connecting this Beauvais character to Commissioner Gilbert. What I do see is a lot of circumstantials and conjecture."

"Captain Irons, this is solid. I have arrested and gotten righteous convictions on less."

"Not this time." He knuckle rapped the board, smearing some of her notations. "Show me a link from the dead guy to Gilbert. Then we'll green light your warrant."

The first thing Heat did when Irons closed his office door was to tell her detectives to stow their harsh remarks and keep their eyes on the ball. "Have your pity party later over brews at Plug Uglies. Right now we need to find a work-around for this roadblock."

"We need a Wally Work-around," said Feller.

Heat quelled the laughs with, "I said later, Randall." Thinking and thinking, she tapped her pen on her lips then said, "OK. We dig deeper into what we've got. Detective Rhymer. Run Alicia Delamater through your contacts at Customs to see if she used her passport yesterday or today. Her lawyer says she left the country, and I want to talk to her."

"On it."

And then an afterthought came to her. "And, say, Opie. Just in case she hasn't gone yet, run a list of cruises operated by Gilbert Maritime leaving New York or Jersey and put out a Watch and Advise for her." If Keith Gilbert was making moves to disrupt Heat's investigation, he might provide the transport for one of her witnesses.

"Detective Feller. Pay a visit to Port Authority motor pool. Use your personal charm to get them to show you the requisitions for names of employees who checked out that Impala. I want those two dudes sweating in our box, and soon." She noticed Rhymer still hanging around. Polite to a fault, he waited until she'd finished and raised a finger to be called on.

"Something just jumped in my head." His Virginia hills accent made it sound like a question. "It's the phone link. Beauvais had Gilbert's home number, that's what started all this."

Showing some impatience, Ochoa said, "Yeah, but Irons hit us with a catch-22 by not letting us get a warrant for Gilbert's phone records. Plus we never found a phone of Beauvais's, so that's pretty much a dry hole."

"Understood," said Rhymer. "But that phone in Jeanne Capois's purse. She had a text from Beauvais, right?"

Nikki got right there with him. "Brilliant. If we can trace that text to Beauvais's phone, we'll have his number and can run that without a warrant. Now that's a work-around."

Ochoa turned to his partner. "Why the hell didn't you think of that?"

Raley shrugged. "Just giving these other men their chance to shine."

Fifteen minutes later, Detective Heat stood Captain Irons back in front of the Murder Board and pointed to her latest posting. "We have come up with your link, sir. A phone call was made from Fabian Beauvais to Keith Gilbert's home number on this date."

Wally interrupted. "Hang on; who the hell authorized a warrant for you to search Keith Gilbert's phone records?"

"We didn't search Gilbert's records. We searched the deceased's—after tracking Fabian Beauvais to his pay-as-you-go cell phone."

"He had a burner?" Irons made it sound like a criminal accessory.

"It's not at all uncommon for low-income people to use short-term cell phones, Captain. Nor is it a crime."

"Fine. But he called the home number. Once. You call that a link?"

"Which is why," said Heat, "the series of other calls that ensued over the next few days—including calls originating from Keith Gilbert's personal cell phone to Fabian Beauvais are so . . . persuasive. Wouldn't you agree?"

Wally Irons was a survivor. True, he played checkers instead of chess with his career strategies, but even a blundering donkey found its feed bucket eventually.

"You're dead sure he's your man?"

"I am, sir. And beyond that, I am already losing potential witnesses, both to homicide and to flight." She faced him squarely, hoping to deliver the argument that hit him where he lived. "So to delay action risks calling our leadership into question, if there's an inquiry."

All he needed to hear. "Let's do this."

The same plainclothes team from PAPD that had shut out Heat and Roach earlier that morning bypassed the strategically vulnerable revolving doors and came out the wider sliding-glass exit that baggage valets used at the Widmark. The security detail made instant note of Detective Heat, who stood by their commissioner's Suburban. Gilbert followed them through and was slower to register her presence, but when he did, his face flashed with anger. Then a realization by the candidate-to-be that media was photographing and videoing all this caused him to relax his presentation. He actually smiled at Nikki as he drew near, but with his weathered facial crags and goatee, it struck her to be a pirate's grin.

"You are fucking relentless," he said, appearing casual for the photo op, but white strings of saliva on his tongue belied all that. "What the hell are you up to?"

"Doing you a favor." He furrowed his brow at that and she continued. "I will give you an opportunity to come with me quietly or . . ." She nodded to both ends of the circular driveway where Detectives Raley, Ochoa, Feller, and Rhymer stood beside their unmarked cars, which were blocking the exits. With each stood a half dozen uniformed patrol officers. ". . . Things could get very awkward."

"I don't understand this. Haven't you asked me all your questions already?"

"I'm not here to ask you questions, Commissioner Gilbert. I'm here with a warrant to arrest you for the murder of Fabian Beauvais."

Keith Gilbert had gauzed the fingerprint ink off his hands with alcohol swabs and sat in a private holding cell awaiting his attorney before he would be questioned formally. Even though Heat had deftly leveraged his arrest to avoid an ugly scene in front of the press line at the Widmark, news spread quickly, and now a nightmare swarm of media vans and spectators jammed West Eighty-second Street outside the precinct.

So many requests for interviews, both on and off the record, flooded in that Heat stopped taking press calls and began ignoring texts and e-mails, only scrolling through them every ten minutes or so in case one was from Rook. She had left him a brief voice mail, just to let him know of the arrest, making sure not to end by urging him to call. Nikki did not want to appear needy, although she ached for him to make contact. Especially after their uneasy moments that morning about the task force job.

When she saw Wally Irons stride out of the men's' room smoothing the button line of the clean white uniform shirt he'd brought on a hanger in that morning, Heat was not surprised. For all his blind spots, the captain constantly had his finger to the wind and now he had cannily reckoned that the most advantageous direction for his future was well away from a murder suspect. Also, the man could not resist the brightness of TV lights. It was like he was part moth. Legend had it that years before, he had knocked over a child in his hurry to a press podium. Heat appeared at his office door while he tied his tie in a mirror and asked him if he was sure he wanted to deal with the media so soon. As he always did, he wrapped his answer in the flag of duty. To the mirror, he said, "Somebody has to stand up and let the people of the city know their NYPD is acting without fear or favor."

"I wouldn't use that catchphrase, sir."

"I got it from you."

"I got it from the *New York Times*."

"Even better," he said. Heat only hoped the briefing she gave him had taken hold half as well as the slogan. She had her doubts.

Ten minutes later, Nikki stood way off to the side as the Iron Man chinned the bundle of microphones set up at the front door of the station house. "Good afternoon. I am Captain Wallace Irons, commander of the Twentieth Precinct." He paused while photo shutters whirred and clicked. "For the record, that's W-A-L-L-A-C-E and then I-R-O-N-S. I have a brief statement to make, which is that following an investigation into the death of a Fabian Beauvais—"

"Can you spell that for us?" asked a woman from Eyewitness News.

Momentarily thrown, the captain said, "I'll provide all that detail after my statement. Now. Following our investigation into the death of Mr. Beauvais, we have made an arrest of our prime suspect, Keith Gilbert." Although the reporters already knew this, a murmur of energy ran through the crowd accompanied by an even larger flurry of shutter clicks. "I will not be discussing evidence we have against the suspect, but, as you all know quite well who Commissioner Gilbert is, I am here to personally assure you that your NYPD acts without regard." Realizing his gaffe, he amended, "This is to say, without regard to stature."

A stringer for the *Ledger* asked, "How will this affect the Port Authority's ability to get ready for Hurricane Sandy? Wasn't he pretty much it?"

"Mm, I would ask Port Authority about that one."

"When and where did you arrest him?" called out a reporter for 1010WINS.

"Commissioner Gilbert was taken into custody without incident today after a speaking engagement . . ." As the Iron Man detailed the arrest, Heat allowed herself to relax a bit, pleased that, as agreed, he would limit his comments to the nuts and bolts of the arrest and procedural aspects, rather than revealing evidence and holdbacks.

A hand rested gently on her shoulder and she turned to see Rook. There was something unsettling in his expression. Then he leaned to her ear and whispered, "Nikki, don't hate me, all right?"

"Hate you? Come on. . . ." The weight he seemed to be carrying concerned her, but she smiled and discreetly leaned her body against his. "Why would I hate you?"

"Because I have something to tell you." She turned to face him, and Rook whispered again in her ear. "You've arrested the wrong man."

SEVEN

N ikki studied Rook's face anew, waiting for the gotcha smile or the way he playfully narrowed his eyes when he was pulling her leg. She got neither. All he said was, "Seriously."

And he looked it.

"Well, you can't be. Or, if you are, you're mistaken."

"I'm telling you, Gilbert's not the killer."

Heat noticed a tabloid freelancer edging toward them, trying to surf their conversation and said to Rook, "Not here." She took his hand and led him inside, past the Hall of Heroes memorial in the vestibule, and into the precinct lobby, which was all theirs but for the duty sergeant behind the bulletproof reception glass and the ever-present odor of a disinfecting cleaning agent. The row of orange molded plastic chairs was empty, and they took seats beneath the big STOP sign, commandeered from the traffic division, that demarcated the boundary between visitors and cops.

"I know you've had all day to dream up some alternate scenario," she began, still holding his hand as they sat there, thighs touching, "but you've missed a whole lot in your absence." Heat didn't need notes. Sometimes a blessing, sometimes a curse, she carried a nearly eidetic mental picture of the Murder Board, and quickly recapped the day, pretty much as she had earlier for Wally Irons on her warrant quest. Nikki ran it all down for him, in order: The discovery that their two infamous goons were searching for Beauvais in a Port Authority Impala; finding the body of Jeanne Capois behind the trash cans, the home-invasion housekeeper victim tortured and horribly abused; her purse, probably stashed in a hurry on the run, yielding the warning text from Fabian Beauvais about "KG." She let go of his hand and placed hers on his knee. "I swear, Rook, after I saw that, I kept thinking, if you were with me, you'd have Gilbert in Sing Sing by now." Surprised that he hadn't interrupted, but merely nodded as if waiting her out, she continued, filling him in on bracing the commissioner in the empty banquet hall at the Widmark Hotel, and, finally, "what really brought this home—are you ready?—the smoking gun of multiple phone calls between Beauvais and Gilbert, who claimed he never knew the man."

Heat didn't get the reaction she'd expected. Rook was elsewhere. Deep in some rumination, his eyes roamed the vending machine across the lobby, and not like he was deciding on which Snapple.

"I tried to call you," she said.

He came back to her. "Yeah, well, I'd gone full immersion."

"What does that mean?"

"Nik, don't get me wrong, I love my ride-alongs with you, but at a certain point, I have to break away, throw out the orange cone, and be the journalist I am." She caught her hand gripping into his knee and brought it back to rest on her lap. He didn't seem to notice. "I am officially on assignment with this story, you know. That's a core deal— home plate for me—and I have to protect it. When I'm rolling with you, I benefit, for sure. I get a ton of insights and observations. But it's too easy to lose my objectivity. If I lose that, I'm not a journalist anymore. I need to keep my independent eye."

What was going on here? she wondered. Rook spoke so calmly and clearly about this, but the effect of what he was saying—about independence and breaking away—planted a kernel of anxiety deep inside her that took root fast and grew with every sentence he spoke. More comfortable (or, at least, safer) with facts, Nikki shifted the direction this had taken. "All right. Writers' solitude. I've seen you work, I get that. But what could you possibly conjure up that makes you think I don't have a case?"

"Just to mention, when you say 'conjure,' you make me sound, I don't know, like some conspiracy whack job."

She was trying to keep this from descending into an argument, but that one deserved a pushback. "Come on, Rook, do you need me to make a list of all the wild speculations you've spouted?"

"Only to get outside the proverbial box. To stimulate you to new thinking. It's not like I went all Area Fifty-one."

"The other day at the planetarium you suggested the unknown body fell from outer space. The next day you were pitching voodoo."

"Well, let's not get anecdotal. This is different. I have some solid, rather eye-opening facts, if you'll hear them."

"Of course I will. Glad to." No she wasn't. She wanted to run away. To anywhere but this moment.

He fished a notebook out of his sport coat. She couldn't help notice he'd switched from his usual black Moleskine to a bright orange Rhodia from France. One more *différance* to absorb. She made an irrational decision to pitch the Clairefontaine pad he gave her. "Let's start at the slaughterhouse," he said. "People like Fabian Beauvais don't just show up out of the blue to choke chickens."

"Nice," she said. "No, I'm sure there's word of mouth in his community."

"Agreed. But. There are also referrals. What's one thing every immigrant needs, especially if he's illegal? Someone to get him through the maze. Red tape, housing, jobs. And discreetly. Under the radar." He opened the notebook to one of the early pages. "The slang is Gateway Lawyer. Now these are not your Park Avenue barristers. They're not even up there with the *Accidentes* personal injury guys you see on bus ads. These are bottom-feeders, for sure, but they serve a role helping the margin class."

Outside, the urgency of reporters vying to get called on caught her eye through the window and told her the press conference was winding down. "Is this going to be a civics lesson?"

"Getting there. The whole coincidence of the slaughterhouse manager pointing us to the Hamptons never went down easy for me."

"Why not? It's what happened."

Rook continued without acknowledgment. "So I did some research. Our friend Jerry, the GM of the chicken plant, has a job-referral arrangement, which sounds suspiciously like a kickback deal, with a Gateway Lawyer by the name of Reese Cristóbal. Remember Fabian Beauvais had a rap sheet for a trespassing arrest? I'm going to let you guess what attorney handled his case. Reese Cristóbal. I guessed for you."

"So far, this is all good background but—"

"Reese Cristóbal is a very busy man. He not only has strong ties to the illegal immigrant community—the night Fabian Beauvais got arrested for trespassing for his Dumpster dive, a couple of other guys got busted with him. Also immigrants. Also repped by our Gateway Lawyer."

"Which would only follow if he's handling a lot of these cases," she said.

"Correct. But this was a first offense for Fabian. I found out the pair he was consorting with had more interesting records."

Nikki cocked her head. "How did you get information on them?"

Rook grinned. "Please. Do I have to carry my Pulitzers for investigative journalism around with me?" Already chiding herself for not checking on Beauvais's fellow arrestees, Heat urged him to continue. He referred to notes again. "Bachelor Number-One, Fidel 'FiFi' Figueroa had a disorderly conduct reduced to malicious mischief for lobbing a stink bomb into a crowd. Oh, and the crowd? It was in Washington Square. At a campaign rally for Keith Gilbert."

"Go on," she said.

"Ah, the sweet sound of your undivided attention. Bachelor Number-Two, Charley Tosh, was arrested for B and E and vandalism. To wit: In the middle of the night, he broke into, and thoroughly trashed, a storefront at Sixty-third and Lex. The Keith Gilbert campaign headquarters. Are we recognizing a pattern here? From your expression, I'd say so. And know why? This was not random stuff. They were paid for their pranks by a very active political action committee. This PAC has very benign initials. It's registered as the CBP. Want to know what CBP stands for? The Committee to Block the PATHole."

He glanced up from his notes. "Don't blame me, these political wonks can be very snarky. Ever watch Bill Maher?"

In spite of herself, Heat's curiosity piqued. "Is that 'PATH,' as in Port Authority?"

"Indeed, but not the train. The PATHole in question would be a certain commissioner from the Port Authority planning to run for the U.S. Senate."

"Rook, so what? Those two did dirty work for a PAC with a sketchy name—"

"—Specifically, against Keith Gilbert's campaign."

"But that wasn't Beauvais. He was only Dumpster diving."

"With those two characters. You lie down with dogs, you're gonna get fleas. And if you ask me, the ransack of Gilbert's campaign HQ seems awfully reminiscent of the job we saw on West End Avenue. Except . . ."

"Except what?"

"Well, at the campaign office, somebody left a grumpy on the fund-raising chairman's desk."

She made a sour face. "You read the police report?"

"No, I got that from Keith Gilbert's public information officer today."

"Wait. You talked with Gilbert's press aide?"

Rook gave a no-biggie shrug. "I knew Dennis when he was dean of the J-school at Hudson University. We met up this afternoon. That's why I had my phone off."

"Rook. I can't believe this. You talked to one of my prime suspect's staff? About this case?"

"I did. It's called getting both sides."

"What did you tell him about the case? Because you have to know it's going straight to Gilbert and his Dream Team."

"Are we getting paranoid?"

"No, we are getting annoyed." Completely floored, Nikki fixed him with a look of indignation that unnerved him.

He got busy flipping ahead in his notebook and said, "I sense resistance, so let me get to my closer." He came to a dog-eared page. "Remember at the slaughterhouse how some of the workers seemed a tad shy of the police, and slipped out the rear?"

"Of course."

"Well, I went back there today and made friends in the alley."

"You paid them?"

"Please. That would be insulting. I handed out Dunkin' Donuts gift cards. And worth it, too, because one of them opened up to me." He tapped a name in his book. "Hattie Pate. Hattie was friends with Fabian Beauvais. Guess you kill a few hundred chickens, you get to know somebody. Anyway, she said Fabby came in all freaked one day.

She asked what's wrong, and he told her someone was out to kill him."
He paused. "Shall I repeat that?"

"Go on."

"Beauvais told Hattie he'd been doing some freelance work for a
bunch of guys. Some sort of ATM theft ring. They turned on him all of
a sudden and said they were going to—quoting now, 'fuck him up and
kill him dead.' They knew where he lived, so it was Hattie who turned
him on to the SRO where he moved and we found his hidden ten grand.
Gee, is it possible money's why they were after him?" He stared at her,
nodding and grinning while she processed his information. "I'll say it
again, you've got the wrong guy."

She was so absorbed chewing over Rook's story—and his indiscre-
tion with the press flak—that she hadn't noticed the news conference
had broken up and that Wally Irons now stood a few feet away. "What's
this?"

"Nothing," said Nikki, jumping in ahead of Rook. "I'm just bringing him up to speed on the case." The captain didn't totally appear to
buy that, but his cell phone lit up and he moved on into the precinct.

When Irons was gone, Heat shifted in the god-awful molded seat
to face Rook. "I'll grant that you raise a lot of interesting points. But I
hear nothing that changes the case I have against Gilbert."

"You call a death threat nothing?"

"No, and you damn well know I'll check it out." She patted his
notebook. "I want Hattie's contact info so I can get on this. But for
now, that's hearsay, and hearsay doesn't trump the evidence I've got on
Gilbert."

"Take a step back like I did, Nikki. Can you really call it evidence?"

"You bet I can."

"Because I can recontextualize everything you've got." It struck her
that, up to that morning when Rook got blindsided by the news of the
task force, he would have said, "We've got" instead of "you've." He
mimed tracing a square in the space between them with both hands and
said, "I could reframe everything in a scenario that shows that the only
connection Gilbert had to Beauvais was coping with a political dirty
trickster who was harassing him and his campaign."

"Wow, you could be Keith Gilbert's press aide now, Rook," she said with no small amount of sarcasm. "Spinning the whole thing to make the poor commissioner look like the victim."

"Maybe not a victim, but clearly he was victimized."

"Then riddle me this. Why did Gilbert deny knowing Beauvais?"

"Who knows? Maybe it had nothing to do with the killing. Or maybe he got pissed at being harassed by the Haitian. Maybe Beauvais was going to blow the whistle on the mistress. Or Keith and Alicia had a love child; another John Edwards situation. So Gilbert threatens him—just shooting off his mouth in the heat of passion—and then that ATM theft gang ends up killing him for stealing their ten grand. That would sure make me a little circumspect."

He closed his notebook and slapped the palm of his hand with it a few times while he mulled an idea. "I think you need to look harder at the two brutes from that SRO. You know, just because Beauvais got himself killed doesn't mean he was a good guy."

Valid point. Nikki often caught herself falling into the natural trap of sanctifying murder victims.

"I'm just saying, step back. Maybe things look one way, but mean another. Isn't it possible that Keith Gilbert had nothing to do with Fabian Beauvais's death but was merely orbiting the periphery?"

Instead of opening up to possibilities, a gloom enveloped her. Nikki had grown accustomed to, and even grudgingly enjoyed, Rook's diverting conspiracy speculations. It was like listening to his brain popping popcorn. But this had a different tone. His assertion that something bigger might be going on didn't pass the Redenbacher test. This felt like a challenge to her whole case.

And not diverting at all.

Detective Feller sat waiting on the other end of a blinking light for Heat when she and Rook came into the bull pen. While she took the call, Rook dropped his messenger bag on his borrowed desk and drifted over to the Murder Board to survey the updates.

"Know what this case is for me?" began Feller, who was checking in from the Port Authority's Central Automotive Headquarters in Jersey City. "Bridges and tunnels and bridges and tunnels. Oh, and tunnels."

"Boo hoo. I've got two dozen phone messages sitting here from reporters, all of whom want me to be their confidential unnamed source on Gilbert's arrest."

"Conference them all with each other, that's what I'd do. Then stand back and watch the lightning bolts arc out of the phone."

"You about done?" she said.

"About. Got a bit of the unexpected over here. Motor pool ran the registration through their system, and there is no record of anyone signing out that Impala for the last month."

"How can that be?"

"Because—are you ready? The car's been stolen."

"Stolen when?"

"Well, now it gets strange. They just discovered it and reported it today."

Nikki finished the call, sidled next to Rook and uncapped a marker to post the stolen status of the Impala. When she had finished he said, "Are you tense?"

"No, why?"

"Did I detect a certain extra degree of squeak in your block lettering, or is that my imagination?"

"Could be," she said. "Lord knows it's plenty fertile."

Before Rook could respond, Wally Irons leaned in from the doorway of his office. "Detective? Gilbert's attorneys are in Interrogation-One with him now. Everybody's ready to roll."

Heat entered the box alone. Captain Irons, who she had invited out of protocol, was too big a coward to sit in (thank God), and Rook, who very much wanted—and expected—to take part, got some bad news from Nikki outside the interrogation room door. With such a high-profile, high-stakes case, the lead detective could not afford to put a foot wrong. Topping the list of stumbles would be allowing a reporter to take part in the formal homicide interrogation of a government official in the watchful presence of his opportunistic Dream Team.

The first thing she noticed was Keith Gilbert's smile. Far from looking like a man who had just had his necktie, belt, and shoelaces taken away, he gave off a relaxed, nearly genial vibe. Nikki took the lone chair that stationed her back to the mirror of the observation room.

Across the table from her, flanked by his trio of suits, Keith Gilbert looked more like a tycoon judge on *Shark Tank* than a murder suspect. Detective Heat decided she would have to change that.

"Keith Gilbert, for the record, this is a formal interview. Just as you were informed at the time of your arrest that anything you say can and will be used against you, in this meeting you remain under caution. . . ." Nikki continued to recite the boilerplate, not only to keep every move legally unassailable, but also to make the statement that this was her party. With A-list criminal attorneys present, she knew, going in, that there was only a slim chance of getting anything damning on the record—certainly no confession. But her hope was that somewhere inside those narrow odds there lived a prospect that a careless slip would come, or that one of his answers would conflict with a prior statement, or that a new piece of useful information would tumble. From such small things big convictions came.

Frederic Lohman, senior partner of Lohman and Barkley, fanned the air with one of his arthritic hands as if shooing gnats. "Detective," he said equably in his signature near-whisper, "I think I can save us all some time if we stipulate that my client has been properly Mirandized and that, indeed, his right to an attorney has been fulfilled with some adequacy." The old lawyer let out a hoarse chuckle which his side of the table joined, including Gilbert, who somehow still managed to appear tan and robust under the sickly fluorescents that washed everyone else out. "We can further economize time by informing you respectfully up top that no statements will be made, nor will any questions be answered, by Commissioner Gilbert."

Nikki replied coolly, matching Lohman's understated tone. But her message's forcefulness couldn't be missed. "And just as respectfully, counselor, if economizing time becomes the priority of this meeting, I'll be sure to let you know. Meanwhile, the prime concern is getting answers to questions I will be asking your client concerning his role in a homicide. You may do as you like, but my agenda is not yours to set."

Having been in so many rooms like this with so many clients over five decades, the attorney took the pushback the way he always did. As if he didn't hear it. Lohman merely waited with a neutral expression.

She opened her file and began. Determined to visit every detail, she went back to the beginning, holding up the photo of Fabian Beauvais and asking if he knew him. "Asked and answered," replied the lawyer. Next she displayed the sketches of the two men who fled Beauvais's rooming house. "Asked and answered."

It continued like that, until, after a few minutes, Keith Gilbert started fidgeting and said, "Are you getting the idea, Detective?" Lohman put a scarecrow hand on his sleeve to no avail. "What's the point of this?"

"To gather facts. And to give you a chance to cooperate—"

"—I have been cooperating—" Gilbert jerked his arm away from his lawyer's cautionary touch. Nikki liked to see this and hoped his frustration would make him careless. "Tell me when I haven't cooperated, huh?"

Heat obliged. "Do you call it cooperation by making evidence disappear, obstructing an investigation?"

"How so?"

"Keith." From Lohman.

"No, I want to hear." He flexed his head side to side and she heard the soft crackle of a neck vertebra. "In my role as a commissioner, I am sworn to uphold the law of the land, and I want to know how I have obstructed."

"Let's see, Commissioner. A vehicle registered to the Port Authority, a Chevrolet Impala, was being used by two persons of interest in this case."

"Let's hold right there," said the lawyer. "All this is fine stuff, very entertaining. But, Detective Heat, you do recall this victim was not killed by a Chevy Impala, right?" He smiled at his colleagues, enjoying his own joke. "I believe he was dropped from an airplane, and that my client was twenty miles away in Fort Lee, New Jersey. So what's our issue?"

"Continuing, Commissioner," she said, pointedly shunning Lohman. "This morning I mentioned the use of the Port Authority vehicle to you. Four hours later—what a surprise—the Impala in question is not only missing from the motor pool, but somebody at your

Port Authority just happened to notice—this afternoon—that it was stolen a month ago. I'd like an explanation why that remarkable coincidence doesn't smell like obstruction."

Frederic Lohman brought up something grisly with a ragged cough, and said, "My client is not required to theorize on your speculations."

"No, Freddie, I want to answer that. My reputation's in question here." Ignoring the don't-do-it headshake from his attorney, Gilbert went on. "I never deal with the Automotive and Technical Center directly. I only know they have a lot of vehicles to account for. My guess about the timing is that the Impala probably came up stolen as they took inventory of assets for Sandy preparation. That would have less to do with me, and more with the hurricane, I assure you."

"Shall I be assured like when you said you didn't know Fabian Beauvais?"

Lohman knocked on the table as if it were a door, a first in Nikki's experience in that interrogation room. "All right, I am going to strongly counsel my client exercise his right to silence," he said with a glare to Gilbert. "And Detective Heat, your innuendos do not become any more credible through repetition. In fact, I expect we will be out of here soon due to the motion we have filed now that new evidence raises serious and fundamental doubts about your case."

She didn't know exactly where Lohman was heading, but it was more than his theater of relaxed confidence that began the slow rise of warning chimes inside Nikki. He was holding something. But what? "I'm not sure what you mean by new evidence," she said, testing the waters, "but if you've retained a private investigator, those findings will have to wait to stand the test of a public trial."

"Really? When a specific and credible threat was made against the life of the deceased by someone other than my client? To wit, a credit card fraud and ATM theft ring with motive, means, and opportunity to do so?"

Those alarm bells rang louder.

Frederic Lohman raised his tangle of eyebrows. "You don't know about this? That surprises me. Detective, your own, ah . . . let's call him friend . . . Jameson Rook, the respected investigative journalist, has uncovered sufficient evidence for me to file a motion for immediate release on own recognizance without bond. I expect we should hear quite soon because Commissioner Gilbert is so vital to the preparation for the coming natural disaster."

Rook? What the hell did he say in that meeting with Keith Gilbert's press aide? How many other of his people did he talk to about this case? Heat's brain spun. She had intended to rock them in this session, but now it was she who'd been shaken. While Nikki tried to gather herself, the lawyer continued in his offhand monotone, "Now the release on OR is only a start. We're going to press hard for a bench dismissal based on these new facts. Of course, that's a tougher road, but worth a wild shot. We all take wild shots, don't we, Detective Heat?"

Her cell phone buzzed on top of the file beside her. The caller ID said it was the DA's office. Across the table, they were all smiles. The room indeed had become a shark tank. And to Nikki, it felt like it was filling with water.

Minutes later, Heat stood peering through the glass watching Keith Gilbert get processed out. Not to Rikers Island but, as his fossil of a lawyer repeatedly claimed, to fulfill his irreplaceable role at the Port Authority leading storm crisis preparation. Rook looked on behind her, and, as the shipping magnate fastened on his nautical racing watch, he said, "I swear, Nikki, I did not tell them anything."

She didn't turn to him or even raise her voice. "Funny coincidence, wouldn't you say?"

"Well, sure, I know how it looks. Especially when you're already in a twist because I met with Gilbert's press guy."

"Today."

"Give me some credit here. I know better than to divulge inner workings of a case to somebody connected to your suspect."

"They got it from somewhere. And they kinda said it was from you. No, they actually said it was."

"They're lying." He gave her a eureka look. "Or they have an inside source. Maybe a mole at *First Press*. I'll bet that's it."

Wally Irons interrupted, joining them at the window. "Talk about a travesty." He shook his head. "I put my face out there in public, and now this? Makes me look like a dumbshit."

"Sir, nobody's unhappier about this than I am," said Heat, "but it's just a setback. It's an OR release. We still have a case."

"Yeah? Sounds like you'd better start plugging holes. Beginning with asking your boyfriend to excuse himself from the precinct premises." The captain left on that note, retreating to his office so he wouldn't have to deal with Rook himself.

"Did he just throw me out of here?"

Heat witnessed a brisk round of handshakes between Gilbert and his Dream Team as they paraded out. Then she turned to Rook. "Probably best for all concerned."

"What?" His head whipped to her. "Did you really just say that?"

"It's orders, Rook."

"But I can help. Especially now that this has blown up."

"You've already done plenty for one day."

"Nikki, are you saying you don't believe me?"

Angry and disheartened as she felt, Heat knew better than to take it that far. "I'm saying my commander has asked you to go. We'll sort the rest out later."

He gave Nikki a pained look. Disappointment, it seemed, was a team sport.

The first call Heat returned when she got back to her desk was to Lauren Parry. "Bad news up top," said the medical examiner. "Forensics can't verify the bites on Beauvais's trousers as any breed or specific dog. They'd been laundered and there was no dog hair or DNA. But I also had the lab study the abrasive indentations on Jeanne Capois's wrists. They were absolutely consistent with the disposable zip-tie handcuffs found near the planetarium following Fabian Beauvais's crash.

"Got something else that's interesting," said her friend. "Under the victim's fingernails we found the usual defensive residue of human skin from scratching her assailant or assailants. Got it all tubed and tagged for DNA potential matches."

"Let's hope," said Nikki. Lauren kept it clinical when she talked about normal defensive residue, but Heat found it difficult to remain detached. All she could envision was a woman brutally hauled behind some trash cans clawing against hope to survive.

"We also found some unusual fibers." Nikki scrawled in her notepad as Dr. Parry continued. "Both under her fingernails and, as Forensics found, snagged on the clasp of her watchband, we've got black fibers of ripstop nylon mixed with spandex. Nikki, these suggest the kind of materials you find in police uniforms. Most especially, police tactical uniforms."

"You mean like from ESU or SWAT?"

"Inconclusive, of course. We're going to do some more testing on these, but I wanted to give you the preview."

And with that short phone call another puzzle piece landed on Heat's table—an orphan with no place for her to fit it. Why would Jeanne Capois's attacker be wearing a tactical uniform? Was this about something that was going on with her or her boyfriend, Fabian Beauvais? Or both? The two guys Nikki chased from the SRO had a military demeanor. But how did that profile connect to Keith Gilbert beyond a Port Authority car they had been seen using? It seemed the more information Heat got, the more it muddied her thinking, rather than clarifying it. The only thing Nikki could be certain of was that a guy falling from an airplane was complicated enough. And this went deeper than that. What was the context here? Heat didn't have it yet, but, as Rook would say, there was a story to be told. Figure out the story, figure out the murderer.

She decided it was time to fill in some blanks.

Reese Cristóbal, the so-called Gateway Lawyer that Rook mentioned, worked out of a storefront office on West Thirty-eighth near the hansom cab horse stables, not exactly a neighborhood must-see on the tourist maps. Heat found a parking spot and badged herself to the receptionist in the tiny suite with the cracked window facing the street.

After she shook the attorney's clammy hand, she knew his peppery cologne would linger for the rest of the day—a dinnertime reminder of the visit. Cristóbal wore a short-sleeved, pink dress shirt with a harmonious tie that probably came with it in a boxed set. He returned to his place behind a stack of papers on his messy desk. Nikki took the sole guest chair and worked not to stare at the hair plugs. "I'm trying to make contact with a few of your clients. Fidel Figueroa and Charley Tosh." When he didn't respond, she said, "I'll wait, if you need to check your files."

"Correction, Detective. Former clients. And I don't need to check my files because I remember them well, and they are so freaking gone. I got no idea where they got off to, and I don't much care."

"Well. That's pretty top of mind." Her gaze went to the transplants rimming his forehead.

"I don't do a lot of criminal casework. Mostly, I'm assisting the huddled masses in transition, et ceter-yadda, et ceter-yadda. You know, landlord issues, securing identity docs, ICE hassles. But if a client gets in a bind, I help. These two, Tosh and Figueroa, abused the situation. I dig them out of a trespassing jam, only to find it's a fucking scam. They're getting paid for it as dirty tricksters for some political action assholes. Do I look like I need any trouble getting tangled up in that? No."

"I don't understand. What kind of trouble?"

"I am not in the business of helping undocumented cretins come to this country and throw rocks at a man who will be our next U.S. senator."

"You're talking about Keith Gilbert?"

"None other."

This had gone where she hoped it would, to the anti-Gilbert PAC. The attorney's protectiveness of the candidate intrigued her, so she stayed on that road. "Are you a supporter of Gilbert's?"

"He's going to be the one. Get aboard, I say."

"Are you involved in his campaign?"

"No."

"Do you know him? Have you ever met him?"

"Huh . . . I'd have to think." He made theater of searching his water stained ceiling. "No."

"Funny that you remembered Figueroa and Tosh, but you don't remember whether you met your favorite political candidate."

"Funny?" He shrugged. "Just had to think, is all."

110

It wasn't the stables Heat was smelling, but a lie. But she'd follow up on that in time. Right then, she had other things to pursue. "Do you also recall a client named Fabian Beauvais?" When he furrowed his brow, she showed him the picture.

"Oh, yeah sure. Misdemeanor trespass. Got busted with the other two. But he wasn't 'with them-with them.' Good kid. Smart. But that kinda works against you when you don't know your reality."

Heat couldn't let that go. "Excuse me, but doesn't that sound a lot like knowing your place?"

"Hey, if it craps like a duck, right? Why do you want to know about him?"

"He was murdered."

"Mm, tough break. I didn't know him. Before the trespassing bust, I mean."

She sniffed another dodge. "Didn't you place him at a job?" Nikki waited then prompted him. "At a chicken slaughterhouse?"

"Huh, did I? I'd have to look it up, but glad I could help him out." The lawyer stood up. "Hey, listen I'm late for some rent hearing up in Mott Haven. Can we do this some other day? Maybe make an appointment next time." Whether the rent hearing was real or a fabrication, there wasn't much she could do about it, with apologies and good-byes, he applied another dose of cologne to her hand and hustled out the door.

Out on the sidewalk, Heat watched him speed off in his silver Mercedes G-Class SUV. Nikki figured, for a storefront immigration lawyer, Reese Cristóbal was doing pretty well.

Back at the Twentieth, Heat discovered Feller had just returned from New Jersey, so she was able to gather her full squad for a late briefing. She shorthanded the release of Gilbert and skirted the captain's banishment of Rook from the precinct. Word on that had circulated on its own, and her crew had enough compassion—or sense—not to comment on it. "I'm not suggesting the killers are cops," she said after relaying the fiber news from OCME and Forensics. "They could be security cops, mall cops, or just buffs who bought from an army surplus. Detective Rhymer, I'd like you to show sketches of our two goons at army-navy shops. I know the clothing could have been bought online, but street-level is a good start.

Feller asked, "What about PAPD?"

"Smart. And since Port Authority is becoming your thing, why don't you make a friend at PAPD who'll run Beauvais and Capois through their data bank to see if there are any hits. Arrests, tickets, citizen complaints filed against a cop, basically anything. Roach, have you gotten any traction on those MetroCard swipes in Chelsea?"

"Indeed," said Raley. "When we went through Jeanne Capois's purse a second time, we found something on the back of a grocery receipt in her wallet. She had used it to jot down an address in Chelsea on West Sixteenth Street."

Ochoa added, "It's an apartment not far from the subway stop."

"And, ironically, the Port Authority Inland Terminal Building. Before you get excited, it's no longer owned by Port Authority, but by Google. I Googled that, increasing a seemingly infinite loop of irony."

"Before you get pulled into a time warp, Rales, why don't you give me that address? I'll pay a visit tonight on my way home. I'd like you and Ochoa to go interview Beauvais's friend Hattie Pate at the address Rook left."

Before she released them for the night she voiced what swirled within all of them. "I don't need to tell you this case is far from cleared. I won't say it's in jeopardy, but we can't sit on what's up here." She indicated the Murder Board over her shoulder. "Let's pretend this is square one and get more."

"Higher, farther, faster," said Rhymer.

Ochoa shook his head. "Don't. Just don't."

She gave the taxi driver the address in Chelsea and settled into the seat burdened by a downer day and her own bleak thoughts. The surprise turn the case had taken and its collateral fallout was bad enough. The underpinning that kept her brain swirling had a name, and it was Jameson Rook. After the years of intimacy and happiness they had enjoyed together, not to mention the deep respect she had for his character, she had cause to believe him when he said he hadn't shared any inside information with Gilbert's man. Then how did this happen?

She took out her phone and opened up the text message Rook had sent her shortly after he left the Twentieth. BTW SINCE YOU BROUGHT UP VOODOO, I ALSO DID SOME RESEARCH ON THAT EARLIER TODAY. NOT AS FRINGY-SATANIC AS PEOPLE THINK. ONE OF THEIR BELIEFS IS THAT THERE ARE NO ACCIDENTS OR COINCIDENCES. EVERYTHING HAPPENS FOR A PURPOSE—R.

Nikki wondered what purpose she could she find in this. Not in sending the text, that was obviously a makeup ping. But what reason was there to find in Rook's dissent and intrusion? Even if he hadn't been the direct cause of Gilbert's release without bail, he'd been more than a loose cannon. She couldn't escape that recurring feeling he was working against her.

Ever since news of the task force job came out.

Heat didn't want even to think he would be trying to undermine her chance for the task force for his personal reason of keeping her in New York.

But she couldn't stop.

So she touched the TV screen to resume the seat-back news video she had switched off before, just to get some distraction. "Hurricane Sandy Slams Jamaica." So much for escape. The *Eyewitness News* report said the storm had become a Category One, moving northward, pounding Jamaica with eighty-mile-per-hour winds. Footage rolled of people walking bent into the sideways force of rain. A reporter in a yellow slicker made his obligatory stand-up report, shouting against the howl of nature from the seething breakwater about dead and missing by the dozens, buildings caving, others being swept out to sea in the surge. The raging hurricane continued its track over the Caribbean, with computer models still predicting landfall in the U.S. Northeast sometime Monday or Tuesday. Like most New Yorkers, Heat looked at the gentle mist reflecting the night-scape on the sidewalks and found it all hard to believe. But a lot could happen in five days.

When the cab let her out at Eighth Avenue at Sixteenth a new unsettling wave rolled through her. After she scoped out this address, Nikki worried: should she go to her place or to Rook's? Their issues would all need to be confronted eventually. For the moment, that meant later. Heat double-checked the address and walked on, asking herself why the hell she ever went into the trash for that Parisian jewelry bag.

If she had been paying attention to the street instead, she might have seen them coming. By the time the man in the black SWAT uniform tackled her from behind, his partner had already yanked her gun.

EIGHT

Surprise delayed Heat's reaction. A split second of "what the—?" was all it took, and she toppled face-first, toward the sidewalk. But in the blink after that split second, training kicked in. With a vengeance.

A primary rule of close combat: Don't get pinned. Nikki spun during the fall to present her back to the ground. On her twist around she jammed a sharp elbow to the ear of the man behind her, which not only stunned him but also pushed him off-line so he would not land on top of her.

When he hit the pavement with an "Oof," she had already continued her roll, flinging a leg behind the knees of the man beside her, the one who'd taken her weapon. He had her Sig Sauer in his hand but pointed where she had been, not where she was. The leg sweep took this guy down hard. The back of his head made a coconut smack on the concrete. Heat sprung into a crouch, ready to lunge for her pistol, but by then the other assailant had gathered himself up and he threw himself on her.

Like his partner, he was big and built like granite. But his bulk also made him slower than Nikki. Once again, she swiveled to land on her back, and when he reached out to put a hand on each shoulder to pin her, she rained a rapid-fire barrage of punches up to his undefended face, a face she then recognized from Beauvais's SRO. He pulled back a fist to strike her, but during his wind-up, she lunged the crown of her forehead into his nose and he cried out. The punch never came.

Movement. The other man, also from the SRO hallway, was hauling himself up onto his knees, dazed, and with blood streaming from the split skin on the back of his shaved head. In the ghosty light, she saw him start to bring up the Sig Sauer. Nikki struggled to free herself from under the moaning hulk. Finally getting to a squat, she gauged there was too much distance and not enough time to jump for the pistol. She made a no-look reach and tore at the Velcro on her ankle holster. The ripping sound gave the man an instant of hesitation. Heat filled it with .25 caliber slugs from her Beretta Jetfire. The air cracked twice and his face lit up with muzzle flashes as the bullets entered just above his eyebrows.

Beside her, a whoosh of cloth. A black tactical boot kicked Nikki's wrist and her back-up piece flew from her hand, clattering into the parking lot of the public housing complex. Without waiting, she dove for her Sig in the dead man's hand. Inches from reaching it, two pairs of hands grabbed her from behind, snatching her up onto her feet. Another big man had joined the attack, and both of them dragged her across the sidewalk toward an idling van. She struggled mightily to free herself. Heat knew if they got her in that thing, she was as good as dead.

Another axiom from Nikki's combat training: To unleash surprise, think in opposites. She made a point of wrestling harder the closer they brought her to the side cargo doors. No match for their brute strength, she was conditioning them to work against her resistance. Then, a yard from the open doors came their surprise. Heat reversed her struggle, unexpectedly charging in the direction they were pushing her. The flip in momentum hurled all three of them at the vehicle. But Nikki was the only one prepared for the shift.

When the two men smacked into the side of the van on either side of her, Heat broke free and ran.

At ten on a drizzly weeknight, this block was hopelessly quiet. Apartment vestibules were empty and locked; the big office building on the left slept; no cabs or cars to flag for help. Ahead, at Ninth Avenue, a pool of bright light reminded her: The hotels. The Dream and the Maritime both had a vibrant night scene. And security. But then she came to an abrupt stop.

A silhouette approached her from that direction; a dark paramilitary form. Half a block away, but coming. Walking. Taking his time, however also bringing his hand to his hip. Something about his ease made him seem even more menacing. Nikki cut a quick turn and shot across Sixteenth to get some leeway on the opposite side. She almost got killed.

The attackers' cargo van bore down full throttle and nearly creamed her, speeding the wrong way on a one-way street. Heat took advantage of the blow-by. They were going too fast to turn around. So she reversed field and doubled back the way they came, toward Eighth. But the van didn't bother to turn around. She heard protesting gears and the thundering of the engine. Heat glanced back as she ran, only to be blinded by white back ups as the Express 1500 raced toward her—full speed—in reverse.

The driver had skills. Even going backward at an insane clip, the tires followed the gutter line expertly, and soon the thing came beside her, pacing her. The cargo doors banged open and the attacker whose nose she had flattened hung out of the hatch, poised to either jump or simply ape snatch her as they drove by. Lungs searing, Heat calculated her chances of making the corner, determined not to go, not like this. And for a flash, she wondered if this is what it had been like for Jeanne Capois right before the torture.

At Eighth Avenue a taxi approached with its roof light burning. Nikki reached the corner shouting with her arms raised, but the driver never looked her way. She ran out into traffic but the few other cabs that came by were all taken on a misty night in New York. A frantically waving pedestrian got ignored; just a drunk or a tourist. She thought of flashing her badge for a stop but at night that was chancy. Besides, the van was still in play. The driver had backed it out into Eighth and roared toward her again, this time, headlights-first.

Heat dashed over to the sidewalk, sprinting toward Fifteenth, no plan. Just get away. Ahead at the corner a food delivery man was getting ready to chain his bicycle to a standpipe. "Hey, hey!" she hollered. "NYPD, taking this." He mustn't have understood, or didn't buy it, because he gave Heat a shove to defend his ride. Just what she needed. Losing steps to the Take-A-Masala guy. She plowed past him, mounting his bike and yelling, "Call 911. Officer needs help."

Nikki ate up sidewalk knowing full well if she took the street, she'd be roadkill under that van.

The van.

Beside her again. Running parallel, matching speed, holding steady. The passenger window opened. A pair of black sleeves came out, forearms bracing on the sill, hands clasping a Glock aimed at her. Heat jammed her brake pedal. The van continued past. A shot barked from the window. The miss sang off the stone wall beside her. Heat's brake pop made her lose balance. Some noise ahead, a big clatter. Fighting to stay upright, she yawed wildly in the saddle. Almost good. Almost . . . A few yards up, the source of the racket. A night-demolition crew rolled a barrow of construction debris from a loading dock right into her path.

The impact bounced Nikki off the big gray refuse tub and she landed on the sidewalk looking up at the front bicycle wheel spinning over her head. The demo workers rushed to her, lifting dust masks off their faces, helping her up. "Whoa, lady, you all right?" A bullet ripped through the upper arm of the one closest to her.

"Down, down, down." Heat yanked them to the deck just as two more shots hit some fractured pieces of drywall in the bin, snowing powder down on them. Her companions froze, panicked and bewildered. Nikki took charge. "NYPD. You." She pointed to the one who wasn't bleeding. "Push, come on." Seconds mattered. "Come on." She grabbed him by the coveralls and pulled him to the debris tub with her. She took one of the other man's palms and clamped it over his wound. "Squeeze. Stay close." She gave a three count and they rolled the container back into the loading dock, using it for cover. Three more shots hit it but didn't penetrate. Thinking now of cover. Tactics and cover. Get inside the building, get behind that metal door. Quickly. But halfway there, the wounded man passed out and hit the ground. Heat scanned the loading dock. Time for new tactics.

Nikki sent her Officer Needs Help text and waited for them to come. A prolonged half minute that stretched all her senses. Wondering how many there were. Wishing she had a gun. She tried not to think of the odds. Only of making her stand. The voice of her training instructor echoed across more than a decade: "When met with superior force respond with shocking vigor." Heat listened, dissecting the night, ready to do her TI proud.

She knew to expect a calculated assault. And not just because these guys liked to put on tactical wear. Their escape from Flatbush in those dual cars showed planning and training. So did the execution of her takedown tonight: the stealth; the van skills; the redundancy—like positioning that cool customer to block her escape toward the hotels. So she got into their heads, following their playbook, anticipating their way in. Which was why when the Glock eased around the corner leading to the loading dock, right where she knew it would be, she was ready for it. But Heat held back. Held back knowing the visual peek-around was still a beat-count away. More arm would show first. And it did. In fact, two arms because both hands gripped the pistol in a textbook isosceles brace.

Now.

Heat lashed out the nine-foot length of flexible metal conduit like a bullwhip. Her cast landed perfectly. The galvanized steel cable encircled both his wrists twice, strapping them together. She gripped her end with both hands and used her full body weight to yank. Her pull jerked his left forearm into the corner of the concrete wall and it snapped. He screamed as he fell forward. She pounced on him to get the Glock before the belting could loosen on his wrists, but as he crashed to the ground the gun broke free and skittered out of reach. Nikki crawled for it. But he got his good hand clear and clutched her jacket, holding her back. A shot fired from outside the loading dock, and the air beside her ear sizzled as the slug passed. The guy's grip not only kept her from the pistol, he held her in place as a target. She reached down to her waistband for the hammer she had taken from the construction worker. With one swing Heat put the claw end into her attacker's temple. She tried to pull it out for another blow but it was stuck. No matter. His grip slackened for good.

Four more rounds put the Glock out of reach in the kill zone. Heat rolled away, retreating to the hide she had made behind the debris bin. She signaled the conscious worker hiding with his buddy behind the tool chest near the electrical panel. He nodded, reached up, and pulled the main. The loading dock fell dark except for light-bleed from the street.

Again, Heat waited.

He came in a low crouch. She could see his reflection in the convex mirror above the service elevator. He crept closer. Cautiously. Mindful now that his task held peril. This was the one whose nose she'd broken. Nikki took only slow half-breaths, not letting any sound give her away. But he had to know where she was. And he was right. He got to the side of the bin. She could hear him swallow. Crouched in the darkness, she was lost in shadow to him, but in the mirror, backlit by the streetlights, she could see he was merely an arm's length away. One more step. That was all she needed. He took it.

She switched on the laser level. Nikki missed his eyes at first, but she quickly adjusted her aim and blinded him with the tool. He fired wildly at the light source, but she had already moved, sprung up from her crouch with a nail gun. He couldn't see anything but he heard her coming and swung an arm to deflect her. The pneumatic tool fired. In that light she couldn't tell what she hit but he gasped and yelled "Fuck." Heat had to get that gun away. He was already bringing it toward her. She slapped her free hand on it and was able to push it aside, but he held strong. He punched at her, landing a hard blow to her cheek that dazed her.

Unable to get the gun free, Nikki pressed the air nailer against his wrist and fired. Pulled back. Fired again. Nails are painful. Nails between joints are excruciating. The pistol dropped. Disarmed, he ran out moaning.

Sirens coming. Lots of them.

Armed with her attacker's Smith & Wesson, Detective Heat switched mode, just like that, to offense. She wanted these guys. For what they did. For what they knew.

Cautiously, rapidly, she picked her way past the debris container that had shielded her and hopped over the body splayed on the concrete with the hammer lodged in its head. She flattened her back against the wall of the loading dock and braced the gun in both hands. The cargo door of the van slammed just outside, and she heard it roaring off. She swung around the corner onto the sidewalk to try for the tires but it was too long gone. Across the street, a quarter block west, a dark gray Impala idled. A man stood at the open driver's side door. This was the cool customer who'd blocked her escape earlier. Their eyes met. In the orange tint of the streetlights, his features were passive. A living death mask.

"NYPD, freeze." Nikki brought her weapon up to aim. With a chilling casualness, he raised an assault rifle and laid down a hail of bullets that sent her diving for cover behind the engine block of a parked car. When the firing stopped and the echoes from the G36 trailed off into the night, Heat shook the windshield glass from her hair and rose up, ready to return fire.

But the Impala was already turning the corner down on Ninth Avenue. Before disappearing around it, Heat could swear she saw an arm raise up from the driver's side and give her the finger.

Forty minutes later, Lauren Parry knelt beside the body on the floor of the loading dock. "Nikki Heat, you did this?"

"Would it help if I said he had it coming?"

The ME glanced again at the claw hammer, still embedded in the man's head, and then back to her. "Remind me never to mess with you, girl." Lauren, who constantly nagged her friend not to get herself killed, chuckled. Her laugh was as false as Nikki's vacant smile.

Heat still inhabited the adrenaline wasteland. After the hormonal tsunami receded, it left her body shaky, her emotions hollow, and her focus dulled. All reserves had been tapped and she subsisted now on pure will. She was relieved to be able to account for her weapons. Her Beretta 950 found its way home to her ankle holster courtesy of a teen from the housing projects who violated his mom's curfew to smoke some weed in the parking lot, found the Jetfire, and turned it in to the crime scene unit working the body of the attacker she'd killed with it. CSU had located her Sig Sauer near his corpse, and she'd have that back soon enough. Detective Feller knew a few things about adrenaline dumps and handed her a Snickers. Randall had arrived on the scene shortly after the first responders, having heard the ten-thirteen call go out. The street veteran said if he'd known that she was the officer needing help, he would have beat them all there, and Nikki believed that. He told her that the plate numbers she got from both vehicles had been boosted from airport rental cars, so good luck there.

"I figured when I saw the Montana tags on the Impala," she said.

"Makes sense that the Cool Customer wouldn't be driving that thing around with Port Authority tags on it."

"Cool Customer, indeed. That G36 he was firing must have packed a hundred-round drum. CSU had to send out for more numbered cones to mark the shell casings. They ran out."

While he went around the block to check on getting her Sig released, Heat took another bite of the candy bar in service to her blood sugar. Then came another boost. Rook arrived.

He had been her first call when things all settled and the wounded construction worker got patched and ported in the ambulance. Nikki phoned just to let him know where she was—at least that's what she told herself. But she really needed to hear his voice. She craved a connection to life after coming so close to losing it. And even though she'd told him not to come by, there he stood, beaming on the sidewalk as if he wanted a candid look at her before he broke and ran to her arms.

They buried themselves into their hug, whispering each other's names, and then kissing. PDA be damned, she thought, I've earned this moment. The tensions they'd been dealing with didn't exist right then; all she wanted was to hold him and be held. He touched his thumb tenderly to the red mark on her check and she assured him the paramedics checked and she was fine, nothing broken.

"You know," he said, "I don't think I've ever kissed a woman standing over a corpse before." Nikki laughed, but it started to turn into tears and she put her head against his chest just to get calm and not break down. He seemed to know she needed that and they stood together quietly a few moments until she stepped back, nodding that she was OK now.

They relocated to the sidewalk to let Lauren Parry continue her work. He said, "Apologies to Peter, Paul, and Mary, but now we know what you'd do if you had a hammer." Which made her laugh, but then she noticed his eyes were moist now.

"Hey?" She took his hand. "I'm all right."

The precinct's remaining Crown Victoria pulled up beside them and the man who needed all that room hauled himself out of the driver's side. "Heat, you're going to give me a fucking heart attack," said Wally Irons.

"No, I think the pork chops and fried dough are pretty much going to take care of that," muttered Rook to Nikki while the captain waddled around to them.

Before Irons even checked on her, he gave Rook a disdainful head-to-toe and said, "I'd ask what you're doing at my crime scene, but I guess I can let it go, considering."

Rook said, "You're a big man, Wally," and took an elbow from her.

Heat filled in her captain on the events. The exercise forced her to relive the unpleasantness, but it also helped her organize the main points for the report she would have to write. It also spared her a second recap to Rook. She finished by telling him Detective Feller would ride herd on Forensics to run prints on the two deceased and on the Smith & Wesson dropped by the man she air nailed.

He bobbled his head. "Sounds like you've got it all buttoned down."

"It's the job, sir."

He looked off up the empty midnight street, watching life beyond the cordon and said, "You think this is related to the Gilbert case?"

"I do." Beside her, Rook cleared his throat but wisely chose not to speak.

"Heat, I want some hides on the wall for this." He came back to look at her. "Meantime, I've tried this before, but I'm not taking no. I'm putting a radio car at your doorstep all night. Period."

She thought about the assault force. Saw the passive menace on the face of the Cool Customer. And said yes.

Irons felt good about that. Until Rook said the car should be at his place overnight.

Heat was up and dressed, pacing the kitchen on her cell phone when Rook shuffled out of the bedroom the next morning. After indulging in a long, hot, therapeutic bath to soothe the morning-after soreness of her street battle, she had already brewed a thermos of coffee and taken it down to the officers in the blue-and-white outside his loft. Nikki poured him a cup of French roast from her second pot and smooched a silent air-kiss while she listened to Zach "The Hammer" Hamner's dour phone call to start the workday.

"This is not going to be one of our usual friendly chats," he'd begun when her phone rang exactly a minute after seven. Zach was so damned earnest, she couldn't tell if he was kidding, or if he truly felt they had a cordial relationship. "This is an on-the-record, official caution, Detective. Are you hearing me?"

"Yes, Zach, I hear you."

Rook glanced up from booting his laptop at the counter and whispered, "Is that The Hammer?" She nodded and rolled her eyes. "Tell him you killed a man with a hammer last night. That'll lighten things up."

Nikki held up a shush finger and turned away so she wouldn't laugh as Zach pressed onward. "In my capacity as special assistant to the commissioner of Legal Affairs, I am informing you that the department has been put on notice that an unlawful arrest suit is going to be filed by Keith Gilbert's attorneys. I don't need to tell you what cost such a lawsuit would carry. Not just in hard dollars, but in embarrassment to everyone here at One PP."

"Are you saying they're threatening? That's chest beating. Why don't they just file if they really have a case?"

"An indulgent stance when you're not in my chair," he said. "I want your assurance that you have a case."

Nikki said yes, but didn't feel it would be wise to share everything her squad had gathered. Maybe she didn't have a law degree, but Heat knew what an abundance of caution was, too. "I've got solid stuff, Zach. I've got forensic evidence. I've got phone records connecting Gilbert to Beauvais, even though he denied knowing him. I've got the doctor who treated Beauvais, who ID'd Gilbert to him as the guy who shot him."

"Tell me you have the gun."

"I have a search warrant in-process."

"What's the delay? No, let me guess, Wally Irons."

"You win."

Zach Hamner didn't laugh. The Hammer never laughed because he wasn't human. But this time, his sourness had cause; he was feeling pressure. "We have to get this right, Heat. *You* have to get it right. A dropped ball will hurt the whole team, but a fumble on your end will have most serious repercussions vis-à-vis your viability for future endeavors. You know what I'm talking about, right?"

"Yes, of course, the task force." She saw Rook look up from his screen and quickly back at that mention. Would this open discussion, or just be the elephant in the kitchen? Nikki yearned for friendly contact and came around the counter to drape an arm on Rook.

"Fine then," said The Hammer. She heard papers shuffling on his desk. "Let's cover some bases. Keep digging. And bring in that doctor for a sworn statement. I'll see what I can do to move along the search warrant for the gun."

"That would be helpful."

"All I can say is, this better be airtight. Let me hear you say it." When Heat didn't respond, he said, "Detective?"

Nikki didn't reply because she was too transfixed by what she happened to see on Rook's MacBook. It was a security camera still photo. Two men—both dangerous-looking, with prison time written on their faces—were leaning into the foreground of the shot, which had the slightly fish-eye effect you got from a wide-angle lens. Heat had seen many pictures like this before. This pair was caught in the act of installing a dummy keypad and card skimmer to steal PINs and account codes from ATMs. But that's not what gave her pause. What made Heat momentarily speechless was who she saw standing lookout in the background: Fabian Beauvais.

"Hello? Did I lose you?"

"No, I'm here." And then, trying to sound like she still believed it, Nikki said, ". . . Airtight."

NINE

N
ikki set her phone on the counter and quietly examined the image on the computer screen of Fabian Beauvais with the two thugs monkeying with the ATM. She paid special attention to the pair to see if she knew either of them as her ambushers from Chelsea. Not only did she not recognize them, they were totally different breeds. The Chelsea gang, including the SRO duo, had a paramilitary flavor, clean-cut, disciplined, even dressed in uniforms of a sort. The two in this picture with Beauvais were street players. Urban gangstas, wild-ass freaks born to raise hell. "When did you get this?"

"Now. Came as e-mail overnight. Looks like I got two files. The other one's a video. Want to see what it's about?" He didn't need an answer. Rook had already executed his trackpad clicks.

Street surveillance video came up, shot from an elevated cam, probably bracketed to a lamppost. It had no audio, but the texture, although grainy, was sharp enough to make out Fabian Beauvais running up an urban sidewalk toward the camera, throwing panicked glances over his shoulder at the two men chasing him. Seconds after he ran out of the frame, his pursuers stopped right under the camera. One of them raised a pistol and fired. Heat counted three muzzle flashes. After the shooting, the two thugs—the same gangstas from the ATM still photo—cocked their heads to look off-camera in Beauvais's direction and then backed away, jogging out of the shot the same way they'd come into it.

"Whoa," said Rook. "Was that Dodge City or Queensboro Plaza?"

"Again," was all Nikki could muster. She'd been too unsettled by the first play to study it and wanted a more clinical look. In the second screening she focused on detail. Beauvais carried something under an arm; a light-colored bag or, perhaps, a manila envelope. She'd missed that before. He had on a different shirt than the still photo from the ATM, suggesting it was a different day. The two running him down were also dressed differently. The way the shooter drew and fired: pulling the piece from his waistband; holding the pistol flat, like a John Woo gangster; and hurrying his rounds, told her he wasn't police or service trained. Sideways shots look sexy and work for speed in close quarters, but, especially for a moving target gaining distance, department trainers drilled Heat's cadet class to take the time to cup and brace: stabilize, sight, squeeze. This wasn't an idle observation. It told her these guys were not part of the professional group that went after her the night before.

She didn't need to ask for a replay. Rook said, "One more," and rolled it again. The impression Nikki got on this viewing was that Beauvais clutched the bag or envelope under his arm like it mattered. You want to lose time in a footrace? Carry something. He was running for his life but wouldn't give up his package for speed.

After it timed out, Rook sat back on his barstool and folded his arms, watching her. He didn't say anything, but his manner felt the same as outside the loading dock the night before when Irons asked her if she thought her attack was related to Gilbert. Then, as now, he remained silent but acted like a horse pawing the stable floor when it smelled smoke. Nikki picked up her coffee mug. It felt cold in her palm so she replaced it beside her phone. "It's inconclusive, you know that," she said at last.

"In what way? It kinda looks to me like our guy getting chased and shot at."

"Oh, are we being smart-asses? Not now, OK? Of course I know what it looks like. But did he get hit? Beauvais was out of frame."

"Three shots, Nikki."

"And he was hauling it. And the shooter was showboating his weapon. I've seen veteran cops miss when a perp is on the run."

"But not you," he said, attaching an impish grin to it.

"Don't try to make up to me with flattery." Then she caved a little under that smile of his. But just a little. "Hey, I never looked at the time stamp. When was this?"

Rook brought it up and read the embedded digital code. Then he did some silent math, moving his lips. "The morning before Beauvais went to Dr. Ivan to get his bullet wound fixed."

That timing could fit. If one of those slugs did hit home, and it caused the clean graze described by the Russian medic, a span of forty-plus hours from wound to treatment put this incident in the zone. Even though this challenged her gut feel about the case, Heat clung to her detective's core value of objectivity, allowing the potential that some street thug, and not Keith Gilbert, could have shot Beauvais. She turned again to the screen in time for a replay of the three silent jerks of the gun in the shooter's hand, thinking that whatever was going on, there certainly was a complicated context to what her Haitian friend had been doing with his days. What the hell was Beauvais up to?

Nikki kept hoping for the lightbulb clue that explained everything, but all she kept getting were these orphan leads that confused more than clarified. She told herself to be patient, that she just hadn't gotten the story yet. And that, at the end of the day, it would all make sense. As long as she didn't lose heart and give up the hunt.

And then, she asked a basic question. "You got this in e-mail. From whom?"

He told her without hesitating. Like it was nothing. Like it was a no-brainer. "Raley shipped it over."

". . . Raley. Just shipped it over, you mean, like it was just lying around?"

"No, of course not. He had some free time, and I asked him to scrub some security video." He tilted his head toward her. "Is this an issue?"

"Only that Detective Raley doesn't have any free time because he works for me doing the assignments I give him."

"OK, so it's an issue."

"Irons banished you from the precinct."

"Which is why I called Raley instead of going in myself. There's no quit in me, Nikki Heat."

"And did it occur to you that I might need to sign off on you poaching my detectives for your personal use?"

"Agreed. But last night when I got the tip from Beauvais's friend Hattie about this . . ." he gestured to his screen ". . . you were busy playing Bob the Builder with your attackers, and I couldn't reach you. So I called Rales and asked a fave. Is that really so wrong?"

An ache cinched her back muscles like barbed wire drawing tight. It didn't come from her street skirmish. Just days ago Heat thought Rook was going to give her an engagement ring. Now he was giving her fits. Knowing a crossroad when she'd reached one, Nikki decided she had plenty of battle in front of her without opening a flank with Rook. For the greater good Nikki knew she had to eat it—to do what she did so well—which was to compartmentalize her feelings for the sake of the job. So she shrugged it off.

But there was one conversation she needed to have.

Since the radio car had been assigned to her anyway, Heat hitched a ride in the blue-and-white from Tribeca up to Chelsea. The officers thanked her for the French roast, joking that she had spoiled them for mystery muck they get from the street cart. When they dropped her at the same corner where she had been attacked barely ten hours before, Nikki declined their escort offer. But, as she walked past the driveway of the housing project, which was still wet from the blood hosing it got from CSU, she glanced back and got a wave from both unis as they kept watch from their patrol unit.

Raley and Ochoa looked a little bewildered when they pulled up in front of the brownstone on West Sixteenth to find Heat standing there waiting for them. The ambush had kept her from checking out the address Jeanne Capois had written on the grocery receipt, so Roach had offered to take the assignment that morning. But Nikki decided to show up, too. She had a reason to pull her surprise visit.

She crouched on the sidewalk beside the Roach Coach. Raley rolled down his passenger window and said, "Heard you had a night."

"Let me think . . . Oh, right."

From behind the wheel, Ochoa joined in the Downplay Game. "Listen, I need some carpentry done. You work on wood or just human flesh?"

The ball having sufficiently been tossed around the infield, they popped the latches on their doors. "Sit tight," she said, causing her detectives to exchange more puzzled glances. "Change of plan. I'm

taking this interview. I want you guys to run checks on these two."
She gave them the printout she'd made at Rook's of the ATM screen
grab. "Of course, that's Fabian Beauvais in the background, but I want
to know everything about the pair up front." She paused and leveled a
meaningful stare at Raley. "Sean, I understand you are already familiar
with this photo after having done some freelance work for Rook without authorization."

He blushed. "Hey, I was at the station late, anyway. It was Rook, so
I thought . . ." he read her unhappiness and let it trail off. His partner
wasn't so cowed.

"What's the problem here? Guy's doing his job, helping out."

Heat turned to him, quiet, but firm. "Are we debating this? We're
not debating this." He blew some air and squeezed the steering wheel
while both men looked straight ahead at nothing over the hood of the
car. "Point made, it's all good. You've got your assignment. Let's meet
up at the Murder Board in an hour."

The Roach Coach departed without a word or a nod. Great, she
thought as she watched it drive off; now they were both pissed at her.
Kind of like she was at herself.

Waiting, buzzing, then waiting again, no answer came to Heat's vestibule
call up to Apartment Three. After pressing the other apartment buttons on the aluminum panel with no response, she rang up the building
superintendent. He lived at another property on Bleecker Street, so she
waited fifteen minutes while he made it up from his Greenwich Village
neighborhood. Not too many years ago, she would have phoned the
tenant, but, as was more often the case in digital times, there was no
landline listed to the place. The super accompanied her to the door with
his ring of keys and stood by while she knocked. Nikki announced,
"NYPD, please open up," knocked again, then put an ear to the door
but heard nothing. She also sniffed, however, but got no telltale decay
odor.

The super advanced to the lock but Heat signaled him to step aside,
which he did, taking three steps back. With one hand on the butt of her
Sig, Nikki turned the lock and pushed the door wide open. Once again

she said, "NYPD." This time it echoed off the bare hardwood floors and empty walls of the apartment.

The super peered in and said, "What the fuck?"

Nobody home. Not even a home.

The homicide bull pen at the Twentieth was shy one detective when Nikki Heat began her morning briefing. She had already phoned ahead to dispatch Randall Feller to Brooklyn to pick up Dr. Ivan, expatriate physician and auto-parts courier. If Zach Hamner wanted to cover his ass with a sworn statement about treating Fabian Beauvais's gunshot wound and hearing him name Commissioner Gilbert as his shooter, she was happy to provide the paper. Knowing Feller's weariness over bridge and tunnel runs, she'd told him to look at the bright side. "Hurricane's coming. How many times can you go to a doctor's office and pick up new wiper blades?" He actually laughed as he hung up.

She began her meeting with good news. "I'm getting my search warrant for Keith Gilbert's gun, which is registered to his address in Southampton. I'll be driving out there as soon as the physical docs arrive. It's taking forever because every lawyer in the DA's office is scrutinizing it to make sure the language is Dream-Team-proof." Even though she felt upbeat about the warrant, the mood of the bull pen was mixed. Rhymer seemed fine, but Raley and Ochoa were still in a sulk. Nikki attempted to lighten things up. "Roach, I think I saved you boys some wheel spinning." They were attentive but passive when she recounted her visit to the vacant apartment in Chelsea, and it was Rhymer who raised a hand.

"Did you get an ID on the tenant?"

"The name is Opal Onishi. Her lease shows her occupation to be a food stylist, but the document is four years old, and her employer at that time is no longer in business. Hello, economic downturn."

"Cell phone?" asked Ochoa, breaking his silence.

"Straight dump to voice mail, so it's turned off. Would you keep trying it?"

"As long as it's authorized by you," he said. His partner extended a be-cool hand to him to wave him off.

Nikki let that one go and kept to business. "Meantime, Detective Raley, would you run a check on Opal Onishi for priors and get a photo of her from DMV?"

"Might want to check Facebook, too," said Rhymer, sounding very Southern. "If she's a poster, you might get a line on her."

"Very good, Mr. Rhymer. You want to handle that one?"

"No, I've got it," said Raley, volunteering, but with a passive-aggressive bite to it.

Nikki turned to the whiteboard and posted blowups of official-looking ID photos under the police-artist sketches of the goons from the SRO. "We have names now for this unsavory pair." She markered each name as she said it. "First, is Stan Victor. Mr. Victor left Chelsea last night with a broken nose and some three-inch galvanized framing nails in his wrist. His partner, Roderick Floyd, left in a coroner's van." In red marker she printed DECEASED in all caps. "These are the two men Rook, Detective Feller, and I encountered at the flophouse rented by Fabian Beauvais. A third, who also died at the scene, was one Nicholas Bjorklund."

She posted a third picture, too, beside the others: a photo ID of the man she had claw hammered. She printed DECEASED in red under him, too, and then went back to the podium to refer to notes. All eyes followed her, mindful and—in spite of chafed feelings—respectful of her ordeal battling those formidable men.

"All three have similar profiles," she said and flipped open her notes. "All were late thirties, all were career military. Victor distinguished himself by receiving a dishonorable discharge in Iraq, citing sadism and cruelty to a Republican Guard prisoner. All three men returned to combat in Afghanistan and, perhaps, Pakistan as contractors—aka: mercenaries—until about a year ago when passport control shows they reentered the United States about the same time. Detective Rhymer. I'd like you to visit the last-known addresses for Victor, Floyd, and Bjorklund. CSU is already at all three places, dusting and tweezing. Make a pest of yourself."

"Will do."

She withdrew another blowup from her file and posted it. "We still don't have anything on the van's wheelman, but we do have a street-cam capture of the driver of the Impala while demonstrating the urban tactical capabilities of the Heckler & Koch assault carbine." She posted the photo and somebody behind her, probably Opie, whistled. The picture showed the face of a man she'd nicknamed the Cool Customer illuminated satanically by the brilliant tongue of flame radiating from the G36 as he emptied his C mag at her.

"Does he even have a pulse?" asked Rhymer. "Dude's laying down lethal fire, but he looks like he's chilling at the fishing hole." Cool Customer, indeed.

"We don't have any ID on him yet, but this photo is circulating now. It's out to NYPD, Homeland, FBI, DOD, and Interpol." Heat's eyes lingered on the eight-by-tens; then she addressed the group. "As we work these guys I want to know a couple of things. What is such a highly trained collection of contractors doing in New York City? And why come after me? And Fabian Beauvais? And Jeanne Capois, if—as I suspect—they also killed them? And who are they working for?" Keith Gilbert's head shot loomed over her shoulder. "I have an idea, but I want proof. I want to find a solid connection."

Ochoa raised one finger. "Miguel?"

"Kinda not how you usually go at it, is it." The detective didn't make eye contact with Nikki. He remained slouched back in his chair, concentrating on the toes of his shoes as he spoke. "I mean, you always tell us to keep an open mind . . ."

". . . Beginner's eyes," added his partner.

". . . And now you're pushing for proof against Keith Gilbert when there's other leads, too. All I'm saying."

That was saying a lot. That was saying her case leadership had come into question. Not only that, it was being challenged within the squad. Quietly, but a challenge nonetheless. Had her reprimand so upset these two that they would rift-out on her like this? "Let's talk about it."

"Yeah, let's." Detective Raley went up to the board. Space was getting tight but he found room and put two mug shots up: one of each of the pair from the ATM who had also chased and shot at Beauvais in the video from Queensboro Plaza. "Let's talk about these thugs.

Thug-One: Mayshon Franklin. Twenty-eight, in and out of prison three times, not counting juvie. Convictions for assault, weapons possession, and credit card theft."

He moved to the second photo, and the tougher-looking character. "Thug-Two: Earl Sliney. This is our shooter from the video. Age, thirty-seven. Older than his partner, but apparently no wiser. Also a juvenile offender; also numerous stretches as a guest of various states. A deuce in Colorado for check fraud and ID theft, a bid in Florence, Arizona, for an armed home invasion robbery; closer to us, he stacked five years upstate at Dannemora for kneecapping a drug dealer who shorted his cut. Earl Sliney is currently at large with a warrant for a recent murder in Mount Vernon, New York. He shot and killed an elderly woman hiding in her bathtub trying to call 911 during an armed home invasion." Raley strode back to his seat. The move reminded Nikki of an improv comic she and Rook saw once who dropped the microphone and exited the stage after he scored the un-toppable laugh.

Nikki sat on the front table and took a moment to consider Roach. And how the pressure she felt could sometimes create harm where she least wanted it, to those who least deserved it. It had been on her mind all the way back to the precinct. It had been she who told Raley and Ochoa to take point on the home invasion case. And from that work came the receipt in Jeanne Capois's purse that led them to Chelsea. And in her irritation, she'd thoughtlessly bigfooted them on the sidewalk and sent them away.

Would an apology make that right? Or maybe this wasn't pushback about her smacking them down. Maybe they truly had doubts. Maybe they smelled something about this case she was missing. "You like these guys for this," Heat said, not challenging, not buying, either.

"We like being open to that," said Ochoa.

Raley nodded. "We feel like things went one way in a hurry."

"Way big a hurry," repeated his pard. "Just noticing what we're noticing, boss."

Roach, her best detectives, were kicking the ball back by feeding Heat her own training lectures. "All right, fine. Tell you what. Follow this thread. See if you can track these two. Relatives, known associates, the usual. Obviously, they're stealing bank card skims, so I'd start there. Maybe you can get more hits from the same source of the ATM still photo. By the way, where'd that picture come from?"

Nobody said anything. Then Rhymer cleared his throat. "Um, got a call from Rook yesterday after he got his tip from that woman at the chicken place."

Thinking back, trying to recall the name, she asked, "You mean Hattie?"

Rhymer nodded. "Yeah, exactly, that's the one. Anyway, Rook asked me to call some of my old pals in Burglary and Fraud to surf for Beauvais in their ATM perp database."

"Wait a minute," said Heat in disbelief. "Rook. Rook called and asked you to do that?" First Roach, now him? Nikki thought, *Et tu* Opie?

The detective shrugged. "Sort of felt like the same thing you'd ask for, if you were around."

Heat dismissed them to tackle their assignments. She returned to her desk and felt that tug of barbed wire pull snug across her back muscles again.

She almost called Rook. Not to share IDs on Thug-One and Thug-Two, but to reopen the conversation about enlisting her crew as a personal research team for his article. She didn't call because she knew where that would go, which was the same no-fly-zone she decided to avoid at his kitchen counter that morning. So she busied herself with follow-ups while she waited for the search warrant to make it uptown from the DA's office.

Still no Alicia Delamater sightings. Either Gilbert's mistress had slipped past U.S. Customs, or her attorney lied and she never left the country. There's a stretch—a lawyer being untruthful.

She located an address for Hattie Pate, Fabian Beauvais's pal from the chicken slaughterhouse who'd tipped Rook off about the ATM crew and the Queensboro Plaza gunplay. She put it in a group text to Raley and Ochoa for them to investigate. Nikki didn't add a smiley face but hoped the gesture would thaw the chilly air between them.

In her renewed sense of open-mindedness, she e-mailed the Real Time Crime Center and asked them to run Fidel "FiFi" Figueroa and

Charley Tosh. Figueroa and Tosh, the Dumpster divers who got arrested with Beauvais had, according to Rook, a history of dirty tricks and harassment against Keith Gilbert's campaign. She didn't know exactly what she could learn from them, but it wouldn't hurt to close the loop.

Detective Sergeant Aguinaldo of SVPD returned her call to confirm that she would meet Nikki at Cosmo in Southampton to facilitate the service of the warrant and the search for Gilbert's handgun. Also, after the Russian doctor named the commissioner as Beauvais's shooter, Heat had asked her to run a check on reports of gunfire the night of his treatment. "Sorry," said Aguinaldo. "I'm afraid there are no reports in that time frame. Which doesn't surprise me. I mean, we'd already know. 'Shots fired' would be big news in the village." The news blanketed Heat under another layer of worry about making her case airtight. And kept the door open that it could have been Earl Sliney who shot the Haitian, and not her prime suspect.

"Thanks for checking, anyway." Then, never one to give up, Heat said, "Would I be pushing my luck to ask you another favor?"

"Name it."

"That patrol officer you told me about."

Inez Aguinaldo was right there with her. "The one who encountered the man staggering to the LI-Double-R?"

"Yes, what do your uniforms call it?"

"Catch and release. When I talked to Officer Matthews he wasn't certain it had been Mr. Beauvais, but he did say the man had an accent and acted sick. You're thinking maybe it wasn't sickness?"

"Maybe he'd been shot," said Heat. "Could you—"

"—Talk to him again? You bet. I'll even see if he can join us when you get to Beckett's Neck."

If Fabian Beauvais had been shot while in the Hamptons, that would end the speculation about whether one of Earl Sliney's rounds tagged him on that Queensboro Plaza security video. It might also put a lid on the internal discord that had arisen about this case. First from Rook, and now from the go-to guys in her crew who'd had their heads turned, either by doubt about the evidence or aggravation at her.

Since Gilbert's gun would be a key link in that chain of evidence, when Nikki got word the search warrant was just blocks away she started to saddle up to be set to leave the instant she got it in hand. During a ritual desk check, her phone rang. OCME. She paused to take it.

Lauren Parry said, "Just finished the postmortems on your two Dead at Scenes from Chelsea. First, cause of death. —Nikki Heat." Thankfully, the ME knew her friend, and could tell from the lack of response that Nikki was on a mission. So she skipped the wisecracks and got right to the rest. "Roderick Floyd, the one you shot. He's got scratch marks on his neck and cheeks. In your incident report from last night, you didn't mention scratching him."

"Correct. My only physical contact was a takedown with my right leg to the back of his knees."

"That would follow, because these excoriations look days old."

"Lauren, you thinking Jeanne Capois?"

"That would be consistent with the appearance and age of the scratch marks. We'll lab his DNA against her fingernail residue, but here's why I called. You've never heard me go out on a limb like this, but I know what we'll find. I am confident that Roderick Floyd was one of her attackers."

After Nikki hung up, she stood in front of the Murder Board, letting her gaze bounce back and forth from the photo of Roderick Floyd, the paramilitary killer of Jeanne Capois, to Earl Sliney, the street player who fired at Fabian Beauvais on video. What she tried to reconcile was how—or if—they fit together. They had such different backgrounds, such different profiles: one, tactical; the other, a hoodlum. The only common thread Heat could see was their history of home invasions. The information she'd just gotten from the medical examiner all but confirmed Floyd as part of the crew that broke into the apartment on West End and killed the owner when he tried to stop them with a baseball bat. They had also chased after Jeanne Capois, torturing her behind some trash cans near a prep school.

Sliney had a fugitive warrant for a home invasion homicide. Were those home invasion dots connecting, or were they just dots? Was this tactical crew working with the street thugs? Or did they even know about each other? Heat simply couldn't see a pattern emerging—yet.

She knew something was there, but every time she got close to seeing the horizon, it was as if a swirl of angry clouds kept the view hidden from her.

Every administrative aide in the station house knew the importance of that search warrant. So much so that one held the door while the other rushed in to hand deliver the paper to Heat when it arrived. As she inspected the doc to verify the date and signatures and seals, Detective Feller called her name. "Trying to get to the Hamptons," she said, brandishing the warrant.

"I think you're going to want to hear this." And when he told her what it was, Heat turned from the door and followed him into the conference room.

Her gut flipped the instant she walked in and saw the Russian sitting with his elbows propped on the conference table. Ivan Gogol's chin rested in both hands, the corners of his mouth were pushed downward, and an ominously blank yellow tablet sat in front of him with a capped stick pen resting on it at an angle. "I cannot write this statement."

"Mr. Gogol," she began gently, softly—hopefully, "is there something I can help you with? Would you like a translator?"

"*Nyet*, I cannot make this statement because is lies." Heat felt herself go flush. Detective Feller whispered a curse and turned away in frustration.

Nikki tried to see what could be salvaged here. Maybe if she broke it down in pieces. "Well, we don't want you to go on record with anything you don't feel comfortable with." She rested a hand on his sleeve and, even though she landed on an archipelago of moles, she left it there. "Let's start with what you will attest to."

"Nothing. I will swear to nothing." He pushed the pad away like a disappointing meal.

Dauntless, she pressed on. "Let's take this a step at a time. You told us you treated Fabian Beauvais for a gunshot. That much is true, right?" She eased the pad back to him.

He pulled up into a shrug and left his shoulders like that, nearly touching his ears, as he said, "I cannot be sure. He was black man. His name, I can no longer be sure." Heat took the photo of Beauvais from

Feller and held it up, but before she could ask him, Ivan said, "Is him? Not him? I cannot be sure now. Very traumatic night. I had been sleeping, you know, I startle awake."

No sense prolonging the agony. "Mr. Gogol? Mr. Gogol, please look at me. Thank you. I need you to think about this before you answer. Just yesterday you told us that this man here," she tapped the Beauvais picture, "had been shot and that you treated him, and that he told you the name of who shot him was Keith Gilbert. Isn't that the truth?"

"I don't remember."

"Mr. Gogol."

"This man say many things. Maybe delirious or drunk from getting in bar fight and shot that way. Yes, that is what I think happened. The drinking."

Nikki stared at Ivan Gogol. His wasn't the face of a liar. What she read on him was fear. Almost panic. Someone had said—or done—something to turn him into a wreck. Heat's concern for him blended with her own as she witnessed a critical piece of her case—her airtight case—deflate before her eyes. "Ivan, if you are at all afraid, please know that the NYPD will provide you with—"

"Enough. I will say nothing more." He pushed the pad away again with such force that the pen slid off the table and clacked somewhere below on the linoleum. Nobody reached to pick it up. It was going to be of no use.

TEN

The old salts working the Atlantic off Long Island didn't have Doppler radar, computer models, or satellite imagery to predict a brewing storm. They smelled the air, watched the birds, or consulted the *Farmers' Almanac*, if the pages hadn't been torn out in the privy. Of course, they also got surprised a lot. In 1938 the Long Island Express slammed into the Northeast killing about eight hundred people who got little advance notice. So much for red skies in the morning.

Detective Heat only had sunshine and sixty-two degrees to ponder as she drove past the exit for the Fire Island National Seashore. Instead of scoping out weather telltales, her attention went to patrolling side and rearview mirrors in case a certain Impala or vehicle yet-to-be-detected seemed to be following. After the attack in Chelsea she knew Captain Irons would insist on a uni driver or even try to make her take a blue-and-white to Southampton, so Nikki ducked out to her plain wrap Taurus right after the busted interview with Ivan Gogol to ensure some needed solitude for the trip.

Could it really have been only two days before that she covered this same road with Rook? So much had changed in that span, and little of it for the better. Notably Rook, not riding along. Whatever he was doing at that moment, she only hoped it would not result in further disruption. Nikki pushed to stay positive. Sure, the Russian doctor had crapped out, yet she had her warrant. But the situation felt much too fluid to let her relax.

Heat had begun by seeing Beauvais's planetarium crash and the home invasion on West End Avenue as two different cases. But then came the connection between the Haitian couple as lovers. And now—thanks to Lauren Parry—the forensic nexus between the SRO goons and Jeanne Capois tied them together, as well. However, the rise of Earl Sliney as the possible shooter jumbled things. Nikki wondered, was she really working one case, or could she possibly be back to two?

Along the drive she'd spot-checked the AM radio for updates on the hurricane. The latest report said Sandy had crossed Cuba as a Category Two with wind speeds of 114 miles per hour, causing the unconfirmed deaths of eleven people. The eye didn't make landfall on Hispaniola, but, as it churned north, Sandy's powerful swirl dumped twenty inches of rain and killed about fifty souls in Haiti. As of eight that morning, NOAA had tropical storm warnings out for southeast Florida, and the entire Eastern seaboard of the U.S. had started getting serious about disaster readiness.

When the newscaster said, "We go now, live, to a joint news conference with the mayor, the governor, and a commissioner of the Port Authority," Nikki cranked up the volume. Hizzoner sounded like his usual easygoing self as he announced he had already opened his Office of Emergency Management Situation Room and that all city agencies were synergizing in response to the coming weather event. The governor cited regular discussions with FEMA and the president, who was monitoring the situation closely. The MTA was preparing to move buses and trains to higher ground in the next twenty-four hours. The mayor chimed in that citizens could also expect to see workers sand bagging subway entrances and fastening plywood over sidewalk ventilation grates to prevent flooding. That image gave Nikki her first visceral feeling about a storm that had seemed so abstract until then. And the feeling she got was not just of impact but something more portentous: inevitability.

A reporter asked the governor if the charges against Commissioner Gilbert would adversely impact readiness. The question was followed by a pressroom full of murmurs.

"I'll answer that," said Keith Gilbert. Heat pictured him stepping to the microphone, sparing the governor from a perilous moment. "Shortly after I was sworn in last July, well before anybody even knew about this storm, I led the Port Authority in a readiness drill, rehearsing for an emergency such as this. We did it in full-scale, war games style using JFK, Newark Liberty, and the Bayonne Bridge as venues. Three months ago. This is how we roll. We plan. We prepare. Now we execute.

"I am about to activate the PA's Emergency Management Office," Gilbert continued. "Our highly trained personnel continue to inspect all assets for readiness and function. Maritime and air terminals are stepping up precautions. Construction at the new World Trade Center is battening down. Also, with an anticipated landfall early next week, I am ordering that, this weekend, critical staff—and that includes Operations and PAPD—will all be working." The room started yelling out questions all at once. He didn't call on anyone. Instead, he delivered his sound bite.

"One more comment to more directly address the reporter's question. Twenty-one years ago, an event called The Perfect Storm lashed the north Atlantic. Now, we see that disparate components could similarly be gathering, poised to fall into place and create a perfectly larger catastrophe. You know I'm a sailor. I am. A sailor who's weathered all kinds of seas. Anyone who's sailed with me knows one thing. I know how to keep my eye on what's important. And to know a real storm from a passing squall."

During his dramatic pause, Nikki shook her head and muttered, "Politicians."

Just as she had two days before, Heat pushed the call buzzer outside the security gate at Cosmo, Keith Gilbert's mansion on Beckett's Neck in Southampton. Moments after, a voice she recognized asked, "Help you?"

"Danny, hi, this is Detective Heat from the NYPD. We met on Tuesday?"

". . . Yeah?" he replied through the tinny speaker. From his detached tone she couldn't tell if that meant "So what?" or "Yes, I recall."

"Would you open, please? I have a search warrant."

When he came out, Danny ogled the document like it was radioactive. His gaze lifted from it to Nikki and then over to Detective Sergeant

Aguinaldo whose unmarked SUV was parked parallel to Heat's Taurus. "This is kind of above my pay grade. Mind if I call Mr. G?"

Nikki thought about it. "Sure, OK. But do it here, though." She didn't want Danny out of her sight behind a heavy gate so he could potentially interfere with the search. He nodded blandly and flipped open his cell, walking a few yards to the side for privacy.

"I don't think there's going to be a problem with this guy," said Aguinaldo in a low voice. "I mean that paper's all you need to go in. If there's an issue, I'll just call for someone to watch him out here while we execute your warrant." Heat appreciated the other detective's calm take. Instead of exerting small-town bullying—of which Heat had seen her share over the years—Inez Aguinaldo had a cool, professional air. That sort of thing was beyond training. It was how she came wired from the factory.

"There's a dog, too."

"We do dogs," Aguinaldo said with a smile. "Listen, early for lunch, but I brought two panini from Sean's Place on Hampton Road."

"Thank you, very thoughtful."

"I've got your choice. Grilled ham and Havarti or grilled ham and Havarti."

"What do you recommend?"

"I'd go with the first one."

Just then Heat's cell phone buzzed. She flashed Aguinaldo the caller ID. "Gilbert's lawyer. This should be interesting."

"I hear you have a warrant," breathed the voice on her phone. Frederic Lohman always sounded like he should be wearing a nasal cannula for supplemental oxygen.

"I do, Mr. Lohman. Your client has a Ruger .38 Special registered as premises-only to his Southampton address through the Suffolk County sheriff. He volunteered the information that he had the weapon on his self-initiated visit to my precinct. I have the paper. I'm getting the gun."

"That's a mighty big piece of property there, isn't it?" Just when Nikki was about to jam him for hindering, he surprised her. "Which is why we are going to tell you exactly where to find it. Notice I said 'we'?" He coughed without bothering to cover his mouthpiece and said, "I have conferred with Commissioner Gilbert, and my client has directed his caretaker to escort you directly to the weapon in the interest of full cooperation."

Slightly aback, Heat didn't want to say thank you, but she did. "You're welcome. Wipe your feet first." He chuckled, then added, "Remember this gesture, Detective." And then he hung up.

The detectives did wipe their feet. It just seemed the thing to do when entering a twenty-million-dollar home. What struck Nikki first was the silence. In the high-ceilinged broadness of the entry and main living room, there was no echo. The absolute cushion of the rugs absorbed all sound inside, and the double-insulated glass kept the outside out. Even the soft rolling of the Atlantic waves foaming on the adjacent beach were dampened—unless, of course the motorized patio windows fanned open. In season, of course.

Heat had no issue with wealth. She just never felt impressed with someone just because he or she had it. Nikki's mother, who spent her postcollege years tutoring piano in some of the wealthiest homes in Europe used to tell her, "Money magnifies," which was to say it only enlarges your nature. Give a million to a meth addict, in a year you're not going to see anything but a lawn full of weeds and a mouth with fewer teeth.

Danny led them past the winding staircase through a showplace kitchen that included an actual curved-glass, refrigerated deli counter full of sausages and cheese, shelves lined with canisters of color-coordinated pastas, and a collection of pepper mills through the years. That led to a den, which was recessed a step down and done in darker, more clubby colors than the airy off-whites and ecrus of the rooms they'd passed through. Without being overly precious, this shipping magnate's home office was designed and decorated to appear exactly like the fantasy image of a captain's quarters on an early twentieth-century luxury liner. Portholes with brass framing gave onto the infinity pool, and beyond it, the sea. The beadboard ceiling felt low and enveloping. A stand-up desk, angled for a view of the room dominated one corner. A heavy wooden executive desk overlooked the hearth and was flanked by wing chairs of bottle green leather and finished with hammered brass nails.

They watched the caretaker go to a built-in cabinet of the wet bar. He opened one glass door and felt around the inside frame on one side, and, not finding what he was looking for, did the same on the other. "Huh. He said the key was in here."

"You've never gotten it before?"

He looked at her like she was nuts. "Nobody comes in this room but Mr. G." He closed that cabinet and opened the door next to it. He reached in and Heat heard a small metallic tink against a coupe glass. "Gotcha." Danny came out with a small key looped on a circular leather thong. As he went to the big desk and knelt beside one of the large file drawers, Nikki thought about the choice of weapon on Gilbert's registration. If you were going to get a handgun for home protection, the revolver was a good option for the amateur owner. The mechanics were uncomplicated—pistols jammed—and the Sturm Ruger .38 Spl +P had a concealed hammer, which made the weapon easier to draw and clear without snagging.

The small latch clicked and Heat came around the desk beside Danny. "I'll take it from here, thank you." He did his habitual shrugnod and stood away, giving her access. Nikki drew the brass handle back and looked inside. She turned to the caretaker and said, "We're good from here. I'll give you the key on our way out."

It took Danny a few seconds to comprehend he was being dismissed, but then he left the room. Aguinaldo studied Heat, and when Nikki tilted her glance downward, the other detective came around the desk to look inside the drawer.

There was nothing in it but an empty holster.

Back outside on the driveway, Inez Aguinaldo returned a casual wave to the officer in a black and silver Southampton Town police cruiser that was U-turning on the shoulder to park behind them. She said to Nikki, "I have to say you were pretty chill in there."

Although she may have seemed unfazed, the instant Heat saw the empty holster it had felt like a pinball was suddenly released in her brain and that the shiny marble was bouncing around up there, tripping lights and dinging bells in a quick succession of questions: Where was the gun? *Ding.* Why did Gilbert cooperate with the warrant if he knew it was gone? *Ding.* Did he have any idea it was gone? *Ding.* Did he know, and merely act cooperative as a pose of innocence? *Ding?* Was it somewhere in the house, or somewhere in the surf? *Ding-ding.* "Chill is all relative, Detective Aguinaldo."

"I don't believe for a second that Gilbert forgot where his gun was," said the local. "I mean, you saw that office. It's as orderly as the Smithsonian in there. Everything in its perfect place."

Perfect. There was that word again. Kind of like the elements of a storm.

The mansion was too large for Heat to search by herself, and her call to Captain Irons was met with a belly laugh. "You want me to commit resources out of town during the ramp-up to a hurricane?" he said. "Maybe next week, Detective. After the big blow." Nikki hung up wondering if his big blow referred to the storm or what he was doing to her case.

She turned and took in Cosmo, not just the sprawling house but also its vast acreage and numerous outbuildings full of potential hiding places. Heat didn't know where that missing gun was. But one thing she did know: The why was just as important as the where.

There are two different police departments in Southampton. A confusing bit of municipal legality that separates jurisdictions of the Town of Southampton from the Village of Southampton. Officer Matthews of the Southampton Town—not Village—Police Department shook Heat's hand and met her gaze with the innate cheerfulness she had seen in more firefighters than cops. One of those aged-to-perfection veterans, Woody Matthews gave off the vibe of the guy who would fix your flat in the Kmart lot on his day off, or be found in a tent flipping pancakes at the town fair. He looked at the mug shot he had already been shown by Detective Aguinaldo, but it was the additional picture Nikki showed him that Roach had found on the floor in Jeanne Capois's room that got him nodding. "Yes, I can now say that's definitely the man I saw."

The patrolman also confirmed the date he encountered him. It had been earlier the same night Beauvais asked Ivan Gogol to stitch him up—if the Russian doctor's original story held true, which Heat believed it did. "Detective Aguinaldo said that he might have been shot?"

"That's possible. Did you see any evidence of blood on him?"

"Negative. I can say for sure, I would have responded to that. Now he was sort of hunched-up, though, with his arms crossed like yay." The officer bent to demonstrate, his leather belt creaking like a saddle. "The guy said he was sick, and I'm not out to bust chops, you know? I just wanted to make sure he was all right. I even offered him a ride to the train, but he declined. I got a drunk and disorderly call at one of the taverns on the highway, so I let it go and rolled to the D&D." Catch and release, thought Nikki.

"Did he seem scared, like he was being followed?"

Officer Matthews brushed his fingers through his short-cropped, salt and pepper hair. "Again, that is definitely something I would have keyed into." Heat believed him. He was one of those local types who put on the uniform every day to help, not hassle.

Heat asked to show where he found Beauvais. He spread a map on the hood of his car and tapped North Sea Road near the cemetery. "That's literally on the other side of the tracks from here," she observed.

"Correct. His direction of travel to the train station was coming from the north."

Which was odd. Odd enough, thought Heat, to qualify as an odd sock. If Fabian Beauvais had been coming from either Keith Gilbert's or Alicia Delamater's, he would have been walking from south to north, not the other way around. "What's up North Sea Road?"

"It's a lot of residential," said Detective Aguinaldo.

"Right," continued the officer. "Some nice homes up that way. Not like all this, but middle to upper-middle class. Wooded lots and two-car garages. Let's see, a liquor store, which is where I first thought he might have been coming from. But he could also have been a kitchen worker from the seafood place. Everything else up there would have been closed that time of night. The tree service, Conscience Point, the general store. . . ."

"Hang on," said Heat. For a second, the word almost slipped by

Nikki. But as it started to float away, it suddenly turned like an arcing boomerang and returned to her full force, slamming into her mind. "What is Conscience Point?"

Nikki pulled into the parking lot of Southampton's municipal marina at Conscience Point fifteen minutes later and parked beside a public works truck that was unloading sand bags to brace for the storm. Inez Aguinaldo got out of her unmarked SUV and led her counterpart on a brief walking tour of the Parks & Rec moorage, which amounted to a humble, yet tidily kept green between the road and North Sea Harbor. Three T-shaped docks jutted out from the seawall and a row of slips ran at a right angle down the shore's walking path.

Two months after Labor Day, most sat empty. The few remaining sloops and cabin cruisers belonging to diehards trying to extend the season were in the process of getting hoisted out now. A crew operating a diesel crane with a sling lift worked at a feverish pace to get the boats dry before Sandy came knocking. Heat kept to herself, watching the cascade of water sluice off a winched-up Ensign 22, observing the layout of the grounds, contemplating the pair of Parks & Rec buildings situated just off the blacktop, noting the trash bins and the white six-hundred-gallon fuel storage tanks across the lot. Listening and seeing, the detective tried to be open; to let this place speak something to her.

The two detectives sat on top of a picnic table, eating their panini, watching the three-thousand-pound Ensign swing on a crane toward a carrier on a flatbed. Finally, Aguinaldo asked, "Can I be of help? Is there something specific you're looking for?"

"It's like playing *Jeopardy*," said Heat. "I've got the answer, I just need to guess the right question." The answer, Nikki explained was: Conscience.

"That word has had me scratching my head ever since we found it. 'Conscience' was written on a scrap of paper stuffed in a fat envelope of cash hidden in Fabian Beauvais's closet. Not insignificantly, Keith Gilbert's address and phone number were on the same piece of paper. But 'conscience' was in pencil, like it was added later."

"You're holding back on me, Detective Heat. I think you already know your question. It's 'What is a meeting place for a payoff?'"

Nikki watched the boat hull settle gently against the padded supports of the carrier and said, "It had occurred to me."

More than that, Heat had spent the last few silent minutes playing out its viability in her mind. "Here's a what-if: What if Fabian Beauvais had some personal leverage, some reason to extort or blackmail Keith Gilbert? I don't know . . . Maybe, working for Alicia Delamater, he learned about their affair and threatened to expose that." As she spoke, Nikki realized she was building her scenario on one of Rook's theories and that there would, no doubt, be some crow eating and a sexual favor trade-off as a result. That would have to wait for tonight, she thought, with some relish. "That accounts for the phone calls between Beauvais and the commish. And the ten thousand in cash."

"Calls to negotiate the payoff and the place to make it. Here."

"Conscience," said Heat.

Detective Aguinaldo picked up the what-if, in complete sync with Heat's thoughts. "So they meet here that night. The money gets paid. But something goes wrong."

Heat took the handoff. "It's not the agreed amount, or Beauvais says something to piss off Gilbert, or vice versa, or Gilbert never intended to pay—or to let him live. Think of all the things that can go south fast in a deal gone bad. Either way, Gilbert brought his gun, and whatever happened, didn't finish the job. Beauvais runs, wounded. Gilbert gets the hell out of here."

"But if the ten grand was some kind of blackmail," asked Aguinaldo, "why didn't Beauvais expose Gilbert after he shot him?"

"Not sure." Nikki felt comfortable enough with the other detective to speculate aloud. "What about this? He's an immigrant, right? No standing in the community. He got his money—through an illegal blackmail. Figures he'll survive the wound. Why put himself out there by getting into the justice system against a power broker?"

". . . Who already tried to kill him."

"And may be highly incentivized to finish the job," said Heat. "Sure would explain how a shooting in the Hamptons leads to smashing into the planetarium in New York City."

"If we know for sure there was a shooting here."

A breeze stirred and Nikki turned to look at it ripple the surface of the harbor. And wondered if the Ruger was buried in the silt out there somewhere.

"That's a lot of water," said Aguinaldo.

"Did Gilbert keep a boat here?" asked Heat as they walked back to their cars.

"Doubtful, but I can check."

"I've asked you to do a lot. I have to get back to the city. Mind another favor?" Heat gestured to the scattering of homes nestled behind evergreens and rail fences off the rural road surrounding the marina. "If you can free up the personnel, could you have somebody knock on a few doors around here, Detective Aguinaldo?"

"It's Inez," she said, opening her notebook.

Rook texted Heat while she was buying a cup for the road at Hampton Coffee Company. Her first reaction was a twinge of melancholy that they had devolved from personal contact to voice mail to IMs. He might as well be in Switzerland. But she cheered up when she read his invitation. STILL IN THE MOOD TO BE IN THE MOOD FOR THAT ROMANTIC ROOFTOP DINNER? Making sure to be immediate, she replied yes. He pinged her back, asking if they could do it at her place. He had his reasons, and she had a roof, too.

Nikki hit the highway with a smile. She wanted to see his face by candlelight when she told him she'd poached one of his wacko theories. She suppressed the tingle she felt about what else the night would bring. For now, she was happy things might be settling back to normal between them.

On the way out of the Hamptons she started counting the round blue metal signs posted a half-mile apart that read: COASTAL EVACUATION ROUTE. Those warnings had been there for years, but she never really noticed them. Like so many things.

What had she missed in this case? Asking herself that, as she did at some point during every investigation, Heat succumbed to the detective's disease. To always feel something got overlooked or was lost in all the complexity and lies. But what experience had taught her was to just push forward. That there's always more going on than you think, but the answer is usually simpler than it appears.

Nikki passed another sign indicating she was still on the evacuation route and wondered if she was leaving a hazard zone or heading toward one.

The answer to that came during her debrief of Detective Rhymer shortly after she returned to the precinct late that afternoon. Opie had spent the day with CSU combing the apartments of the known members of the hit squad that had attacked Heat. So far, they had found nothing to connect Bjorklund, Victor, or Floyd to the Port Authority commissioner. As they talked, Heat's cell phone started to come alive with texts and e-mails from friends and colleagues. Their content only gave hints. Brief messages said things like, LOW BLOW! or DIRTY POOL! And from Lauren Parry at the ME's office, WTF?! Lauren's contained a hyperlink to one of the scummier Webloids, *city's-edge.com*, a step down from the *Ledger*, if that was possible. Nikki clicked on it and it opened to the blog's front page. WTF was right.

The headline, big and bold, screamed:

HEAT SNAP?

Underneath was a half-screen picture of Nikki confronting Keith Gilbert outside the Widmark Hotel prior to his arrest. The caption read, CELEBRITY COVER-COP NIKKI HEAT SNARLS AT A COOPERATIVE AND CONFUSED COMMISSIONER KEITH GILBERT JUST BEFORE SHAMING HIM WITH AN AWKWARDLY PUBLIC MIDTOWN ARREST. IS THERE FIRE, OR DID SMOKIN' HEAT SNAP? It got worse.

The article, quoting only unnamed insiders and sources preferring to remain anonymous, painted a picture of a formerly stellar NYPD homicide detective with a penchant for obsession.

People in the know have come out about Neurotic Nikki's single-mindedness. Like flogging her murdered Mom's case over ten years, always at the expense of other investigations. "Don't get in her way when she's on a tear," said one ex-cop. It seems Heat has no problem multi-tasking when it comes to the bedroom, though. Although romantically linked to über-journalist Jameson Rook, a buff gym buddy was shot dead in her tony Gramercy apartment not long ago. When responders arrived, the hunky stiff was naked in her foyer. "I think she kinda cracked," spoke another on background only, fearing retribution from the swingin' dick. "But cut her some slack. Her mom got knifed and her dad's turned into a lush."

Is this what Keith Gilbert meant when he invoked Steinbrenner to mask his threat to throw her over a wall? Maligning her family? She stopped reading and immediately picked up the phone to call her father. The sad reality was, Nikki had to look at the clock to see if it was early enough in the day to reach him while he was still sober.

"Hi, Dad, it's me, Nikki. Listen, just thinking about you. Hoping you're all right." She paused. What do you do in these situations: leave a message telling him not to read a paper or answer any e-mails or calls? "Give me a ring right away when you get this, OK? Love you."

As Heat ended her voice mail, a sharp rap on the captain's office window startled her. She turned to see Wally Irons standing inside his fishbowl, with one hand holding the ballpoint he'd used to tap the glass, and the other holding the phone to his ear. He used the pen to point at Nikki and then jerked it back to beckon her in. He wore the expression of a man whose sloppy joe had started coming back up on him.

"She just came in the office, I'm going to put you on speaker," said Irons who then cradled his handset, accidentally disconnecting his caller. "Fu-uck." Then he turned to Nikki. "It's Zach Hamner from One PP; park yourself." The line purred again in a redial instant and he stubbed a finger down on the speaker button to answer.

"Heat?" asked the voice of The Hammer.

"Right here." Nikki tried to sound nonchalant, but all her defenses were on high alert. Irons and Hamner despised each other, so having them together on a call, combined with Wally's dyspeptic look, signaled a DEFCON-3 event. Her first thought was that this would be about the sleazy article. She wasn't that lucky.

"I hear there was no gun," said Zach, getting right to it, actually, helping Heat relax a little because she was prepared to address that.

"A bit of a surprise after his lawyer called to help us locate it in the house. But it happens." Captain Irons emitted an audible sigh and grimaced some more. She ignored him and continued, "I'm not sweating that."

"How can you not? It's physical evidence in your case."

Nodding at the speaker grid on the gray phone, she said, "Which has disappeared. Or been hidden. Or lost. I'm not happy about it, but it just means we have to recover it. Or chalk it up. In any event, I see this all in keeping with Gilbert's duplicity. Embracing the search to appear innocent and cooperative, knowing the whole time that I'd spend half a day chasing my tail to find an empty holster."

"Must be nice to be so blasé."

"Uh, anything but, Zachary. Listen, this is the pick-and-shovel work we do out here in the field. It's a setback, but that's all. I continue to get new and promising leads on this guy." She almost told him about Conscience Point, but that was still so theoretical it would only feel more speculative, rather than less. Nikki tried to remember when she ever had to work so hard to sell a case, but sell she did. "The missing gun is one detail we'll work around." She didn't like the sucking pause from the downtown end of the phone line. She disliked it even more when he filled it.

"To this office that gun is more than a detail. As is your Russian doctor who's not even a doctor. What happened to him naming Gilbert?"

"He spooked. Somebody got to him."

"There's a pattern. No gun, your witness recants . . . You still don't have a link to Beauvais and Gilbert and an airplane."

"He owns a helicopter."

"Which he couldn't have been in because he was giving a speech when your Haitian took his skydive."

"So one of the goons he sent to attack me did it."

"Oh, you didn't tell me you had proof they were working for him." The weasel's sarcasm made her wish he was there. If Zach had balls, she would kick them.

"Gilbert is solid for this."

"Heat, I know this is a passion for you," said The Hammer, "but my passion is keeping this department from embarrassing and costly lawsuits."

"Yeah, well, mine is putting away killers." Something slipped its chain inside her and she leaned over the phone to add, "Even if they play golf with your bosses."

Irons lurched forward in his chair. "Detective, that is out of line."

"If you're rich and connected, you get a free pass?"

"And insubordinate." Wally checked the light on the telephone to make sure his objections were on the record and added, "Careful now, somebody's living up to her tabloid rep." Heat cut him a sharp look, but decided she'd done enough damage with her outburst.

If the senior administrative aide to the NYPD's deputy commissioner for legal matters took offense though, he didn't sound it. In fact, when he finally spoke again, he came across as downright laid-back. "I think we'll all do ourselves a favor to take a breath here." Nikki, who had bolted to her feet in the exchange, sat back down.

Zach's calm tone gave her a sense that since his second official caution of the day had been voiced, the worst was over. At least until he said, "So I'm taking the pressure off this right now. I got the consent of the brass here, and I've conferred with the DA. We are withdrawing all charges against Keith Gilbert."

ELEVEN

Surrounded by her squad, Heat stood craning up at the TV on the bull pen wall watching live coverage of Keith Gilbert's statement to the media about his dropped charges. The whole thing, although hastily called, had the taint of orchestrated theater, and it turned Nikki's stomach. Tie loosened, shirtsleeves rolled perfectly to the let's-get-to-work spot, the commissioner had posed himself in front of the Emergency Response magic board in the Port Authority's Hurricane Sandy Situation Room. Why didn't he just wrap himself in the flag positioned behind him next to the blinking green lights marking bridge and tunnel status?

Rook called her cell phone. Heat stepped away from the cluster of detectives to take it. "Are you watching this?" he asked.

"It's like a highway accident. I tried not to, but I just have to look."

"Thanks for calling to let me know."

"I would have," said Nikki, "except apparently, Gilbert knew before I did. Hang on, what's he saying?"

Up on the TV, Gilbert was addressing a reporter who was offscreen. "There never was anything to this, so it never concerned me—beyond my thoughts and prayers for the victim of this crime," he said. "I hope the NYPD will now be able to concentrate its resources on bringing the true killer of Fabian Beauvais to justice while I concentrate on the looming storm headed our way."

Rook scoffed in Nikki's ear. "Where's the patriotic music? This guy should have some John Williams or Aaron Copland backing this." His cynicism was welcome, but little comfort to Heat. Rook not only didn't believe the commissioner was responsible, his own investigation may have created the first tiny crack leading to the collapse of her case.

For her own sanity, she tried to put that in her back pocket for now. Gilbert himself made it more difficult to do so.

"Commissioner," asked another reporter, "A source told me you had planned to sue NYPD for wrongful arrest. Is that still in the works?"

Keith Gilbert smiled a wan smile and slowly wagged his head from side to side. "Let me say this. Now is a time to be present-and-future focused. Ultimately, the NYPD and the DA did the right thing. This didn't add up, and they knew it. Even a top investigative journalist, Jameson Rook—who, ironically is the romantic partner of the lead detective of this case—raised huge doubts as recently as today on a blog posted on *First Press-dot-com.*"

Her detectives, nearly in unison, rotated a 180 to regard Nikki. She turned from them and whispered into the phone, ". . . What?"

Rook cleared his throat. "Ah, maybe this would be a good time for me to hang up."

"Don't you dare."

"Nikki, there is nothing in that post we haven't already discussed. And, just so you know, I did not publish it. The magazine did without telling me as a teaser because this is such a hot case. You believe me, don't you?"

What could she say? Something to start another argument? "I can see how that could happen," is where she found both truth and neutral ground.

"I'll help you forget all about this at dinner, I promise."

"That would be a welcome change." And then she added, "Whatever you're making, just no crow, all right?"

When she had gotten out of her car an hour before upon returning from the Hamptons, Nikki felt every ache, scrape, and bruise from the prior evening's street fight, and had planned to call it an early end of shift. The intervening events changed all that, so she convened her crew for a regroup session.

"We're back to the Murder Board and, I guess, the drawing board, too," she observed, but without a bit of whimsy. The four detectives seated around her weren't smiling, either. "Before we break camp, let's share what we've got."

She began by filling them in on the missing gun and her theory about Conscience Point. From there Nikki shared the medical examiner's certainty that the scratch marks on the late Roderick Floyd would most likely confirm her hit squad member as one of Jeanne Capois's killers. Heat also mentioned her frustration at trying to link the quasi-SWAT crew that went after her and Capois to the gangsta pair that shot at Fabian Beauvais. When she admitted she was open to the fact that any one of them could have done Beauvais, Roach looked to each other, not at her. Oh, well.

Detective Raley recapped his efforts trying to get a line on Opal Onishi, whose Chelsea apartment Heat had found empty that morning. "Got her DMV photo," he said, handing the picture of the young Japanese-American woman for Nikki to add to the gallery on the Murder Board. "Age twenty-six. No arrests. No warrants. I went back to her crib and the neighbors said she cleared out late Monday night."

"Same day Fabian Beauvais made his planetarium plunge. Same night Jeanne Capois bought it." added Ochoa.

His partner said, "You are correct, sir. Neighbors didn't know where she went, so I spent the day tracking Opal Onishi's jobs over the past few years. Turns out she's an NYU film school grad. She started as a gopher at Food Network on *Iron Chef* and moved up to her current position hauling equipment for Location Location. That's an AV company in Astoria that rents sound and camera gear to movie and TV shoots around the city."

"Why do you suppose Jeanne Capois would be carrying Onishi's address around?" asked Heat.

"Housekeeping job, maybe?"

"From somebody humping an hourly-wage gig?" said Feller. "Doubtful."

Raley shrugged. "I dunno. Be nice to ask Opal Onishi. But I called her boss. He told me she hasn't come in all week."

Heat said, "Go over there first thing tomorrow and talk to her coworkers and friends. And, Sean? Nice job." He acknowledged the shout-out, but barely. Body language told her that he and Ochoa were still peeved. "Miguel, you're up."

"Trying to chase down the two dudes from the ATM crew that

shot—sorry. Shot *at*—Beauvais." It sounded like an honest slip, and may have been, but when Ochoa dropped that preposition it resonated palpably in light of the hour's developments. Nikki wondered how many more blows she could absorb, and just wanted to get home to be with Rook and start fresh in the morning.

He pressed on. "Both still at large. Thug-One, Mayshon Franklin, has no active warrants, so he's not getting a lot of love. However, Thug-Two, Earl Sliney, is still a wanted fugitive for his home invasion murder. His case got kicked up to New York State Police Bureau of Criminal Investigation. I got the name of the BCI detective holding the jacket. We ended up trading calls and e-mails." Ochoa slid the cuff back off his watch. "We finally set a time for a call this evening, so I expect I'll have my what's-the-what before too long."

Detective Rhymer shared his day in the Bronx at the various apartments of the three men from Heat's hit squad. "All three sort of lived in the same block on Bathgate, so it made it easier to cover the venues simultaneously."

"Bite me," said Feller. "I spend half my life on bridges and the other half in tunnels. Opie gets one-stop shopping for three crime scenes." The others chuckled, but Rhymer seemed preoccupied.

"What you holding, Detective?" asked Heat.

"I made a progress check with CSU when you were in the captain's office on your . . . um, call. First off, at Stan Victor's place—he's the lucky fella you got with the nail gun—they found an index card with the home invasion address on West End Avenue where Jeanne Capois worked as the housekeeper and where they killed the old stockbroker." He paused and kept his face to his notes. "They also found your addresses, both here and at your home in Gramercy Park. And a list of your habitual spots. Rook's loft, your gym, your Starbucks."

In the dead quiet that had descended over the room as they reflected on the surveillance implications, Heat said, "Well. They went to a lot of trouble. Glad I made it worth their while."

Nikki backed up closer to the Murder Board, which had grown so full of pictures and congested with marker notes in all colors and sizes that it looked like one of those urban buildings that, unbidden, becomes a tagger's paradise. She declared to the group, "And guess what? I'm not done. Legal Affairs may have wimped out, but I am not erasing this. Instead, I am digging in. Gilbert is dirty, and the fact that he's flipped from own recog to no recog changes nothing. He's not going anywhere. The storm will keep him around, and tomorrow, or the next day, or the one after that, we are going to find the thing we don't have up there yet. . . ." She paused and surveyed the history of the case on the whiteboard, then continued, ". . . And we will do exactly what he hoped for in his press conference: Bring the true killer of Fabian Beauvais to justice. And I know who that is."

When she turned back to face her homicide squad she guessed only half of them were with her. That was a start.

When she unlocked the door to her apartment, she almost called "Lucy, I'm home" to set a lighter tone with Rook, but something gave her pause. Heat knew the feel of her own place—the sounds, the scents, the atmosphere—through many years and countless moments. She'd known it as a party space and a work space; a love scene and a crime scene; and all shades in-between. What was off?

The quiet? No, not that, because it wasn't exactly quiet. The city ambience of car horns and far distant sirens seemed too present, as if a window were open.

Heat dismissed the notion of going downstairs to the cruiser posted across Twentieth Street, but mindful of Detective Rhymer's briefing, she closed the door quietly and rested her hand on her holster as she crept forward. Nikki reached the end of the rug where her entry hall met the corner turn to the kitchen and saw a white cocktail napkin on the floor. She chanced a peek around the edge and saw another napkin two feet away. A doorman's taxi whistle drifted across the square from the Gramercy Park Hotel and one ply of the far napkin lifted in a breeze to wave hello and then settled at rest. The warmth of a fond remembrance enfolded her and she took her hand off her gun. Then Nikki stepped around the corner and smiled.

A line of cocktail napkins led across the floor like paper stepping-stones from the hallway, through the living room, to the open window.

When she stuck her head out to look up, The fire escape was lit by votive candles to the roof. Nikki thought, this day could turn around yet, and started climbing.

Rook took her by the hand when she reached the upper rung and held it in a courtly manner that began playfully but became genuine as she stepped onto the flat of the rooftop. "Looks like you had no trouble finding me. Talk about a paper trail, huh?"

"I seem to recall you using that method once before."

"Hold that thought," he said. "It's the theme of the evening."

"It's Thursday. Since when does Thursday have a theme?"

"You're the fancy-ass detective. You figure it out." He stepped aside so she could take in the *alfresco* dining spot he had created for them. Two chairs at a table covered by a white linen cloth reflecting pools of dancing candlelight had been grouped in the center of the roof. To the side, a card table with more candles was set with covered dishes and the makings of a bar.

"I don't exactly know." She took a stab. "Romantic, open-air dinner?"

"Congratulations." He held her in both his arms and smoothed her hair. "You win. You are the worst detective ever. Our theme tonight is Beginner's Eyes." As he led her over, Rook said, "Tonight, we are going back to our beginnings, Nikki Heat. Remember our first time? Of course you do, I was magnificent, a stallion. I digress." He gestured to the bar, which amounted simply to a bottle of tequila, a shot glass, lime wedges, and a salt shaker. "Our first drink 'that night'?"

"Oh my God, yes. We had margaritas."

"Hand margaritas, to be precise. The heat wave caused a power outage, and we sat by candlelight much like this, getting liquored up the old-fashioned way."

She laughed, "I needed that so bad."

"And the drink, too." He flicked his brows. "And what night of beginnings would be complete without the first meal we had up here on this very roof? Which is basically why I wanted to do this here."

Nikki rested a hand on each stainless cover and guessed, "Quesadillas and smoked salmon." She raised the lids and laughed again, seeing she was correct. "Rook, what a great idea."

"Oh, I've got an endless supply of them. Here's one." He drew her to him for a kiss. But Nikki started getting ideas of her own and thrust forward, meeting his mouth with an eagerness that took him by surprise. Rook didn't seem to object, and they held each other in the night, ignoring the food and the drink and the candles, exploring each other. They kissed with the passion that still attracted them over years together—and something else.

"Mm. Beginner's mouth," he said with a grin when they parted at last, making her laugh once more. This is what she missed; this is what she needed. She stared at his face—yes, his ruggedly handsome face, as he liked to point out—and thought about the art of his laughter. Rook's laughter may have been his greatest gift to her, keeping her sane by banishing earnestness and lightening her up when she needed it most. Which was most of the time.

He held her chair and she sat. While he busied himself laying out the makings for the hand margaritas she surveyed the squarish form, the size and shape of a jewelry box, in his side-coat pocket, and the flutter she hadn't allowed herself to feel for days tingled within her. Rook sat beside her, took her hand, and with unself-conscious intimacy licked the web between her thumb and forefinger before he shook salt onto it. He poured her a shot of Patron, which she hoisted to him. Then Nikki licked the salt, downed the tequila, and bit the lime wedge he held out to her.

"Your turn," she said, and set him up the same way. Licked him, salted him, poured for him, and then teased him with the lime before putting it in his mouth while he sucked the juice from it.

After their second round, he said, "You going to tell me what the hell happened with Gilbert, or make me suffer?"

"I hadn't planned on mixing business with all this."

"Bullshit. It's in our DNA, Nik. Spill, so we can move on to more pleasant topics."

"OK, fine, but I'd like another one of these." As he obliged with another shot for them Heat downloaded it all. No doubt the *reposado* had something to do with the ease she felt unburdening her cares. Of all the items, he seemed most interested in the missing Ruger from Gilbert's study.

"That is Grade A weird," he said. "Combined with his lawyer offering cooperation finding it . . . ? If he knew the .38 wasn't in that drawer, then why?"

"A mask of innocence. Wake up, Rook, you've been around." His interest grew when she told him about Conscience Point, and she paused there to let the cogs of his conspiratorial wheels engage without interruption. Who knows? Maybe he'd leave the dark side and put his efforts in support of her case, after all. Nikki thought she'd nudge him along. "There is now an official nexus between those guys who came after me last night and Jeanne Capois."

"DNA come in?"

"That's still cooking in the lab." She told him about the index card with the home invasion address. Seeing the impact of that, she added the detail of the surveillance information they had gathered on her. When he started to look over his shoulder, Heat said, "Does that bother you?"

"Hell, no. A squadron of crypto-SWAT, black ops, rogue commandos stalking us? Just my thing. As long as they don't waterboard. I have very small nases."

"Not to worry. There's a radio car out front."

"What if there's a sniper?"

"Come on, Rook. Who goes around worrying about a sniper?" He checked the higher rooftops anyway. She said, "I am not going to run scared and I am not going to give up on finding out how Gilbert pulled this off."

"You always love a high degree of difficulty."

"Just because something's difficult doesn't make it impossible."

"True," he said. "For instance, did you know a French author published an entire novel—two hundred thirty-three pages—using no verbs?"

"Snapple cap?"

"Snapple cap. An education inside every lid. More tequila?"

"We should maybe pace ourselves," she said. "Speaking of difficult, but not impossible, are you done publishing blogs and articles that make my life miserable?"

"Are you calling me difficult?"

"But not impossible." She leaned in to kiss him again. "OK, one more."

"Kiss or shot?"

"Surprise me." Rook kissed her, then poured. Before she drank it, her cell phone rang. "Ochoa. I'd better. . . ."

He agreed and threw back her ounce while she answered.

"Sorry to call you so late," said Ochoa.

"You kidding? You guys can call me anytime." She tried to sound bright and, yes, conciliatory but didn't get a response. "Where's your partner?"

"I'm on, too," said Raley."

"Hey, Sean. Good. Got the full Roach." Nikki heard herself pushing too hard. Whether it was from the tequila or trying to rekindle lost camaraderie, she decided to dial it back to business mode. "Going to put you on speaker because I'm with Rook." She pressed the button. "What's up?"

"Just got off my conference call with the state BCI inspector handling the fugitive warrant for Earl Sliney." By reflex, Heat reached for her notebook the way ex-smokers go for phantom packs, but she'd left it downstairs. Rook pulled out his and handed it to her with a pen. "Sliney's been off the grid, but they caught a break because, apparently, he's traveling with the other guy from the Queensboro Plaza video cam."

"Mayshon Franklin?"

"Right. Well, Mayshon screwed up day before yesterday and shoplifted some beer at a package store up the Hudson in Rhinebeck."

"Got his picture taken by the cash register cam," added Raley. "And they pulled his prints off the glass on the beer case."

Ochoa dovetailed right in to the narrative. "Database spit him out as a known associate of Sliney's, who has a brother living in that area, a small town called Pine Plains up in Dutchess County. State and county vanned up and raided the brother's place. They'd missed nabbing these dirtbags by six hours."

Nikki asked, "Did Sliney's brother say where they went?"

"Nah, either he doesn't know or he's throwing up a wall. But that's not the reason we called."

"It's about what we learned about the brother," said Raley with some weight attached.

"Yeah...?"

Ochoa said, "Earl Sliney's brother works at a farm up there. His job is he flies the crop duster." After the shortest pause, he continued, "So what we're saying is that Earl Sliney's brother had access to an airplane."

Even slowed half a step by the tequila, Heat quickly calculated the math of Roach's intel: Fabian Beauvais worked the ATM theft crew with Franklin and Sliney; Sliney was already known and wanted as a murderer; security video depicted Sliney popping off three rounds at Beauvais, who was on the run from him; Beauvais had a gunshot wound; Sliney's brother had a plane; Beauvais fell from the sky.

A familiar claw grabbed hold of Nikki's gut. She wasn't liking at all where this was going. Not liking the bright, shiny, and new probabilities of Earl Sliney versus Keith Gilbert as the killer.

"It's food for thought," she said and found out what it sounds like when a Roach sighs on a conference call. "I'm not saying it's not viable stuff. It's just—"

"—It's big," said Ochoa, jumping on hard.

Heat bobbed her head. "Agreed. So what we do is put it with all the other pieces and see how it shakes out."

"What needs to shake out?" Raley's question was as valid as it was tersely delivered.

"Look, I'm not shutting your theory down, fellas. You know that, don't you?"

After an interval of whooshing street noise rising on their end, Ochoa said, "What are we doing, then?" His voice carried the subdued consternation of both partners.

Because she needed to be open to the possibility that they could be on to something, and because she wanted to reconnect with this pair that she liked and admired so much, she said, "Here's what you're doing. Set your alarms for early-early and be in Pine Plains by sunup. Go to that farm and brace Sliney's brother, Roach style. Check out his whereabouts on the morning of the planetarium fall. Get his story and get corroboration. Check out the plane. What condition is it in? How many seats? See if there's logs or flight plans. I don't know the rules for rural aviation, but you may get lucky. What I'm saying, boys, is work this. Follow the hot lead, right?"

Only slightly mollified, they said that was all they wanted to hear and said good-night.

"So," said Rook after Nikki plopped her phone on the table. "Sounds to me like they're still hacked off from this morning when you bitch-slapped them on the sidewalk in Chelsea." He caught her reaction and froze to backpedal before he bit into the lime wedge. "Perhaps I should explain. It's true that I spoke to Detectives Raley and Ochoa on another matter today and that incident came up. But in a purely informational way. The inference that your interaction constituted a bitch-slap was purely mine."

Nikki set aside her annoyance about being gossiped about and went for the money. "What other matter did you discuss with my detectives?"

"See, I should never do the *reposado* and talk murder. It's a bad combination."

"Don't try to joke your way out of this, Rook, tell me."

He folded his arms and leaned back in his chair to consider. "All right. I was going to let this go until tomorrow, not wanting to add another log to the pyre of your case, but I heard that Keith Gilbert had filed a restraining order last month against—wait for it—Alicia Delamater."

"And this was from a good source?"

"Yes, but I always verify. Hence the call to Roach. And it checks. So things may not be so cozy around Beckett's Neck. Not like that puffed-up, hack mystery novelist neighbor says."

"You're pissed because he said you should stick to magazines."

"I don't think it's ignoble that I found his judgment harsh."

Nikki didn't hear that. She'd slumped in her chair and raised her face to the sky conducting some secret dialogue with herself.

"Heat, I know it's not good news. It blows the mistress theory right out of the sky—meaning no disrespect to the late Mr. Beauvais." He leaned forward and put his hand on her knee. "Hey?" She lowered her chin and stared at him. "Can we just put this whole business on hold and enjoy the rest of our night?"

Nikki shivered, wishing she'd brought up a sweater. Or maybe never come up. "You mean like talk more about our day?"

"You want something to eat?" He started to reach out with a fork. "The smoked salmon is from Citarella."

"Maybe talk about how my case is unraveling before my eyes?" He put the fork down and gave her his attention. "Or how my squad is whispering and giving me the buffalo eye when I walk in the room? Or how about the meat grinder I walked into with One Police Plaza?"

"They'll get over it. Zach Hamner has no feelings. He isn't even human. Probably hangs his suit of human skin over the shower rod at night." When she didn't crack a smile he said, "Are you worried he'll kill your shot at the task force?"

There it was again. The elephant had joined them on her Gramercy Park rooftop. In a small voice she spoke her reality. "I think I can kiss off my chances with that task force."

He shrugged. "Could be a blessing in disguise."

A fuse lit deep in the back of her skull. "Rook. Are you saying that blowing a promotion is a good thing? Or good for you?"

"No, for us. —Hey, I'm not saying I want that." He raised his brows in thought. "Although. . . ."

"What."

"That job would mean gi-lossal lifestyle challenges. But all open to discussion, right?" Trying to keep it casual, he poured her a shot. "Think I got your last one."

Nikki didn't want another drink. Adrenaline and bile had made her suddenly sober. "This doesn't feel like it's about lifestyle challenges, not anymore."

"I know what you're going to say. Fair's fair, and that I travel, too."

"Fuck logistics."

"Huh. *So* not what you were going to say."

Heat smacked her palm down on the table. "Will you stop? Just stop being cute for once and deal with me?" He corked the bottle. She had his attention. "Tell me how this is all open to discussion? It never got there. You've seen to that."

There. It was out. Nikki had held it down for days. Denied it.

Avoided it. Ate it. At last she'd given voice to the beast, and there was no reining it in.

"You're going to have to explain that to me."

"Rook, please. The moment you found out about my offer to be on that task force you started picking away at my evidence."

"I did not."

"What do you call it?"

"Investigative journalism. Kinda what I do."

"Know what I call it? Sabotaging my case. Either because you're pissed that I didn't tell you about the promotion—"

"—That's ridiculous—"

"—Or so you could keep me from getting it. Or both."

"You know, Nikki that is so not me."

"What else can I conclude? That's when it started. You didn't just get contrary. Contrary, I can deal with. You dug in. You got destructive."

"By looking at other possibilities in the case?"

"By undermining me. First by cozying up to Gilbert's aide; then you poach my limited resources—Raley and Ochoa, even Rhymer—to act as your personal research assistants. Which planted doubts with them, and now look. You heard Roach. They're pulling the opposite way now because of you." Nikki had lost all restraint. She knew she should count to three or walk it off, but the fuse sizzled and burned toward the powder keg. "Even tonight, you can't stop. You have to keep grinding with the restraining order against his mistress."

"I'm sharing my discovery. I'm collaborating."

"What did you call my case, a burning pyre?"

"I'm sharing evidence. Which you choose to ignore. Like the airplane Roach called about."

"Do you expect me to believe some crop duster flew into Manhattan and dropped Beauvais over the Upper West Side without showing up on radar?"

Rook said, "Radar isn't perfect."

"I want to believe in perfect radar."

"Just for argument's sake, let's rule out Sliney's brother and his plane. How then did Keith Gilbert manage to drop the Haitian from the sky without detection?"

Nikki's beast fed off anger; Rook's from sarcasm. "Oh, I know. Gilbert is sailing pals with Sir Richard Branson. Maybe he asked Richie to cruise Fabian Beauvais up to the Kármán Line on his Virgin Galactic spacecraft and launch him from under a wing."

Heat's hand found the shot glass in front of her and flung the tequila in his face. "Go."

Liquor dripped off his nose and chin and onto his shirt. He made no move to wipe it. Rook stared at her, speechless, astonished, hurt. Nikki already felt a tide of shame begin to rise, but her anger remained stronger. Before the balance could shift, she repeated more quietly but still firmly, "Go."

Still stoic, Rook stood. He hesitated, perhaps wondering if he should say something healing or righteous. While he waited, Heat saw the outline formed by the small square box in his jacket pocket. The wave of anger then mixed with the backwash of shame. The swirl created a sort of undertow, dragging Nikki down. Helpless to do anything but founder, she watched Rook turn and go. An impulse to call out to him came and went because the feeling to attach to the words never materialized.

She had gone too far.

Whatever the evening was to have been, it would now not be. Could not be. That was her dark thought watching him descend the fire escape and disappear rung by rung out of this moment, and perhaps, she wondered, out of her life.

TWELVE

Heat got there early and paced the hallway. At 7 A.M. most practices in the medical and professional building weren't open yet, and when the elevator up the hall finally chimed, it broke the dead silence like a fight bell. Lon King, Ph.D., a psychologist who offered services through the NYPD counseling program, didn't usually have office hours until nine, and Nikki thanked him for agreeing to meet her. After unlocking his suite, he asked her to hold in the waiting room, then disappeared behind his closed door to prepare as if some magic would be lost if the switching on of lights, the hanging of a jacket, and the adjustment of blinds should be witnessed.

"It's been a while," said the shrink when she took her seat on the couch and he settled into his easy chair on the other side of the coffee table.

"Almost two years, I think." Heat listened to the pillow-soft sounds of York Avenue drifting up twelve floors while she thought about where to begin. She never felt comfortable here. It wasn't him, she liked Dr. King enough. It was the whole idea of counseling. She had originally come to him against her will when Captain Irons used psych leave as a tool to suspend her without all the nasty paperwork.

Painful as that had been, Nikki found it helpful, and had come back a few times when she felt her compass spinning and needed some guidance. Or solace. As was his way, he sat passively and waited for her. Nikki delivered the opening line she had formulated in the taxi ride uptown. "I'm dealing with a bit of a challenge."

"I assumed so. If you, of all cops, would ask for this time in the midst of your usual caseload and preparation for a hurricane, it must be quite a challenge."

"It's why I hoped to see you early."

"To fit it in." He smiled. "Nikki, you do know that I can't solve your life in fifty-five minutes."

"Give me sixty. I'm a quick study."

"Why don't you begin by telling me about the trigger for this session?"

The shame stirred again. The shame that had become her stalker and kept her tossing in bed until it enveloped her and found its way inside now shifted like a serpent whose scales etched her damaged soul. "I threw a drink in my boyfriend's face last night."

King's reaction was muted. A listener first, the shrink's countenance matched the ambience of his office: buttery light, placid tones and textures. A neutrality designed to evoke. Personally, he fell on the scale somewhere between taciturn and meditative. But he knew her and, therefore, the significance. "That's profound. You have spoken in here before about how you prize self-control."

"I lost it." She had been eyeing the box of tissues and snatched one.

"Let's try to understand why."

"Where do I start?"

"I think you know where."

And she did. At least she thought she did. So that is where she began, with finding the receipt for the engagement ring and her candidacy for the international task force. "I hid the promotion from him, I guess, because of the proposal I thought was coming, and I knew my travel would be an issue."

"You didn't tell Rook."

"I didn't think I could."

"But you also didn't turn down the promotion."

Seeing him reflect on that, Nikki started to feel that she had made a mistake coming there. She didn't care if passing through discomfort was the path, and that the best way out was always through, and blahdy-blahdy-blah. She wanted relief, not more agony. "Let me tell you what else this is all wrapped up in," she said, hearing a desperation in her eagerness, but feeling the need to be understood.

Heat talked about the case. Not all the details, of course, but the psychologist nodded an awareness of it when she mentioned Keith

Gilbert. The crucial thing, she said, was that Rook seemed to be with her, a partner as he always was, right up to when Captain Irons spilled the beans about the task force.

"That was a turning point. From that moment on, it was like he had become an adversary. Not only refuting the evidence I was gathering, but actively working to develop contrary leads for his article."

"He was on assignment?"

"Yes."

"On the case you're working?" She nodded and he asked, "Isn't that different for you two? Except for those profiles he did?"

"Yes, but this goes beyond his journalistic zeal. He not only seemed to be pulling against me, he planted doubts in my squad, and, as a result, I've got issues with some of my detectives."

He asked her to describe those, which led her to describe her conflicts with Raley and Ochoa. "The upshot of all this is that I've now had my arrest pulled. I've never been called into question like this."

"I have a lot of great cops sit here and tell me about their firsts. Setbacks top the list."

"They've got it wrong."

"I'm reading a defensiveness I've never seen before. Is there some part of you that worries you may be wrong?"

"No."

"All right. What about, perhaps, that you may have missed a step along the way?"

She started to say no but held back. ". . . Well. OK, honestly?" He watched her, just patiently letting her come to it herself. "I admit I may have pushed it. Not cut corners, I never do that. But in a few instances, I may have made some slips in judgment or hurried things where I wanted them to go instead of waiting them out or closing all the loops."

"Why is that, do you think?"

After an eternal moment of air conditioning hiss, she said, "Maybe this got to me on some personal level."

"How?"

"I don't know. The case. I can't explain it, it's a feeling."

"Feelings are what we do here, Nikki." He smiled encouragement.

"I got a few buttons pushed."

"Rook?"

"For sure."

"What else?"

"I don't know." Nikki slid forward, the scooched back, trying to center herself on the couch. "Lately, I've been feeling like a crash-test dummy for stress. Everywhere I turn, there's one more thing pissing me off. Rook, One PP, my own squad. I just wanted to run this case."

"Your way?"

The implication hung there between them. "I've always been a collaborator, Dr. King. And open-minded about an investigation and new ideas."

"Always been. What about now?"

She didn't speak. Her look told him they both knew the answer.

"A couple of observations." He set his Circa notebook on the side table and crossed his legs, signaling a new mode. "One of the issues we have dealt with in prior sessions is the murder of your mother."

"Well, that was solved about two years ago."

"Closing a case doesn't settle all that's happening within you. In fact, it could be part of this issue." He picked up his notebook again for a glance. "When I reviewed my notes after you phoned last night, I recalled that I asked you once—and this was before you solved her murder—what life would be like without the sense of purpose the pursuit of your mother's killer gave you. Have you had difficulty adjusting after that?"

"I hadn't really thought about it."

"Do. Try it on. That sense of mission was a convenient way to sublimate. It's not uncommon to replace rage with purpose. And when the purpose goes away, what comes back? Rage in trauma victims doesn't get relieved by externals like case closure. It defers. Like squeezing a balloon, the pressure moves elsewhere. Is this case really any different than any other? Maybe you're still working it out."

"I don't go around feeling rage."

"You threw a drink in Rook's face." The serpent beneath her skin moved again and she lowered her gaze.

"Now, don't feel judged. On the upside, it's nice to see someone as controlled as you be spontaneous. Also, rage is human. Rage lives somewhere in all of us. I'm sure it has helped us survive from prehistoric times to now. But we're not cavemen anymore. In daily, civilized life rage can be toxic. And a waste of good scotch."

"Tequila."

He allowed his version of a chuckle and his eye line went to the clock she knew sat over her shoulder. "Before we run out of time, I want to discuss you and Rook." Hearing his name, Nikki felt her skin bristle like the onset of a rash. "You say he was going to propose to you last night?"

"I thought so. I'd found that receipt, and he gave all the signs and set up a very romantic evening for us. I even think I saw the box in his pocket."

"How do you feel about that? The possibility of marrying him?"

"Hold on, are you saying I created a scene to derail his proposal?"

"Who knows? The subconscious is an impish little bastard. But I'm interested more in your feelings about this relationship." She had come there seeking some measure of relief and now she found herself being prodded into even deeper distress.

As if he were reading her thoughts, King said, "I know this is hard, but you came here because of your incident with Rook. Let's talk about him." Heat gathered herself and gave a willing nod. He consulted his notes again. "You've been together, what, three years now? Mostly, the relationship has been good for you?"

"Yes, of course."

"And I can only imagine the challenge of two strong-willed high achievers sharing both careers and romance. In fact, when he took on your recent murder case as the subject of his investigative piece, it kind of set you up for conflict, didn't it?"

"I see that now. When he mentioned it, I assumed he'd just ride along."

"And write up your findings like dictation?" He let that sink in. "It might help if you recognize you are living the quintessential modern relationship, Nikki Heat. Passion and career demands are a volatile mix. This quarrel over your case may be the tip of an iceberg. Especially when you have needs and ambitions that conflict with his."

"The task force?"

"It's a lot to consider. But consider it, you must. And seek to resolve. Think you're going to talk with him about this?"

"If he's still talking to me."

"Do yourself a favor before you do. Ask yourself this: Given what you've just gone through, can you see a long-term future with Rook when it's only going to get more demanding?" He stood and said, "In case you're wondering, I can't answer that for you. I only ask questions."

It's always back to *Jeopardy*, she thought.

Wally Irons snared Heat as she passed his doorway on her way in. "Where's your two guys, Starsky and Hutch?"

"Assuming you are referring to Detectives Raley and Ochoa; right about now they're up in Dutchess County following up a lead."

"Oh." He held up a memo and put out his lower lip in an unconscious pout. "I was going to announce this to your squad, but seeing as you don't have a quorum for roll call, here. You tell them." He handed her the sheet of paper. "All leaves and vacations are canceled in light of the approaching hurricane."

"There goes my weekend in Lahaina."

"No leaves, not even for the weekend," he shot back, trumpeting his total lack of irony. As she entered the bull pen he called out, "And Heat. No more letting personnel leave the city for a Friday fuck off without my OK." It wasn't his snippy tone that made her flare. Or shouting into her squad room at her like that. It was one more instance of the armchair administrator calling shots. Nikki took it to his face.

"I think we had better be clear on something, Captain." His eyes popped at the unexpected confrontation. Behind her, Detectives Rhymer and Feller swiveled their desk chairs to rubberneck. "Sean Raley and Miguel Ochoa are seasoned investigators who were working very late hours last night and took the initiative to call me to request permission to explore what they see as a promising lead upstate. I will back these detectives for their tenacity and heads-up play. I will also be respectful and honor your request for the sign-off. But I will not let you characterize the work of these men as a 'Friday fuck off'." She left him there and went to her desk, reading the emergency status memo.

It said that Sandy had crossed the Bahamas and begun a more north-northwesterly course. Even though it had diminished from just one mile per hour shy of a Category Three hurricane to a Cat One, it remained potent and dangerous with wind speeds of eighty. Up the Eastern seaboard, North Carolina, Maryland, DC, Pennsylvania, and New York had already declared states of emergency, with New Jersey and Connecticut expected to follow suit. In anticipation of possible landfall sometime Monday into Tuesday, the mayor had officially opened New York City's Office of Emergency Management's Situation Room. Not only were leaves and vacations canceled, but also all police, fire, and sanitation workers should be expected to be ready for deployment, as ordered, for public safety and civil order.

Heat shared the memo with Feller and Rhymer, who were back to working their phones, beating the bushes for anything that would resuscitate the stalled Beauvais-Capois murder case. She didn't think it would be too early to try Rook, so she stepped outside onto Eighty-second Street for some privacy and called his number.

It didn't go straight to voice mail, which told her the phone was on. And it delivered the full complement of rings before she heard his outgoing message, so at least he hadn't pushed the decline button to reject her. Hearing his recording, Nikki's mouth went dry. After the tone, she kept it short and as pleasant as she could manage given her stress level. "Hey, it's me. Storm's coming, thought I'd check on you. Call me so we can talk, all right?" She almost hung up but added, "I'm here" first.

She looked up at the sky, which was brilliant blue with only a few vaporous clouds the morning sun hadn't burned off yet. No hint of the cyclonic pinwheel feeding off humid water a thousand miles southeast. The storm made her think of the Emily Dickinson poem Rook joked about in happier days—at the chicken slaughterhouse. The one that called hope the thing with feathers that sings such a sweet tune. And in her mind, she recited her favorite stanza:

And sweetest in the Gale is heard;
And sore must be the storm
That could abash the little Bird
That kept so many warm.

Then her iPhone buzzed with a text from Rook. It said he thought they should take a breath and get some space. He'd be in touch. He didn't say when.

Not one feather on that.

When Raley and Ochoa checked in later that morning they were southbound on the Taconic in the Roach Coach. "What did you learn at the farm?" she asked.

"Not much from Walter Sliney, that's for sure."

The speakerphone picked up Ochoa, whom she could envision behind the wheel. "Total doucher."

"Understandable, though," said Raley. "He was icing us to protect his brother."

"Who murders old ladies." Another addition from Ochoa.

"So no leads on Earl Sliney or Mayshon Franklin?"

"Correct. But state police lifted prints that confirm Thug-One and Thug-Two definitely crashed there, so at least there's a trail to follow, and they are on it, big-time." Raley added, "Good rapport with the BCI lead, so if they get a handle, we'll know it soon as they do."

Since they hadn't brought it up, Heat initiated. "What about the crop duster?"

"I'm not a pilot," said Ochoa, "but that plane looked viable."

Raley, obviously in accord, filled in the detail. "I kind of expected some bucket of bolts biplane rusting under a haystack. The plane is in top condition. It's a Piper Pawnee Ag aircraft converted to a tandem two-seater, which would allow room for the pilot and Beauvais's body, if the scheme was to fly him out over the Atlantic and dump him in the ocean."

"Is that your theory?" Sensitive to recent tension, she asked without judgment, only as a point of information.

"It's one. I'll admit, it's a little bit like the wood chipper in *Fargo*, but that fits the IQ profile up here."

Ochoa chimed in, "The plane not only has the room, it's got the range, about four hundred miles."

Picking up the rhythm of partner-talk, Raley added, "And it would be an easy in and out from that farm. No tower, no flight plan to file, no logs. Just load and go."

Heat still had her doubts, but post-shrink, she consciously led with her usual open style. "Let's factor that in then. And fellas. Nice work. Thanks for the initiative."

She got left hanging in another one of those awful midair voids waiting out their reply. "Boss?" said Ochoa at last. "Rhymer and Feller called. They told us about you getting up in Fat Wally's grill for us."

Detective Raley sounded loose. Like his old self. "Just want you to know we're good."

And then, overlapping him, Roach said, "Way good."

Nikki hung up. May the healing begin.

The subject line on Lauren Parry's e-mail screamed, "Toldja!" Nikki clicked it open and read the synopsis of the lab results from testing residue under the fingernails of Jeanne Capois and the DNA of Roderick Floyd. High-confidence match. Heat wrote her friend back and busted her chops. "No coroner should ever use a smiley face emoticon."

Her own smile faded after she walked over to post this news on the Murder Board and saw that it was already sort of up there. The medical examiner's e-mail had provided confirmation but no momentum. Worse, it only reminded Heat that a puzzle piece she'd long been holding still didn't fit anywhere. Nikki's board was replete with floaters, orphans, odd socks, coincidences, contradictions, and names of the deceased—all proving that this was indeed about more than one man falling from the sky. Sounding to herself more like Rook than Rook, Heat believed that when this scattered array of disparate pieces finally did come together, it would expose a conspiracy of some kind. What kind? She wasn't sure. Nikki found the notation for RODERICK

FLOYD—FINGERNAIL DNA, took a marker, made a check mark beside it, and called that progress. For now.

Coming back from grabbing a Greek yogurt from the break room, Nikki heard her iPhone purring on her desk and lunged for it, fearing she'd miss a callback from Rook. But the 631 area code told her it was the Hamptons.

"Detective Heat, it's Detective Aguinaldo; sorry I missed your call a bit ago, but I think you'll forgive me when I share my reason."

"Hey, no problem, Inez." Heat set her Fage cup down and cleared space for notes. "I didn't want to be a pest. Just making my rounds; you know how it goes."

"Well it goes a bit slower here in Southampton Village, but yes. When you called I was back at Conscience Point. I wanted to knock on some doors after we were up there yesterday, but I couldn't clear any officers, so I went up there myself this morning."

"No explanation necessary. I appreciate you making the effort."

"A number of folks weren't home. Being that we are so low and coastal, people are heeding the warnings and caravanning to the mainland. The Cross Sound Ferry just announced they're going to cancel Monday service because of Sandy, and you can imagine the backup of vehicles waiting to get on a boat at Orient Point." Heat calculated the number of cars she had already seen leaving the day before and could only guess that the exodus now must be looking like the fall of Saigon.

"But I got an interesting piece of news for you. Know how the road forks left to Scallop Pond Road? Of course you don't, but it's right near the marina, take my word for it. One of the residents there said that the night we're talking about, he heard what he thought were kids setting off M-80s, you know, firecrackers."

"How many?"

"Two. And pretty close together. Bang. And then bang. I asked him to time it out for me."

Nikki jotted down two bangs. "Is this the right time frame?"

"Perfectly in the hammock."

"Your witness. Is this person reliable?"

"Solid. Bright guy. Does PR for one of the vineyards on the North Fork."

"And he didn't call it in because he thought it was firecrackers?"

"Exactly. You get a lot of that up there, kids being kids. He did step out to investigate, and said he heard two cars speed off, so he thought, why bother, they're gone anyway."

Heat tapped her pen on her lips. "He said two cars?"

"I circled back on him to confirm. Definitely two."

"He say he heard anything else. Voices? Shouting. A cry?"

"I asked. He said that would have made him call it in."

"Inez, this is very helpful."

"Not done yet," said the Southampton detective. "I'll keep on this, even if I have to put on my waders."

"Tell me you do not have waders," said Nikki. She could hear Inez Aguinaldo laughing when she hung up.

Heat spent the next ten minutes in a near-meditative state, sitting in a chair, staring at the Murder Board. The exercise, which she employed whenever she felt "this close" and yet "that far" from a solution helped her clear away the noise of a case and let the graphic elements before her eyes speak to her. Well, she hoped they would. They didn't always. In fact, sometimes they downright mocked her.

"Detective Rhymer," she said when she'd had enough and stood to stretch.

"What's up?" Opie asked, crossing over from his desk to join her.

She tapped a blank spot amid the riot of pictures and notations. "There's too much white on my whiteboard." There was a name above the open space. "You were checking on the whereabouts of Alicia Delamater, right?"

"With no joy. Same as last update. No customs dings, not using her credit cards, her cell phone, nothing." Nikki beckoned him to her desk and he followed, waiting while she went through her notes. She found what she was looking for, copied it onto a pad, and handed the page to him.

"What's this?"

"Alicia Delamater's home number in Southampton. Call it and leave a message."

"All right . . ." he said tentatively and turned the paper around and around between his forefinger and thumb. "What makes you think she's going to call me back?"

"Because you are not Detective Rhymer, NYPD. You are the new senior manager of the marketing firm that just won the account to reboot Sean Combs's White Party at The Surf Lodge in Montauk— And you want to interview Alicia about a job to be the event planner."

He grinned. "Always thought I would make a good creative type."

"I have nothing but faith," she said. "Make us proud."

No sooner had Rhymer gone off to make, or more likely, practice, his phone call, Detective Feller strode up to her desk with a little extra kick. "I just got a hit on your friend from Chelsea with the assault rifle. I forwarded you the bulletin."

He waited while Heat scanned the Interpol rundown of the man she had nicknamed the Cool Customer. One piece of information at the end stopped her cold. She reread it to make sure she had it right and stood, grabbing her keys and her phone. "Come with me. You and I are taking a ride to see an old friend."

On their way out, Heat palmed the form of her gun on her hip just to reassure herself it was there.

It had been almost three years since Heat rode the express elevator to the top floors of the black glass, high-rise near Grand Central. From Vanderbilt Avenue, it looked like any other Midtown office building with sidewalk retail and a mix of law firms and corporate offices filling the tower up to the topmost two stories. Those floors belonged to a company not listed on the lobby directory. That clandestine touch was characteristic of Lancer Standard, which called itself a consulting firm. But that was only another layer of camouflage. Because Lancer Standard's prime-consulting service was mercenary operations.

For years it had thrived—often controversially—as a CIA contractor in Iraq, Afghanistan, and Pakistan. With secret (read: publicly denied) training facilities in the remote Nevada desert and who knew where else, Lancer Standard, Inc. provided freelance commandos, assassins, saboteurs, and personal security for state leaders and business tycoons in the world's hot spots.

After refusing to check their service weapons, an exercise Heat had gone through (and prevailed at) on her first visit, she and Randall Feller were ushered from reception by three gentlemen of lethal handsomeness through the secure, thumbprint-activated, reinforced air lock and up a flight of internal stairs to the penthouse office of the CEO, Lawrence Hays.

Unlike last visit, Hays gave Heat a smile with the handshake upon entry to his corner office. Unlike last visit, Hays was not a prime suspect in the murder of a parish priest. Things like that have a tendency to put a strain on a meeting. He dismissed their minders and pushed a button that closed the door as they sat in the conversation area of his sprawling office.

"Funny," he said. "Human nature. You sat in the exact spot last time."

"Some memory."

"Rely on it." He cocked his head to her and threw his blue-jeaned leg over an arm of the easy chair exactly as he had before. Heat had a sense of recall, as well. It told her Hays still played the aging Steve McQueen down to the close sandy haircut and more than a few hours spent in the gym. "What's the occasion, Detective? I can assume you're not here to try to browbeat me into a false confession this time."

"No, actually, I'm interested in testing the memory you're so proud of."

Hays held up one of the bottled waters resting on the coffee table, which had been fashioned out of the elevator wing from the tail of a Black Hawk helicopter. It was hard not to notice the spray of bullet holes dimpling it. After both detectives declined, he twisted the cap and took a sip, ready to listen. But his demeanor tweaked when she said, "I need to find a man who has done some work for you."

"We don't share information about personnel. Not even to confirm their employment."

"This man is a killer."

"You know, I see that on a lot of résumés. Might even be a plus." He flashed a quick smile, showing off the cocky knowingness insiders like to play up to outsiders. "Hate to shut you down, Detective, but you have to get me behind a closed-door joint congressional subcommittee, and even then, I'm not one to go all Dr. Phil and open up the goods."

"He's operating in the city."

"We don't do that."

Feller hopped in. "Oh, just like you guys don't cross the border from Texas to disrupt the drug cartels?"

Hays appraised the street detective as if deciding if he could measure up to a job. "I go to Juárez for the cuisine. Try *El Tragadero* in Calle Constitución. Best rib eye you'll ever eat."

Heat said, "But Mr. Hays, you do have a domestic entity. What about Firewall Security?"

"Rope-line bouncers and celebrity-threat assessment. Nothing more." He capped his Fiji and stood. "We all happy now?"

Nikki said, "So you've never heard of Zarek Braun?" The tonal shift was striking. For the first-time ever, Heat saw him falter. Maybe it wasn't fear she saw on his face, but something close to it. The cockiness sure got dialed down.

"You're after Braun?"

"So you do know him."

"He's here?"

Heat held out the CCTV capture of Zarek Braun emptying the assault rifle at her, and he sat back down to study it. "G36. The Z-man still likes his toys."

"He was playing with me when that got taken."

"And you're still here. I'm impressed." Hays meant it. Heat decided to ride the unguarded moment.

"Our Interpol report said he was Polish military, an employment gap, then Lancer Standard, and now nothing. Fill in some holes for me here."

He fluttered the photo across the Black Hawk wing to her. "Zarek Braun came on my radar after he mustered out of the Polish army. He was some fucking soldier. Led a platoon of Poland's First Special Commando Regiment in Operation Swift Relief in Pakistan in 2005. Moved on with them to Bosnia, then Iraq, then kicked some ass in Chad in 2007.

"Got into some trouble for being trigger-happy for a UN peace-keeper—which I had no problem with—and so, when he got drummed out, we used him. Mainly for sabotage at first, then for our extraction teams in places I will not name, but you have seen on the nightly news. He had a lot of skills but, man, it was his temperament. The guy kept himself so mellow. I swear he pumped Freon instead of blood."

Heat thought of her nickname for him and pictured Braun's cool, casual air sauntering toward her on West Sixteenth. A trickle of discomfort ran through her and she wondered if her face registered the same uneasiness she just saw on Lawrence Hays. "Are you going to tell me if he still works for you or make me guess?"

"In my business you get a share of madmen acting out. That's the life. Things happen in battle we can't judge sipping mineral water in air-conditioned comfort. So there's leeway. Zarek Braun, though. Braun is in a league of his own. I'm not going to run it all down, but during a covert action we were asked to spearhead called Operation Dream Catcher, we started getting feedback from the field about atrocities and some majorly diabolical shit. So, when I made a trip over there to our little hamlet in our undisclosed location, I had a sit down with him." Hays tapped the photo on the table showing Braun passively emptying the gun. "This is what he looked like through the whole conversation. Long story short, I booted him. That night Zarek Braun set an IED in my base camp. Killed my best bodyguards." The CEO stood and pulled up his black polo shirt to reveal a salad of pinched, discolored tissue, jagged scars, and disfiguration from burns. He let the fabric drop and said, "I don't know where he is now."

"You can find out." Hays gave her a blank look, but she now knew it was personal with him so she pushed harder. "This guy is not only out there in the city firing assault rifles at cops like it was Kandahar, Mr. Hays, I need him for multiple homicide cases I'm working. You want him to pay? I can get him. Will you at least say you'll help?"

Lawrence Hays considered, and Nikki thought just maybe she had reached him. But then he said, "I make it a point of never saying anything." He pressed a button and the door automatically opened to let in their escorts.

––––––––

Feller got out and folded in the side mirror so Heat could snug her car close to the Roach Coach when she double-parked outside the precinct. She was gauging the width of West Eighty-second to make sure she'd left enough room for traffic to pass when her phone rang. "Hey," said Rook. "Can you meet me? I mean right now."

THIRTEEN

R ook was waiting for her just where he said he'd be, in the playground by the swing set. But not so much by the swing set as on it, and when Heat spotted him after her short walk down Amsterdam from the precinct he looked all of eleven years old with one heel planted on the ground, leg extended, pivoting from the chains. All he needed to complete the effect would be to play bombardier with his spit over an ant.

A troupe of marathoners left the running store across the avenue on a training run, and the slapping of their waffled soles on pavement drew his attention Nikki's way as she approached. The late October sun had already set, kids were home having supper, and Tecumseh Playground was all theirs. The awkwardness of the prior night muted the greetings. He kept seated in his swing; she took the empty one beside him, leaving them to sway shoulder-to-shoulder but facing opposite directions.

"Hope you don't feel too exposed here, but I wanted some neutral ground away from work, or your turf or mine." Then he added, "And away from liquids. If you plan on dousing me, you're going to have to push my face into that drinking fountain."

Nikki wished she could laugh, but her soul felt encased in shame. "Not one of my proudest moments." She offered that olive branch and studied him, trying to get a fix on his state of mind. She got it. His brow was set low and he wasn't smiling.

"You know, you hit me where I live when you accused me of being out to undermine you."

Nikki started to speak, desperate to get out ahead of this; to let Rook hear all she had been mulling about her behavior, not just the previous night, but everything leading up to it. If she could just come up with the words to make this right, maybe she could reset them to where they were before. But this was his meeting, and he had something to get off his chest, too. "It's not easy pulling off the balancing act we do," he said, echoing Lon King's observation from that morning's emergency counseling. "The job stress, the hours, the travel, the disagreements. . . ."

He paused and watched another wave of after-work marathon trainers set a course for Central Park. Heat didn't speak, just yielded the moment, even though this conversation was feeling like the prelude to an ending—like the watershed after three years, with each making civilized promises to stay friends on Facebook. It didn't make her feel any better when he finally continued. "But what I always counted on as our glue was the value we shared. And that's trust. When you called my actions and motives into question on this case, you weren't just going after my journalistic integrity, Nikki. You made a laser strike at who we are." Salt stung her eyes and she wondered if she'd feel this same drill boring into her heart every time she passed this playground. But then he took an unexpected turn.

"Which is why I wanted to give you something that would symbolize our trust and cement it for the future." Her chest fluttered as he reached into his side-coat pocket.

"Rook. What are you doing?"

"Something that can't wait another minute. It's why I called and said I needed to see you right away." His hand came out of his pocket, but he wasn't holding a jewelry box. It was a small Ziploc bag. "Ta-da." He beamed triumphantly and held it before her. She looked through the cellophane and found no engagement ring in there. "You can't see what this is? Here, I'll hold it up to the light." He dangled the bag so that it was backlit by the Chirping Chicken fast food sign, which had just come on.

She examined it, dumbfounded. "Is that . . . ?"

He bobbed his chin. "That's right. A bullet. But not just any bullet. A .38 caliber bullet."

Thoughts of both a breakup and a marriage proposal sufficiently elbowed aside, Heat snatched the bag from him and pored over the mangled slug inside it. "Where did you get this?"

"After our little—shall we call it, dustup on the rooftop—I couldn't sleep when I got home."

"Me, neither, I was thinking all about you."

"Yes. Ahem, I also was thinking about the case. Especially your theory about some kind of payoff happening at Conscience Point. So I thought, screw it. I got up and drove out there. Arrived about four A.M. Sat in that parking lot with my flashlight and thought to myself, if Fabian Beauvais's gunshot was indeed a slicer, maybe, just maybe, the slug got lodged somewhere."

"So you found a bullet? How long did it take you?"

"About nine hours. Dug this one out of the banister on the steps to the deck of the rec center. Detective Aguinaldo found a second one about an hour after she showed up."

"What? Rook, I talked to her, she never mentioned any of this."

"Because I made her promise to let me tell you. The one she found got nested in one of the shingles on the side of the building. Very soft wood, so that slug is pristine. She kept that one and sent it to the NYPD ballistics lab to run for you."

"Any sign of the gun?"

"Boy, you want everything, don't you?"

"No, I'm good. In fact, this is one of the nicest gifts you could have given me." 'One of,' she thought.

"Comes at a price, though."

"Yeah?"

"I want your trust. That's what got me out of bed and driving a hundred miles to Conscience Point. To do what you would do. Follow the leads where they go, and let the truth be told." He jiggled the bullet in the bag. "And even if I hadn't found this, don't you know you can always trust me?"

"Yes, of course." Nikki drew what felt like her first full breath of the day. "I am so glad this is behind us." She rested a hand on his thigh and noticed he didn't respond. ". . . It is behind us, isn't it?"

"I want back in the precinct. Divide and conquer's one thing. But getting banished is how this weirdness got started."

Nikki threw "Boy, you want everything, don't you?" back in his face. She chuckled alone. He still hadn't taken her hand. "I'll talk to Captain Irons about letting you back in."

"Good." And Rook stood. "Let me know when, and I'll see you there."

"Seriously? Don't you even want to get some dinner tonight?" He sucked in his lips, hesitating. "Rook, I thought we were moving forward from this."

"We are. I'm just not in the let's-get-together-tonight place yet. Just being honest." Much as that stung, she understood. To think otherwise was to minimize the impact of what she'd done. Heat thanked him for the bullet and walked back to the precinct with it.

On her way up Amsterdam she turned and stopped, watching him walk the opposite way. How weary was Nikki of seeing his back?

Heat woke up the next morning alone, and feeling every bit of it. Her alarm was still ten minutes from ringing, so she opened the app to kill it with extreme prejudice, and while she did, her phone rang in her hand, startling her. The caller ID said it was Detective Raley.

"So. You do wake-up calls now, too?"

"This will help you rise and shine. We found Opal Onishi."

The woman facing Nikki on the couch in Greenwich Village still had pillow marks on one side of her face. Opal Onishi balanced them out with the perplexed frown she gave Heat's badge. "You said Homicide, right?"

"That's my division, yes." Nikki didn't want to tip her yet that she'd found her former address in the purse of a murder victim. She'd hold it back until she got answers to a few preliminaries without that grim spoiler coloring things. So Heat redirected the subject. "I just have a few questions to ask and I'll be on my way. Sorry to wake you up on a Saturday morning."

"No problem. My roommate crashed with her boyfriend, so I was up anyway to feed her cat."

"Your roommate, Erika?" Nikki always did her homework.

"Yeah, Erika. Is she in some kind of trouble? She's not like a crazed killer like in *Single White Female*, is she?"

Heat said, "No, actually we only know of Erika because she works with you at Location Location. That's how we found you here at her place."

Opal, who was still in her mismatched Gap flannels from bed, cleared her throat and folded her legs, pulling her knees toward her chest. "You were looking for me?"

"We tried you at your old apartment."

"Yeah, I moved out of there."

"Quite suddenly."

"Uh, right." She lit a cigarette and waited for Nikki to say something, and when she didn't, Opal filled the void. "Yeah, well, I had a bad breakup with my girlfriend. She was coming around all hours, you know, just being a bitch, so I . . ." Opal finished the thought by sliding one palm off another like a jet taking off from an aircraft carrier.

"I know how that goes." Heat poised her pen over her notebook. "May I ask your girlfriend's name?"

"Ex. Do you have to involve her? She's an actress on a movie that's filming in town." Again, Heat left a space. Opal Onishi filled it with a woman's name that Heat probably didn't need but wrote down anyway. What she really wanted to know was why Jeanne Capois had her address and if it was relevant to the murders. And why the sudden move? Nikki didn't buy the harassing-lover story at all, and picked at that.

She appraised the living room of the East Village one bedroom, which was over-filled with cardboard cartons and stacked furniture. "Did you file any complaints against your girlfriend?"

"With the police? Nah. I just moved."

"At midnight."

Opal seemed smart and came up with quick answers. Some might even be true. "It's easier to double-park a cargo van then. No traffic."

Nikki decided to follow another course. "I'd like to show you a picture and ask if you can identify the person." She placed an enlargement of the photo of Jeanne Capois on the coffee table. Opal stubbed out her cigarette and picked up the picture. Nikki couldn't be sure if it was hesitation or simply an attempt at recollection, but she felt like it took a few seconds too long to answer.

". . . Jeanne." She offered the picture back. "Jeanne." Heat let her keep it.

"Do you know her last name?"

She pursed her lips and shrugged. "Sorry, but I only know her as Jeanne."

"And how do you know her?"

Again, that fraction of waffling gained the detective's notice. Opal said, "I hired her to clean. She's a maid."

Heat noted her use of the present tense. But still, why all the mulling for simple answers? "May I ask when she did housekeeping for you?"

"Gee, I'd have to think. I dunno, three weeks ago, last time?"

"How did you hear about her?"

A pause, then, "Through a service or something, yeah. I don't remember the name."

Nikki offered, "Happy Hazels?"

Quickly, this time, jumping at it, Opal said, "Yeah, that's it. Happy Hazels."

This was all feeling improvised so Heat kept at it. "Did you pay her cash or check?" A long shot, but a paper trail from a check register might be useful.

"Cash."

"How much?"

"Wow, you bear down." Then she searched the ceiling. "I guess, what, fifty bucks?"

"You tell me."

"Fifty. Why are you asking about Jeanne?"

"She's a victim in a homicide investigation." Heat watched her reaction, always crucial, but especially when there's a sense of something being off. Opal Onishi's face grew slack and she sat, staring into the middle distance. To Heat's mind, a strong response, considering the hesitation at recalling her name.

"Fuck . . . What happened to her?" Unguarded at last.

Nikki kept it in simplest terms, for now. "Jeanne Capois was found beaten and strangled on the street uptown." She turned to a blank page, wanting to take advantage of the openness shock always brought. "When Jeanne came to your place, did she mention any threats against her?"

"No," she said, low and dazed. She gave the same reply when she quizzed her about whether Capois seemed agitated, worried, or talked about being followed. Then Nikki brought out the photographs and sketches, She presented them, one at a time, to Opal, who had slid to a spot on the couch beside her. The young woman shook her head to each one: Fabian Beauvais—no; the four mercs who had attacked Heat a block from Opal's old apartment in Chelsea—no; the gangstas in the ATM shot—no; Keith Gilbert . . . Hesitation.

"Opal, do you recognize him?"

"Of course, he's that politician. Kind of a dickwad, if you ask me."

"You have no other reason to know of him?"

"No, why should I?"

Heat smelled something here. Rather than jam her, she offered an escape hatch. "Opal, I talk to a lot of people in my job. And I sort of get a sense when someone is not being open with me."

"Are you accusing me of lying?"

"I'm saying if there is anything you aren't sharing, for any reason, this is the time to tell me." She read her interviewee, sitting again with her back against the armrest of the couch with her knees pulled into an upright fetal position. "If you are afraid of someone, I can give you protection."

Opal Onishi digested that but said, "I answered all your questions, right?"

At the door Heat gave her a business card. "In case you remember anything." Or, she thought, watching her take it, if you decide to tell me why your hand is shaking.

Rook met Heat on the sidewalk outside the precinct at nine that morning. "What did Wally say?"

"Don't worry about Wally, just come in."

"You threaten him? Maybe say I'll do him dirty in the press?"

"If you must know, I haven't spoken to him. He's not in yet. Look, don't give me that face, this won't be a problem. Trust me, I know how to handle Wally Irons."

Good enough for Rook. He held the door for her. But she didn't budge so he closed it again. "What?"

"Irons isn't the only one who needs to be dealt with. I have a condition, too."

"Go on. . . ."

"You have an article to write, and I will honor my commitment so you can keep riding along. But—I have enough stress without adding to it if you're going to go around bruised or harboring an attitude."

"I hear you. And just you watch. I can be a team player. I can even still be your court jester."

"Good." she said. "Now, we can hash our personal stuff out when all this gets settled. But, until then, Rook, I need to know we can move forward without any more drama."

"Are you telling me to behave myself?"

She smiled. "See? We're back to normal already." Heat pulled the door open and went in. He shrugged then followed.

It sure didn't feel like a Saturday when they entered the Twentieth. Although Nikki and her homicide detectives worked plenty of weekends when the casework called for it, today the entire station house was in force, not just her section. In the Homicide Squad Room, the big TV on the wall was on, but muted. Raley, Ochoa, and Rhymer were on phones or working their computers. Occasionally one of them would glance up at the storm-track animations or to shake his head at the obligatory live shots of some poor correspondent getting pelted by sand and wind, or dodging palm fronds.

While Heat updated the Murder Board, Rook stared at the crawl on the bottom of the screen beneath the silent video of the Office of Emergency Management team answering press questions from its Brooklyn HQ. The ribbon of text said Connecticut's and New Jersey's governors had joined the rest of the region in declaring states of emergency. The Jersey governor had gone so far as to order evacuations of the barrier islands from Cape May up to Sandy Hook, and to tell Atlantic City casinos to close by four Sunday afternoon. Amtrak canceled service on many of its East Coast routes. It was too soon to tell where the hurricane would make landfall, but Delaware, Maryland, and New Jersey seemed likeliest targets. New York's mayor was holding off on evacuations pending more data, but expected Lower Manhattan to be most vulnerable to storm surge, especially Battery Park.

"Not going to stop for a formal meeting," said Heat to the group. "You guys are busy, and I don't want to slow you down. Just a few quickies." She summarized her meeting with Opal Onishi that morning. The feeling she left with was that she was hiding something and Nikki wanted to look deeper into her. When she told them about Rook and Detective Aguinaldo of Southampton Village PD recovering two slugs from a building at the Conscience Point Marina, Nikki got a big reaction, especially from Raley and Ochoa.

"Could make me think twice now about Earl Sliney as the Beauvais shooter," said Raley.

"Me, too," added his partner. "Not ready to give it up, but sounds like it could be righteous. Maybe."

Heat and Roach triangulated a moment of speechless reaffirmation, and all three appeared relieved to have tensions ease. Then she asked them to call the ballistics lab to set up a meeting for her later. "I want to be the squeaky wheel on the slug Inez Aguinaldo delivered there and to drop off the one recovered by Rook."

"Jameson Rook is . . ." boomed Ochoa in a hoarse TV promo voice, "The Bullet Whisperer."

Rook picked right up on it. "I see lead people. . . ."

Their hissing and belittling of Rook—and his enjoyment of the crap they were giving him—made Heat happy that he could live up to his pledge not to harbor resentment. She brought things back to business, asking Opie about his attempt to lure Alicia Delamater out of hiding. Rhymer said he'd left The Surf Lodge party message as bait the afternoon before. Still no Alicia callback.

Feller slid into the room. "Got something you might be interested in. Remember how Records came up with a prior on Fabian Beauvais?"

"Yes," said Heat. "It was from a while back. A misdemeanor trespassing bust for Dumpster diving. It's top of mind because I've been trying in vain to connect with Beauvais's so-called Gateway Lawyer, Reese Cristóbal, so he can put me in touch with the accomplices."

"Well, your favorite detective went all old school on ya. Real Time Crime Center came up with the last-known addresses you requested, so I went knocking on some pretty seedy doors." He referred to notes. "OK, one miscreant . . . moved back to Jamaica ten days ago."

"Oh, ouch," said Rook. "Just in time for the hurricane."

Feller tapped his notepad. "However, his other accomplice, Fidel "FiFi" Figueroa, is also going to get a taste of Sandy, because FiFi is here."

"Can we go see him?" asked Heat.

"Be stupid not to." Detective Feller gestured to the hall. "When I said here, I meant right here. He's in Interrogation-Two."

"I was told there would be a reward of a monetary nature" were the first words of Fidel Figueroa when Heat and Rook entered the interrogation room. Feller, who was already in there leaning one shoulder against the wall behind the wiry man, simply shook no to Nikki.

"Actually, although we value your cooperation, there is no reward, Mr. Figueroa."

"FiFi. Everybody calls me that." He hooked two thumbs to indicate himself. "Fidel Figueroa. FiFi."

Rook said, "Wouldn't that be *Fih Fih*?" The silent reproach of the entire room fell on him and he held up a surrendering palm. "But who am I to edit another man's gangsta handle?"

FiFi kept to his talking point. "So, no money?"

Back when she was a uniform, Heat had arrested scores of guys like Figueroa, usually working street corners on Eighth Avenue off Times Square. If it wasn't selling counterfeit sunglasses and handbags, it was running short cons like Find the Pea to fleece unwitting Nebraskans in a rigged game. They came in all sizes, shapes, ages, genders, and colors, but all shared the dodgy moves, quick eyes, and body ticks of the career hustler. And they were always seeking the elusive one-up. Even in a police department interrogation room. "Let's call it banking one for good citizenship," she said.

The guest brushed his knuckles across the graying line of his chin strap beard then said, "Hey, worth a shot, huh?"

"Why don't you just tell her what you know about Fabian Beauvais?" said Feller, pushing himself off the wall and looming over the grifter. Heat got a strong manifestation of Randall's history as a street detective, knowing how to take physical intimidation right up to the line—and effectively.

Fidel scooted his chair an inch away and cowered. "Sure thing, the Haitian. Smart dude, that guy. Rough life, but had the touch, you know?"

"I don't know," came back Feller. "Why don't you tell me?"

Nikki hoped the hustler wasn't playing them because this was her first real opportunity to get a sense of her victim's activities. Maybe FiFi would also give her some red meat, too. What that constituted, she would only know through careful listening. This bullshit artist gave her a lot to wade through.

"He had *astucia*. Cleverness. Some guys grow up getting shit on, and all they get is mean." He brought his forefinger just close enough to his thumb to make a crack to peek through. "These many, just this much, get clever instead. Fabby was new—maybe off the boat just a coupla months after the big quake. That's when he joined our, um, enterprise."

"Picking through trash?" said Feller with a sniff. He took a seat on Figueroa's side of the table and rested a boot on the man's chair. This time FiFi didn't shrink. On the contrary, he gave him a derisive side-glance.

"You don't know, man, you have no clue. You think we were like these hoboes or some shit? Fuck that, man. We were pickers. But not for cans and bottles."

This felt like it was heading somewhere. Nikki took the contradictory route, seeing now how conflict opened him up. "Well, what else do you call it, climbing into trash bins? I sure as hell wouldn't call it an enterprise."

Rook fell in step. "No shit. An enterprise? That's usually a business undertaking that calls for slightly more resourcefulness than fishing for empties to recycle."

"What about scoring hundreds of thousands? Millions. Would you call that an enterprise?"

"I would," said Heat. There were numerous ways to get a witness to talk. Intimidating, cajoling, inducing, begging. She read FiFi as a man who needed to boast. So she fed the hungry egotist. "And you personally know of such a thing?"

"Know it? Hell, I worked it." He checked himself in the observation mirror and said, "This may get me busted, but what I've seen? Whoo. Mind-boggling."

"I can be boggled," said Rook. He asked the others, "Anybody else?"

"I worked on a team for an organization that sent hundreds of us out in the field, day and night, to harvest the good stuff out of the trash."

Nikki shrugged. "Help me here. The good stuff?"

"ID stuff. Bank stuff. Credit card stuff. God, are you people dense?" Of course not, but playing it sure kept him rolling. "Any piece of paper that goes out in the trash with a name, an address, a birth date, a social, a club or union membership, Christmas card with momma's maiden on it, preapproved credit lines, computer passwords—I shit you not, people throw away papers with their fucking passwords on it." He laughed to himself. "We'd go out in the city like a little army every night and find all kinds of stuff."

Feller asked, "And do what with it?"

"Turn it in, of course. For money."

"Where?" Heat hoped for an address.

"Different places every time. A box truck would come. We'd trade, they paid." He laughed again, so smart about life, this one. "They hauled it off to some place to process it, don't know where." He read her skepticism. "Honest, I don't. All I know is it got sorted and used for, you know, fake IDs, credit card fraud, the whole buffet. They bought everything off us. Even shreds."

Rook asked, "What good are shredded documents?"

"You're kidding, right? Idiots think they're safe just 'cause they shred. Guess what? Most machines people use are strip cutters. And then what do they do? Put the neatly cut strips in a handy plastic bag for us to pick up and deliver."

"But they're shredded," he persisted.

"In strips. Clean slices—no security. They've got tons of people, you know, illegals and such? Sit in a big room and put that stuff together like jigsaw puzzles for pennies an hour. Worth it, too, because why shred it in the first place if it's not valuable?" He gave a knowing nod and rocked back in his chair with his arms folded.

Nikki now had a direction forming and followed the path to it.

"And that's where you met Fabian Beauvais?" FiFi gave her a you-bet grin. "And what about him was special, this, this . . . ?"

". . . *Astucia*? The man was a genius. Example. One day he shows up with a cooler on wheels. I say what are you doing, you bring some Bud Lights for the crew? No. It's empty. He goes into an office building pretending he's doing sandwich delivery. Every fucking office building in Manhattan has these guys walking the halls, so who notices another immigrant hawking turkey wraps? Nobody. He'd go in with the empty cooler in broad daylight, bust the padlock on the blue recycling bins in the copy room, or wherever, put the papers into his cooler, roll it out the front door, thank you very much, and sort it all out later."

"That's bold," said Feller.

"Worked great, too. Until the bulls caught him boosting some of the docs, you know, keeping a stash for himself. They were ripshit, man. After they moved him up the chain, let him work ATM skims with them, and all."

After she and Rook and Feller mind-melded over this bit of news, Heat said. "What do you mean, bulls?"

"You know, the ballbusters. The enforcers for the enterprise that kept us pissing our pants if we got greedy. Or talky."

The door from the observation room opened quietly over Heat's shoulder and Raley stepped in, handed her some head shots, and left. "FiFi, I am very impressed with how much you know. Really blown away." She slid the two pictures of Beauvais's ATM street *playahs* across the table toward him. He started working his head up and down before they reached him.

"That's them."

"The bulls?"

"Yeah. This one's Mayshon something. And that bad boy's Earl. Earl Sliney. That dude's a freak. Laughing one second, and bam, turns on a dime . . . Scary shit." He pushed Sliney's picture away like it carried a curse. "When it went bad with him and Fabby, it got ugly. Said he was going to kill him. Meant it, too."

"Do you know what documents Fabby—Fabian Beauvais stole?" Nikki held her breath after she asked. So much rode on this.

"No idea." She tried again, had to. But he still said no.

One more thing and we're done. "Do you know if Earl Sliney killed Beauvais?"

"Don't know who killed him. Only what." He arched a brow. "*Astucia.*"

Something about Keith Gilbert loved a front page. Heat found his smiling picture filling the bulldog edition of the *Ledger* on the rack at Andy's when she waited for her turkey sandwich and bought a copy of the rag to read on her walk back to the precinct. The headline read: KING ME, and the *Ledger* exclusive announced that the powerful New York ex-governor and former UN ambassador known as "The Kingmaker" was giving his endorsement to Gilbert's senatorial bid.

Even though the nod virtually ensured him a party nomination and a fat war chest of election funds, the candidate-to-be took the PR high road. "*'This approval means more than anyone can know' commented Commissioner Gilbert in a written statement. 'But the time for politics will have to come some other time. Right now I have a job to do keeping the citizens of this region safe from a storm of historic proportions, and that shall be my sole focus.'*"

Passing through the precinct lobby Heat tossed the tabloid on the visitor chair beside the hooker waiting for her pimp to be released. Maybe *she'd* swallow that.

Lunch talk in the bull pen centered on guessing what documents Beauvais took that cost him his life. "Maybe it doesn't matter," said Rhymer. "Maybe just the fact that he ripped off the ID theft network was enough. I mean, come on, we've all seen how heads of crime families mete out punishment to keep the soldiers in line."

"Did you just say 'mete'?" asked Ochoa.

"It's a legitimate word. Ask our writer."

Rook hung up the phone at his desk and kick-rolled his chair over to the group, spinning a circle on his trip. "Mete, as taken from the Latin *meta*, meaning boundary or goal. Plus-ten for Opie." He scooted over beside Heat. "This just in. Remember Hattie? My new bestest friend from the poultry slaughterhouse?"

"So much for my turkey sandwich." Nikki wrapped the remainder and set it on her desk.

"I just talked to her."

"How'd you manage that?" asked Raley. "We've been calling and calling, and dropping by her apartment and work, and she's been MIA."

"Count the Pulitzers. I'm just sayin'." Raley gave him two middle fingers to count. Rook continued. "Since they were friends, I wanted to find out from Hattie if Fabian Beauvais ever mentioned any documents. Guess what? He did ask if she could hide something for him. Hattie said yes, but Beauvais never said what it was or gave anything to her. And right after that, he got shot at in Queensboro Plaza. End of conversation."

"Hang on, though," said Nikki. "The slaughterhouse manager told us Beauvais showed up at work, injured. Meaning after he'd been shot. Where was Hattie?"

"Away helping her niece through a home detox. She never saw him."

"So we still don't know what he was holding, or where it is now," said Ochoa.

"Without rekindling a squad conflict here," said Heat, "can I at least throw out the most no-brainer of possibilities? That Beauvais got some goods on Keith Gilbert?"

To her surprise, it was Rook who first jumped in. "Just to keep that ball in the air, it sure gives a reason for some sort of payoff scenario at Conscience Point."

"But what about Sliney then?" Ochoa's question had an air of protest.

His partner said, "Could be parallel tracks, Miguel." Raley held his arms out like train rails. "Beauvais rips off Sliney's people, Sliney goes after him, track one. Beauvais shakes down Gilbert, Gilbert goes after him, track two."

"If that's true," said Detective Feller, what do you suppose the Haitian had on him? A love letter from a mistress? Evidence of a love child? Some medical secret that would harm his candidacy?"

"Kenyan birth certificate." said Rook. "Aw, come on, don't say you weren't thinking it, too."

On the walk to her car to drive to the ballistics lab, Heat did what most New Yorkers were doing that day. She made a sky check and found it difficult to believe that in twenty-four hours those hazy, mundane skies would darken with the leading edge of a hurricane. Even with her attention drawn upward, she heard the crunch of sidewalk grit under a shoe, a little too close. She palmed the butt of her weapon and spun.

Heat found her own image reflecting back in Lawrence Hays's aviators as he stood before her, grinning. "You know, even with your hand on that Sig I could still draw and shoot you before you cleared leather. If I wanted to."

"I might surprise you."

"You'd have to."

She assessed him and felt no threat. He even took a step back and kept his hands visible. "To what do I owe the pleasure?"

The CEO of Lancer Standard seemed to be enjoying himself. He held up the first two fingers of his right hand, a plain-view sign of non-lethal intent, and dipped them into his front-jacket pocket. He came out with a slip of paper and offered it. When she opened it, she saw a Bronx address written there. "How recent?" Nikki asked.

"You're welcome" was all he said. Then Hays strode off toward Amsterdam Avenue. She noticed the slight limp, verification that this was personal.

Heat put the assault plan together quickly, first dispatching Roach, Feller, and Rhymer up to the Bronx neighborhood to stake out the address in case Zarek Braun left. While they positioned themselves to observe, Nikki coordinated with the Emergency Services Unit to rustle up a SWAT team, then contacted the Forty-eighth Precinct about setting up traffic control. The idea was to keep people out and create choke points to keep her suspect in. None of this was new; Nikki had organized these raids more times than she could count.

But this one carried an extra crackle. "No room for mistakes," she told the incursion team—and herself—as they armored-up in the staging area around the corner from the house. She envisioned Braun's calm expression emptying the HK at her. Played back the mental picture of the scars and burns on the torso of Lawrence Hays. "Always think cover. Always just think."

ESU had already taken survey photos of the building before she got up there, and she spread them on the hood of her Interceptor to familiarize herself with the ways in and of the exposure hazards. Next Heat knelt behind a junker refrigerator on a corner patch of lawn to scan the block with binoculars. This was an economically depressed area with a mix of abandoned duplexes and run-down saltbox cottages. In the growing dark she could make out Halloween decorations on some of the graffiti-tagged neighborhood doors. "You've cleared the surrounding houses?" she confirmed with the ESU commander.

"Affirm."

"Don't want any kids walking into this." Satisfied all was ready, she said, "We'll go in five." Heat rose up from her hide and saw the worst possible thing she could see at that moment. Captain Wallace Irons, who must have bought his body armor at a big and tall came waddling up the street tugging Velcro and checking his sidearm.

When he reached her, Wally said, "What the hell is he doing here?" Rook finger waved from where he was standing off to the side in his personal bulletproof vest that read JOURNALIST instead of NYPD.

"Observing."

"This is a police-only, restricted area."

"Yes, sir, I know, but I have everything in hand. Rook is going to lag back with you while I go in."

"Change of plan," said Wally. "I am leading this incursion."

"Sir, with all due respect—"

"Then you will respect a direct order from your commander, Detective." He took in the staging area looking to Heat more like a cloddy equipment manager hanging with the jocks. "Don't you think I hear all the talk? How I'm an armchair cop? Well, that gets put to rest here and now." He swiveled his head. Protruding from his flak vest he could have been a turtle poking out of his shell. "Where's my ESU CO?"

"Here, sir." The commander of ESS-3 stepped forward.

"You boys in position?"

"Yes, sir."

"That the house?"

"It is."

"Show me your position map." Wally bodychecked Heat aside and the ESU leader performed his show-and-tell using the chart Heat had marked up. Irons asked no questions. After the briefing he turned to Heat. "You're backup."

"Sir, may I ask you to reconsider?"

The captain persisted, talking right over her. "Stay here. Make your move when I go in." He turned back to the ESU commander. "Follow me." And just that rapidly, just that recklessly, just that narcissistically, the Iron Man hustled across the street where he crouched behind a parked car, paused, and led the Go Team to the front door of the cottage.

"What the hell is he doing?" asked Feller.

"Wally being Wally," said Rook. "I wonder if he'll wear the body armor to his press conference."

"Get ready to move," said Heat into her walkie. "He's at the door."

Captain Irons's voice echoed across the empty street. "NYPD, open up!" An instant later, the ESU battering ram popped the door and Wally led the charge inside. Heat and her detectives trotted to cover and made the parked car. That's as far as they got.

A bright flash filled all the windows of the house and was instantly followed by a deafening boom.

FOURTEEN

While Nikki Heat sat on the curb the next morning waiting for the bomb squad to give the all-clear to go inside the house, she watched the sun rise grimly through wood smolder and thickening clouds. Rook found a spot beside her and handed over a coffee from the bodega that had just opened outside the restricted zone. Although he had remained on scene all night, they had not spoken since the blast. She had immediately kicked into emergency leadership mode—fire-walling her personal feelings about the close call so she could manage the crisis and its aftermath. In this interval before the next phase, they sat in silence, sipping their drinks, awaiting the magic of caffeine.

At last, Rook said, "So I can assume when you said you'd handle Wally Irons for me, this isn't what you meant."

She paused. "Dark." Then, turning to him, said, "You may be more cop than I knew."

"Hey, you said I could only ride along again if I could be me. Here I am."

Captain Irons had been the only fatality. The ESU team that entered with him heard the telltale metallic click when he rushed over to read the message written on the strip of duct tape on the wall, and took cover. Two made it out the door, the other dove into the empty fireplace. The SWAT officer said he yelled to the captain to stay put, not to move, but in his inexperience and panic, Irons tried to get out, too. Human-flight instinct sealed his fate. The instant he took his foot off the pressure plate that was rigged to an explosive device under the floor, he was cooked.

Heedless of their own safety, the pair of officers who'd bailed out the front door heroically reentered through the flames and hauled their wounded comrade out. Kevlar and his leap into the hearth saved his life. Surgeons spent an hour extracting nasty shards of glass and pieces of wood from his calves, but he'd probably be released from Bronx-Lebanon by lunchtime.

NYPD Counterterror had joined in the sweep of the small box of a house. Commander McMains made the trip there from the OEM hurricane HQ in Brooklyn along with the mayor and the chief. A bomb and a dead precinct captain became top priority, and the Counterterrorism boss needed to assess the degree and scope of the threat. There would be no conversation about the task force that morning. When the site had been declared safe, Cooper McMains came out of it and rested a hand on Heat's shoulder. "You sure you want to go in there?"

When Nikki got inside, stepping on glass and plaster and nails, holding a handkerchief over her face in a useless attempt to filter the fumes, she understood what he meant. The duct tape that had been on the wall above the gaping hole in the floor had been recovered way across the room. A CSU tech had sealed the charred and disfigured specimen in a plastic evidence bag. She held it in her hands and concentrated on not letting them tremble as the other detectives and Rook watched. There were two words written in black Sharpie on the tape: BYE HEAT.

For Nikki, this was just chilling confirmation of what she already knew and had tried to avoid thinking about until later. But for the hubris of Wallace Irons, that could have been the last thing she saw before she died. Heat passed the specimen around, and nobody said a word. Until Rook broke the charged silence. "He left out the comma."

The duct tape went off to Forensics for prints. Nobody disputed whose they would find. "Thing I want to know," said Ochoa, "is if this Zarek Braun knew you were coming, or if he just thought maybe you might come."

"A lot of bang for a maybe," said Detective Feller. "I'm thinking setup."

Of course Heat had already made the triangulation between getting the address and the detonation. When Hays gave her that paper, was he priming the fuse? Or did Zarek Braun know it was only a matter of time before she tracked him and set the booby trap for that inevitability?

Commander McMains came to her when she stepped outside.

"Nobody will think less if you decide to stand down. It's been a hell of a night for you, Heat." She didn't answer, just squared her gaze to his. "I didn't think so," he said. "Obviously, this is still your case, but let me assure you that we're heightening the APB for this Zarek Braun and all available resources will be on this."

"Thank you, Commander." But she knew by how quickly he got called by the chief back to the motorcade headed for the OEM Situation Room that Braun would be looked for with half an eye. His key word was "available" resources. With a Category One hurricane bearing down on the city in less than twenty-four hours, Heat knew this would be her battle to wage.

That didn't mean she would be alone. With all recent differences forgotten, Raley and Ochoa came to her first, offering split shift, 'round-the-clock Roach protection. Soon after, Rhymer and Feller did the same. The solidarity meant everything to her, she told them. "But I want us to focus on taking this to him, not hunkering down for protection."

Heat tasked Roach and Rhymer to canvass the neighborhood with pictures of Zarek Braun, Fabian Beauvais, and just to be thorough, Lawrence Hays, which she had downloaded from an antiwar Web site and texted to them. "Talk to residents, talk to shop owners. Get a sense of when Zarek Braun was last here, if anybody was with him, did he have girlfriends or boyfriends, what he was driving, the works."

She put Detective Feller on checking him through the RTCC. "See if there are any hits on disturbance calls or neighbor complaints on this street. A guy like Braun might be the type to get in a beef with someone over nothing, or just creep somebody out. Don't overlook the smallest thing, even a hassle with a meter maid over an opposite-side parking ticket." Eager to be useful, Rook went off with them, barnacling onto Raley and Ochoa.

Lauren Parry stepped out of the house and told her friend she should go home and take a nap because her enhanced team of MEs would be a long time painstakingly collecting the remains of Captain Irons.

Heat said, "Thanks, Mother," and said she'd hang there nonetheless. Nikki felt a quarter-inch from meltdown and worried what would happen if she stopped working.

The bomb squad sergeant gave her the prelim on the device. As expected, a pressure-sensitive plate had been cut into the floor with a bath rug placed over it as camouflage. The explosive material was C-4, military grade, with the primer set to trigger when the pressure came off the plate. She tried not to imagine herself on that rug, reading that message, but it was hard. Would she have run for cover like the captain, or would she have held it together? Thankfully, she didn't need to know.

Zach Hamner phoned and Heat was surprised that the caller ID was his office at One PP, not his cell. "You working on a Sunday?" she asked.

"It's storm watch, Heat, there is no weekend here." As if he took a day off, anyway. Heat imagined that Zach Hamner probably went to the beach in his suit and tie. He nearly—but not quite—sounded compassionate as he checked on her after the ordeal.

"I'm fine. But I'm not the one OCME is working on in there."

He asked her how Irons managed to get in that position, and when she told him, he muttered, "Fuck. . . ." And then he sniffed and added, "A boob to the end."

"Excuse me, you asshole." The trauma of the ordeal started to boil over, and The Hammer was the lucky caller. "Wally Irons was a lot of things, but you know what he is now? A cop who died in the line of duty."

Zach started to retract, but she plowed him down. "So listen to me, you fucking little fuck. If you say anything to malign a brother cop who gave up the ultimate sacrifice, I will come down there personally and feed you your goddamned BlackBerry. Right after I stuff your balls down your throat." Then she saw Lawrence Hays hanging around her car and hung up.

"I'm saving you some trouble, Detective."

"How did you get into my crime scene?"

Hays ignored that, like accessing a restricted area was nothing to a man like him. He just stood there with his arms folded, his butt resting on the trunk of the Taurus, waiting for her. "When I heard the news, I figured, if I were Nikki Heat, I'd come looking for the guy who gave me this address. Here I am." He took off his aviators so she could see his eyes.

What assuaged her wasn't what she saw there. This guy was so schooled in psyops, he could adopt any attitude and appear credible. The fact was, though, it made no sense for him to set her up. Unless Hays was working with Zarek Braun. Her gaze drifted down to the scar tissue peeking through the V in the neck of his polo shirt. "I think we're good," she said. "For now."

"Smart." He slipped the sunglasses back on and said, "Now. You want an assist?"

"As in?"

"Come on, you know what I do."

"Mr. Hays, if you're offering your professional services, I decline. This is a police matter, and NYPD is capable of handling it. Besides, I think one mercenary operating in this city is enough."

He took a moment to survey the thin scrim of smoke still curling off the house and said, "You'd better hope so."

Her squad reassembled two hours later following the neighborhood canvass. "You called it," said Feller. "Real Time Crime DB had a ping. Two weeks ago, a guy living in one of the row houses up the block called in a beef about a foreigner making lewd sounds and gestures to his teenage daughter. The Four-eight sent a uni, but the citizen said there must have been some mistake."

Ochoa said, "We did a door knock at the home of the complainant. The family was jumpy, seeing how they just got let back in after the all clear. But they ID'd Braun from the photo."

"Even better," continued Raley in full-Roach overlap, "the foreign dude freaked them out so much—which is why they lied to the uniform—that they kept tabs on him."

"May I?" asked Rook. "I so seldom get mistaken for a detective." He opened a page of his notes. "Last time they saw your Cool Customer was Thursday. He came by with a big duffel bag and some power tools. Ran a circular saw for about an hour, did some hammering, and left with the tools but not the duffel." He closed his notebook. "Sounds to me like a booby trap installation."

"Thursday. You do know that's before we saw Hays," observed Feller. Heat told them about the CIA contractor's visit and her feeling Lawrence Hays was an unlikely, and to move on. Nobody disagreed.

Detective Rhymer's cell rang, and while he stepped away to take the call, Raley asked if Heat knew what would be happening next at the precinct. "I hate to get practical, but has anybody told you who's coming in to replace . . . you know?"

"I don't think anyone's thinking that far ahead, Sean. My best guess is One PP's focused on storm watch and little else. I'd be surprised to hear anything before Sandy's done."

"Hey?" said Opie, sounding a lot like the TV Opie. "Guess who that was."

"No," said Heat, reading the triumph on his face. "Really?"

Rhymer slipped his cell phone back in his pocket. "Alicia Delamater will be happy to meet me to pitch concepts for the secret Sean Combs reboot party."

At two that afternoon not a single drop of rain was falling on Manhattan's Upper West Side. Sandy still churned off the Georgia and Carolina coasts, tracking northeast with enough menace to cause the mayor to order evacuations of the most flood-prone zones in the city. A mix of urgency and fatalism filled the streets with some New Yorkers hurrying to stock up, get sheltered, or leave before the subways and trains shut down at seven; the rest took it in stride and carried on as normal, either ignoring reality or just content to ride out nature's spectacle when it arrived the next day.

The latter group was not about to let an annoying tropical cyclone keep them from Sunday brunch at Daughters of Beulah. Sidewalk service at the trendy Columbus Avenue bistro had been closed due to the arrival of forty-mile-per-hour winds, but every inside table was filled, and the mimosas and Bloody Marys flowed in denial-reinforcing volume.

While he stood near the curb outside, a strong gust parted Detective Rhymer's sport coat and he scrambled to yank his badge off his belt, since few marketing directors carried a police shield. He had just pocketed it when a cab pulled up and a woman, dressed to impress, got out.

After handshakes and introductions, he pulled one of the ornately scrolled brass handles to open the door for her and they entered in a swirl of air that shook the potted palms in the reception area. "Our party is complete now," he said to the hostess. When Nikki turned to face them from behind the podium Alicia Delamater's eyes actually double blinked like a vaudeville comedienne's.

"I've got the perfect table for you," said Heat. "At the police station. It's much quieter. We'll actually be able to talk."

Alicia Delamater didn't share Detective Heat's desire for a nice chat. She sat with her hands folded on the interrogation table doing what most people did in that room—trying at first not to look in the mirror, but then surrendering to glimpses, which became glances, which became lingering self-appraisals. To Nikki, that was the magic of the magic mirror: the spirit-crushing view of the guest reflected back in one of life's low moments.

But it still didn't open her up. This woman's relationship with Keith Gilbert was Heat's best chance yet to get inside to find out what was going on with him, with Fabian Beauvais, with Conscience Point, and more. It presented a tricky dynamic. Alicia was not a suspect or even charged with a crime. But she was involved somehow, or she wouldn't have gone underground. For now, Nikki just wanted knowledge. Any scrap to run with and gain some new traction. She had invited Rook into the interview because that day in her house at Beckett's Neck, Delamater seemed attracted to him. That allure had, unfortunately, not translated into any advantage. And so the three of them sat. One of them making mirror checks but not speaking.

And then Rook spoke—going back to one of the first interrogations he and Nikki had ever done together—to play the perfect card. "So what now, Detective? Time for the Zoo Lockup?"

Both women's heads whipped to him: Alicia's in nervous disquiet; Nikki's in stunned admiration. He didn't wink, didn't have to. Nikki took the baton handoff without missing a step. "Well, I didn't want to resort to that, but maybe it's been long enough."

"What's the Zoo Lockup?" If she saw her reflection now, Nikki thought, she'd melt.

Rook started to rise from his chair. "Want me to call down and tell the sarge we've got another live one for the cage?"

"What are you talking about?" Alicia's mouth had gone dry. "What about cages?"

"Actually, it's one cage," said Rook. "With an assortment of colorful types waiting for processing."

"Colorful . . . ?"

"They don't call it the Zoo for nothing," said Rook ominously.

The picture that painted freaked the woman out. Of course she had no way of knowing there was no such thing as a Zoo Lockup, and that it was a total bluff created years ago by Heat, fabricated to loosen the tongues of novices to the criminal system. "You can't do that. Can you do that? What if I want my lawyer?"

Nikki said, "Sure. You can wait for him there."

"In the Zoo Lockup," said Rook.

"But it's Sunday. It could take him hours. . . . Maybe he evacuated."

"Alternatively, we could just talk," said Heat.

Alicia didn't need to think too long. "Fine."

Rook sat. Heat picked up her pen.

"Let's start with why you lied to me."

"I didn't lie to you. About what?"

"You said Fabian Beauvais hurt himself with the hedge clippers."

"That's what he told me."

"He'd been shot."

"Then he's the one who lied." Delamater's answers came a little to defensively for Nikki's taste. Was she lying again, or was she just scared of the Zoo? She came at her from another angle.

"Have you ever seen Keith Gilbert with a gun?"

"No."

"What about the night of the intruder? The Southampton police said you were there when they arrived and that Gilbert had a handgun."

"Oh, wait, yeah. That. But Keith isn't a gun guy. I thought that's what you meant. He was just trying to protect me."

Rook said more than asked, "From a drunken crime novelist?"

"We didn't know it was him."

"What's a mystery writer gonna do?" said Rook. "Tease you with a scary cliff-hanger?"

Heat put a hand on the table between them. "Rook, I've got this." Actually, she was glad for the sidetrack. It gave her what she wanted, which was a chance to hairpin turn back to the Haitian in hopes of shifting her off-balance. "During his time working on your property, did you and Fabian Beauvais have a good relationship?"

"Sure. We got along fine." Then she reconsidered. "'. . . Relationship?' You mean like sleeping together?" Heat's turn not to reply. The woman kept going. "No, never. Not like that. But we were friendly. Ish."

"Did he ever open up to you about having any papers?"

"You mean, like, immigration papers?"

"Alicia, I'm not here to bust you for sleeping with the help or hiring an illegal. I want to know if Mr. Beauvais talked about possessing any documents."

"No, why would he tell me that?" Again, that defensive oversell.

"So he never talked about documents he had or gave you a package or file to keep?" Delamater shook no. "I can't hear that."

"No."

"Did you ever see him with one? Maybe a file, a small bag, or a thick manila envelope?"

"Again, sorry." But then the eyes trailed off. Not to the mirror but to the ceiling. Heat smelled something and persisted.

"Maybe it slipped your mind. That happens. Think about it."

"I don't need to. No."

Nikki smiled and said, "OK, good, good." Which made Alicia relax. Which was just what Heat wanted before she jerked her chain.

"What blew up your romance with Keith Gilbert?" The woman's features widened and blotches surfaced on her neck. "Come on, Alicia, I know about the restraining order. What happened?"

"That is . . . that is very personal."

"And it's why I am asking you. He wanted you out of his life for some reason. Did he catch you in bed with Fabian?"

"He did not!"

"Then what turned?"

"Do you have to ask this?"

"Did his wife find out you were crossing Beckett's Neck for more than a cup of sugar?"

"No. I mean, she never knew."

"Did you push him? Play me, or trade me?"

"I didn't push anything. It was him. He just fucked me over." Heat's pressure had touched a nerve. "It was so exciting, having our little affair when I worked with him. Dangerous and new. . . . Hot. But it got too tough to manage a relationship in the workplace, you know? It got to be a distraction. Too large to handle." Nikki didn't turn but sensed Rook's slow swivel to her.

"Go on," said Heat.

"So then he gets the idea I could quit Gilbert Maritime and have a place in the Hamptons near him. Close, but under the radar, if the wife should ever decide to show up. So he bought my house, helped me get my business going, and it was all fun and games—until that bastard cut me off. Asshole scumbag." Alicia Delamater had started slowly but became hostage to a juggernaut of growing rage. "Know what he called me? A political liability. See? It wasn't his wife. His goddamned career was his wife. And I couldn't compete. How do you fucking compete with that? Tell me. Huh?"

The outburst ended in tears, racking sobs with Alicia cupping her face in both hands. Maybe it was the all-nighter in the Bronx that lowered her own guard, but the testimony hit close to home for Nikki, too, who still felt Rook's unspoken scrutiny. She hoped to hell he would have the grace to keep it unsaid.

They could have held Alicia Delamater on a ticky-tacky charge, something like lying to a police officer. But her attorney would have had her sprung, and what was the point? Heat did the next best thing, which was to tell her she was still considering whether to charge her with hindering an investigation and to remain at the Midtown extended-stay hotel where she had been hiding all this time.

"What's your take?" asked Rook when she'd left.

"Smoke screens and dodges, that's my gut. The fact that she's no longer in bed with Gilbert doesn't mean she's not part of this somehow. I want to find out more."

"Do you really think she'll open up later?"

Nikki wagged no. "She'll only have time to come up with better lies. And show up with her attorney. No, I want to find out without relying on Alicia Delamater's help. I want some search warrants."

"On what grounds?" Rook's undercurrent of skepticism annoyed her. But she checked herself. With fatigue and emotions swirling, this was not the time to pick a fight or get offended. So she answered plainly.

"Access to material evidence, lying, her admission that she hid from us."

He sucked his teeth. "After the DA pulled your arrest, they're not going to go for search warrants on that foundation."

"No, but I think I know who will. Your old poker buddy."

"Judge Simpson? Don't you owe him money from the last game?"

"Perfect. Then he'll take my call."

After Heat completed her conversation with Horace Simpson, who agreed to her request for a search warrant of Alicia Delamater's Manhattan rental, she made one more call. This one went to Detective Sergeant Inez Aguinaldo in Southampton, who began by offering her condolences to Nikki and the precinct after the death of the captain.

Nikki thanked her and said, "I know I've been leaning on you a lot, but I'd like to press my luck."

"Name it."

"And I'm sure you're busy with your own ramp-up to Sandy."

"Tell me what you need, Detective Heat. I'll make the storm wait."

So Nikki voiced her request for Aguinaldo to search Delamater's house at Beckett's Neck.

When she told the Southampton investigator what to look for, she asked, "Won't I need a warrant?"

"Oh, right," said Heat. "That's my second favor."

The other detective laughed and told her she knew just who to call. "That's the virtue of a tight community."

Nikki finished the conversation feeling fortunate to have crossed paths with Inez Aguinaldo, who, at each step, obliterated the cliché of the small-town cop. She placed the phone back in its cradle and rotated her chair so she could reassess the Murder Board on the other side of the squad room. The latest addition was a purple line drawn with an arrow from Zarek Braun to a new name in handwriting she could hardly recognize as her own: CAPT. WALLY IRONS.

Tilting her head, she peered into the darkness of his office. In the coppery glow of the sodium streetlamps spilling in the window, Nikki made out a familiar shape: the reflection, in dry cleaner plastic, of his media-ready, dress uniform shirt. The light began to slowly diffuse as in the form of a headless ghost-man; however, it was no apparition. Just a blur from bone-deep fatigue. The aura faded away and, the next thing Heat knew, a hand was gently rocking her shoulder while a voice from a distant tunnel asked her to wake up.

Her eyes popped open and she arched up in her task chair. Roach stood over her. "Sorry to startle you," said Ochoa. "My BCI man just called. They've cornered Earl Sliney and Mayshon Franklin."

The cobwebs dissolved and she got to her feet. As she grabbed her coat, Raley asked, "What about him?" Across the bull pen, Rook had his head down on a desk.

She called out, "Rook," and his head gophered up. "We're rolling." Through his walrus yawn he called shotgun.

FIFTEEN

They convoyed with gum balls lit but no sirens across the Williamsburg Bridge to Brooklyn; Heat, Rook, and Feller leading Raley, Ochoa, and Rhymer in the Roach Coach. Behind them the Manhattan skyline set the low ceiling ablaze like a CGI special effect and the car got buffeted by forceful gusts advertising the imminent arrival of a hurricane.

Rook scrolled his iPad and called out occasional tidbits about the storm. "Whoa, with the freak convergence of meteorological factors and the full moon tomorrow night, they say there could be storm surges of eleven to twelve feet. Know what that means, don't you? Ocean-view dining in Times Square."

"If I have to sit back here," said Detective Feller, "can I at least have some quiet?"

The silence that followed lasted a full ten seconds before Rook finger-swiped another Web page and horse chuckled. "Are there any fans of irony here? The Metropolitan Opera announced it's canceling performances of *The Tempest*, due to—wait for it—the hurricane. Gotta love it." Another burst of wind pounded the Taurus and he hollered at the window, "'Blow, winds, and crack your cheeks! Rage! Blow!'"

"Uh, Rook?" said Heat.

"Yeah?"

"First of all, that's *King Lear*, not *The Tempest*. And second? Put a sock in it?"

"You didn't tell me to put a sock in it when I hit Alicia Delamater with the old Zoo Lockup."

"No, that was . . . That was timely," Heat exited the bridge onto Broadway and looped back toward the East River passing Peter Luger's.

"I was thinking you'd say 'inspired.' See what history gives us?"

He twisted to Feller in the backseat and explained the bluff he had pulled out of the Nikki Heat playbook.

Detective Feller gave him a thumbs up. "I do the same thing to spook the amateurs, except I call it Cellmate Lice Buddy."

"Ew," blurted Rook. "I'll confess now to anything." Which made all three laugh, at least until they saw the roadblock of flashing lights up Kent Street.

At the staging area beside the defunct Domino Sugar plant on South Third, Detective Ochoa shook hands with Senior Investigator Dellroy Arthur. "Pleasure to meet you in person," said the BCI lead. Heat immediately noticed the plainclothes detective's badge, the state police's distinctive "golden stop sign," which had a mourning band across it just like hers. He told them all he was sorry for their loss, never mere words among the law enforcement brotherhood. Heat thanked him for the wishes and the solidarity, and then they did what cops do—got to work.

"Here's how it came down," began the SI. "NYPD got a call that someone had cut through the fence around the bicycle course they're creating over there." They all turned toward Havemeyer Park, a vacant lot that was in the process of being developed into a BMX pump track complete with moguls and dirt berms. "Patrol showed up and observed two men drinking beer and riding the course. The pair evaded the officers on their bikes, but the unis pursued and saw them enter that construction site." Heat and her group pivoted up Kent, where the concrete skeleton of a ten-story building jutted up into the blustery night.

Heat asked, "What put them on your radar?"

"Simply put, shots fired. That brought out the incident squad from the Ninetieth, which interviewed the responding officers, who ID'd Earl Sliney as one of the perps based on our APB. His companion fits the general description of his known associate, Mayshon Franklin." The state detective fired up his iPad and they gathered around while he stylus-walked them through the street map to indicate street closures and exit chokes. "We've got them boxed on the ground. Unfortunately in this wind we can't bring air support."

"How do you know they're still in there?"

"More shots fired. They're somewhere on an upper level from the round I heard." Arthur laid out his plan, which was to employ a dual SWAT team pincer incursion, starting at ground level and clearing each floor to the roof. The construction company had e-mailed him PDFs of the architectural plans and he indicated each phase, and the timing, of each team's movement so they didn't cross fire each other. When he'd finished, the BCI man asked, "Any questions?"

"Just one," asked Heat. "Can you take them alive?"

"Guess that's up to them."

If it hadn't been for his customized vest, which proclaimed JOURNALIST instead of NYPD, Rook might have made the cut. But the New York State Police senior investigator was "not playing games," as he put it, and the writer got ordered to wait at the staging area. "It's my own fault. The bling did me in," he said to Heat, indicating the two Pulitzer medals embroidered onto his body armor.

"Plus no badge, no gun, no training."

"That's right, rub my nose in your so-called superior qualifications."

Heat and Feller joined the first SWAT team; Raley and Ochoa fell in with Team-Two. Dellroy Arthur had done his homework, radio communication was ongoing, and the incursion teams were first order. None of that minimized the danger of entering a dark construction high-rise at night with a howling wind obscuring sound and blowing objects at you out of nowhere while armed suspects—one, a killer who shoots old ladies—waited God knows where.

Methodically, over the space of thirty minutes, stairwells, elevators, air shafts, and port-a-potties were cleared on ten of the ten floors. That left only the roof. Air support would have made the job so much easier. Or a taller building in the vicinity that could put observers on its top floor. The teams waited at their entrance points on opposite corner stairwells for the go, when they would storm the rooftop simultaneously. After confirming readiness, the green light came.

They burst onto the surface and quickly found cover behind the bulky AC units on one side of the roof, and stacked metal crossbeams on the other. What they hadn't planned was for Sliney and Franklin to be astride their bikes, pedaling like mad for the edge of the building instead of laying down fire. While Heat and each team ran at them shouting to freeze, she tried to picture the iPad map to recall how close the nearest building was. And how far down.

Whether they had some Thelma and Louise death pact, or had seen Matt Damon leap from too many heights into windows and make it, Sliney and Franklin sped forward without hesitation. The men made no sound. No whoop, no rebel yell, no scream. They simply pedaled their fiercest until they ran out of roof.

Neither one hit the ground.

Coming off the ledge, it was clear they would not make the other side. Sliney must have realized that quickly because he made an X Games midair dismount and desperately wrapped both hands around the cable of the construction crane next to the building. In a wild junction of flashlight beams, they saw him grip it, but he wore no gloves. His momentum, gravity, and friction combined to skin the meat off his palms as he cried out in his horrific slide down the braided steel. The giant lift hook at the bottom of the cable stopped him. The point snagged under his jaw and tore his neck open wide, leaving him to swing lifeless, head thrust back, in the fifty-plus gusts.

An interrupted scream and metal-on-metal impact brought all the lights to whip below to the seventh floor. Mayshon Franklin had stayed with his BMX, but a burst of wind had thrown him back into the side of the building where he crash-landed atop the construction-site elevator. From what Nikki could make out in that light, it appeared the bike had bent around the hoist and its gear works with the rider blanketing it, spiked there by the handlebar poking up out of his lower back.

When Mayshon Franklin moaned, Heat called out, "He's still alive," and bolted for the stairs.

With Franklin living, but destined for prolonged surgery and complete sedation, Heat left Williamsburg when the OCME van transported Earl Sliney's remains to the Brooklyn Borough morgue in East Flatbush at one-thirty in the morning. She insisted her squad get some sleep and to make sure their homes were buttoned up for the hurricane, a Category Two monster, just three hundred miles away at that hour.

With a third-floor apartment in a protected block, Nikki felt reasonably certain her place would survive.

Just for peace of mind, she had put in an earlier call to Jerzy, her building super, and he cheerfully agreed to keep tabs on it. So instead of going home, she set out for the Twentieth Precinct to crash for the night. Rook had made use of his long wait in the staging area to check on his loft as well. Then he called his mother to make sure she was OK. After receiving a blustery vow that no piffling storm would dare take on Margaret Rook, star of Broadway, summer stock, and Sardi's, he rode back to Manhattan with Heat.

He dozed against the passenger door. Heat craved sleep, too, but the task of holding her lane in the wind lash crossing the East River kept her plenty alert. It felt about the same as her trip over, but something new had been added to the swirl of skyscraper-devouring clouds and the buffeting of the car: a humid scent of the tropics. It made her reflect once more on inevitability. And how you can name a beast and even know it's coming, but little can be done to stop it.

Early the next morning, after four hours of openmouthed sleep on the break room couch and then raiding her file drawer for the emergency wardrobe she kept there, Nikki made a breakfast of peanut butter on an apple she had sectioned. Rook came in looking too rested for a man who'd slept in an empty jail cell. He held two Grandes of Starbucks heaven. "Is that home cookin' I smell?"

She slathered a slice of her apple and held it out. "Offer you a Pink Lady?" she asked, knowing full well she was setting him up.

"In a heartbeat, if we had more privacy. But hold the thought about the peanut butter." He took the apple and they sat there in the lounge watching Channel 7's coverage of Superstorm Sandy. "I liked it better when they were calling it the Frankenstorm," he said. "Monster hurricane, Halloween . . . So what if it sounds too flip? I say, if we're going to get pounded by a hurricane two years in a row, we're allowed to laugh it off."

He saw Keith Gilbert on-screen, live from the Port Authority Emergency Management Office. "Shutting up now," said Rook, using the remote to turn up the volume.

"Landfall," said the commissioner, "is predicted to come about twelve hours from now, give or take. Best guesstimate for location is still slightly south of New York metro, but that would still put the city and the harbor in the powerful upper-right quadrant of the cyclone. Port Authority is therefore closing LaGuardia Airport at seven-fifteen P.M. JFK, Newark Liberty, Teterboro, and Stewart International will remain open, but with all flights canceled. Maritime facilities are closed. . . ."

Nikki watched her prime murder suspect smoothly presenting his best face and virile composure in the looming crisis. As if reading her mind, Rook said, "You do know that all this macho chill only enhances his appeal as a candidate. Hell, watching this, it's a shame he can only run for senate in one state. I'll bet he could get elected from New Jersey, too. He's a slam dunk."

"Not everything is inevitable, Rook." With that, she picked up her Starbucks and strode to the bull pen to get to work.

Her squad had already assembled when she got there. She invited them to coffee-up fast and then gather at the Murder Board. While they hustled out to empty bladders and re-caffeinate, her desk phone rang. "Peace offering," were the first words she heard. It was Zach Hamner. "So, please don't hang up."

"Go ahead."

"I just processed an order to relieve you from duty."

Nikki sat on the edge of her desk. "Am I being dense here? In what world is that a peace offering?"

"Because I am turning this over to your precinct commander."

"I don't have one. He's dead."

"That's my point. But you will have one tomorrow. An interim white shirt they're plucking from cubicle land. This order to place you on administrative leave came through my office from the deputy commissioner of Personnel. But you know how it works here in the Puzzle Palace. Somebody else squeezed somebody else's balls up the food chain, and, suddenly, you're tapped for the sidelines."

"What sidelines?"

"Specifically, your orders are for desk duty on Staten Island, TFN.

So that is my peace offering to you. A gift of twenty-four-hours' notice." The implications took a lap in Nikki's head. Gilbert or his lawyers got to somebody at City Hall or One Police Plaza, and this is the monkey wrench that got thrown in to the gears of her case.

"Heat, you still there?"

"Uh, yeah, I'm just sorting out what to do." And how fast she needed to do it. She looked at the wall clock and became short of breath. "This is good info to have."

"I thought it would be." He paused, then continued, sounding small and contrite. "And sorry I said what I said. You know. About Irons being a boob. That was totally douchy. I apologize."

Funny thing, she thought. Boobs can become heroes and assholes can show some heart. "Thank you, Zachary."

"Gentlemen, we have not a minute to waste," Detective Heat began when everyone had formed a semicircle. She recapped the heads-up call from The Hammer, which elicited universally pissed-off faces and a smattering of curses. Nikki called a halt. "I'm with you—obviously more so—but getting mad isn't going to help."

"This won't shut the case down," said Feller.

"Really," said Ochoa. "Do they think we're just going to drop it because you go to Staten Island?"

Heat said, "Of course you are capable of keeping it going. Especially this group. But we need to see this for what it is."

"Round one," said Rook.

"Exactly. This is the opening salvo in an orchestrated legal and power offensive. The idea is to dismantle progress one piece at a time and, eventually, to 'make it go away.'"

She took a moment to register contact with each of them. "We can't let that happen. This case has been a difficult one from the start. A lot of contradictions. A lot of conflict—even in here. Which is fine. It's what you get with cops who have passion. I want that. But now we have entered a new phase." She walked to the board to point at Captain Irons's name up there as a murder victim.

"We need to drill down." Nikki turned to look at his name again and milked the silence. Then she selected a new red marker from the cardboard sleeve. "This squad has twenty-four hours to be brilliant. Twenty-four hours to live up to its reputation as the top-clearing homicide squad in the NYPD."

Heat opened the red marker and used it to draw a circle around her earlier translation of Fabian Beauvais's tattoo: "Unity Makes Strength." Then, in that same red ink, Nikki divided the board into four equal quadrants. She wrote a name in each, going clockwise: "Raley. Ochoa. Feller. Rhymer." Capping the marker, she squared herself to her detectives. "Your assignment today is to examine every case detail inside your square. If you aren't the detective who brought in the lead, become familiar and dig into it. If you did bring it in, go back over your own work and be critical. 'What did I overlook?' 'What didn't I ask?' 'Who didn't I talk to?' 'What do I know now that I didn't then that opens new lines?' Talk to each other. If you have an expertise or hunch, poach that item from your colleague and run with it."

Their attention was rapt and she took advantage of it. "Four victims: Fabian Beauvais, dropped from the sky; Jeanne Capois, tortured; Shelton David, home invasion victim; Captain Irons—line of duty. This is a bear of a case on the worst day to work it. But we all know that the solves don't get handed to us. They come by donkeywork." She tapped the whiteboard. "Something already up here could bring this home. Be diligent. Be thinking. Be cops."

The squad flew into its work without hesitation, all of them going to their desks, except Rhymer, who lagged behind to faithfully copy the items listed in his box into his notebook. Raley, the media king, brought his iPhone to the mix and made a photo capture of his section. In short order, the bull pen filled with the buzz of investigators working phones to call back eyewits, confer with other divisions and precincts, and to debrief each other about leads and clues. Heat worked as liaison and free-floater, connecting thoughts and waving off the obvious time wasters. Rook self-directed, cherry-picking from the board and free-associating on Internet searches.

Shortly before two, Heat came to Rook's desk. "Mayshon Franklin is out of surgery and in recovery. You mind getting a little wet?"

The first thing the prisoner saw when he opened his eyes was Heat's badge. He couldn't help but see it because Nikki held it so close that it was almost touching his nose. It had taken him longer to come out from under his anesthetic than she and Rook had expected, and they spent a quiet hour waiting in bedside chairs listening to the hiss of rain against the window. Far from lost time, it ensured she would be there on wake-up when the haze of pain meds might dull Mayshon Franklin's instinct to clam up, lie, or ask for an attorney.

With Earl Sliney, the state police's fugitive now off the board, BCI Senior Investigator Dellroy Arthur had broken camp, happy to leave his accomplice to NYPD. Heat obliged. "Mayshon Franklin, you are under arrest," she said, removing her shield once she knew it registered.

His eyes were glazed, searching but not making optical sense of his world yet. He tugged lightly at the manacles connecting him to his jail-ward bed. Then he licked his dry mouth and said, "Earl?"

"Earl Sliney is dead, Mayshon."

He closed his eyes, nodding an of course to himself, and then opened them again. "How?"

As Heat tried to decide how to put it, Rook stepped up behind her and said, "Human Pez dispenser." That only confused Franklin, and Heat didn't want him to lock up. Plus, she only had so much time before he would fatigue-out and go under again, so she got to it.

"Look up here, Mayshon." Nikki held up the ATM security cam freeze of him and his crew and tapped Beauvais. "You recognize him, right? Mayshon, eyes here. Good. You know him?"

Franklin nodded weakly. "We have video of your friend Earl shooting at him a few weeks ago. You were there." He nodded again, which was encouraging because she wanted him unguarded. "Did he hit him?"

"No, shot at him."

"Right. We know he shot at him. Did any of Earl's bullets hit him?" Mayshon shrugged and winced at the effort. "Can you answer yes or no?"

"I don't know. Mighta hit him, mighta not. I dunno." He took a breath that stuttered on the intake and his eyes drooped.

"Stay with me, Mayshon, you're doing great. Almost done." His lids fluttered to half-mast and Nikki pressed, aware of the short time she had before he zoned. "You and Earl were chasing him, and he had a package. What was it?"

"He stole."

"What did he steal?"

"From the boss." He smiled dreamily. "Y'all don't steal from the boss."

"What's the boss's name, can you tell me that?" He made a face, mimicking a child in trouble and wagged his head on the pillow. She'd come back to that. "What was in the package?"

"Bad stuff, I dunno. Stuff meant for the shred net."

Since he claimed he didn't know what was in it, she didn't want to waste time flogging that. "Tell me about the shred net." One eye closed. His other lifted like a stoner's in a music video. "Mayshon. Where's the shred net?"

"You don't know? You're the police."

"Tell me, help me understand you better, Mayshon."

"Flatbush. C'mahn, you know." His speech became increasingly slurry.

"Where in Flatbush?"

"Flatbush, there ya go." He closed his eyes and muttered in a singsong, "Mar-co." And then he chuckled, answering in the same cadence, "Po-lo. . . ."

"Mayshon, don't play games with me, just tell me where."

Again he sang, "Po-lo," then didn't say anything, and she thought she'd lost him. Then he chuckled again and said, "Whirl ride."

And then he slept.

Working his iPad in the hall after the floor nurse ordered them to step out, Rook made a spin move on the polished linoleum. "Ha-ha, knew it. Thug-One wasn't jerking your chain. Look." He held the tablet out for Nikki to read his search hit. "Marco Polo Worldwide—as opposed to 'whirl ride'—Spice Distributor and Wholesaler in Flatbush, New Yowk." He watched hope cross her face and her wheels starting to turn. "I wouldn't call ahead."

"No," she said on her way to the elevator. "Let's surprise them."

When they pulled out of the garage of Brooklyn's Woodhull Medical Center,
the rain surprised both Heat and Rook by still seeming relatively light.
Shouldn't it be more torrential? The wind, however, remained prolific,
seemingly limitless. On the drive down Marcus Garvey Boulevard
toward Flatbush, plastic bags, tree branches, chunks of billboard, even
price numbers ripped from service station signs flew across their path,
prompting Rook to say something Nikki only half heard about falling
gas prices.

She was busy trying to sway the acting precinct commander of
the Sixty-seventh to provide backup at Marco Polo Worldwide. He
was understandably reluctant to release assets during a citywide emergency, yet was no match for Heat, who invoked the name of Zach
Hamner as her next call, if that's what it took. The acting PC offered
two patrol teams to meet her at the west end of Preston Court in fifteen minutes.

Heat's Taurus had been blocked in back at the Twentieth, so she
and Rook arrived in the drug impound undercover car she had commandeered in her haste. A pair of blue and whites was waiting for
them outside the U-Haul parking lot on the corner of Preston at Kings
Highway. "Don't want to jinx it," she said to Rook, "but we're only
about three blocks from Fabian Beauvais's SRO. If this turns out to be
that shred net, and he ripped them off, it's an easy walk."

"Or run," he said.

More than simply functioning as backup, the patrol officers had
good local knowledge. Preston Court was a down and dirty industrial zone, a partially unpaved, two-lane alley lined on either side by
low-rise weathered brick and concrete warehouses, mounded quarry
materials, and metal-scrap lots bordered by chain link and razor wire.
The spice distributor sat a hundred yards east between a tire recycler
and a boiler-system repair company. The ranking uni, a sergeant, said
all the business on that stretch of Preston loaded their materials in and
out the front doors, so there was only a narrow service track running
behind the buildings, an easy route to plug with a patrol car on each
end. Heat told the sergeant she liked his plan and dispatched him and
the other team to the back, keeping one of the uniforms to go in the
front door with her and Rook.

On the drive up the block, they passed a flatbed stacked with hollow automobile bodies in front of a crusher yard. Next door, outside a vacant hulk with a red and white sign advertising thirty thousand square feet for lease, a handful of young Latinos crouched with cupped hands around their smokes as if the hurricane were a minor inconvenience. When they made the undercover cop car, they ran in all directions. Pulling up to Marco Polo Worldwide Spice Distributors, Rook scoffed at the sign. "If this isn't a front for something, I'll eat a tablespoon of cayenne." Indeed, the sad building looked anything but international, a double-height box of exposed concrete blocks topped by rusty corrugated steel panels.

The front door was unlocked, either through sloppiness or thanks to the smokers, and the three entered. They found the reception area unattended. Clearly it got no walk-in customers. Dingy framed photos of herbs drying on foreign hillsides graced Masonite paneling straight out of a Khrushchev-era basement bomb shelter. Inside the dust-caked display cases, bowls of dead and decayed spices were laced with cobwebs. From their pallid color and texture, they might have been delivered by Marco Polo himself.

The door to the side of the counter opened, and an imposing guy ripped with muscles stepped in, hastening to pull it closed behind him. "Help you?" he said in a voice an octave higher than anyone expected from his roided body.

"Interested in some spices," said Rook. "I'm just mad about saffron."

Both the officer and the muscleman gave him strange looks. Heat's focus stayed on the hard body, whom she saw stuff something in his back pocket and cover it with his untucked shirt tail. "I'd like to speak to the manager. Is that you?"

"We're closed."

"The door was open." She parted her coat to show some tin and Sig Sauer. "Are you the manager?"

"No."

"Who is?"

"You have a warrant?" As soon as he asked it, the inner door behind him opened wide. A slender Asian man holding an unlit cigarette and a disposable lighter stood in it. Behind him they could see a portion of a large, open warehouse with about a dozen foreign men, women, and children off-loading garbage bags from a box truck. Muscle Man gave the guy with the cig a shove back inside and pulled the door shut.

"Won't be needing a warrant. I just happened to observe illegal activity. That girl I just saw is working in violation of child labor laws," said Heat, approaching him. "And you are under arrest for carrying an illegal weapon." She reached in his back pocket and pulled out a telescoping billy club. While the uniform frisked and cuffed him, she said, "I think I'd like my tour now."

An hour later, still handcuffed, but seated in a stained executive chair in the middle of the warehouse, the muscleman, Mitch Dougherty watched glumly as his workforce of forty-six illegals called him names in foreign tongues as they filed past to be processed by Social Services. SSD personnel had braved the weather and arrived with two buses to transport the dozens of abused and malnourished aliens to emergency shelters and to get a health assessment.

To use the term Heat had heard from FiFi Figueroa, Mitch was only one of the bulls, an enforcer. But he was inside, and that meant he must know who ran the business. And what a business it turned out to be.

Ana, a young woman from Honduras who spoke excellent English, approached Nikki on behalf of the other workers, desperate to share the story of their plight. "I am like most of these women. We have been abducted from our hometowns and brought here against our will."

In the case of Ana, she was taken one night in La Ceiba by gangs who first raped her, then smuggled her to America to be a prostitute. "Sadly," she said, "it is true for some of the boys as well, although many of the men and women were not kidnapped, but were tricked to come here. Who does not want to come to America for education, si? That is what they told some, and then they arrive, and there are no identity papers or no colleges, and they are then forced to work for pennies in this living hell and live in the squalor of the rooms they keep us in."

Heat scanned the lineup of vacant-eyed souls. Of course she knew about human trafficking—the underground industry of human servitude that kept the moral outrage of slavery alive and well in modern times. But here she saw it in the flesh, en masse. Men, women, and—as she learned from Social Services—children, as young as nine, caught in the historic form of abduction, abuse, and enslavement for the enrichment of their captors; and all who supported the system. Here before her were forty-six lives. What made her shudder was the certainty that they were the proverbial grain of sand on the beach.

Exhilarated by her rescue from bondage, Ana led Heat and Rook around the warehouse, describing the setup and the jobs done by each team. "That's how they divided us, by specialty. And by literacy. You'll see what I mean."

The wide-open, twenty-thousand-plus-square-foot building was subdivided by task. In one end, plastic garbage bags were mounded high, filling one end of the immense, hangarlike space. The rest of the concrete floor was sectioned off by planks of wood that defined square borders where sorting was done. All work was done by hand. One team sorted each bag into raw materials that were carried to its designated section. An area each for: credit cards and credit card receipts; ATM cards and receipts; personal mail, which was then organized by type—bank statements, preapproved credit lines, mail order and Internet invoices that used credit cards, newsletters from professional organizations and clubs, and birthday cards to harvest dates of birth; cardboard shipping cartons with name and address labels; and hard goods, which included everything from discarded clothing with names and phone numbers, to luggage tags, and old technology—especially computer hard drives and old phones.

"This was all sorted on hands and knees all day and into the night. And then the trucks would come and bring more and more."

Rook asked, "What happened to the good stuff you found?"

"Yes, the useful material with names and information that could be used to make IDs or to do fraud were boxed in those plastic bins and transported elsewhere to the people who would make false accounts or fake credit cards and such."

"It must be worth millions," he said to Heat. But she was looking elsewhere, across the huge room.

"Ana, what is that back there?"

"The confetti pile. Come, I will show you." She led them to the back corner where they saw the shredded material FiFi had described. Shredded documents, which had been emptied out of plastic bags, laid out on the floor, and painstakingly—almost impossibly—assembled like jigsaw puzzles into completed car loan and mortgage apps, résumés, anything that got shredded for security from identity theft. "This is where they made me work," she said. "Because they said I was patient and smart."

Ana coughed back a tear and then kicked apart one of the nearly complete docs, a credit report for an apartment. It swirled to pieces in a mini gyre and drifted to the floor like snow in a globe. She liked it so much she kicked another and another until she collapsed. Nikki held her to comfort her and beckoned a social worker over.

But as quickly as she had crumbled, Ana sat up, wiping the tears, declaring she was fine. Heat said, "Ana, we can do this when you feel stronger, but I would like to ask you to look at some pictures."

"I will do it now," she said. "Truly, I am fine. I am free." She smiled. Nikki took out her cell phone and scrolled to a photo of Fabian Beauvais. "Oh it is Fabby!" Ana was so excited she tried to take the phone. "He worked here, too, you know." And then her face clouded. "Fabian was tricked to come her from Haiti after the earthquake. They told him he would have a better life. This was his life." She turned to the room as the last of the forced laborers left for the shelter. "But Fabian, he got out. He got away. And helped his fiancée break free, too."

Heat put her phone away. She couldn't bear to carry this conversation any further.

"Here's how it's going to go, Mitch," said Heat as she pulled up a chair to put herself knee-to-knee with the bull in charge. "I'm going to give you a chance to tell me now who runs this little . . . enterprise." She gave Rook a glance and saw that he caught the FiFi reference. Her casual air was a total mask. Nikki knew it was just a matter of time before word got to the leader of this sweatshop, and she wanted that name immediately before he could flee. But she couldn't show her neediness, so she toyed, holding her notebook like a secretary from the *Mad Men* steno pool. "First name, last name, please."

"I can't."

"You mean you won't."

"Damn straight I won't. Know what they'll do to me if I talk?"

"What did Fabian Beauvais take from you guys."

"I said I'm not talking."

"That's too bad. Because I was going to offer you a plea deal. Hurricane special. Because, you see, Mitch, we are really good at finding things out. What do you think we'll learn when we check your cell phone for calls?"

He looked up at Rook, who said, "Oh, yes. Any call to you, or from you."

"Mitch, don't you think we'll figure out who you work for?" Heat let him stew on that for a while and snapped her fingers. "Wait, I have a terrific idea. Do you shred your papers, Mitch? Because I am going to have our Crime Scene Unit go through your trash. Here at your little office and at your home. What will we find, Mitch? Check stub? An e-mail you printed carelessly?"

Rook tagged in. "Lucky you like to work out, Mitch. New York prisons have the best weight facilities. A piece of advice? I'd be careful who spots you. Some of those lifers act clumsy, but I think they just like to see what happens when heavy iron lands on a throat."

Mitch started to squirm. He gave Heat a nervous look, and she said, "Don't listen to him. Nobody's going to bother you in the exercise room. A build like yours, someone will most likely test you out in the recreation yard or in the chow line. Put a shiv in a big fella like you, that's going to buy some gangster a lot of cred." She patted his knee. "Too bad. You had a chance to take the deal."

As soon as she stood, Mitch said, "OK."

On their rush to the car Rook called to Heat in the lobby near the display cases. "Wait." She stopped and turned.

"Wait? Really?"

"Gotta do one thing. I'll hate myself if I don't." He held up a pause finger and ran back into the warehouse. Nikki stepped in the doorway and watched him jog past Mitch and the officers who were about to lead him off. He arced around a mound of old PCs and stopped at the confetti pile. He paused over it a beat, then turned and opened the back door. The howling winds moaned and lifted the piles into the air, grabbing at them with greedy force and sucked the shreds out of the warehouse, scattering them into the maelstrom.

When they were gone, now just ticker tape in the storm, Rook pulled the door closed. He passed Heat on his way out again and said, "Whoopsie."

The high tide wasn't supposed to crest for almost two hours, but when they passed Wall Street just past 7 P.M., the wheels of Heat's car were rim-deep in East River overflow. The TAC frequencies were lively, to say the least. They heard reports that the Brooklyn-Battery Tunnel had begun to take on seawater, that numerous residents were stranded in elevators in the downtown-most high-rises because Con Ed had cut power as a precaution, and that the entire façade had shorn off an apartment building in Chelsea, exposing all four stories of front rooms to the street. "Would not want to be the guy sitting on the can with the *Ledger* in that building," commented Rook, who then gave a jaunty wave. "Hello, New York City."

Heat appraised him and said, "How old are you?"

"Go ahead, hate me for my highly visual imagination."

On Beaver Street the power was still on when Nikki parked, but the streetlights didn't keep her from bumping the curb with her front tire because it was submerged. She checked her mirrors and gave the block a full rotation. All the retail shops were closed, as was the Delmonico's restaurant on the corner. Nobody was out driving, and the only vehicles on the street were parked cars and a UPS truck, all of which were empty. "I'm not seeing our boys."

"Bet they got slowed by the storm."

Detective Ochoa confirmed over his cell that the Roach Coach had indeed fallen victim to a road closure. "The FDR and Henry Hudson are both NG," he said. "High water was supposed to be ten-to-twelve, but now they say it's rising over a foot above that. Rhymer and Feller are tailing us, but, with the streets like they are, I can't see us there for maybe an hour." All Heat could imagine was her suspect up there in his apartment making his escape out some back way.

"You up for this?" she asked Rook.

"What? You're not ordering me to stay behind in the car for once?"

"No," she said with a sly grin. "You're going to give me a pony ride to the door so I don't wreck my shoes."

He actually offered to do that, even came around to the driver's-side door and crouched for her to hop on. She gave his ass a swat and he gave up that notion. They slogged ankle-deep to the front of the apartment building, a prewar terra-cotta, twelve stories tall. Heat shielded her eyes from the whipping wind and rain and tilted her head back. The penthouse lights were lit.

"NYPD, open up." Detective Heat banged once more and listened. She heard movement inside and stepped back, then launched herself forward to deliver a kick to the sweet spot of the door. In the blink before it landed, the dead bolt slid and it started to open. Her momentum carried her sole into the wood and the door flew about six inches before it slammed into someone behind it who cried out.

She came in with her gun drawn and took position over the man cringing on the floor. She handed Rook the Beretta from her ankle holster and told him to hold it on him while she checked the other rooms. "It's wet," he said.

"Don't worry, it'll still fire." When she came back a moment later, she holstered and came around to cuff the attorney.

Reese Cristóbal wept. Sitting cross-legged in his foyer, blood streaming from his split lip onto his champagne carpet, the Gateway Lawyer blubbered like a toddler. Heat tried to raise her detectives, but cellular service had gone funky, either through excess call volume or equipment damage. Nikki decided to give them ten more minutes. She turned to her prisoner. "So how low are you? Putting yourself out there like some community asset, saying you're placing immigrants in jobs and smoothing the transition for them, and all the time it's a cover for your ID theft ring. No, forget that. It's more than a cover; your position guaranteed you a ready supply of slave labor to pick through the trash and gather your stolen documents." At first it looked like he was nodding agreement, but the man rocked back and forth, keening and moaning.

"Welcome to your reality, counselor. You are cooked; you know that, right? You are not only going down for human trafficking and every related civil rights and abuse charge we can throw at you, plus ID theft and bank fraud. . . ." His sobs grew louder so she spoke up to drown them. ". . . I am going to see you tried as an accessory in the attempted murder of Fabian Beauvais by one of your bulls. And who knows? Maybe you had something to do with his killing, too."

"No!"

"And his fiancée, too. Wasn't Jeanne Capois also enslaved in your shred operation? Maybe you'll also go down for her."

Cristóbal's whining mixed in perfect pitch with the eighty-mile-per-hour winds roaring between the buildings in the Financial District. "No, no, I'll cut a deal."

"That's not your choice."

"I know things." He finally brought his gaze to hers. "Things you want."

Was he acting, or was this the break Nikki had hoped for—if not the smoking gun, at least the hot trail? She tested him. "Tell me about Beauvais."

"I know all about Beauvais."

"What did he steal from you that was so dangerous?" When he didn't answer, she asked, "What about Keith Gilbert? What's his connection to all this?"

He licked his mouth and smiled broadly, and when he did, his lip parted again and blood dripped off his chin. With the wind and rain and flashes of lightning, he could have been Dracula. "Deal first," he said.

Heat checked her watch. Nearly an hour had passed, and still no backup. She checked the window. Water had risen to the chassis of her undercover. Any higher, she might not be able to start the engine. Cristóbal was scum. Heat needed to get him to swear a statement before he lost his fear and did too much thinking.

She turned to Rook. "Let's get him to the First Precinct."

There were whitecaps on Beaver Street as they crossed to the car and got him into the backseat. Relieved when the ignition fired up, Nikki said to Rook, "Change of plan. It's worse than I thought out here. In all this, Ericsson Place is too far to go. I'm thinking One PP is closer."

"You're the skipper. Want to cast off?"

The car filled with high beams from behind. She checked her mirror and made out the form of a black armored vehicle pulling up. "May be our lucky day. Looks like we've got backup, after all."

But when Heat registered that the BearCat drawing alongside did not have NYPD or National Guard markings, instinct took over. She threw the transmission in low gear and floored it. Her tires spun until they made purchase, and the car slogged forward, churning water. "Down, down," she yelled just as the rear windows shattered with automatic rifle fire.

SIXTEEN

Heat jerked the wheel and made a sharp right up William Street. Too busy driving, Nikki couldn't turn to see, but she knew Reese Cristóbal had to be dead. She reached for the two-way and keyed the mic, "One-Lincoln-Forty, ten-thirteen, officer needs help." She released the button. After the squelch came a blizzard of radio calls stepping on each other. "You hit?" she asked Rook?

"No." The car filled with light again as the BearCat followed in pursuit. He twisted in his seat for a rear view. "Shit."

"One-Lincoln-Forty. Ten-thirteen, officer pursued by heavily armed suspects in armored vehicle. Moving north on William, passing—" She called over the wind to Rook, "What's our cross?"

"Wall Street—No, Pine, Pine."

A short burst of automatic gunfire flashed from the passenger side of the assault truck and took Heat's side mirror clean off. She steered sharply to the right, then left, then right again to become a weaving target. "You hit?"

"Stop asking me. I'll let you know."

Back on the two-way. "One Lincoln-Forty, taking automatic fire. Ten-thirteen, William and Pine. Do you read?" Nothing but garble. She might be getting heard, but there was no way to know. Heat ditched the mic and said, "Hang on."

A restaurant-linen-and-uniform delivery truck started to inch into the road across their path with its flashers flashing, driven by someone who must not have been able to see in the cyclone. Nikki whipped the wheel to the left and her vehicle responded, clearing the front of the truck, with Rook's door taking a mean, shrieking scrape as she passed. Behind her, through the gale, she heard the throaty blast of the BearCat's horn as it got blocked.

"Ha-ha, denied," said Rook. "Where now?"

"We keep going to One PP. When we reach Fulton, I can cut up to—forget that." Ahead of her, a car had struck a light pole that toppled and jutted across the intersection, barring the street.

"Can you squeeze by on the sidewalk?"

"Not sure," she said, squinting through the sideways rain. "Don't want to get wedged."

"I dunno, might make it."

"And also might get wedged." They both made another rear check and saw no headlights. "Plan B." Heat turned a right down Platt.

"Whoa, check it out." A small car floated sideways past Rook's window. "Now there's something you don't see every day."

"Not liking this, Rook," she said in a low voice. "Not liking this." The tide had risen significantly, coming up the top of her wheels.

"Maybe we should have risked the wedge instead of driving where? Toward the river?"

"Um, not helpful?"

"Just observing."

"Just driving." The engine became swamped and died.

"Not anymore." While she tried to restart, the sky to the north lit up with a huge blue flash followed by another. "Lightning?"

One second later, the entire block fell into pitch darkness. The two-way crackled with multiple calls about an explosion at the Con Ed station on Fourteenth and advisories that all of Manhattan was blacked out south of Grand Central. Rook said helpfully, "I have a little squeezy flashlight on my key ring." He indicated the backseat. "I'm thinking Mr. Cristóbal won't miss us if we get out and walk to—" He stopped short as the car blazed with daylight.

The BearCat roared back, charging toward them. "Out, out, out," called Nikki, but the flood had risen halfway up the doors and the resistance from water pressure made them impossible to push open.

Bang!

The impact threw them hard against their seat belt straps and deployed both airbags. Still conscious, Nikki wiped a trickle of blood from her nose and shook off the stupor from her face crashing into the inflated sack. Beside her Rook was coming out of it, too. Behind them the three-hundred-horsepower Caterpillar diesel revved. The BearCat rode high enough not to be bothered by the up-tide. Six tires securely gripped the wet pavement and the assault vehicle pushed them forward by its reinforced front-impact grill.

Helpless to do anything but go along for the ride, Heat pulled the hand brake to no avail. The black machine shoved them slowly but relentlessly off the street and down the ramp of a parking garage. In the fearsome blare of the BearCat's head lamps, they saw their fate ahead of them. Submerged cars bobbed on the incline. The whole place was inundated by tidewater and filling fast.

White-water rapids cascaded down from street level into the underground garage, which had already filled enough to swallow the dozen or so cars they could see floating around them. Heat's plain wrap banged to a stop when it crunched against the tangle of autos blocking the ramp. Still, the BearCat's engine revved louder and louder, pressing them in place. Their attackers' strategy was clear and chilling: to brace them there, trapped, to drown in the rising tide.

It wouldn't take long. With the back windows blown out, the flow had already begun to gush over the side doors with impunity and both of them sat with water above their laps. "Can you move?" she asked.

"Yeah."

Nikki undid her seat belt and got on her knees for a quick check of the situation. Because of the incline of the ramp, all she could see of the truck out the rear was the black steel ram on the reinforced front grill, which meant anyone up in the truck would be high enough not to see over it to them. The water had risen even more and Reese Cristóbal's corpse bobbed up to her seat back. The back half of his head was gone. She fended the body away and said, "Come on, let's move. We're going to try an end around."

"Problem." He gave her a wide stare. "Seat belt's stuck."

"Is it your hands? Did you get hurt?"

"No, it's the buckle. I keep trying and it won't unlock."

"Move 'em, let me." Heat had to put her chin in the water to be able to reach the fastener. Somehow it had jammed from the impact or because of all the wet. "Damn." She brought her face up and the look they shared in one instant spoke volumes about how bad it was—and how little time they had.

"Can you squirm out?" He tried. Sideways, upward, nothing. "Reach down. Can you put your seat back?"

Rook leaned down for the release, needing to submerge his right ear to do it. "Fuck me. That's jammed, too." He pressed his feet against the fire wall and shoved backward with all he had. Still no good. "You got a knife?" She shook no.

The car shifted slightly in the flow and more surge rolled in. The swirl was up to his chin now and Heat had to press her head against the roof liner to get air herself. He closed his eyes briefly. When he opened them he said, "Get out while you can."

"No."

"Don't be stupid. Why both of us?" He shook his head and made a small wake with his chin. "Stupid. You go. Maybe you can take them out and come back before. . . ." He left it there. They both knew there was no time for that.

"Try again. Harder."

He reached down and did his best. "Not budging."

"One more try," she said, trying not to panic. And he did try.

He craned his neck to keep his mouth clear and gripped her hand. "I love you, Nikki Heat."

"Fuck you," she shouted. "Fuck you, Rook, you are not dying." And all the feelings, all the built-up anger—all the rage—her shrink had tried to get her to confront, erupted. Nikki gulped some air and dove under.

Heat knew it would be pure desperation. But desperation was where they were. In training, she had heard about it. She had even watched a slow-motion demonstration video on the Internet proving it would work. That wasn't her concern. Nikki wanted only one thing: For it to work *now*.

She grabbed the sash just above the buckle with her left hand and tugged it as far away from his body as she could. When she had cleared enough room for it to fit, with her right hand Nikki brought her Sig Sauer down, carefully aimed it away from his thigh, pressed the muzzle against the seat belt—and pulled the trigger.

The gun fired.

Underwater, and in that oscillating light, she couldn't see if it worked. But she didn't have to. The belt in her left hand went slack. Heat yanked the fabric loose from the eye of the buckle and felt him rise and float free.

They crawled out the wide-open back window swimming butterfly strokes across the trunk to keep low enough not to be seen over the hood of the BearCat that loomed over them gunning its engine. Nikki mimed for him to follow her, and she slipped into the water. The current caught her by surprise. Rook snagged her by the collar to keep the jet from propelling her forward into full view of their attackers.

Heat collected herself, filled her lungs, and submerged. Grabbing hold of the BMW next to them, she pulled herself hand over hand under the width of its bumper until she reached its opposite side. Her searing lungs cried out for oxygen and, when Nikki broke the surface, she inhaled too greedily, choking on briny water. Rook emerged seconds later, also gasping. They signaled each other they were ready, then fought the stream, hauling themselves up the incline, using car-door handles as grips. At one point she caught movement in the passenger window of the truck and saw Zarek Braun staring right at her. He said something to his driver and then brought up his HK assault carbine, swiveling it to the gunport.

"Gun." Giving up on stealth, Heat churned her knees against the cascade with Rook hauling it, too, right on her tail. They managed to get far enough behind the vehicle to get in Braun's blind spot so when the short burst from the automatic weapon came, it only spit lead into the painted brick wall behind them. If they could just reach the sidewalk, they might escape, but the BearCat shifted into reverse backing up the ramp. Soon it would be even with them, making them easy targets or blocking their way out.

Heat knew there was no point shooting. The truck had ballistic glass windows and steel plating capable of resisting a full AK-47 maga-zine. Which gave Nikki an idea. She hollered, "Stay close," and changed course, running right for the BearCat.

Pilot fish avoided getting bitten by sharks by riding on top of them where they can't be reached. If bullets from the outside couldn't pierce the armor, neither could they from the inside. She hopped on the rear bumper and lunged for the roof rack. Heat extended her free hand to Rook, who snatched her forearm so she could lock onto his wrist. His wet shoe slipped on the runner, and the motion of the vehicle nearly pulled them both off. But she held strong until he could get a foot on the metal.

The side and rear windows still exposed them, in fact, she could see Zarek Braun coming toward them through one of them. "Up top, fast." Rook grasped the top rail of the metal ladder and climbed up, two steps at a clip. Heat rolled onto the roof beside him just as the truck backed out onto the street.

It stopped, idling.

Heat and Rook panted, alive for now, barely hearing their own breaths in the tempest. Sirens in the night offered hope, but that faded as they wailed off into the distance away from them.

Somewhere beneath them a latch popped. Nikki drew her Sig and put her head on a swivel scanning 360s for movement. "There," said Rook. A Glock came up from the driver's side. It fired wildly over their heads and then disappeared. Heat waited. Didn't take the bait. Held for what she knew would be coming. And when a top slice of Zarek Braun's head popped up on the passenger side with his assault rifle, she fired. Nikki figured both her shots ended up misses, but it got him to duck and take cover inside.

She checked her cell phone. Waterlogged. Dead.

"Mine, too," said Rook.

They felt the BearCat jar as the transmission kicked into drive. Heat said, "Get a grip."

"Oh, if I had a nickel," he replied.

The driver floored it, and the motion forced their bodies backward. But halfway up the block, he slammed the brakes, and momentum carried them the opposite way. Both of them nearly slid off right over the windshield. The truck then lurched into reverse, at speed. The wheelman executed an abrupt turn, which slammed the rear tires against the curb. Heat and Rook both got bounced up and down, but managed to stay on for the next forward acceleration that sped them down the block and into a hairpin right onto the next street. Centripetal force swung Nikki's legs over the side. Rook let go of the bar with his near hand and clutched her jacket while she swung one knee over the rail and used it to haul herself up and roll flat again beside him on the black steel plate.

A prolific rooster-tail wake churned behind them on Pearl Street. Heat figured their speed at near seventy. At one of the numerous alleys around there, this one named Coenties Slip, the driver hit the brakes hard and steered them into a sharp left that felt like it would roll the truck. This time it was Rook's turn to slip over the side. Only one leg went over, though, and he made a quick recovery just before the BearCat plowed through the park benches and cement chess tables in the neighborhood plaza at Water Street, nearly sending both of them off the top.

The truck stopped there. Idling again.

An angry bear at rest.

Heat shivered. The temperature was mild, in the sixties, but she was soaked through. Her fingers were growing numb. She forgot all that to listen in the maelstrom for what might come next. Rook caught her eye when they both detected some kind of movement below.

It all happened quickly. Another latch popped. Both went on high alert. Then a lightning bolt must have made a direct hit near them. The brightest light and loudest concussion split the air, blinding and disorienting them. By reflex, their hands went to defensive mode, covering eyes and ears after Zarek Braun tossed out the stun grenade.

His angle of opportunity had been poor, tossing from a side portal. The flash bang didn't get high enough to detonate on the roof, but exploded yards away in the little square. Still near enough, though, to get the effect he needed. A three-count after the fireworks, the driver hit the gas and then the brakes. Heat and Rook, disoriented and no longer holding on, flew off the back, landing in the water.

Ifs count a lot. If Braun had made a better throw, they'd both be paralyzed in pain. If Heat had been looking to the right at the time of the flash, she might have been totally blinded. If that square hadn't been waist-deep in water, she might have broken something. The ifs were with Heat, and she would take every one of them.

Trying to blink the halos away, she hoisted Rook to his feet and drew him to the side of the van that shielded him from Zarek Braun. She knew he would be out there ready to finish the job. Listening, buying time to clear her eyes and ears, she tried to go to the Zen place, to calm herself.

Screw that.

Heat's rage dealt the play. With her Sig Sauer in one hand and her Beretta Jetfire in the other, Nikki burst around the rear of the truck with both guns blazing. The passenger door gaped open and she made out the silhouette of Zarek Braun splashing for cover behind a planter wall. She spun in a crouch at the open door and called freeze just as the driver swung his Glock at her. Heat fired one shot at him and his head jerked backward into the mist of blood decorating the window behind him.

Rounds from the G36 slapped the water beside her legs. Nikki hoisted herself up into the BearCat and pulled the armored door closed and heard pops like hailstones dance on it. She got on her knees and leaned across the driver's body to open the other door. She called for Rook to get in, but he was already hauling out the corpse and doing just that.

"Can you see?"

"Well enough," he said. Then he hit the gas, gunning it straight for Zarek Braun. But the front end smashed into the planter wall he was taking cover behind and the BearCat lurched to a stop. "Maybe not so well, after all."

Heat pointed. "He's running that way. Go, go, go."

Rook found reverse, backed clear of the planter, and chunked the transmission into drive to follow the fleeing killer. But, in his blurriness, he rammed the planter again. By the time the vehicle got back on track, they thought they had lost Braun. Then, up Water Street, they saw muzzle flashes. Rook accelerated toward them, drawing close just as Braun kicked an NYPD harbor unit patrolman out of the Boston Whaler he'd been patrolling the streets in, and took off with the outboard at top speed.

"Rook. Stop."

"I can catch him."

"Just wait." She hopped out and ran to the officer, who was down. In a draw between saving the life of a brother-in-arms or capturing a killer, she would take her chances on finding the killer later.

"Officer, I'm on the force. You're safe. Where are you hit?" She bent and rolled the man over faceup in the water. He had a clean shot to the temple. Even though she knew he was dead, she felt for a pulse. Rook helped her carry him to the truck and they resumed their pursuit.

Heat said, "He can't have more than a block on us. Two maybe."

"Detective?"

"Yeah?"

"That was the right thing to do."

She kept her face to the window searching for signs. "Someday, that could be me." And then she added. "But not today."

"Got him!"

"Where?"

"See how the counter-wake is slapping the walls of that drugstore?"

Rook stopped and backed up. Heat shined the side spotlight down the alley. In the distance, she made out an indistinguishable form.

"Not sure." Nikki's mind raced, running maps and odds through her head. "Pier Eleven's down the block. He might be making a run for the river. Let's go, let's go."

Rook tore off after the outboard, whose churn they could by then make out like a pale apparition in their headlights. The tide had reached its peak, and the water grew deeper as they got closer to the East River. The truck, which had performed like a champ, began to labor. "Come on, baby, come on," said Rook. "How close?"

"Almost to South Street, almost there." But then the machine lost its match with Nature. The engine died. Heat opened her door and stood on the running board, shielding her eyes from the storm, trying to follow the beam into the swirling night.

The outboard had reached Pier Eleven, and was slowing to a stop. That bastard was less than a hundred yards away. She indicated the dead officer to Rook and said, "Use his radio to call another ten-thirteen." And then Heat grabbed something from the floor of the truck and left.

SEVENTEEN

Spindrift pelted Nikki's face, filling her mouth with a brackish taste. The howl of Sandy's fury isolated her from any sound other than the wind and spray lashing violently at her ears. Though she ran as hard as she could, the tide measured thigh-deep in that neighborhood. Still lower than it had been farther downtown, but fighting the ferocious wave chop coming right off the East River made Heat feel like the trailing contestant on *Wipeout*. Underneath the FDR, she caught five seconds of shelter, adjusted the sling of the backpack, and sloshed on.

A tiny, shallow-draft Boston Whaler was not engineered for superstorms. Ahead of her on Pier Eleven, Heat saw its bow lift in a gust, turning its flat bottom into a wing that caught air and pointed the craft skyward before it flipped back upside down and then pinwheeled directly at her. She ducked behind the metal generator unit at the head of the pier and watched it sail overhead and crash into a concrete support of the highway overpass behind her.

When she came out from behind the machinery, Nikki spotted Zarek Braun recovering from his capsize. He saw her, too, as he hauled himself up from the churning water that covered the pier. Just when Heat thought she had him bottlenecked on that wharf, he turned and kicked a massive wake of his own, running to her left. Was he foolish enough to try to swim for it?

No. He was heading for the gangplank to Slip A, one of the docks where the water taxis come and go. No taxi tonight. But she did see a boat tied to the heaving berth—a twenty-four-foot Zodiac military pro Responder. A man on board caught a glimpse of Zarek Braun waving a circle in the air and fired up the twin Mercury 150s on its transom.

The floating dock took a swell, and Braun toppled facedown on his first step off the gangplank onto the lurching platform. Nikki reached the top of the gangplank, braced on the metal railing and called a freeze that got carried away unheard in the whirlwind. Zarek Braun rebounded from his fall and pivoted toward her with his assault rifle. She fired one round that went astray when the dock pitched, moving him sideways and down. He got on one knee and replied with a flaming burst from the G36 that sent Heat diving behind a soda vending machine.

His aim was off, too. All his rounds went high.

Heat made a rapid peek around the corner just as another surge knocked Braun off-balance. This time, he lost hold of his assault rifle. It slid away from him in the radical pitch and came to a stop against the safety fencing at the far end of the dock. Seizing the moment, Nikki sprung to her feet and started down the heaving gangplank toward him. But she lost her footing in a sea roll, too. Heat landed on her knees, gripping the banister with her left hand and clinging to her Sig Sauer with her right.

When she hauled herself up, she looked in disbelief as her Cool Customer lived up to his nickname. Instead of backtracking for his carbine, he turned his back on Nikki and strolled toward the waiting escape boat with out so much as a glance at her. He knew what they both knew. It was impossible to get off an accurate shot with the river tossing them about in a hurricane. But at the bottom of the gangplank, Heat braced and fired.

Zarek half turned but kept his stride. Another yaw of the dock as it strained against its pilings sent the HK skimming back her way. She grabbed it, aimed, and pulled the trigger.

It was empty.

The mercenary gave her a smug nod and laughed as he hopped into the black Zodiac. Nikki started weaving toward him with her Sig up. Braun pointed to something down inside the boat, and his accomplice, whom she recognized as the man she had shot with the nail gun in Chelsea, reached over with his unbandaged hand and brought up a fresh G36.

Proving she could be a cool one herself, Nikki stopped and holstered her weapon. That confused Zarek Braun as he took the HK from his partner. In the moment he hesitated to wonder what the hell that was about, Heat underhanded the flash-bang grenade she had brought along in the backpack and lobbed it into the Zodiac.

Back at the Twentieth Precinct, just before dawn, Heat stood in the faint light of Observation-One staring through the glass at her prisoner. The shiver she felt wasn't from the still-damp hair tickling the back of her neck. It came from watching a paid assassin sit under the lunar wash of fluorescents with such inverted tranquility he resembled a wax replica of himself at Madame Tussauds.

She could have easily killed him hours before on that dock. Even with all the heaving and pitching, Nikki had the drop on him, and at that range, she had three nines left she could have parked in his head, with one left for his boat wrangler, if he'd gotten any ideas. Who knows? She might have worn a medal for it, cashing the chit of a double cop killer.

But Heat wanted this prick alive.

And she got him, flash, bang, boom.

Now came the harder part, and she knew it: trying to get a mercenary with psyops training to give up the man who hired him. Heat assessed him again and quietly composed herself, becoming mindful of her breathing. The room still had a tang from the old days when they allowed smoking in there, and her own clothes—the same ones that she had changed out of and balled into her file drawer the other day—weren't the freshest, either. But they were dry.

Sandy had moved on in the overnight after making landfall near Atlantic City. The former hurricane was now somewhere over Pennsylvania, but the city was still reeling, and through the door behind her, Nikki heard the early-morning bustle of the precinct's forces in response mode.

She had a different job to do. And it was time to jump in.

Zarek Braun's concentration never left the spot he had chosen under the mirror. Not even when he heard the sucking sound as Heat came through the air lock that buffered the observation room from Interrogation-One. "Something different about you this morning, Mr. Braun." She ducked her forehead toward his and squinted into a playful face. "What is it, now? Is it the orange jumpsuit? Not as flattering as your black phony SWAT outfit, is it? No, something else . . . Oh, I know. The manacles. You are incarcerated." She tossed her files onto the tabletop and took her place. "Just as you will be for the rest of your life. Which may end up being shorter than you had planned."

That brought his eyes off the wall. She winked. "That's a topic yet to explore. First, I want to ask you some questions. Number-one is sort of a public safety issue. Are there any more members of your urban black ops cadre out there? Because I would sure like to get them off the street." His gaze drifted front again. "That's OK, because we're finding out lots about that from your boat skipper in the other room. I just thought I'd give you a chance to get ahead of the rush for leniency from cooperative goodwill."

She could have put Braun and his Zodiac captain, Seth Victor, in the same interrogation box together to play them off each other. Her decision, though, was that the Cool Customer would have intimidated his underling into silence. So she went with divide and conquer. Maybe Victor didn't know as much as Braun, but his paranoia about getting sold out might loosen him up. This one would be a challenge, though; she knew that before she came in.

"Look, let's keep it real. We both know you're going to try to stonewall here. And, unlike you, we don't go for torturing our prisoners. Although, I have thought of it, Zarek." Addressing him by his first name brought a tiny flex to his mouth. "Not so much a thought, as a fantasy." Heat brought up a hand to count off fingers. "Let's see, you killed my captain. You killed a patrol officer. You killed Reese Cristóbal. You killed Fabian Beauvais, too, didn't you?" She waited. The Cool Customer remained passive. "And you also killed Jeanne Capois. And the old man she kept house for. Look: out of fingers. Am I leaving anybody off?"

He seemed amused by some private joke. Then he spoke. "You have lovely eyes. Bedroom eyes." His words came softly in a Polish accent, which, under other circumstances, Heat might have found sexy.

"And you know what they see ahead for you? Let me lay it out. New York does not have a death penalty, I'm sure you've thought that through. But guess what we've been busy doing. Letting our pals at

Homeland Security do some checking on you. We like to cooperate. Not just with each other but with our allies in foreign lands. A little birdie told me about Operation Dream Catcher. You were a bad boy in the desert. A very bad boy. Let me ask you something. If our friends in Afghanistan want an extradition so they can repay you in all the ingenious ways they can imagine, what do you think I should tell them?"

A minuscule flare of his nostrils. A scalp flex that moved his ears. Small tells gave away his unease and let her know she'd had some impact. So Nikki tested it for the money. "I want you to tell me about Keith Gilbert. I want to know everything. I want you to tell me why Keith Gilbert wanted Fabian Beauvais dead. I want you to tell me how you killed Fabian Beauvais for Keith Gilbert."

She gave him an opening to respond, but he didn't take it. "Did you notice there's a theme here? Keith Gilbert. Wealthy men have no problem hiring men like you to do their scut work. Keith Gilbert even told you to kill me, didn't he? And you tried. Twice. Oh, and how did that work out for you, Zarek?"

Heat sat facing him, waiting. And waiting some more. She stood. "Fine. You keep it zipped like that, being all cool. Styling your orange duds and your bracelets and chains. Know what I'm going to do? Go Google the weather forecast for Kabul."

When she left Interrogation, two a half hour later, she found Rook waiting for her in the ob room. "These guys are hard core," he said. They watched Seth Victor picking at his wrist bandage through the magic mirror. His face was still swollen from the broken nose Heat had given him in Chelsea. The effect made him appear even more stoic than his unit leader in the next box. "You know, in my prior, somewhat nutty ramblings about roving bands of rogue black ops mercs out on the streets, dishing out justice, I always figured it would be a little more satisfying to meet them. Like they'd have some swagger and élan."

"You mean like an action figure?"

"Exactly." And then he realized what she'd said and turned to her. "Was that a shot?"

"If the beard fits."

Anyway, these guys are just punks with army-surplus gear. Lethal enough, I grant you, but swagger? Élan? I think not." Inside the box, Victor turned toward Rook. Even though they both knew better, it seemed like a reaction. "I think we should find another room."

Out in the hallway Rook said, "I made it to Gramercy Park. Your apartment's fine."

"What's it like out there?"

"Not good. Storm's past, but now we're getting the nasty back ass of it. Power is still out below Thirty-ninth, subways, tunnels, and some bridges are closed; they're still putting out house fires in Breezy Point . . . Oh, and somebody put a roller coaster in the ocean off the Jersey shore." He led her into the break room and indicated the clothes on the coat rack. "Got you these from your apartment."

"Oh, great. Thanks."

"It's the least I could do after you saved my life."

She pulled the outfit off the hook. "Oh yeah, this suit definitely makes us even."

"I beg to differ, Detective Heat, but I think we are finally even for that bullet I took for you."

"You know, I don't see it as even. I see it as your turn to take another one." And she stepped into the ladies' room to change.

The voice of Keith Gilbert echoed up the hall from the bull pen as Nikki returned in her refreshed wardrobe. She looked up at him in front of the forest of microphones on TV when she stepped into the room and thought she saw something on his face that went beyond weariness from running the PA's emergency sitch room overnight. Did she see stress? A twinge of fear?

Rook came up behind her and voiced her thoughts. "Do you think Commissioner Gilbert knows that his soldier of fortune's fortunes have turned unfortunate?"

"Oh, so you're with me now on Gilbert?"

"When did I ever doubt you?"

The news from the press conference was grim. Over ninety deaths in a sixty-mile radius, forty-three of them right there in New York City, mostly in Queens and on Staten Island, which took a wallop.

Kennedy, LaGuardia, and Newark airports were closed. All seven East River subway tunnels had flooded and were closed. Same with the Midtown, Holland, and Battery Park automobile tunnels.

"Got breaking news here." Ochoa lofted the phone on a stiff arm toward the ceiling. "Feller and Rhymer calling in from da Bronx."

Nikki muted Gilbert's press briefing. "Put them on speaker so we all can get it at once." She, Raley, and Rook circled Ochoa's desk. "Whatcha got, Detectives?"

"We found Zarek Braun's crib," said Feller.

Another chill, a good one this time, raised hairs on Nikki's arm. "How'd you manage that? Neither of these guys carried ID, not even a wallet."

"Hence the term, going commando," added Raley.

"Correct, but as all of us who have endured long hours of stakeout know, you need to do something to pass the time."

Detective Rhymer said, "Before you start with the dirty jokes, we combed through that Fort Knox on wheels they were driving and found a *Sports Illustrated* Swimsuit Edition stuffed in the driver's side pocket." He paused. "Huh. Still no dirty jokes, what's wrong with you guys? Anyway, your deceased BearCat driver, Mr. Bill Santinelli, was a subscriber, and—employing all our savvy and cunning as professional investigators—we went to the address on the magazine label. By the way it's off Bathgate. Same block as the rest of his crew was living when I checked their places out."

Everyone thought the same thing—about Wally Irons walking into an IED trap. "You two should hold," said Heat.

"Not to worry. Bomb squad sniffed it and passed it a half hour ago while you were in with Zarek Braun." Randall Feller cleared something from his throat. "By the way, if he's still hanging around, I'd like to soften him up for you."

Everyone on that call felt the same. Heat steered them away from that black hole. "Are you sure Braun lived there, too?"

"Affirm. Got some picture ID here with numerous assumed names. Driver's licenses, fake passports, even a private gym card." They could hear door hinges squeak and the acoustics change as Feller stepped outside. "I'm walking to the detached garage, which ESU is still clearing so we can't go in yet. But, standing here looking in, I can see all sorts of ordnance, ammunition, tear gas, flash bangs."

"Zip cuffs?" asked Ochoa.

"Don't see any right off, but I would bet on it. The infamous Impala is also parked in here under a tarp. And there's a big space here with some wide-track tire marks that I'm sure belong to a BearCat."

Heat said, "Just before you called we got a trace back on that 'Cat. It was reported stolen by Mexican police last year."

Rook said, "That explains how Braun got it. You can't just buy those things on eBay. I've tried."

"Hang on, hang on." The phone rustled on Feller's end and they heard muffled chatter. Then he came back on. "The bomb sarge found a wallet on the workbench. No picture ID in it, but there's a paycheck stub from the chicken slaughterhouse. It's made out to Fabian Beauvais."

Feller and Rhymer hung up to resume their search of Braun's hideout up in the Bronx. Before Heat got involved in other things, Roach led her to the Murder Board. Like the other detectives, they had taken to heart Nikki's directive to drill down on every aspect of the case. Since both of them felt a proprietary interest in Jeanne Capois and her unresolved connection to Opal Onishi, that's where they had put their initial efforts.

Ochoa began, "I read over the notes from your interview with Onishi." He took his pen out of his teeth and tapped the woman's name in his quadrant on the whiteboard. "Squirrelly, that one."

"You think?" said Nikki. "If we ran a polygraph on her, we'd probably have to order in more ink."

"Yeah, my antenna was up all over. So I thought, what's in that interview that I could at least run some kind of check on? So I left word with the Happy Hazels. Remember, Opal told you that she hired Jeanne Capois through that agency?"

"I sort of prompted her with that, but, yeah."

"But no. It took awhile because of all the craziness with the storm, but the happiest Hazel called me back about a ten ago. She never referred Jeanne Capois to anyone other than her boss, the old man from the home invasion."

"Shelton David," said his partner.

"And she has never heard of Opal Onishi. I'll admit," he said, "that it's not so much a lead, as a confirmation of a lie."

"At this point, everything helps, Miguel." And then she said, "You actually read my notes?"

"Hey, just doin' the fact-donkey dance."

Rook scooted his chair over and said, "The next question is, why? Why lie?"

Heat agreed. "And why move in the middle of the night like some traveling circus?"

"Was she in debt?"

Raley hopped on that one. "No. I ran a credit check on her 'cause I wondered the same thing. It's maybe the most logical reason to make a midnight run like that. Opal's not rich, but she's making all her payments on time. And she's got a steady job."

"We're back to where we started," said Heat. "Wondering what the connection is between Opal Onishi and Jeanne Capois."

"Which is where some of my donkeywork might help," said Raley. Nikki could tell by looking, Sean was holding. "Although I did mine wearing the crown."

"As my King of All Surveillance Media?"

"A little more like a commoner. I didn't scrub surveillance vids; I only used the Internet. To Google Opal Onishi. You can find out a lot about people online."

"But don't believe all of it," said Rook. He felt their stares and dismissed them with a wave. "I reveal too much. Go on."

Rales said, "What got me started was, in your interview—which I also read, thank-you—Onishi said she had been sleeping with an actress on a film shoot, she's referencing old films, and we knew she went to NYU film school. Anyway, that got me thinking: gopher on *Iron Chef*? Rental clerk for movie equipment? That's not career work for a film grad, that's the J-O-B job you do to pay for your passion. Film." He had their attention but could see they were only partly with him. "Maybe it's better if I can just show you." They followed him to his desk where he clicked on a bookmark that brought up a page of search engine hits.

"Check this out, she's got her own site." He opened the home page to a full-screen pose of Opal Onishi standing at the gate of a Cherokee reservation, resting her arm on an Arri Amira camera body presenting a defiant look to the viewer.

Nikki drew closer to the monitor. "What's this about?"

"It's about Opal's other life. As an independent documentary filmmaker."

"And a serious one, too," said Rook. "Look at the films and subjects she's made." Raley obliged by scrolling as he read. " '*Village of the Slammed*—Gay violence and bashing in New York's Greenwich Village; *Heart of the Bully*—Chronicle of the aftermath of spousal violence; *Tribe and Punishment*—Exposing corruption and abuse on Native American reservations.' That must be where that home page pic was taken."

Raley swiveled his chair to Heat. "So, it looks to me like the Gen-Y kid who's been fetching coffee and schlepping stage lights is really a Michael Moore in the making."

Heat made the connections in a blink. "Kind of makes you wonder what her latest social justice project was. But I have a pretty good idea." She went to her desk to grab her keys. "If anyone needs me, I'm off to the East Village to visit an indie filmmaker."

EIGHTEEN

"You keep waking me up," said Opal Onishi when she opened the door to let in Heat and Rook. "You know, it's polite to call first. The power's all fucked up, but my cell works." She thumbed the home button to check for bars and held it out as a visual aid. Heat ignored it and instead surveyed the living room. The surplus furniture remained stacked, as before, but the cardboard cartons had been razored open revealing their contents: kitchen gadgets in one; surge suppressors and orphan TV remotes in another. Some of the boxes were empty, and their contents covered every open surface in the room.

"I see you've had time to move in since my last visit."

"Yeah, sorry for the mess. Wasn't expecting company, and I was up working on a project. At least till the lights went out."

Rook said, "What's the project, *American Hoarders*?"

"You're not a cop, are you?"

"No, this is Jameson Rook. He rides with me sometimes."

"The writer. Cool." Opal scooped up a few of the tall stacks of papers that filled the couch, end to end. "Here, sit here."

When they sat, Nikki said, "So you're trying to finish up your next documentary."

She got back a cautious reaction. "Yeah . . . How'd you know?"

"Detective." Heat side-nodded to the bundles of paper—drafts of screenplays—and four milk crates filled with DVDs, both sleeveless and in jewel cases. Fanned across the coffee table in front of a Mac Cinema Display were stapled forms entitled EDITING CONTINUITY in boldface with grids containing lists of time codes, shots, and scene notes marked by highlighters.

"What gave me away?" Onishi chuckled and then lit a cigarette with an Ohio Blue Tip. She didn't sit, but stood because it seemed to relax her, one hand on her hip and the other taking a satisfying drag.

"Actually, to be truthful, we checked you out online."

"If one were to be truthful," added Rook with a calculated degree of innuendo as an attachment. "You have some impressive reviews. I checked you out on *Cultureunplugged* and *Documentarystorm*. Your film on gay bashing won a Doxie Award at South by Southwest."

"Ancient history. That was my senior project at NYU." She acted dismissive but seemed flattered by Rook's notice. "Independent documentary film doesn't get a lot of mass awareness, which is cool, really. It's a passion. As an investigative journalist, you should screen it. I have a DVD of it here somewhere."

Nikki said, "I'm more interested in the project you're working on now."

"*Tribe and Punishment*?"

"Stop lying to me, Opal. You know the one I'm talking about. The one Jeanne Capois was helping you with."

"The maid? Helping me on a film?"

"Stop. The. Lying."

"Looks to me like it's called *Smuggled Souls*." Rook held up one of the pages of editing notes.

"Hey, that's private." She snatched it from him and tossed it in one of the empty cartons—a futile gesture since the title appeared in bold-face atop every other piece of paper that was visible.

"Opal, we checked," said Heat. "The Happy Hazels did not refer Jeanne Capois to you. And we know now that she was a victim of human trafficking. I am forming the reasonable assumption that she had something to do with a film you are making, and I want you to cut the crap and tell me what it was."

"OK. This is true." Onishi stubbed out her smoke and sat on one of the boxes, lighting up another. "Jeanne came to me a few times. Helped me out with some background stuff, you know, keeping it real. That's all."

Detective Heat had done enough interviews in her career to know the dodges. One was the straight lie, which was what she got from Opal last time. Now she was getting the lie hidden inside a truth. Suspects and witness did that when they wanted to feed you enough to satisfy you, hoping you'd move on. Nikki wasn't budging, and needed to call her out. "I did a records check and didn't see any calls to you from Jeanne Capois."

Just as the woman started to relax, Nikki pulled the rug. "But I did another one before I came here and recognized several calls that turned out to be from the home phone of her employer, Shelton David. Including one the night she was murdered. The night you moved out of your place in Chelsea like it was on fire." The cardboard box gave in a little under Opal's weight, startling her. Nikki ignored the distraction. "Did she share something with you that made you afraid?"

"I am not afraid."

Heat waited out her defiant glower through the smoke curl. After a few seconds Nikki spoke quietly as she laid out the crime scene death shots of Jeanne Capois in front of Opal, one by one. "Here is where they killed her. It's a trash storage area behind a prep school." She set out another. "Here is a close-up of what they did to her hands and fingers to make her talk." Then another. "This discoloration on her neck is where they choked her." Then one more. "This is what they did to her eyes. Poured antifreeze into them until they sizzled. See the discoloration?"

"Stop it! Don't!" She swept the pictures off the coffee table and turned away from them, covering her face. Nikki didn't know what sickened her more: seeing the photos again or using Opal's vulnerability to get what she needed from her. It didn't matter. Heat had a job to do.

"Whatever Jeanne Capois shared with you so you could make your movie got her killed. And you know that. Make it right. Will you help me get these guys?"

Opal Onishi didn't answer yes or no, but simply began in a very distant voice to narrate, as if doing a voice-over in one of her docs. "Jeanne Capois was special because she was just like all the others. A girl who grew up in poverty but raised with hope. Like a lot of the Haitians I have interviewed over the past year, hope is not just aspiration, but takes form in tenacity. It is how you survive, it is how you keep going in the face of life's unrelenting assault. Political corruption, violence, hunger, disease, squalor—even an earthquake does not stop them from seeking a better way." The ash fell from her cigarette and she absently ground it into the rug with her slipper, then turned to them.

"Jeanne told me she and her fiancé had been told a major hotel chain in the United States was looking for servicepeople to do the work the Americans were no longer willing to do. The man who met them at the patisserie in Pétionville bought them banana cakes and *presse cafe* and told them the hotel company had health insurance, training for advancement, and a weekly wage that surpassed what they could scrounge in a year in Haiti. They would also provide the transit to New York. Since Jeanne and Fabian had both lost family in the 2010 quake, they decided to take a chance and go.

"Everything changed once they boarded the ship, where their possessions were confiscated and they were locked in the holds below. They were trapped aboard for weeks as it went port to port. Jeanne said they knew where they'd been by the other people who came down into the holds with them. Dominicans, Venezuelans, Colombians, Jamaicans, Hondurans, Mexicans. Even a group of prostitutes the captain won in a card game in the Caymans."

"Was this a cruise ship?" asked Rook."

"A cargo vessel."

Nikki said, "I'm going to guess who owned it."

"If you guessed Keith Gilbert, you would guess right," Opal said. Nikki reflected on the visceral reaction Onishi had voiced last visit when she flashed his picture in the array. "The stories I got from other people enslaved by this ring—and it is slavery, let's call it what it is—were all transported on ships owned by Gilbert Maritime."

"I want to see these interviews," said Heat. "Starting with Jeanne's. And get transcripts, if you have them. If you don't, we can transcribe them."

Rook asked, "Did you also interview Beauvais?"

"No, I didn't." Then she held up her hands in a staving gesture. "Whoa, whoa, let's all hold on here. I'm cooperating, right? Like I'm not ducking your shit anymore, OK?"

"And?"

"And this material is mine. This is what I was afraid of when you came around before. I've spent a year making a film. I've got more interviews I want to do, more writing, and tons more editing. If I let this raw footage out and it starts circulating before I'm ready, I can pretty much kiss off my funding and distribution."

Heat felt pressure. Half a day—or less—before the interim precinct commander arrived and took her off the case. Desperate, but trying not to show it, she pushed buttons. "I guess I was wrong. From your résumé, I kind of had you figured as someone who wanted to help fight oppression and injustice."

It was a valiant effort, but Opal tapped out another cigarette, played with it, unlit, in her hand while she mulled, then said, "If the film releases properly, it'll do just that. Besides, I don't think you can make me." She turned to Rook, fishing for support. "Don't I get some protection as a journalist?"

He shrugged. "Might be debatable whether your indie project gets First Amendment protection. But I do have some perspective to share."

"Yeah?"

"Ever hear of Mary Ellen Mark?" Opal shook no. "We're going back thirty, thirty-five years here. Mary Ellen Mark was, and still is, a respected photojournalist who managed to gain access to Mother Teresa's mission in the Calcutta slums. She's going along, doing her job, snapping pictures of Mother Teresa and her volunteers working their asses off cleaning the lepers, mopping up after the sick, comforting dying kids, physically picking up and carrying the malnourished men and women she'd find collapsed in the gutters or sleeping in sewage. Mary Ellen got some great photos, too. Know what Mother Teresa said to her? She came up to her very calmly and said, 'You should put down your camera and do some work.'"

While Opal thought that over, Rook tapped her shoulder and added, "And if that's not good enough, imagine the media buzz and word of mouth *Smuggled Souls* will get if your film is instrumental in taking down a corrupt power broker and a human trafficking ring."

Opal Onishi cocked an eyebrow and smiled.

Jeanne Capois was alive. At least on film. And in that digital form, the twenty-something Haitian immigrant had achieved a sort of immortality. She exuded a goodness and quiet grace that filled the screen and the entirety of Detective Raley's media kingdom back uptown. Her Creole notes flowed musically around her even after she had spoken her words. The warm French flavor stood in sharp contrast to the disturbing testimony she was offering.

The backdrop was a bookcase—very Ken Burns-style—with her eyeline a few degrees off the camera lens as she spoke to her unseen interviewer, Opal Onishi. The young woman did not smile—this was all too intense for that—but Jeanne Capois looked like a person who commonly smiled, and made others join in just for seeing hers.

Nobody in the small room spoke. Not Raley, not Rook, not Detective Heat, who took notes and jotted time codes off the digits scrolling in a corner of the monitor so that Rales could assemble a highlight reel of the most damning allegations.

When the interview ended and the screen went dark, all three sat in silence, hearing only the cooling fans of the equipment and Rook muttering a small "Fuck."

Nikki swept aside a tear before the lights came up then tore the relevant sheets off her pad for Raley to edit by. Heat smelled that she was inches from the truth. She stood and said, "Let's go get this guy."

Detectives Rhymer and Feller had returned to the bull pen when Heat and Rook came back from their screening. They were particularly animated and it took some work for Nikki to adjust to their manic chatter after what she had just experienced. "Did I score something new, or did I not?" asked Feller.

"You did," said Rhymer. "Actually both. I was there. But it was mostly him."

"Maybe one of you could do me a favor before they try to pull the plug on this case anytime now, and just give me a report."

"I'll take this," said Feller, flattening a palm on his chest. "My quadrant—the one you assigned me from the Murder Board for drilling down—included the interview we conducted with Fidel "FiFi"

Figueroa. Lots to sift through there, but, skeevy as he is, the man gave us some good intel."

"Is this you getting to the point?" heckled Ochoa from his desk.

"Remember, Detective Heat, how he used a term to describe Fabian Beauvais?"

"*Astucia*," said Heat.

"Plus-ten for you. It occurred to me that you can't go around exhibiting balls like that, bluffing your way into office buildings with a sandwich cooler to steal documents without setting off a few alarms here and there."

"It's an odds game," offered Rhymer.

"Exactly. So I thought, let me take two elements." Randall held one hand to the sky and said, "Fabian Beauvais and his *astucia* right here. . . ." And then held his other hand up. "And bad shit involving Keith Gilbert here." He brought the hands together and interlocked his fingers. "So I got on the blower to the Real Time Crime Center and asked the detective on duty to run a computer search for incidents and complaints at the Gilbert Maritime tower on Madison, Midtown. Took a while to get back to me with the hurricane and all, but after we wrapped at Braun's commando post in the Bronx, I get the call. A trespass complaint weeks ago. No arrest, but officers responded, so it was in the database."

Nikki said, "I'm interested now."

"Just wait. We paid a visit. The building's closed like everything else today, but security's working. I get the security chief to look at the mug shot of Fabian Beauvais. Guess what he says."

" 'The sandwich guy,' " said Rook.

Feller made a slow rotation to him and said. "My punch line. I tell the whole friggin' story and you steal the punch line."

Rook shrugged contritely. "Sorry. . . . Inside thoughts, inside thoughts."

Rhymer, ever earnest jumped in. "Can we not lose track of the fact that we have established that Beauvais did work Gilbert's corporate HQ to steal documents in his cooler?"

"It's an important piece. Thorough work, you two. After the interview Heat just watched, she certainly knew why Beauvais was targeting

Gilbert. What she didn't know was what kind of information he had gotten on him. At least she didn't know yet.

Rook arrived at Nikki's desk. "What's up?"

"I'd like you to do something for me—that is, if you're not too busy."

"I smart with your implication. Don't you think a small word of acknowledgment is in order for me getting Opal Onishi to give up her raw video without a First Amendment battle?" Rook searched her face, and all he got was a flat stare. "Apparently that will have to wait. What can I do?"

"You know your old girlfriend at CIA?"

He enjoyed this moment. "Hm. You're going to have to be more specific. Which one?"

"Rook."

"Yardley Bell, yes."

"See if she's reachable. I have a favor to ask her."

"And that would be?"

"The one I will ask her when you get her on the phone for me."

"Right."

As he moved off to make his call, Sean Raley delivered a thumb drive to Heat. "Here's the edit you asked for of the Capois video. I'd call it the greatest hits, but it's more like low moments in humanity."

"Not many lower." As soon as the memory key left his fingers he rushed back toward his video realm. "You on a mission?" she called to him.

He turned, walking backward so he wouldn't lose any time talking. "Got an idea from something in my quadrant that put me onto some video."

"You look like you think you're onto something but won't tell. Are you onto something?"

"Could be useful, could be a bust. I need to scrub it to see if there's anything."

"Go to it, King."

But Detective Raley had already hurried out in his eagerness.

———

Inez Aguinaldo had called to alert Heat that she was en route with evidence from her search of Alicia Delamater's property at Beckett's Neck. When the lead detective from Southampton Village PD arrived just after noon, Nikki couldn't take her eyes off the brown paper forensics sack in her hand. But to show some grace for the courtesy and effort the Hamptons cop had extended, she minded her manners rather than ripping it from her like a three-year-old going for the presents at a birthday party.

After a hello to her buddy Rook—the bullet whisperer—and squad introductions, Heat thanked her for driving in. "Yeah, it was surreal, if you want to know. A ninety-minute trip that took me five hours. Thank God for all-wheel drive. Had to badge my way over the Throgs Neck Bridge just to get here. But I know you're up against the clock, so let's share our Sandy horror stories later, and get to the goods."

"If you insist," said Nikki, getting a laugh as she lunged for the property bag. Detective Aguinaldo held it open for her, and the squad tightened the circle around Heat as she reached in with a gloved hand and brought out a Sturm Ruger .38 Spl +P in a plastic Ziploc. "You get this at Alicia Delamater's?"

She nodded. "Last night. A half hour before the lights went out and the Atlantic Ocean creeped in her front door.

"Tell me it's his," said Nikki.

"Make and serial number is a match for the handgun Keith Gilbert has registered with the Suffolk County sheriff. We didn't do prints yet. I figured you'd want control of the lab process so there's no potential inter-department contamination for his defense attorneys to plead. As for ballistics, same deal. Plus your techs can probably turn that around faster than we could."

"You guys what, farm yours out to Korea?" said Rook.

Aguinaldo chuckled. "Might as well. The main thing is, I knew time was of the essence; want to get this in your hands right away."

As Nikki signed the chain of evidence voucher, Feller nodded toward the Ruger and said, "So I guess it's no longer the virtual smoking gun."

"Let's not get ahead of ourselves," cautioned Heat. "This is only one piece of many. And we haven't labbed it yet."

Detective Aguinaldo needed to hustle back to Southampton, and Nikki thanked her wholeheartedly her for all of the valuable assists all along the way. Handing Inez a thermal copy of the receipt for the revolver she asked, "Just out of curiosity, where did you find it?"

"In her home office trash can. Hidden under the plastic liner."

"Amateurs," said Ochoa. And the other detectives agreed.

Nikki drifted back to a week ago and said, "You never know what you'll find in a trash can."

Feller said, "Yeah, but she's got the whole ocean right there. Why keep it?"

"No kidding," said Rook. "Has no one ever heard, 'Leave the gun, take the cannoli'?"

Heat's e-mail chimed. She stepped to her desk, read the screen, and hung her head. "'S up?" asked Ochoa.

"From Zach Hamner at One PP. The interim precinct commander is on his way. With my orders for administrative leave. He'll be here in less than one hour." She typed a short reply and hit SEND. "Which means, I guess I'd better not be."

NINETEEN

A scramble. Nothing else could describe the charged atmosphere in the Homicide Squad Room of the Twentieth Precinct. Nikki covered the phone and alternately called out directions or hollered answers to questions from her crew, all the while keeping a compulsive check on the clock.

She finished her call with Yardley Bell of the CIA with both pretending to agree that they should get together sometime. "I hear you're up for the new task force," Rook's former girlfriend had said, causing Nikki to wonder if he had told her, or if Agent Bell was just that damned looped in.

"That's a can I'm kicking down the road for the moment," said Nikki. Heat thanked her for agreeing to do the favor, knowing she now owed one to the ex. "Ya do what ya have to do," she muttered to herself after she'd hung up.

Rook saw she was off the call and sauntered over. "You going to tell me the favor now?"

"Doesn't matter. She's not into three-ways." Then she craned to search the room. "Anyone seen Raley?" That sent Ochoa disappearing up the hall on a search.

"First of all, I beg to differ about Yardley. And second, I'm reckoning you have less than ten minutes," said Rook.

"You don't need to tell me, I'm pedaling as fast as I can." Nikki went over her mental checklist one last time. She had sent Detective Rhymer and a pair of policewomen off on their assignment forty-five minutes before. On the precinct cell phone she'd signed out to replace her waterlogged 4s, Heat received a confirmation text from him of a mission accomplished. Feller and a team of uniforms were in holding outside Zarek Braun's and Seth Victor's cages, at the ready. Now that she'd secured major help from Yardley Bell, she had one more call to make, but that would wait for the caravan.

"I think we're set to roll." Heat called in a loud voice. "Once we have the complete Roach."

"Then everyone grab your car keys," said Raley as he jogged in on the heels of his partner. "Sorry to keep you waiting, but, trust me, it was time very well spent." He held up his laptop and said, "I'll fill you in on the road."

Detectives Raley and Ochoa departed the bull pen for the Roach Coach. Nikki texted the green light signal to Feller while Rook gathered her files and the thumb drive. "Ready?" he asked.

In the sudden quiet of the empty squad room, Heat paused, ever-thorough, and ran her checklist one more time. With a parting glance to the Murder Board she said, "As I ever will be."

A deputy inspector with gold laurels and oak leaves pinned to his starched white uniform shirt stood in the doorway. He peered through the glass wall into Captain Irons's office, which sat dark, as it had since his killing, then turned his attention to the bull pen. "I'm looking for a Detective Heat."

Nikki approached him and said, "I'll let her know."

And then she and Rook double-timed out past him to the car.

Storms never just came and went. Nikki knew all too well that every tempest left its destruction; all fury spawned repercussions. En route to her objective, the caravan of four police vehicles led by Heat, who'd appropriated Captain Irons's former Crown Victoria, got a firsthand look at the aftermath of a super-storm in New York City. Uptown, the wet streets now reflected dazzling sunshine that intermittently broke between pinwheeling clouds on the rear end of Sandy. Heavy traffic slowed them at a detour around West Fifty-seventh Street where the arm of a construction crane at a new high-rise had collapsed in the monster winds and wagged precipitously seventy-five stories atop the site. Elsewhere, the sidewalks teemed with residents and tourists antsy from being cooped up and eager for a chance to restock pantries and assess the damage. Marathoners training for Sunday's upcoming race weaved down the sidewalks in defiance of doubters that the event would even be held.

The effects were more evident below Midtown where the power outage lingered, creating an exodus of citizens heading north to use uptown as their supermarket. Two major hospitals down there, Bellevue and NYU Langone, suffered generator failures and had to mount heroic-scale patient evacuations to health facilities outside the blackout zone.

In spite of the delays, blockages, and roundabouts of the journey, the small convoy finally arrived at its destination. Under a spot shower falling in the milky light, Heat got out for one last huddle with her squad, reviewing the choreography once again. Before going inside, she bent her head back for a look up at the height of the Port Authority office tower, and the rain felt good on her face. To everyone else, it was the last gasp of the super-storm. To Heat, it marked the leading edge of the torrent she was about to unleash upstairs.

Gaining access to the Port Authority Emergency Management Office came easily enough—if you planned ahead. Which is just what Heat had done. She was too experienced to come all that way with her entourage only to be turned back. So Nikki had phoned Cooper McMains, the commander of the NYPD Counterterrorism unit to discreetly secure entry for her entire group. The bond of trust that had developed between the commander and the detective was strong enough that he did not ask her the reason for her visit, nor did she volunteer it. She knew McMains to be not only one of the most trustworthy cops she'd met, but one of the smartest. In her heart, Heat believed he had her mission figured and was tactful enough not to carry the conversation further into potentially uncomfortable zones.

The result of laying such groundwork was to witness the utter shock on the face of Port Authority commissioner Keith Gilbert when Nikki Heat and Jameson Rook strode into his situation room during one of his press briefings. "Thank you," he boomed mid-question to the gathering of media, some of who reacted with dismay at the uncharacteristically short shrift when he stepped away from the podium. Gilbert was so taken aback that, for a moment, he waffled in place, unsure of which direction to go—to Heat, or away. Nikki decided to help the man decide.

"Commissioner Gilbert," she said, marching forward directly to him. "Detective Heat, NYPD. You remember me, I'll bet."

The commish smiled the politician's smile—the one that gets pasted on when there's a chance a picture might be taken. And God knew there was a press pool's worth of lenses surrounding them both. He put out his hand and when she took it he gave a hard squeeze then pulled her close so he could speak low in her ear through his grin. "What the fuck do you think you are up to?"

With a hand that still felt rubbery from the previous night's rodeo on the roof of the BearCat, Nikki returned a bone vise of her own. "What I'm paid to do, Commissioner. I catch murderers."

Behind her, the public information officer for Gilbert's campaign approached Rook. After greeting each other Rook said, "A little out of your area, aren't you, Dennis?"

"How so?"

"This isn't exactly a political event."

The PIO chuckled. "My friend, when you're ramping up for a nomination, everything is a political event. I've got a video guy here getting footage of him for future ads."

"Tell your guy to keep his lens cap off," said Rook. "He may get some unexpected candids." He moved over beside Heat, leaving the flak to wonder what that meant.

When he joined her, Keith Gilbert had turned his back to the press pool to square off with Nikki. His face was empurpled with suppressed rage. Still, he maintained a hushed tone. "What are you, some kind of a stalker? Use your goddamned head. Look around. You've come into my situation room in the middle of a crisis." Heat scanned the nerve center. Clearly the immediate danger had passed sufficiently that the other commissioners, officials, and their lieutenants were running things just fine on their own.

"Seems like things have slackened enough for you to do your media thing against this nice backdrop."

"Your guy's getting some sweet footage, too," added Rook with a thumbs up to Dennis and his shooter across the room.

"As usual, Heat, you're out of line and your timing sucks."

"Think so?" said Nikki. "I think my timing may be just about perfect."

"Hear me loud and clear. You are not going to make a scene in here. Especially not now." Then he saw something over Heat's shoulder that made his forehead tighten enough for the weathered creases to go smooth.

Across the room, Detective Rhymer stepped through the glass doors accompanied by two uniformed policewomen escorting Alicia Delamater. His spurned mistress gave him a hard glare that he broke off to sweep the area. All he saw were too many underlings. And press.

"Not in here."

"No," said Rook. "You can't have a situation in the situation room." And then, to explain, "*Strangelove*. The movie, not you and Alicia."

Gilbert put a hand on the shoulder of a woman who wore a headset. "Josephine, take over for a few, OK?" Then he turned back to Heat. "There's a more private room."

Nikki said, "I know."

Keith Gilbert speed walked to a side door then up a short corridor as if he could, through swiftness, shake the police and the ex. But when he opened the door to the conference room he lurched to a halt. Because inside, Nikki Heat had arranged a tableau to greet him. Detectives Raley and Ochoa had entered moments before to set up the monitors and audio playback in the high-tech boardroom, and stood with arms folded. At the far end of the long mahogany table sat a pair of urban mercenaries in orange, flanked by standees Randall Feller, plus two uniformed NYPD officers holding M16s pointed to the floor. It wasn't lost on Heat that they were guarding the very man who had put the mourning bands on their badges.

The dumbfounded commissioner remained in the doorway as Detective Rhymer, Alicia Delamater, and Rook filed in. Gilbert turned to the aide at his elbow and said, "Get Lohman."

"Good idea," said Heat. She gestured to the chair of honor and closed the door when Gilbert sat on the edge of the cushion, not quite ready to lounge back in the command pose he customarily adopted on that leather throne. "I'd want Frederic Lohman, too. I'd want the whole Dream Team. My guess is that it will take your lawyers a bit of time to get here. But look who I'm talking to. You've got all the latest data, so you know they're a long way off." His expression changed as if solving a puzzle and he started to rise. "And if you try to leave, we can always conduct this out there."

"That'd make some campaign ad," said Rook.

The commish sat down. Detective Heat left her spot by the door. "Alicia, I want to thank you for coming."

"Like I had a choice when your detective and those other two showed up at my hotel this morning." She indicated the policewomen whose backs were visible through the glass as they stood sentry outside.

"Legally, you could have refused," said Gilbert. It sounded like parental disapproval wrapped in a scold.

"Yeah? Well maybe I'm glad I'm here."

Perfect, thought Heat. Just what she'd counted on. Animosity, still raw and smarting. Once she knew Delamater had hidden the gun, Nikki hoped Alicia would still be pissed enough to give up her old flame as Beauvais's shooter. Especially in exchange for dropping charges on illegal possession of a firearm. Get 'em while they're hot, thought Nikki. She set a clear plastic evidence bag containing the Ruger on the table. Both Gilbert and Delamater went a shade paler.

Alicia whispered an "Oh my God. . . ."

"Where'd you find that?" said Gilbert as he cleared some phlegm. "Certainly not at my house." So this is how bad it gets when it goes bad, thought Heat. If there had been a bus in that room, Ms. Delamater would be wearing tread marks. But then, Nikki—and everyone—got a surprise. Everyone, that is, except Keith Gilbert.

"Oh. . . ." Alicia's mouth quivered as she lost her words.

Gilbert tried to shut her up. "Alicia. Stop. Right there." To Nikki's dismay, the lost woman responded to being directed, and began to consider his instructions. She might have just done that, stopped and asked for a lawyer. Except Keith had to add one more thing. "I'm serious, bitch. You've fucked up enough already."

Alicia reacted with a small jolt, as if slapped by an invisible hand. Then a resolve came over her and she rotated her head to Heat. "I was there that night."

"At Conscience Point?" Nikki gave her a sympathetic face to counter Gilbert's bullying. "It's OK, let it out, Alicia." Rook offered a handkerchief from his pocket, which Delamater took without noticing, and dabbed her eyes.

"Yes. I was there for his meeting—"

"Alicia."

"No, I want to say this." Her stance was so firm, it went beyond plea bargains or concerns about hiding a gun. "I was at Conscience Point for his meeting with Fabian."

"Beauvais?" asked Nikki for the record.

"Right. Keith told me about the blackmail. I didn't know what it was about, just that Fabian was putting the screws to him about some shit he'd dug up, and he wanted hush money."

Heat gave Gilbert a preemptive glance and said to her, "You're doing fine, keep going. You followed him in your car?"

"No." Nikki, Rook, and the other detectives flicked eyes at one another. This was veering from the scenario they had painted. "I was already there. Waiting."

"Alicia, I'm pleading with you, you don't have to do this."

"Mr. Gilbert, let her speak." Heat went back to her. "Alicia, why were you there waiting?"

"Because I had the gun."

That surprise sent more furtive looks around the table. "You brought the gun for Mr. Gilbert?" asked Heat.

"No, he didn't even know I'd be there."

"Why don't you just tell me what happened."

Delamater nodded. Done with tears, a resolve had come to her as if this was her pivotal moment to say what she needed to, or regret it every eternal dawn of her life. "I knew he was meeting Fabian, so I got there early. I parked on the lawn behind the marina offices so they wouldn't see my car and waited in the dark under the stairs.

"Fabian got there first, about a half hour before he said. He sat across the parking lot on the steps of the rec center like he told Keith he would." She tilted her head Gilbert's way. "When Keith pulled up and got out with the money, ten thousand, I think it was, and Fabian came forward . . . I stepped out and fired."

"Oh, Alicia, don't," moaned Gilbert.

Heat asked, "How many shots?"

"Two. It was dark. I was nervous, and I missed. Fabian ran. Keith yelled at me." She mimicked him disparagingly, " 'What the fuck did you do?' then he drove off to catch him. But he got away." That made sense to Heat, and would explain the second car the Conscience Point resident had heard speeding off. It was Alicia Delamater's.

A troubled silence hung in the room. Even the hardened prisoners at the other end of the table seemed riveted. But the same way something noisy refuses to get ground in the garbage disposal, elements of this story felt way off to Heat. It was out of whack enough that she wondered if this was some fabrication the two had cooked up. Didn't Beauvais say Gilbert shot him? But then again, Heat could understand how darkness and surprise might have led him to that assumption. She'd known seasoned cops to get it wrong in the fog of war. Nikki wished she had more time to reflect, but concern that Delamater would lose her impulse to unload her soul forced her to take a leap and trust her instincts.

"There's something I don't understand," said Nikki. "Why in the world would you do something as drastic as that?"

Gilbert jumped in. "Are you listening? The guy was shaking me down."

Heat ignored him and persisted. "Killing someone—with such premeditation. That is big. You would have to have a very strong reason." She avoided the word *motive*. No sense sobering her with legalities. Alicia didn't answer, just panted as if steeling herself for the next round.

In that interval, another piece of story grit rejected itself, and Nikki addressed it. "Also, can you help me with this? If you did go there with the intent to kill Fabian Beauvais, why didn't you just do it when he got there early?"

"Jesus fucking Christ. It was all to protect me, don't you get it?"

"You egotistical son of a bitch!" blurted Alicia. "I wasn't trying to protect you. I was trying to kill you." Heat had certainly figured Delamater to have been part of the incident in that marina parking lot. But as an eyewitness, at best; an accessory, at worst. Shooting the gun, and not just hiding it, was bombshell enough. But this. This was a twist even Heat had not seen coming. From his face, neither had Keith Gilbert.

"Fuck it. If I'm getting arrested for shooting at someone, at least it's going to be for the right person." Alicia continued to rail, imploring Heat to understand, "Keith and I reconciled after the restraining order. At least I thought we had. But then he cut me off when he officially decided to run for senator. Then he called me that thing again." Nikki silently pronounced the words as Delamater said them aloud. "A political liability."

"Leesh," said Gilbert in a bedroom voice, "we don't need to—"

"Suddenly, I'm fucking off the boat." Alicia clapped her hands together. "Just like that."

Rook jumped into the conversation. "So you used the payoff as a setup to kill Keith and make it look like Beauvais did it?" He turned to Nikki. "Sorry, I just kinda got caught up in this."

Heat said, "Was that the idea, Alicia?" And when she nodded, Nikki asked, "And you wounded Fabian by accident, or were you going to kill him, too?"

"I didn't need to kill him. Who'd believe him? I mean, come on." The ugliness of the statement matched the actions.

"Alicia, Goddamn it, I helped you."

"You helped yourself, as usual. You weren't protecting me. You kept quiet because if it ever got out what happened, all the questions would hurt your stupid campaign. So don't fucking insult me."

Stunning as it was, this version worked for Heat. She could even picture how Alicia got the Ruger. Back when Detective Aguinaldo responded to the prowler call at Cosmo, and Gilbert had his gun out, Delamater was there. Which made it feasible that she not only knew he kept the .38 locked in a desk, but she saw him get the key from the cabinet. Sneaking onto the property weeks later to get it would have been no problem. Even Topper the guard dog wouldn't stop Alicia because he knew her.

The pragmatist in the commissioner weighed in. "Detective, I think what's happened here is that I am now exonerated from any wrongdoing in the shooting of this illegal. In fact, I'm technically the victim, aren't I?"

But the wounding of Beauvais represented only one piece of the entire case jigsaw, and Heat moved forward to the next. "Except with Fabian Beauvais running around as a loose end, you had to do something about that." Heat's attention turned to Zarek Braun and Seth Victor, who remained stoic. "Am I right?"

"Bullshit." Gilbert flung a hand in the direction of the prisoners. "Why are these guys here, anyway?"

"Are you saying you don't know them?" asked Heat.

"Nope. Don't."

"Are you certain?"

Gilbert leaned toward them and glowered. "I have never seen them before this moment."

Nikki moved on. All things in time. "What was Fabian Beauvais's shakedown about?"

"I have no idea."

"Mr. Gilbert, we know that a complaint got called in to the Midtown North Precinct by *your* security at *your* corporate office building when *your* extortionist, Fabian Beauvais, was seen trespassing."

"Trivia like that wouldn't come to my attention."

"I expect not. But the reason for his trespassing was that he routinely stole documents for use in ID theft and fraud. I want to know what he scored that made you want to pay him off, and when that failed, to kill him."

"You're back where you were, Heat, clutching at straws."

Watching Keith Gilbert rock back in his executive chair, the picture of confidence and self-possession, sage words reverberated from her past—the wisdom of her beloved mentor, Captain Charles Montrose, who once said, "Nikki, never underestimate the ability of the devils among us to see only the saints in themselves. How else could they go about their day?" Heat decided it was time to hold up a mirror.

"Fabian Beauvais was planning to get married. His fiancée's name was Jeanne Capois. She's dead now. Murdered." Nikki briefly took in Zarek Braun. The man in charge of that killing registered nothing. "But before she died—and, probably why she died—Jeanne sat for some interviews with a documentary filmmaker. She had some interesting revelations."

Detective Raley started the video selects he had copied to the thumb drive. The beauty of Opal Onishi's interview technique was that it required no setup. Even edited down to four minutes of essentials, Jeanne Capois's story was self-contained. Her lovely image filled the flat screen and, thus, the entire conference room as she recounted the journey she and Fabian had made from Haiti to America by way of the filthy, crowded, suffocating hold of a cargo vessel.

The core of her narration spoke of hopes raised, then dashed, then crushed over weeks that turned into months of squalid living conditions, debasement, and cruelty from their various overseers before landing in New York for hopeless days and nights of soul-robbing labor in exchange for a shitty meal and a putrid mattress in a locked room. "At first, I always asked the others," she said, " 'Why don't you run?' and they would all say the same: 'Even if we could get away, where would we go?' " Their bondage came from deadbolts and violence, for sure. But penniless foreigners, illegals in a strange land with no connections, were doubly captive.

"Fabian said he would make us free, and I believed him. My Fabby, he has intelligence and courage. So we did our labor. And we kept doing it, waiting for our chance. I was afraid they would put me into prostitution like the other girls, but they kept me in the *entrepôt*—the, um, warehouse—sorting papers and putting the tiny shred pieces together to make documents. I was worth more than sex work because I could read.

"We did that all last year. Then Fabian—he's so smart—he got trusted with an outside job. With one of the crews that harvested paper from trash at office buildings. So he did that and then somehow got a side job butchering chickens to make enough to get us away. We have no money, though. I clean an apartment for a nice old man But my fiancé, he says he found out a way to make a big lot of money to get us home to Port-au-Prince and have our lives back.

"From anyone else, I would say big talk. But Fabian is smart and has that courage. He said he knows who runs the boats that brought us all here, and he is going to make him pay for him not to go to the police. He found out he is a powerful, rich man named Keith Gilbert. I hope Fabian knows what he is doing. Sometimes, I think he is too smart." Her chuckle was the last thing on the screen before it went blank.

When all eyes in the room went from the flat screen to Gilbert, he dismissed their stares. Alicia's especially bored into him in disgust.

"Oh come on, are you serious? I deny that."

"It's from the mouth of one of your human traffic victims," said Rook.

"You print that, I'll sue." He turned to Heat. "You try to take that to court, you'll get laughed out. It's hearsay. Reality-show theater. Where's the proof? It can't be substantiated."

"What if it could be?" asked Alicia. His head whipped toward her, but she was leaning the other way, sober faced, to address Heat.

"If it could be, that would be important," said Nikki.

"Let's talk about this then. I'm in trouble, I know it. I didn't kill anyone. I'm so sorry I hurt that man, but I didn't kill him, did I?"

Nikki had been in these conversations so often, she could lip-synch them. So she began. "Are you saying you want some kind of deal?"

"If I told you what Fabian was blackmailing him with, would that be worth something?"

"Do you know what it was?"

"She doesn't. This is bullshit."

"Would it help? What if I said I knew where the documents were?"

Heat said to Alicia, "Ms. Delamater, if you have material evidence to lead to an arrest and conviction in this case, I will offer you a deal."

"What kind?"

"Fuck you both."

"I will personally speak to the DA about making the most liberal deal possible. I can't promise you what, but I can promise it will be the best they can do."

They waited as Alicia, the cast out mistress and political liability, weighed all that. "They were shipping manifests." She fixed an icy grin on her ex-boyfriend, who rolled his eyes. "Shipping manifests, including names of men, women, and children I realize now must have been slaves, or whatever you'd call them." Gilbert dismissed her with a loud exhale, but she went on. "There is also accounting of how much was paid per unit. That must mean people."

"You're guessing."

Unfazed by him, no longer under his thumb, Alicia continued. "There was more. Not only manifests but an accounting printout of bank transfers going back over nine years. I spent a whole weekend reading them after you shut me out, Keith."

"What kinds of transfers were they?" asked Heat.

"They all came out of the big fund generated by moving the units. *Units*, God, that's sick. But the payouts were a million here, a half mill there—millions and millions over time to accounts with weird names. Let me think. Most of the payments went to one called Framers Foremost."

"Alicia," snapped Gilbert.

"Framers Foremost?" said Rook. "That's a super PAC named after the framers of the Constitution. They're a clearinghouse that bank-rolls political candidates." He turned to Gilbert. "So that's it. You were using your ships for human trafficking so you could generate income off the books to launder into a political war chest. Brilliant!"

And then Rook realized what he had said. "I mean, in a completely evil-genius sort of way. Ah . . . Heat?"

"Is that why you were doing all this, Mr. Gilbert? To skirt election laws to launder your campaign funds as soft money to PACs?"

"Enjoy yourselves. This is all talk."

"No, I have the documents," said Alicia. "I noticed some things had been moved in my garage and found a manila envelope hidden under my golf bag a few days after the shooting—after you told me you'd handle everything. I kept it, in case someday one of the things you decided to handle was me. Same reason I kept the gun instead of throwing it in the ocean like I told you I did."

Gilbert scoffed. "You're bullshitting. If you even do have any documents—"

"Oh, I do," said Alicia to Heat. "In a friend's safe-deposit in Sag Harbor."

"Doesn't matter. Doctored papers with no verification? Illegally obtained? By fucking lowlife, Third World scavengers? My lawyers would suppress without breaking a sweat. You've shown nothing here linking me to any of this."

Nikki flopped back in her chair and searched the faces of her squad. "He's right. I hate to say it, but he's right."

"About fucking time." Gilbert rose to leave.

"So there's only one thing left to do." Heat nodded, and Detective Raley bent over the video controls.

"Can I say it?" asked Rook.

Raley said, "You got it."

Rook stood up. "Cue the zombies."

The harsh scraping of a creaking door filled the conference room, but it wasn't from Keith Gilbert leaving. In fact, upon hearing it, he took his palm off the brushed aluminum handle and turned to gape at the flat screen with everyone else.

It was nighttime on the video, and the camera panned across dark forms lying on sand. This was amateur handheld stuff—uneven moves and a rocking horizon. But the audio sounded professional-grade, especially the wolf howl that had to have come from a sound effect recording. Then a familiar—even iconic—musical beat began, and the dark forms all stood up at once, revealing dozens of young people in tattered rags and hokey stage makeup.

Zombies.

When the colossal signature notes of Michael Jackson's *Thriller* sounded, the splash of brass and organ raised gooseflesh on Heat. The song always had that impact, even as a little girl, but more so at that moment as she watched her prime suspect tugging at his goatee, watching the case against him become undead. "You recognize this, Keith?" she shouted over the din. On the giant LED behind her, college students threw their heads back, stomped, and rotated in choreographed unison, lit by moonlight and flaming tiki torches.

"Let me refresh your memory," Nikki said. "That's your backyard at Cosmo. And this is the *Thriller* flash mob one of my detectives found posted on YouTube." Over at the video deck, Raley took a slight bow.

"So? It was annoying then, and it's annoying now."

She took a step nearer so she wouldn't have to yell. "I know. So annoying that you called the police."

Rook did a Vincent Price impression. "For terrorizing yawl's neighborhood."

The music on the video abruptly stopped and the dance lines sputtered to a halt as several Southampton cops arrived on the scene. One of the undead, through a blistered, ash-blue face with one side melting, said something like, "We're just having a beach party" to a policeman.

"I don't see why this is relevant," boomed Gilbert, in a voice still pitched to be heard over the music. But just as he said it, there was a chorus of boos from the college kids. The camera operator panned to the edge of the mob and zoomed to Keith Gilbert who was in animated discussion with another cop, a uniformed sergeant.

He was far enough away that only pieces of his diatribe could be picked out. Snippets came though like "my fucking taxes," and "private property" that were as embarrassing as they were trite. Nikki wondered how many times law enforcement in wealthy neighborhoods had to endure those words. Then Heat saw what she was waiting for and called to Raley, "OK, Sean, right there."

The video froze on a still vignette of the patient Southampton Village police sergeant, the irate Cosmo resident, and several men who were standing behind him. They were in the dim shadows, but recognizable to those who knew Nicholas Bjorklund, Roderick Floyd, and Zarek Braun. The first two men, Heat had killed when they attacked her in Chelsea. The third man was quite alive. Nikki didn't turn, but she heard him sniff back sharply at the other end of the table. Gilbert said nothing. His eyes pinballed in their sockets as he scrambled to access his next lie.

"And just in case you are you still going to contend you never met this gentleman. . . ." Heat signaled to Raley who resumed play of the YouTube show. The camera jounced as the operator drew closer to the complainant and the cop. Just as the lens arrived, Gilbert walked over, put his arm around Zarek Braun's shoulder and whispered something. The mercenary, dressed for leisure in an untucked Nat Nast bowling shirt, nodded in agreement—or obedience. The property owner nosed up to the sergeant and said, "If you won't take care of it, my security will."

And the signature *Thriller* notes blasted, punctuating the threat as the video jumped to a disappointed flash mob dispersing. When the credit said THE END, Rook applauded.

Nobody else clapped, but Heat flashed a smile to Raley, who retained his title as her King of All Surveillance Media for catching the notation in his Murder Board quadrant about the otherwise minor flash mob complaint, and drilling down.

The commissioner palmed the table to steady himself and sat back down. Heat sauntered to the other end of the room and stood behind Zarek Braun. "Zarek, I am going to give you one final opportunity to talk." At the opposite end of the mahogany, Gilbert lasered him with a ruthless stare.

"I have nothing to say."

"You're sure about that? Think. It may be the most important decision of your life." The hired killer didn't reply, except to twist to peer up at her and then turn away in disregard.

"Your choice." Then Nikki said, "Miguel?"

Detective Ochoa went to the door and hand signaled to someone through the glass.

Keith Gilbert had no idea who the man was who entered the room, but he must have been alarmed by Zarek Braun's reaction. Heat watched orange denim bunch at his shoulders at the sight of his former employer from Lancer Standard, Lawrence Hays. "Do you two know each other? It's a small world, I guess."

Heat made her way to the middle of the conference table for a view of Braun, and he of her. "Thank-you for coming on short notice, Mr. Hays."

"Wouldn't pass this up."

"Zarek, I should probably fill you in," said Nikki. "I have been in contact with federal officials about you. CIA, in particular. There seems to be a high degree of interest in you. So, in the spirit of interagency cooperation, I have received the go-ahead to employ this gentleman's firm, a known special services contractor to the United States government, to provide you secure transport today."

The prisoner spoke for the first time, and he did not sound like such a cool customer. ". . . Where?"

"Now, that wouldn't be very secure, would it?" Heat slipped him a sympathetic grin. "But, since you have made it clear you have nothing to offer me, I see no reason to hold up whatever plans the feds have for you. Mr. Hays, are you set?"

"Oh, yes. I've got a Gulfstream 450 all fueled up in Westchester, set to roll. You ready to take a little trip, Z-Bra?"

Zarek Braun stared at the man he had failed to kill and knew all the consequences that would come under his supervision. Zarek could imagine the black hood. The rendition. The lengthy, unspeakable physical and psychological tortures that would leave him gasping, pleading to die. He knew these things because he had inflicted them himself routinely over the years. The whole history of their savage, warring ways played out in the milliseconds of their held stares. The hollow silence of that instant felt like the eternity after the metallic snap of a rifle bolt in the dark.

The mercenary disconnected from Lawrence Hays, passed his glance above Gilbert so he would not see him, and came to rest on Heat. Nikki recognized the dispirited eyes of defeated soldiers from textbooks and war documentaries. But the detective held no sympathy for this one. Especially when she heard his statement.

"I first worked for him providing elite security on his cargo ships to keep the Somali pirates from hijacking them. Now and then I would do other odd jobs for him. For this assignment, he called me in after he fucked things up trying to handle the payoff himself."

"Who called you in?" Heat pressed for detail so that he knew this was for the record. "I want you to say the name."

As his last futile attempt at defiance, he flared. "Him, Keith Gilbert. Did you not understand who I am talking about?"

Nikki took a seat and angled it toward Braun. "What did Keith Gilbert ask you to do? Specifically."

"What it is that I do. Take him out."

"He told you to kill Fabian Beauvais?"

"Jesus, yes. *Jasna cholera*, he said to kill him. Kill him and to make the problem go away."

"Including killing Jeanne Capois?"

"That was not specified. But I am not stupid. When a problem needs to go away, I know what that means, right?"

"So you also killed Jeanne Capois as part of your contract with Gilbert?"

"Yes."

Heat suppressed a lilt of excitement. The Port Authority commissioner had bent over with his elbows on his thighs and practically had his chin on the table while his hit man sang. She tamped down the thrill because she wasn't there yet; there were still details—vital stuff—that were necessary to get on record to lock the case down. If that worked, there'd be ample time to do a happy dance.

"How did you come to kill Fabian Beauvais."

"Can I tell you a funny thing? That was an accident." Zarek laughed alone. "OK, not so funny he died, but I was meant to kill him later."

"Mr. Braun," said Heat, "how did you come to kill Fabian Beauvais?"

"I had him at my hide."

"Up in the Bronx?"

"That place, yes. I needed to find out who else knew about this blackmail, this, how you say . . . extortion information. I worked on him good. But he was stubborn. I thought fuck it. I knew Mr. Gilbert flew in from Southampton on his helicopter, so I had the pilot pick me up after it dropped him off for his speech. So the chopper picked us up in Crotona Park near my place, and I took the bastard for a little thrill ride to loosen his tongue." He paused, sharing a brief, knowing look to Hays. "It is a legitimate technique of interrogation."

Heat had an idea, but needed it said. "Describe it."

"It is a terrifying thing to behold a potential fall from great heights. Men talk. They always do. Beauvais talked. He fought hard, very hard. But he gave up this fiancée. The maid on West End Avenue." Nikki's heart clinched at imagining Fabian's anguish at giving up his lover in terror, and of the indelible picture of Jeanne Capois at her murder scene as a result.

"After the Haitian talked, I brought him in the hatch. The plan was to drop him over the ocean, past the Rockaways. But he still had fight. His hands were zip tied, but he tried to butt my head. I smacked him. A little too hard, huh? Out he went."

And then came the shared thought of the detectives and Rook. Each one rerunning the tourist video taken outside the planetarium that had captured Beauvais's plummet into the glass.

Rook said, "I thought there was no reported copter traffic that morning."

"Only police and government," said Ochoa, who directed himself to Gilbert. "Government chopper. Son of a bitch. . . ."

Nikki steered Zarek Braun back on track. "So Fabian Beauvais's information led you to the home invasion? You and your guys did that, too?"

"Completing the assignment, lady."

"Even if it meant killing an old man?"

"Shit happens."

"And why did you torture Jeanne? Why not just kill her?"

"Because her boy gave up that she was talking to some filmmaker. The maid cashed out before we got a name or address."

"So you followed me to Chelsea," said Nikki.

"Where you killed my two best men."

"Shit happens."

Nikki took a moment to run everything in her head. She'd been through this once before with unhappy results. Satisfied, she stood and surveyed her people: Raley, Ochoa, Feller, Rhymer, and finally, Rook. She wordlessly checked them for assent. They all gave her good-to-go nods.

"Stand up, please," she said when she reached the head of the table.

This time, as Detective Heat read off the charges for his arrest, Commissioner Keith Gilbert, billionaire, power broker, senatorial hopeful, and golf buddy with the mayor, did not bite back. Like Hurricane Sandy, his bluster, too, had become a spent force. This time he knew Heat had nailed him.

TWENTY

That night, with the blackout from the massive arc at the Con Ed plant still darkening the lower half of Manhattan, Rook said he couldn't see the point of roughing it in their apartments and, after several calls, managed to score a junior suite at the Excelsior Hotel uptown, a lovely spot to camp out. He was in the shower when she came in, exhausted from the day, the week, the everything. Nikki announced herself from the bedroom then noticed he must have gone back down to Gramercy Park. A half dozen of her outfits hung tidily in the closet. He'd even brought shoes.

Over the stream of the shower, Rook put on a goofy show for her, singing "Reunited and it feels so good."

"You know," she called through the open bathroom door, "that would be fifty percent less creepy if you weren't in there alone." Which made him stop. But then he started again, only this time, belting out a Vegas lounge spoof of "After the Lovin'." Nikki might have laughed if she didn't feel the shadow of a pending, very big conversation looming over her.

Toweled and wearing one of the hotel's plush terry robes, he joined her in the sitting area and poured them each a glass of Hautes-Côtes de Nuits from the bottle in the ice bucket. "Nice digs," she said after they toasted.

"You kidding? It has everything. Electricity, electricity, and electricity. Plus, it's an easy walk to the precinct. And check out the view." He took her to the window and parted the drape, revealing the twinkling Upper West Side skyline, and more prominently, the Hayden Planetarium directly across the street. "Hm, makes it kind of a busman's holiday, huh."

"A little." It had been just over a week since Fabian Beauvais crashed into that museum; now there was no trace of the event. The giant powder blue orb glowed as usual inside the glass cube that illuminated the neighborhood with its gentle glow. She found the couch and her glass of wine. "Thanks for picking out some clean clothes for me."

"My pleasure. But just to be clear, this suite is clothing-optional. In fact, see this sash?" He waved the loose end of the robe's belt and gave a licentious flick of his brow. "Guess what happens when you pull this."

Heat smiled thinly. "Hey, now there's a turn on." She didn't fault him for being playful. Nikki was busy feeling the weight of the confrontation on the horizon.

He joined her on the sofa and they talked, both deciding against any tube. Besides, Rook had watched the news all night and gave her the summary. Mostly it was about the devastation on Staten Island and along the Jersey shore. Little or no looting, in spite of the blackout. "Oh, and on *News 3 @ 10*, Opal Onishi was Greer Baxter's guest on "Greer and Now," showing clips from her Jeanne Capois interview."

"That's good. . . . I guess." Nikki tried to balance mixed feelings about self-promotion versus getting the message out about human trafficking, and decided it wasn't her call to make.

Of course the only other non-Sandy news was the rearrest of Keith Gilbert. "You know that cardboard crown I gave Raley for being the media king? I should do better than that after he found that flash mob video."

"See? Early on I knew zombies figured into this case somewhere. And you dismissed me."

"Rook, you're like that broken clock you hear about that's right twice a day."

He grinned. "I'm sorry, the only thing I heard was something about me being right." She gave him a swat. "What's happening at the Twentieth with the interim dude?"

"I wouldn't know. I haven't been there yet. We processed Keith Gilbert at the nearest precinct, the One-three. When I was finishing, I got a call to drive to the OEM headquarters in Brooklyn."

"Office of Emergency Management? Why there?"

"Because everyone from One PP is over there. Commissioners, Commander McMains, The Hammer. . . ." Heat looked down and used a finger to scoop a cork crumb out of her glass. "I guess I got back on their radar today. They wanted to meet with me about the job on the task force."

"And they offered it to you?"

She wiped the cork on a napkin and brought her eyes up to meet his, knowing how emotionally loaded this subject was, but getting it on the table, at last. "Yes."

"And what did you tell them?" He held up a hand. "Wait. Don't tell me. I mean not yet. I just remembered. I want to show you something first. Don't move."

Rook dashed out of the room with his robe parting in a most undignified way. She heard the zip of his overnight bag and he came out, hiding something behind his back. Keeping his hand hidden he rejoined her on the couch. Nikki's mouth felt dry. The wine wasn't quenching it.

"OK," he said, "where do I start? Recently, while I was in Paris, I made a quick side trip to one of my favorite jewelers in the Marais."

"Oh, really? . . ." The college theater arts actress in Nikki hoped she sold ignorance to him.

"Why, you may ask? Because . . . last spring I had left him my mother's antique engagement ring to put a bigger diamond in the setting, and I wanted to pick it up." He brought his hand from behind his back and opened a bag—the one she had spotted in his kitchen trash can—and pulled out a small case that he opened and held out to her. "What do you think of the job he did on Mom's ring?"

Nikki didn't need to act at that point. "Rook . . . I'm, I'm speechless."

"Édouard—he's the master jeweler there. Been there forever. Probably designed those candlesticks Jean Valjean stole. Didn't he do a great job?"

"Oh. Very, um, quite." She was struggling to hold her composure, feeling foolish and, yes, crestfallen. "Very, very nice craftsmanship."

"*C'est très bon, n'est ce pas?*"

"Ah." Then she heard a wooden semblance of her own voice say, "*. . . Oui.*"

"Good, because otherwise you might not want to wear it."

At first Nikki thought she'd misheard. She was so blitzed from the week's ordeal, and so caught up in the shock of learning that receipt had been for his mother's ring, that it seemed as if Rook was trying to indicate this engagement ring was actually for her. But that must have been what Rook meant, because he was taking it out of the case and holding the big diamond up to her. She stared at it, flabbergasted, as all the facets sparkled in an infinitely stunning display of pure light. "Rook. Are you saying. . . ."

"I am saying this is for you."

"Your mother's engagement ring?"

"Don't worry, Mom's got a whole box of them. I dropped a quarter in the slot and worked the claw to pick out this one."

They both laughed. "Romantic," she said.

"Just because I ghostwrite romance novels doesn't mean I have to be romantic."

"No, this is plenty romantic. In a twisted, Rook kind of way." Her face grew serious and she said, "I think before we go further we need to clear some air first."

". . . All right. Is this going to be about the task force?"

"In essence, yes." She held a shielding hand up to the ring and chuckled. "Can you put that aside for a second? It's very hard to concentrate."

"That's the whole idea." He flashed it in her face again to tease, then slipped it back in the velvet and closed the lid.

"I haven't figured out how to put this," she said at last, "so can I just spew?" After his affirming nod she embarked. "I've wondered why this task force job was such a flash point. It really got us both at each other."

She paused there to allow him a space to speak, but he just showed agreement, so she proceeded. "I asked myself why. When I heard about it, I knew it was an exciting job and a big promotion. But what did I do? I hid it from you. By reflex. Why? Because I knew it created major challenges for us. Logistically, in our lifestyle, and—here comes: as a couple. There's a concept, right? A couple. Talk about an exciting job and a big promotion."

He held his silence, letting her roll. "That job offer pushed me to define things. Define us." Nikki shrugged a tiny shrug. "And to define me. I don't mean me without you. I just mean, as a test of whether

I am still young enough and independent enough to make choices in my life."

"On your own."

She borrowed a phrase from her shrink session with Lon King. "I can't solve my life in ten minutes in a hotel room. But, even though I don't have all the answers, I do know a few things after this week. Like, I know we are good together. You make me laugh. You shake me out of my earnestness and task-orientation. You're the only one I ever met who also gets bugged by missing commas." She laughed.

"I'm your comma cop."

"My punctuation police."

"Did I hear good in bed?"

"Awesome in bed; are you serious? . . . But, as much as I feel that we belong together, the idea of taking it to the next level scared the hell out of me."

"Wait." He held up the jewelry case. "Are you saying you knew about this?"

"A woman knows." Not prepared yet to bust herself for her trash can revelation, she let it go at that, which he seemed to buy. "So what did I do? I fought with you. I accused you of things."

"You baptized me with top-shelf tequila."

"I didn't know what the upset was." She churned her hands in front of her chest. "It was all this stuff kicking inside me. All the quaint little idiotic theories you always come up with started feeling like attacks, so I hit back." She rested a hand on his knee. "When I almost lost you in the car last night, I freaked. I thought I saw you take your last breath before you went underwater. And you used it to tell me you loved me."

A choking sob escaped, and Nikki fought to hold it together. "Rook, I couldn't picture myself without you. And reflecting on it now, I'm seeing what I was fighting with all week wasn't you. It was the fear of losing my independence. I know it may sound selfish and indulgent—even a bit Self-Help section—but I need to be true to myself. You know, even in a relationship—no, *especially* in a relationship—I need to have that independence for it to be healthy. Does that make sense to you?"

He swayed a few inches side to side, a writer choosing his words. "Well, Nikki, may I make it short and sweet?" After she wiped a tear, he continued, "It so happens that this independent woman you are describing is the one I love."

In the last hour of the day, at the end of a dark week, Nikki could swear she saw a rainbow. "Yeah?"

"Yeah."

"Let's see if you feel that way when you hear about my new job."

Points for Rook—he didn't blink, didn't falter. "Please," he said, and took a long pull on his white burgundy, waiting.

"It's going to mean a lot of long hours, extra responsibility, days and nights apart, broken plans more common than not. It's going to be a ballbuster."

"So you you're on the task force. Congratulations."

"No, I turned it down."

"OK, now you're just fucking with me."

She laughed. "And you just didn't, with the ring?"

He lifted his glass to her. "Touché."

"They offered it to me, that's why they called me there. I said thank-you, but no, thank-you."

"But I told you we could weather this, Nikki. I meant what I said about your independence."

"I didn't do it for you. How indie is that? I did it because there's a job that interests me more. A job where I know I am needed. I turned it down once before, but now I am ready."

"You're taking over the Twentieth Precinct."

"Damn it, Rook, do you ever let anyone deliver their own punch line?"

"Apparently not. Continue."

"They weren't delighted, that's safe to say. But they got it. I saw what happened last time when I passed, and they brought in Wally Irons. Then I got a look at that doofus today, and I could see it happening all over again. To my squad."

"I am with you a hundred percent."

"Tell me that when we have our fifth canceled dinner in a row."

"And this would be new?" He thought a moment and said, "Don't you have to be a captain to command a precinct?"

"I already passed my boards, remember? The Hammer still has my gold bars in his desk drawer from three years ago when I told him to shove them where the sun don't shine."

Rook hefted the jewelry case in his palm. "Is that what you're going to tell me?"

Heat finished her wine, set her glass on the coffee table, then bounced on the couch cushion to face him. "I don't know. Let's find out."

He slid off the sofa, lowering himself on one knee before her. In that instant all the light in the firmament, the sum total of the heavenly glow of the sun, the moon, the stars, the comets, and the planets conspired to fall on the beaming face of Jameson Rook. Nikki's skin chilled with excitement and irrepressible glee and she swallowed hard. Keeping his eyes true, caressing hers while she cradled his, he reached out a hand and she took it, thinking, thank God his fingers were trembling, too. His smile filled her heart, and somehow it grew bigger as he finally spoke.

"Well, Captain Heat. . . ."

A sound came out of her, whether a laugh or a cry, it was born of joy, and that's all that mattered. ". . . Yes, Mr. Rook?"

"I have loved you from the first day we met. And, as unbelievable as it would have seemed to me then, I love you more now—this day, at this moment—than I ever have."

Nikki wanted to say I love you to him, and almost did, but didn't dare interrupt. So she told him with her face.

And he got it.

"Nikki, I believe in destiny. Not only has everything I've ever done led me to you, every time we are apart—whether I'm in Paris or a jungle or across town in Tribeca—I measure everything, every minute, every breath, by how soon we can be together again. Which, in a way, means we are never really apart. But here. Now. Together like this. This is what I want forever. To spend the rest of my life with you. And you with me. Rockin' happiness."

After working some swagger, he paused before he continued. "I want to be your husband. And I want you to be my wife." He started to choke up and some water rimmed his eyes. Rook collected himself, held out the ring, and smiled at her—an angel's smile. "Nikki Heat, will you marry me?"

ACKNOWLEDGMENTS

First off, I am not Richard Castle. It seems proper to get that out up front, although certainly you have already discerned that from the absence of his flair in this section. Normally, Mr. Castle would write this part himself, but circumstances I'm not at liberty to discuss have intervened to make him . . . unavailable by deadline. So it falls to me, this lowly junior editor, to fulfill his wishes by acknowledging those who assisted him with this book. Please bear with me. Searching his office, I found his notes to be less than organized, and anyone I could consult for clarification is too rattled to talk. Here is my best offering gleaned from his work space.

In his Moleskine I came upon a starred page calling Kate Beckett "my muse, my inspiration, and my life." Underneath that, something that looks like it says, ". . . in space they can't hear you scream, but can they hear you say 'I do?' "

Clearly he wanted to thank the Twelfth Precinct. He lists Javier Esposito and Kevin Ryan with "bro" printed beside each. Then Captain Victoria Gates, with a question: "Is it possible for a smiley face to frown?" He drew an arrow from that scrawl to Dr. Lanie Parish, so there must be some smile versus frown connection to her, as well.

There's no doubt he wanted to highlight his mother, Martha, and his daughter, Alexis—simply because he did that—highlighted them, literally. With a highlighter.

On his desk, under a ten-pound slug of iron from a scuba belt he was using as a paperweight, I found a list of names with the heading "Magical" on top. The list follows: "Nathan, Stana, Seamus, Jon, Molly, Susan, Tamala, and Penny." Beneath that, a note to "Thank the wizards in the Clinton Building." One assumes that is not a reference to the presidential library because he had added "Raleigh Studios" to his annotation.

Of all places, spiked to the rotor tips of a motorized toy helicopter (!), were two pieces of scratch paper. The first mentions Terri Edda Miller "for keeping me aloft." The other name appears to be Jennifer Allen and it's printed on a sketch of a hot air balloon shaped like a heart.

In a file drawer, almost hidden under a pair of Slinky eyeglasses, I found a map of the Hamptons with some marginalia acknowledging the Southampton Town PD duty officer for "answering my dumb questions," plus a brochure from the 1770 House in East Hampton with a reminder to thank the manager for the personal tour.

I thought that was that until I noticed the cabinet above his espresso maker was plastered by Post-its. I hope I have the order correct: "My stalwart agent, Sloan Harris; Executive Editor Laura Hopper [my boss]; Ace researcher, Christopher Soloway; Ellen Borakove, for 'all things OCME'; John Parry, for 'the Dutchess County GPS 411'; Clyde Phillips, for clearing writing space; Ken Levine, for blog shout outs and support."

Apparently the author also wishes to acknowledge Lisa Schomas, ABC's *Castle* franchise manager, as well as Melanie Braunstein of ABC, who so ably handles book promotion. This is because I found a note stuck in his blotter that reads: "Don't forget to acknowledge Lisa Schomas, ABC's *Castle* franchise manager, as well as Melanie Braunstein of ABC, who so ably handles book promotion." I'm not a mystery writer, but I do know a clue when I see one.

Although not what one would explicitly consider a note, the screen saver on Mr. Castle's computer monitor consists of a pair of animated inkwells that drift to and fro. One bottle is branded "Andrew" and has a subscript: "Leader, visionary, creator, friend." The other says "Tom," with its ink label reading, "Always half-full." Not notes per se, but I am including them, just in case the names mean anything.

One can only guess. And hope that one's admittedly untrained (and perhaps, unwelcome?) search of Mr. Castle's writing domain has brought forth all the editorial needs for these acknowledgments. If, in the interim, the author himself should—become available—the publisher shall, of course, stop the press run and allow him to revise.

May it please be thus.

Junior Editor, Name Withheld
New York City—May 12, 2014